READERS LOVE SUZAN HOLDER

'I blitzed through this as I just could not get enough…Light and witty, I enjoyed every second.'

'A sweet, heartwarming read…I can't wait to read more from this author!'

'Such a fun read! Perfect for one sitting.'

'I cannot wait to see what comes next from this talented author…a wonderful, heartwarming story that is an absolute must-read.'

Also by Suzan Holder
───────────────────

Rock 'n' Rose
Shake It Up, Beverley

WHAT WOULD DOLLY DO?

SUZAN HOLDER

Harper North

HarperNorth
Windmill Green
24 Mount Street
Manchester M2 3NX

A division of
HarperCollins*Publishers*
1 London Bridge Street
London SE1 9GF

www.harpercollins.co.uk

HarperCollins*Publishers*
Macken House,
39/40 Mayor Street Upper,
Dublin 1, D01 C9W8, Ireland

First published by HarperCollins*Publishers* Ltd 2025

1

Copyright © Suzan Holder Ltd 2025

Suzan Holder asserts the moral right to be identified as the author of this work.

A catalogue record for this book is available from the British Library.

PB ISBN: 978-0-00-873868-6

This novel is entirely a work of fiction. The names, characters and incidents portrayed in it are the work of the author's imagination. Any resemblance to actual persons, living or dead, events or localities is entirely coincidental.

Printed and bound in the UK using 100% Renewable Electricity
by CPI Group (UK) Ltd

All rights reserved. No part of this publication may be reproduced, stored in a retrieval system, or transmitted, in any form or by any means, electronic, mechanical, photocopying, recording or otherwise, without the prior permission of the publishers.

Without limiting the author's and publisher's exclusive rights, any unauthorised use of this publication to train generative artificial intelligence (AI) technologies is expressly prohibited. HarperCollins also exercise their rights under Article 4(3) of the Digital Single Market Directive 2019/790 and expressly reserve this publication from the text and data mining exception.

This book contains FSC™ certified paper and other controlled sources to ensure responsible forest management.

For more information visit: www.harpercollins.co.uk/green

For anyone who has ever been accused of being 'too much' despite secretly feeling they'll never be enough…and for funny, fearless, fabulous Dolly, who shows us all there's simply no such thing as 'Too Much'!
Suzan x

Chapter One

I stared into the mirror and the face of Dolly Parton stared right back at me. I wasn't hallucinating, she was sitting right there, the undisputed queen of country music; bouffant blonde hair, bright blue eyeshadow and lips painted in 'Harlot Red'. I noticed she looked a little more weary than usual, but it was Dolly nonetheless.

Pursing my own lips, I watched Dolly pucker up too as though she wanted to kiss me. I leaned towards her, planting a big smooch right on the kisser and leaving a big cupid's bow of lipstick on the glass. It looked comical but I was struggling to find anything funny right now. With a sigh, I wiped my hand over the red stain and smeared lipstick across my own reflection. Reaching for the make-up remover, I began the de-Dollying process I'd perfected over years of working clubs and bars. Not for me the hallowed stage of Nashville's Grand Ole Opry or a place in the Country Music Hall of Fame. I was a Dolly Parton tribute act – a good one, I'm not doing myself down here – but I was just a copycat performer singing songs written by and made famous by somebody else. Sure, I could belt out the classics and shimmy my tassels but the lack of real creativity in this job had made me start to think I might as well be working '9 to 5'. It didn't even pay all that well anymore so I'd recently taken a part-time job in a shop.

I blinked back tears as I realised my performance income was going to take an even bigger nosedive now I'd lost my very own Kenny Rogers. Damn Robbie, he'd picked a fine time to leave me, hadn't he?

I took a last look at the woman in the mirror, platinum blonde hair piled high on top with cutesy tendrils framing her sad face. Even in despair, I thought Dolly looked glamorous and alluring. That was the best thing about dressing up as the queen of country music – as Dolly, every fibre of my being was set to full dazzle; you couldn't dip your headlights when you performed as Dolly. Even sitting here, in the cluttered, poky storeroom that doubled as my dressing room, my heartbreak had an air of tragic glamour while I still resembled divine Dolly. Once she'd been removed, with the help of half a pot of Nivea, my misery would have nowhere to hide.

I suppose I shouldn't feel bad about taking comfort in mimicking Dolly's look. After all, she was always loud and proud about copying the look herself from a woman she'd seen walking around a town near her Tennessee mountain home way back in the 1950s. A woman wearing figure-hugging clothes, a little too much make-up and heels far too high. Little Dolly thought she was the most beautiful woman she had ever seen, not realising the locals referred to her as '*the town tramp*'. When she heard the names they called her, young Dolly decided she too wanted to grow up to be 'trash' so she could look just like that supposed woman of easy virtue. I'd spent years learning everything I could about how Dolly set about turning herself from a plain Jane into a blonde bombshell, and I knew that once she got famous she would often joke, *'Ya know it takes a lotta money to look this cheap.'* I bet it did! Her custom-made costumes were worth thousands of dollars. I didn't have the cash to splash on couture diamanté corseting and hand-dyed marabou-feather trims. Luckily, I'd been brought up knowing how to use a needle and thread, and had become a dab hand at knowing how to quickly transform a satin pantsuit with a few well-placed tassels and rhinestones.

It was now time to perform the opposite of the make-over Dolly had given herself. I was about to take away everything that made me feel confident enough to stand on a stage and perform to an audience night after night. Piece by piece, bit by bit, I would soon revert to my own 'plain Jane' status and simply be single, soon-to-be-thirty-five, Becky Mooney.

I lifted Dolly's wig off and placed it on the mannequin head on the dressing table. My own light brown hair was pinned up so, as I plucked at the grips holding it in place, it stuck out in all directions even as it fell back down to my shoulders. I wiped away the arches of turquoise blue eyeshadow and peeled off the spidery jet-black eyelashes revealing something I did have in common with Dolly Parton, my green eyes. Me, Dolly and the flame-haired temptress Jolene from the hit song all shared the same unusual eye colour. I wasn't so blessed in the bosom department, however. Sticking my hand inside my shiny pink jacket, I yanked out the foam domes that gave me an impressive Dolly-esque embonpoint. Now my waist didn't look so teeny tiny as it did with them in and, once I'd discarded the matching flared trousers and sky-high platform silver sandals, my thighs would look a bit chunkier too.

It was always a bit depressing to see the normal version of myself reflected in the harsh lights of the dressing room mirror; black hoody over blue jeans, white trainers on my feet ready to run for the last bus back to my flat on the outskirts of Edinburgh. Sometimes, I would have to exit through a bar where the audience had just cheered and whooped as I'd finished a show with a final singalong encore of '9 to 5' and not one person would recognise me. What a way to make a living.

On the bus twenty minutes later, I let myself think about what Robbie had told me just moments before we had to entertain 250 people with our 'Dolly & Kenny Country Music Spectacular'. His timing was awful, that was for sure. The social club had been bursting at the seams with the friends, family and associates of a local businessman celebrating his 50th birthday. We couldn't let them down. No matter what happens, I always try to follow the oldest rule in showbiz, 'The Show Must Go On'.

It was just like Robbie though, I thought to myself bitterly, his timing had always been terrible. I don't think he'd ever come in at the right place in the second verse of 'Islands in the Stream' in all the years we'd worked together!

'I'm moving to Peterborough,' he'd said, although I'd had to ask him to repeat himself as he'd been fixing his 'Kenny' beard in place and all I'd heard was a muffled mumble that had sounded like 'I moo moo piddle butter' which didn't make much sense, even for Robbie.

'Eh?' I'd said as I'd pulled a wide studded belt another notch tighter to cinch my waist in just an extra smidge more.

He'd stopped fiddling with his silvery stick-on whiskers and stood by my side in front of the dressing room mirror, addressing my reflection instead of facing me properly. The coward.

'I'm moving to Peterborough,' he'd repeated and I'd looked back at the two of us stood side by side, a rectangle of lightbulbs framing us, a Scottish *Spitting Image* version of country music's best-loved star couple. I remember noticing a couple of bulbs had blown and one was flickering, which created a distinctly less starry image than the one the real Dolly and Kenny would project. Typical.

There hadn't been time to get into the full-scale, screaming, humdinger of a row this casually dropped bombshell really deserved. The sweaty face of Jock McIntyre, the club's resident emcee, had poked itself around the dressing room door warning us we had just five minutes before the show began. I'd just had time to discover that Robbie was leaving me to be manager of a pub in Peterborough. I'd always figured the bar job he'd had for the last few years in a small club off the Edinburgh Mile was just a thing he did to top up his showbiz earnings. I hadn't realised he saw it as an actual career.

'It's a promotion, Becky,' he'd said. 'It's a big place and I can really put my own stamp on it. It's the chance of a lifetime.'

Robbie's idea of a life-changing opportunity was clearly very different from mine and it was a lame excuse for leaving me in the lurch and I told him so. Not only was he wrecking my singing career by leaving me Kenny-less, he was also presumably ending our romantic relationship. Under absolutely no circumstances would I be moving to Peterborough – I wasn't even completely sure where it was?

'It's not really a *romantic* relationship though is it, Becky? Be honest,' he'd countered, waggling his fingers in the air when he said the words 'romantic relationship' as I attempted to claim he was leaving me heartbroken, bereft and abandoned. 'It's really only ever been a friends with benefits arrangement, hasn't it? For both of us. Don't try to pretend this has ever been some big love affair.'

Robbie spoke kindly, with no malice, and he had a point. My on/off relationship with him for the last six years could probably be described as a case of 'love the one you're with' as opposed to either of us being with someone we truly, passionately adored. There hadn't even been that many 'benefits' on offer in recent months either, now I came to think about it.

As my bus climbed another hill, noisily grinding its gears as it did so, I struggled to precisely remember how we'd even made the transition from singing partners to bedfellows. We'd always got on okay, most of the time, and beneath the Kenny Rogers wig and whiskers Robbie wasn't unattractive, but my murky memory recalled a sparsely attended gig in

Aberdeen as the turning point. A couple of lairy blokes heckling from the bar and too many shots of tequila to comfort ourselves afterwards had been the key to us tumbling into bed and stumbling into being a couple. It wasn't really anything to write a love song about, if I was telling the truth.

So, as I'd taken to the stage at tonight's 50th birthday bash and launched into a jaunty version of 'Two Doors Down' singing about dancing and having a party, I was already beginning to reconcile myself to the fact my relationship with Robbie had run its course. Sweeping my eyes along the row of middle-aged revellers already jigging about to the music and lapping up my dizzy-Dolly Americana patter, I was less worried about the vacancy in my love life and more worried about the impending one on stage. How could I carry on as a solo performer and keep gigging without my 'Kenny'? Punters always loved the well-known duets we did like 'We've Got Tonight' and 'Islands in the Stream' … how would I be able to do those alone? And Robbie's solo renditions of 'Ruby', 'The Gambler' and 'Coward of the County' gave me the necessary time for costume changes. The audience appreciated my Dolly outfits becoming increasingly colourful and star-spangled as our set went on. As more questions popped into my mind, I had to force myself to slap on Dolly's famous megawatt smile and push my worries away as I performed, for the sake of the audience. I knew all too well that no one ever wants to see a downbeat Dolly.

Back to being Becky on the bus, I almost missed my stop as I gave in to fretting for my Dolly Parton future. Having Dolly as my alter ego was more than just a showbiz sideline, and Robbie knew that. How could he do this to me? He must know how hard it would be for me to consider going on alone. Perhaps Dolly and I had reached the end of the country road and I'd have to follow Robbie after all. Not to Peterborough … I wasn't that desperate … although I had now learned it was in Cambridgeshire … who knew? But perhaps it was time to turn my back on showbusiness, enter civvy street and get a 'proper job' working 9 to 5 full-time?

Chapter Two

The next morning, I tumbled out of bed and stumbled to the kitchen in a daze. I'd slept fitfully, dreaming of being marooned on a tiny jagged rock in the middle of a fast-flowing stream of tequila, while Robbie waved frantically at me from the riverbank, wearing a giant pair of bright green spectacles. I blamed it on the midnight cheese on toast.

I yawned and stretched as I tried to summon the energy for a proper day's work at my new part-time job at Grayson's, the jewellers. A late night followed by an early start was never easy and neither was managing the turnaround from Dolly in the spotlight to Becky on the shop floor. I knew which role I preferred but now I was thinking I might well need to make the 9 to 5 job permanent if the gig money I was used to earning as my main income was going to evaporate. The thought made my mood plummet even lower. It had seemed an interesting, quirky thing to do when I'd spotted the handwritten sign for a part-time assistant in the window of the jewellery shop down in Edinburgh's Grassmarket and I'd walked straight in and applied on the spot.

Grayson's looked like The Olde Curiosity Shoppe, a Victoriana-tinged throwback with a bulging bay window stuffed with glittering trinkets, vintage treasures and jewels. The heavy old door had dinged as I'd pushed it open and triggered the big gold bell above it. Inside, softly glowing wall lamps bounced reflected light off antique wall mirrors, glass display cases and the polished mahogany furniture. It had felt like stepping inside a genie's magic lamp.

Gordon Grayson, the old feller who introduced himself rather formally as the *'proprietor of the establishment'* had turned out to be an amiable Scottish gent with old-school manners and a pair of very twinkly blue eyes below the tangled explosion of his black and grey eyebrows.

For the first couple of weeks, I'd loved working alongside Gordon and his lovely wife Morag when she popped in to help. The shop was their pride and joy. They knew so much about the jewellery trade and were happy to try and teach me. Old customers adored them and new ones instantly respected them, they had such a natural way of welcoming people into Grayson's. They were a lovely couple clearly still very much in love with each other and they shot to the top of my relationship goals chart. They teased each other a lot but it was always done kindly and I couldn't help but notice how much they enjoyed being together.

Working at a jeweller's had never been my dream but I was surprised not just by how much I often enjoyed it but also by the fact it seemed to be something I was good at. Other than singing, I'd never really found a skill to be proud of before, but Gordon said I had a good eye and with his help, in the few months I'd been there, I'd learned an awful lot about precious and semi-precious stones, cuts and settings. Grayson's business was built on unique pieces, vintage finds and some dazzling investment jewels. Gordon and Morag showed me how to spot the real deal among all the fake and fashion jewellery, to know it by sight and feel and weight. He had a magpie eye, and while he loved the dark gleam of a real sapphire, or the twinkling charm of an opal, he loved paste and costume jewellery too, but only when it was sold honestly as that. Gordon always said we owed it to our customers to be truthful about what we bought and sold, to find the value in every piece and match it to the right customer. I loved how Gordon didn't just care about the technical side – hallmarks and clarity, patina and provenance – but he also taught me how to find what suited a customer. I'd soon learned, when someone came in glancing at the pear-cut diamond earrings in the corner cabinet, whether they were likely to walk out with them, or if I should direct them to tourmaline clusters or the elegant Art Deco glittering drops instead. And if anyone came in asking to value or sell their grandmother's diamond engagement ring, I quickly learned how to tell if it was more likely to have come from a mass Chinese shipment than a treasured relative's legacy. In addition to all the new things I'd learned, I'd spent my career as a Dolly Parton impersonator covered in rhinestones and crystals, so maybe that was why I was able to spot genuine diamonds so easily? Whatever the reason, it was a talent that Gordon and Morag valued and they'd eagerly welcomed me into the Grayson's fold and made me feel like family.

But now as I slammed the door to my flat behind me I felt my stomach lurch with dread about the day I had ahead of me in the shop. I'd only been working at Grayson's for a few months but an awful lot had happened in that time. I trudged despondently down the three flights of stairs to the street, recalling how the atmosphere had been shattered the day Gordon had received a phone call telling him Morag had been found unconscious in their front garden by a neighbour. We'd closed the shop straight away and rushed to the hospital to find that poor Morag had suffered a stroke.

I'd been able to hold the fort by myself for a little while until we reopened a few days later and Gordon came back into work in between shifts of sitting at Morag's bedside. I'd done my best to keep things going, for Gordon and Morag's sake as much as my own. I actually relished the opportunity to show how much I had learned and it was lovely to be able to help people buy special pieces of jewellery to mark an occasion, or a gift to loved ones. Gordon had taught me never to rush anyone, but to take an interest in customers, try to gauge their tastes and budget, and to find out who the purchase was going to be for.

'The real trick is to match the purchase to the customer, don't just try and shift the most expensive items in stock,' Gordon had told me more than once. 'That way they are more likely to recommend us to their friends and come back and use us again. It's the real secret of being a successful and trusted independent family business.'

Gordon's mantra made complete sense to me. I'd quickly found I wasn't a natural at the hard sell. I didn't like to be pushy and I certainly didn't relish clinching a deal unless I was sure I'd matched the shopper with the perfect item. If I felt someone was stretching themselves too far to afford a diamond engagement ring, I'd much prefer to show them some alternative ideas like Gordon had shown me. That way seemed to work out better for everybody.

But things had changed since then in the twinkly world of Grayson's jewellery emporium. The cosy atmosphere had been punctured by the arrival of Gordon and Morag's son, Guy.

A few days after his mother's stroke, Guy had flown into Edinburgh from Silicone Valley. With a striking sun-kissed quiff, a face full of Botox and a strangulated mid-Atlantic accent, Guy couldn't have been more different from his kindly, well-mannered parents. I'd taken against him almost immediately. I don't see how anyone could blame me. For a start, it had taken his mother to have a stroke before he could haul himself across the ocean, trailing his tiresome Californian wife, JoJo, and vapid teenage daughter, Kourtney, along with him.

'Well, ain't this quaint?' JoJo had drawled as the three of them poked around inside the shop the day after parachuting into Edinburgh from La La Land. They all occasionally flashed sets of enormous white teeth but I figured their smiles were as fake as their gnashers.

I couldn't blame Gordon for treating Guy like the prodigal son but the thought that he might want to take over the family business was ridiculous … and horrifying. I'd overheard JoJo whispering to Kourtney that the place needed a complete make-over for a start.

'It's far too dark and dingy,' she'd hissed at the girl who looked even more bored than usual and simply carried on scrolling on her phone.

Gordon had agreed immediately when Guy offered to 'help out' in the shop despite my hints that we could manage without the input of a 'digital marketing strategist', whatever in the big wide inter-web world that was?

'He and JoJo are family, Becky hen, and this is a family business. We all need to pull together now. That's what his ma would want after all,' Gordon reasoned, not unreasonably, but I was not convinced.

Guy and JoJo's idea of 'helping out' appeared to me much more like 'taking over'. Guy's methods were completely alien to the Grayson philosophy.

'Exclusivity, that's the key,' he kept on saying. 'We don't want every browser and dreamer in here. If they're not ready to spend big, I don't want them through the doors. This is a shop, not a museum.'

Guy appeared to sneer at every potential customer who crossed the threshold as he eyed them disdainfully and assessed their spending power. He took no interest in their taste or style and always pressed for the highest price sale he could get. Worse, I'd seen him deliberately undervalue a couple of pieces that people had come in to sell. I hadn't been in the trade for long but I knew he was ripping people off. There had been one elderly gentleman who had come in to get a price on his late wife's vintage watch. In a voice shaking with emotion, he'd started to talk about her: he obviously hadn't been a widower for long. But Guy had ridden roughshod, given him some fast-talking pitch and the poor soul had left with far less cash for the beautiful timepiece than I knew he was due. I couldn't get the bereaved man's disappointed, grief-stricken face out of my mind.

I had tried to tell myself the Grayson family business was not my problem. I was just a hired hand and, even though I had loved the job more than I expected to at first, it was just a job, I could always find another one. But Robbie's news meant the risk of losing yet another source of income was impossible to ignore, and I could feel my anxiety about the shop was rising. It wasn't just Guy's business methods I had reservations about. Guy was arrogant, entitled and seemed to think I was part of the shop's merchandise he could manhandle. I could deal with lairy hecklers in a club, but Guy's invasion of my personal space was a whole other level of creepy and inappropriate. More than once he'd intimated that he fancied more from me than an honest day's work … even hinting I should be grateful to provide it as part of my duties. He even seemed to expect me to be flattered by his oily attention, inappropriate comments, and wandering hands. For all his talk of modernising Grayson's, Guy was a dinosaur in his attitude to women. He might be the boss's son but that didn't mean he could molest the staff. I needed to find a way to handle him and put him back in his box, if I was going to be able to carry on working with him.

As I made my way through the streets I tried to appreciate all that my beautiful home city had to offer that morning, despite my low spirits. It had rained overnight but now shafts of light shone down here and there, spotlights of sunlight finding their way through any gap they could, illuminating the hustle and bustle of a weekday morning.

The golden light brought a warmth to the traditional dark stone walls of the buildings around me. Edinburgh was a rare place in many ways, and particularly unusual in the way it looked its most beautiful after it had rained, which was fortunate given the local climate. Still, despite the usual rain, most days I felt beyond lucky to live among such brooding, gothic architecture and have a route to work that took me along streets unchanged for centuries, through steeply stepped tunnels and passageways, like I was an extra in a magical movie. But today Edinburgh wasn't casting its usual uplifting spell on me.

I quickened my pace as I walked down through Grassmarket. I was due to open up this morning and it wouldn't do to be late in case Guy or JoJo decided to come in early to try and catch me out. I had the distinct impression Guy would relish the chance to trap me in a corner and give me a dressing down. Or worse.

I was walking so determinedly, with my head down, full steam ahead, that I was almost at the shop before I registered the commotion going on outside. A police car pulled up at an angle right outside the bay window, its blue light silently flashing and jarring horribly with the Dickensian appearance of our little street. What the …?

Sprinting quickly forwards I checked the small square windowpanes in the bay to see if they were broken … had there been a smash and grab? I couldn't see any shards of glass on the floor. Or maybe the cops were there for my new boss? A flash of hope surged through me. I knew Guy Grayson was up to no good: had he pushed his luck too far? Made one shady deal too many or committed some despicable crime like ripping off another poor customer and the law had finally caught up with him? My heavy heart gave a little leap.

Pushing the shop door open, the bell dinged above my head to signal my arrival. Usually I was greeted by the beeping of the burglar alarm before keying in my code to unset it. But not today. Today three people were already inside the store as I stepped onto the parquet flooring and they all turned to glare at me as though *I* was the unwelcome intruder.

'What's happened? Have we been robbed?' My pulse was hammering with the shock of seeing uniformed cops in their fluorescent hi-vis vests standing in the genteel surroundings of Grayson's.

No one replied, but the female police officer glanced towards Guy who stood behind the counter wearing a fixed grim expression on his sun-tanned face.

Why was no one saying anything? I tried again:

'What is it? What's happened?'

This time Guy rolled his eyes and made a noise that sounded like 'Hmmff!'

The male copper cleared his throat then and, without taking his eyes off me, asked Guy, 'Is this her?'

Guy's face remained expressionless, which wasn't that surprising given his addiction to face-fillers, but his eyes slid away from me as he nodded and whispered, 'Yeah.'

Everything happened so fast I didn't have time to catch my breath. The male officer stepped forward and addressed me directly.

'Becky Mooney, I am arresting you for theft. You do not have to say anything, but it may harm your defence if you do not mention when questioned something which you later rely on in court. Anything you do say may be given in evidence.'

Simultaneously the female officer stepped around and grabbed me firmly by the arm.

'Ow, you're hurting me!' Even as I said it I was dimly aware this phrase may not be something that would help my case if given in evidence at a later date. I should have been shouting my innocence instead. But my mind was whirling too much to summon a more sensible reply or even voice the thousands of questions running through my brain. What the hell was going on? This wasn't my life. I was a part-time Dolly Parton impersonator, part-time shop girl ... not some career criminal.

But before I could find the words to tell them there had been some kind of wild mix-up, I was back outside in the street being frog-marched to the police car, a hand placed firmly on the back of my head as I was guided onto the backseat of the police car, and then we were off. I've never liked Mondays all that much, who does? But this Monday morning was an absolute corker.

It was barely 9.05 a.m. and I was under arrest.

Chapter Three

As the police car sped through the city streets on its way to the cop shop I watched ordinary people going about their ordinary business and wished with all my heart I was back there among them. It was all so absurd I'd have laughed if it wasn't for the growing ball of anxiety that was filling my chest as the reality of my situation sank in.

'I don't understand, what am I supposed to have done?' My voice was trembly and the sound of my own fear made tears prickle in my eyes. The officers in the front of the car studiously ignored me and heaped more humiliation on me by doing so. I had no experience of criminality, having always been a goody-two-shoes by anyone's standards so I had nothing to draw on to help me in this alien situation. When I was a teenager I'd been horrified when some of the girls in my class bragged about the shoplifting sprees they carried out most Saturday afternoons. They'd come to school with bags overflowing with cheap make-up they'd pinched from Woolworths on Princes Street. Passing around tubes of cherry lipstick, pots of cream blush, and blue powder eyeshadow, they'd looked pityingly at me as though having an unpainted face and no criminal tendencies was a very bad thing.

I was almost wishing I'd joined in with the pick 'n' mix pilfering brigade now; at least it might have given me some idea of what to expect when you got your collar felt. All I actually had to go on was stuff I'd seen in police dramas or ancient sit-coms. Was the 'good-cop bad-cop' routine a real thing? Would one detective try to gain my trust while another waited for an opportunity to catch me out with a loaded question? Would I be placed in an empty room and then watched from behind a one-way mirror by a team trying to decipher my body language? Was I heading for a long stretch in jail protesting my innocence, would I fester behind bars until I became an old lag?

I wasn't sure where the jailbird jargon phrases popping into my head were coming from ... I wasn't much of a crime drama fan so maybe it was down to those late-night re-runs of *Porridge* on the comedy channel? My mind was spinning out of control now ... were you forced to eat porridge in prison? Horrifyingly, I gave a sudden snort at the very thought and quickly turned it into a bout of coughing in case they thought I was laughing. It really wouldn't do me any favours if the police thought I wasn't taking this seriously.

It wasn't hard to take the whole thing a lot more seriously once I was sitting on an uncomfortable plastic chair in a windowless interview room, being told that I was being accused of theft. Me!? Some kind of jewel thief? I could barely take it in.

A female detective with a very stern expression insisted I had a duty solicitor present. I should have realised that didn't bode well. I resisted at first but, when she doggedly persisted, that was the moment I realised I was in a lot of trouble.

The door opened and a skinny youth with a bum fluff beard loped into the room. This did nothing to help quell my nerves. Were they kidding? Was this some sort of weird reality TV show? Was there a camera hidden somewhere on his red spotty tie? This ... *boy* was supposed to be my legal representative?

The man-boy introduced himself as Calum Crutchley and we had a brief conversation where I told him I knew nothing about anything, which didn't seem to impress him much either. Someone brought us two paper cups of tepid, grey liquid, I had no idea if it was tea or coffee and had no chance to find out as Calum knocked my cup off the table splattering liquid all over the floor as he struggled out of a coat two sizes too big for him. This was going from bad to worse. This was who I had to rely on to help me? ... Calamity Calum?

The detective then told us both she had reason to believe I had stolen items worth thousands of pounds from Grayson's Jewellers. Shocked, I glanced at my Kevin-the-teenager solicitor but he looked just as bamboozled as I was.

There was worse to come. They had CCTV evidence from the back office at the shop. I thought the system was out of action but there I was on the flickering black and white footage, stuffing watches, necklaces, rings and bracelets into my bag and skipping merrily through the door like some modern-day Artful Dodger.

'It's not ... I wasn't ...' My protestations stuck in my throat as I tried to explain.

Then the killer punch. Detective Constable Thatcher had sent a colleague to my flat this morning, she said. My blood ran cold as I realised why I'd been left waiting for almost two hours and I guessed where she was going with this.

'Your neighbour downstairs was very helpful,' DC Thatcher said. 'She gave us a spare key so we gained access to your flat.' Was I meant to thank them for not battering down my door? She carried on as I kept my mouth firmly shut. 'Do you know what we found, Miss Mooney?'

I did. I knew they would have found some of the most expensive items we'd ever had in stock at Grayson's stuffed under my mattress. You didn't have to be any sort of legal eagle to know this did not look good for me and whatever I said would sound like a lame excuse.

For the next couple of hours I pleaded my innocence, tried to make them understand what had really happened, but the circumstantial evidence against me was too strong and DC Thatcher appeared to think she had an open and shut case. I was to be charged with theft. Me, Becky Mooney, no previous convictions or even petty pilfering misdemeanours to be taken into consideration, but now I would have a rap sheet reading 'theft'. The shame was overwhelming.

But Calum Crutchley swung into action at this point, successfully arguing that more investigation needed to be carried out before I was charged. My version of events had to be fully explored, he'd said, stressing there was an entirely legitimate explanation for having high-value merchandise under my bed. He believed me! Perhaps having this young man on my side would not be such a calamity after all? Maybe?

I was released shortly after with a grim warning to expect the police to be in touch. It was a relief not to have been charged immediately or kept in a cell while they carried out more enquiries, but it didn't feel like I was off the hook yet.

I emerged from the front entrance of the station, blinking into the daylight, as though I'd just tunnelled out of Shawshank Prison. The shock of being arrested and questioned had been a nerve-jangling start to the day. All I wanted was a calming cup of tea and a sit down, but my mind was racing. The faces of the gruesome twosome of Guy Grayson and his joyless wife JoJo swam in front of my eyes but the police had warned me to stay right away from the shop while they completed 'further enquiries'.

I just needed to go home. My stomach lurched when I thought of police officers invading my flat and rifling through my belongings but I couldn't blame Mrs Forsyth for giving them access. I squirmed with embarrassment yet again when I thought of how I was going to explain all this to her. I loved my little apartment and I couldn't bear it if, on top of everything else, I now had to find somewhere else to live. Although anywhere would be better than a six-by-eight-foot prison cell.

I tottered on shaky legs to the top of the steps outside the cop shop, spotting solicitor Calum paused halfway down the stairs with his phone clamped to his ear. He looked up and gave a brief nod in my direction as I attempted a smile I hoped showed him my gratitude for saving me from being thrown straight into clink. Suddenly a commotion behind me made us both stop and turn. A man with unruly reddish hair and worn jeans was being manhandled through the revolving police station door by a burly uniformed cop. The two of them barely fitted into the glass compartment together and they burst out with the officer holding the guy by the scruff of his neck and the seat of his denim-clad bottom.

'And this time stay out of bloody trouble!' the policeman growled as he threw the guy roughly in the direction of the steps where Calum and I were still standing. I was glad I'd only encountered the hatchet-faced DC Thatcher and not this muscly monster.

The red-headed man wasn't the young scruffy kid I'd initially taken him for. He looked like he could be well into his thirties and if it wasn't for the fact that he was clearly a no-good wastrel being booted out of a cop shop I would have said he was really rather attractive. I only caught the briefest glimpse of his face, strong jaw and a devilish grin, before he pulled out a pair of dark glasses from his back pocket and put them on. It wasn't particularly sunny so maybe that was why he then immediately misjudged his footing on the stairs. He stumbled down a couple of the steps but managed to stop himself from falling down the rest, sticking out his arms as though he was balancing on a tightrope. I caught a flash of taut tanned skin as his blue-checked shirt fell open and his tight white t-shirt rode up his toned stomach, but hastily looked away before he could see me checking him out. I'd only been incarcerated for a couple of hours, for heaven's sake, and here I was eyeing him up like I hadn't seen a man in years ... what was wrong with me? It might have been a difficult morning but the last thing I needed now was to develop a sexual appetite for petty criminals and vagabonds ... what was I thinking?

The ginger guy turned and fired off a mouthful of colourful expletives in a Scottish accent to the officer who stood with his arms folded looking down with an expression more amused than annoyed. I knew I shouldn't gawk but I couldn't help but wonder what crime the villain could have committed? Was he a shoplifter? A mugger? Was he a political activist who'd been defacing public monuments or glueing himself to traffic lights? He couldn't be *that* dangerous if he was being let loose on the Edinburgh public.

The guy had a rather peculiar smirk on what I could see of his face behind his completely unnecessary shades, as though being thrown out of a police station was merely an occupational hazard for a cool career criminal such as himself. He mockingly dusted himself down and gave the cop a jaunty wave.

'Be seeing you officer,' he called.

'Not if I see you first, Tommy,' the policeman retorted with a knowing nod of his head.

Right, I decided, this was none of my business. I had enough problems of my own and it was high time I was on my way, leaving the baby-faced solicitor, the burly officer and the red menace well behind me.

Turning quickly on the stair to make my getaway my stupid foot slipped off the troublesome step I'd just watched the other guy tackle and, giving a squeal of distressed horror, I fell awkwardly and painfully head first down the remaining stairs. My landing, witnessed by all three men plus a couple of amused by passers-by, left me spread-eagled face down on the pavement with my feet still on the third step from the top. Excellent.

As I scrambled for the scattered contents of my handbag I sensed young Calum was mortified by a flash of my bright pink knickers and the sight of my bum stuck up in the air. I felt like I was moving in slow motion as we all watched one lipstick and two tampons roll, along with my last shred of dignity, towards the gutter.

It was the true criminal among us who moved first. With one bound the ginger demon was by my head grabbing for my bag, like the opportunist thief he was. That did it. I'd had quite enough to deal with already, thank you very much. Springing to my feet in a cat-like move that surprised even me I caught the guy about to make off with my handbag completely by surprise. What a brazen scoundrel! Trying to rob me blind, and right in front of a police station, a cop and a solicitor too!

Snatching my leather shoulder bag out of his grasp with such force it must have left friction burns on his thieving hands I swung it backwards and then landed him with a good clout around the head. I only remembered I'd got my GHD hair straighteners in the bag when I heard the satisfying 'dong' sound as it made contact with his red head.

'Ow! What the …?' He looked affronted as much as in pain, rubbing his unruly ginger hair at the spot where I'd made contact, his face screwing up in shock and pain.

Ignoring his protestations and picking up as much of the debris from my bag as I could, I was assisted by Calum the wonder-boy who finally managed to move his feet and help me. Although he did hand me a tampon with such a quizzical look on his face I did wonder if he'd ever seen one before. No matter, he was helping me and that's what counted.

The cop and the robber were both now yelling stuff I chose to ignore. I was so desperate to get home, I blanked them as they shouted after me, and limped away from the station as fast as I could. What a pair of Neanderthals! At my side though, bless him, holding my elbow supportively, was little Calum who stuck out his hand like a proper grown-up and hailed me a black cab so I could make a decent escape.

He pulled open the car door and practically pushed me inside as I stuttered my thanks.

'What the hell just happened?' I asked him as I clambered in. The question could have been about my shocking arrest, interrogation, surprise release or humiliating tumble down the station steps, all of it was crazy, but I was actually referring to the fact that, after all that, I'd then had to defend myself from being robbed by a brazen bad guy in broad daylight right outside a police station!

Calum seemed to be as bewildered as I was by the turn of events and understood what I was saying. He shook his head wearily as though he had already seen too much crime in his young life.

'If I hadn't been there and seen it for myself I would never have believed it,' he said.

Slamming the door shut as if to accentuate his point I left him standing on the kerb as the taxi pulled away. Well said, Calum! It wasn't him that deserved the nickname 'calamity' after all, it was me! In one sentence he'd actually summed up the entire situation, my disastrous day and the whole sorry mess that was my life.

Chapter Four

My heart was in my mouth as I carefully stepped on each stair up to my third-floor flat. Having lived there for so many years, I thought I knew every creaky spot in this old building, but I managed to find a couple of places that threatened to give away my return home to my neighbour, Mrs Forsyth, who lived on the ground floor. She's a kind and usually cheery soul, pushing seventy and resolutely single with a couple of cats and a surprising passion for martial arts. We've always got on well but I couldn't face the inevitable questions about that morning's police raid.

Once safely inside I clicked my front door into its jamb and stood with my back pressed against it while I tried to get my breathing to return to normal. The climb up the forty-eight stairs (yes, I counted them, it was something of a ritual) never worried me usually but anxiety was making me breathless. Most days I actually relished the opportunity to have a mini workout every time I came home. I needed to be able to pour myself into Dolly's clingy satin pantsuits on a regular basis, and scaling three flights was a good counterbalance to my addiction to marshmallows. I rarely keep them in the house. Seriously. It's a problem. Once I open a monster packet of those pink and white pillowy cubes I just can't stop. Of course, I always buy a monster packet: what on earth would be the point of buying a small one? Robbie used to say it looked like I was inhaling a double duvet once I started stuffing them, one after another, into my gob to console myself if I'd had a bad day. I reckon they are the ultimate comfort food. There's something unique about the simple sweetness and the way they turn from fluffy to gooey as you chew. I'm telling you, it's a problem.

I looked around the hallway for evidence of the police search carried out this morning. The coats on the hooks might have been in a different order but I couldn't be sure. The door straight ahead into the living room was wide open instead of slightly ajar as I had left it. Or had I? Now I thought about it I really couldn't be sure of anything.

I eased myself away from the door and made my way very slowly from room to room. In the living room my eye, as always, was drawn to the huge bay with its floor to ceiling windows framed by white wooden shutters but I dragged myself away from the pretty view over the bowling club's pristine green laid out in the square below. Our row of Victorian houses matched the four-storey terraces opposite, each floor sporting a distinctive large bay window. I have to say, this flat is worth the forty-eight-stair climb. To be this high up but with a huge picture window totally justifies the very reasonable price my parents paid for the place over a decade ago. I would never be able to afford to buy or even rent a place like this by myself but Mum and Dad let me pay a rent I've been able to afford (so far) as long as they can use the second bedroom whenever they come back over from Spain. It's an excellent deal in my opinion.

Back in the room everything looked a bit skew-whiff: my red chesterfield sofa too far back from the big old wooden chest I use as a coffee table, the large potted plants by the shutters also looked odd, as though the leaves were now facing the wrong way. Everything had been moved, adjusted, disturbed.

Turning through the door on my left it was harder to spot any sign of disturbance in the kitchen. The bright blue painted kitchen cupboards and sunshine yellow walls were as cheery as ever. I'm ridiculously proud of how my mismatched blue and white crockery, sourced from markets and junk shops, fits in so well displayed on the high shelf above the breakfast bar. It's the little things that make a place feel like home, isn't it? My attention was suddenly drawn to a drawer left slightly open. Did the police really think I would hide stolen jewellery in with my cutlery?

Next, I stood at the door of the bathroom with my toes on the black and white tile floor. I pictured a young police constable being sent to check for loot but finding himself thwarted by the fact the toilet has a high-level cistern with a long chain flush, impossible to reach without a tall step ladder. It would have been an excellent hiding place for sure, if I had a big enough ladder. But I don't. I figured there was nowhere else to look in there so comforted myself with the thought the invaders spent very little time in my bathroom.

The door to my bedroom was closed. I placed my hand on the crystal doorknob and blew out my cheeks to release some tension. My bedroom has always felt so cosy, a haven to retreat to. While the rest of the flat is full of light with splashes of bright colour, this room is mainly decorated in dark navy with accents of gold. When I moved in I immediately painted the wooden panelling on the bottom half of all four walls a rich deep blue and carried on to paint the window shutters to match. I've never regretted it; the dark blue colour framed my vantage-point view perfectly. I needed help to wallpaper the top half with end of line rolls of paper I'd found on Ebay, an absolute bargain with a beautiful blue and gold Art Deco fan motif. Dad was a dab hand at all that. With my mismatched vintage furniture, a shabby chic armoire, tartan upholstered armchair and fluffy faux fur rugs, throws and golden cushions, the whole effect is opulent and adorable. Well, that's what I think of it. Robbie did once remark it looked like Norma Desmond's boudoir. I took the reference to the ageing, slightly unhinged star of the Hollywood movie *Sunset Boulevard* as a huge compliment even though it probably wasn't meant to be.

Now it looked like Norma had thrown an almighty diva strop and her tantrum had left everything thrown around and upside down. The room was a chaotic mess. Once my haul of stolen goods was discovered the search team were obviously too jubilant to spend any time tidying up after themselves in here.

I'm appalled but I can't just collapse into tears. I can't. I channel my upset into energy and storm around the room, pulling the mattress back into place, putting clothes back onto hangers, straightening and tidying and restoring order to my inner sanctum. By the time things are back to something resembling normal I'm breathless, damp with sweat and desperate to eat my bodyweight in marshmallows.

I'm half a bag down accompanied by several swigs of scotch and starting to feel slightly mellowed by the mallow when I'm made to jump out of my skin by a loud banging on the front door. Not of the house. Not someone safely three floors down well away from me and possible to ignore. No, my own front door of the flat, just a few feet away from where I'm sitting. Are the police back? Who has got into the building without being buzzed in via the intercom?

I want to ignore it or just tell them to go away. My shattered nerves are jangling so loud I think they might be able to hear them, and then the banging starts again. Perhaps Mrs Forsyth has come up to check on me. A voice starts calling my name … 'BECKY! Bex … let me in … I know you're in there … Becky … come on, it's me, Robbie.'

Robbie? It beats me why he thinks that will convince me to open the door. How does he even know I'm here? It's the middle of the afternoon, actually it might even be later than that, I've lost track of the exact time, but I should still be at work as far as he is concerned. Why is he here?

I've forgotten Robbie has a key. Damn it. I'm cross-legged on the sofa surrounded by messy evidence of a marshmallow and whisky binge when he storms into the room and stands over me with a look on his face that looks like a mixture of anger and relief.

'Oh shit!' he says, taking in the scene. 'Monster marshmallows *and* whisky? The situation is more serious than I thought.'

His attempt at a joke breaks me. I burst into tears.

While I sniff and hiccup, he tells me Mrs Forsyth called him as soon as the police left this morning and he's been to three police stations trying to find me since then. I scrabble on my phone as he claims he's been ringing my mobile non-stop. It's dead, I'm always forgetting to charge it. Robbie shakes his head in exasperation as I try to tell him today has been an absolute nightmare and the police have got it all wrong but he waves away my explanation.

'Of course you're not a thief. You don't need to tell me that.'

He's on my side. The relief is enormous and emotion makes my throat constrict. It means everything that he believes me instinctively but I need to tell him what I think has happened. I'm hoping having someone to listen to me will help me get my scrambled brain in order. While we drink fresh cups of coffee I try to explain, bit by bit, how I've been accused of something I know I didn't do. Yes, the police found expensive items of jewellery stashed under my mattress. Yes, the CCTV from the back room of Grayson's shop caught me red-handed stuffing it all into a backpack and leaving the premises. Yes, Guy Grayson has reported me to the police and had me arrested for theft. All of that is true ... and yet ...

'Guy *told* you to take those items and hide them somewhere safe? He actually TOLD you to do it?' Robbie's eyes bulge as he repeats what I've just said.

I nod and take another sip of scalding coffee. It makes me cough. While I try to recover, Robbie's brain is working through the rest of the scenario.

'So he's framed you? Got you to take stuff, made sure you're captured on video and then called the cops?'

I nod slowly. It is the only explanation I've got. 'He told me his dad hadn't kept the shop insurance up to date and while he was sorting it out we needed to be very careful about how much of the really expensive stock we kept on the premises. He said if I could hold onto it for a while it would be the best thing. He said it would only be for a few days while he sorted the policy.'

'So you shoved it all under your bed?'

'Well I don't have a handy jewellery safe I keep for emergencies!'

I didn't mean to snap and could see why he thought it was a bit daft but I'd stood for a long while in the flat the day I came home with my bag bulging with expensive jewellery wondering what to do with it all. There was always a chance someone could break in. It was unlikely in a third-floor flat but certainly not impossible. There had also been times Mum and Dad had 'surprised me' with a trip back to Edinburgh and so I wanted to put the stuff safely out of sight. I'd been trusted to keep it all safe and I was just trying to do that in the best way I could.

'But why? Why would Guy Grayson frame you?'

I shook my head. I was still trying to figure that out, although I had a nagging suspicion it could have something to do with me rejecting his clumsy advances. I didn't really want to admit that to myself, let alone tell Robbie.

Robbie asked if he could make himself a sandwich. The guy is *always* hungry. I told him to help himself and while he foraged in the fridge he started yakking on about his move to

Peterborough. I think his plan was to change the subject to distract me but I couldn't really hear him properly ... I've lost count of the times I've moaned about him only ever starting a conversation with me once he's left a room. What's all that about? Why start speaking from the next room, why not try talking when we are together? Maddening. The other thing that was hampering communication was that he now also had a mouthful of my wafer-thin ham.

'What?' I eventually barked. He was really trying my patience. My shredded nerves had run my reserves low, but I could have sworn I just heard him say the whole thing could be off?

He reappeared in the living room, just visible behind a plate piled high with what looked like the entire contents of my fridge. 'It looks like I'm gonna have to stay in Edinburgh after all.'

He had my attention now and I waited for my heart to leap at this unexpected turn of events. Our Dolly & Kenny show could carry on. Would that mean the Becky & Robbie show would too? But my heart didn't leap or skip, not even a flutter. Robbie looked crestfallen and I just felt sorry for him. He was a mate after all. A good friend, as he'd just proved by instantly disbelieving I was any sort of criminal. We should have stuck to being mates, falling into bed had been a daft idea in the first place and I realised I now just wanted us to be friends and stay friends. I felt bad for him, he'd been so excited about managing a bigger place, making a new start, he clearly thought climbing up the beery brewery ladder was where his future lay. What had happened to scupper his plans?

Between mouthfuls of a triple-decker ham, cheese and beetroot sandwich he explained the situation. Sonny's Bar had been taken over just last year by a husband and wife called Simon and Gill Drummond who'd decided to invest some unexpected lottery winnings on a clutch of venues in different parts of the country. Simon and Gill's hearts were in the right place but they were blessed with more enthusiasm than expertise. Their vision was to establish a small chain that laid on entertainment as well as beer, wine, spirits, cocktails and soft drinks. Create clubs that offered music, comedy and theatrical culture alongside the drinking culture. The idea was a good one, I thought. As a performer I wanted to see more venues opening their doors to musicians, bands and stand-up comedians. It was hard to get a start in showbusiness these days. Yes, you could launch yourself on social media, even create your own YouTube channel to share your jokes or your songs or whatever your 'act' might be but, in my opinion, it was no substitute for honing your craft in front of a live audience. When I was little my parents had a country-music act they performed on a regular club circuit. I spent my childhood and teens watching talented people work a live room. Done well, the buzz for both performer and audience was like nothing else in the world. I'd love to see that sort of circuit come back.

I was distracted from Robbie's lengthy backstory as I recalled childhood memories of schlepping round clubs, village halls, and arts centres watching Mum and Dad, The Moonshine Duo, perform night after night. Once I reached double figures they let me join in on a couple of numbers until eventually we became The Moonshine Trio. Good times, until my teenage inhibitions kicked in.

Robbie was now saying something about Lanzarote. I wasn't clear on how we'd got from Peterborough to Lanzarote.

'Sorry, what?' I focused back on Robbie and his half-eaten sandwich and half-explained story. He sighed and wound back a little.

'Simon and Gill see me as a safe pair of hands. We tick over nicely here at Sonny's Bar. Figures are on the up and I've built up the customer base, so they wanted me to move to the new venue in Peterborough and do the same there. They had someone lined up to take over from me so I could move to the new place and get it up to scratch. It would have been a big challenge but if I'd done well there I could have had a manager role over the whole Drummond empire.'

I could see how crestfallen Robbie was. 'So what's gone wrong?' I asked.

'They had my replacement here all lined up but he's been offered a job in Lanzarote instead. Can't blame him, I suppose, but now he's pulled out they've had second thoughts about moving me. They reckon it's easier to re-recruit for the Peterborough position and leave me where I am. I had some great ideas for the new place though. They loved 'em.'

Robbie took a large, savage bite of sandwich as though he was tearing a strip off the Lanzarote-bound guy who'd scuppered his promotion.

An idea sprang into my head and was out of my mouth before I could stop it. 'I'll do it!' I said.

Robbie gawked at me with his mouth open and a half-chewed sandwich on display. I have to admit I have never found him less attractive.

'You don't even know where Peterborough is!' Robbie spluttered.

I suppressed my revulsion and irritation at Robbie getting the wrong end of the stick and pressed on with the vision that was forming in my mind.

'I know Sonny's almost as well as you, I've spent enough time there after all. I worked in bars loads when I was younger. I know how to pull a pint and mix a cocktail, and I've got lots of fresh ideas too. I love the idea of making it a venue for performers too, the kind of gig that's welcoming for artists and the audience, and I know lots about all that. Sonny's needs to be a real magnet for the arty crowd, we need to build a community that sees the place as its home – both the talent and the audience. The stage might only be tiny but it could be used far more than it is right now: we could have regular comedy spots as well as music nights? How about a free-and-easy night every month, too, where people can just have a go at singing, playing music or telling jokes … proper talent show stuff?'

I was babbling now but as my mouth sped off my brain was catching up with more and more ideas for Sonny's. The place had always been close to my heart. For some reason I suddenly had a vision of how great a hang-out it could be, a real little gem in the underbelly of Edinburgh and all these random thoughts were just bursting out of me.

'You should go to Peterborough like you planned, you're obviously dying for a fresh start and I can't say I blame you. I think it's what we both need.'

Robbie was still trying to swallow down his sandwich and say something but I took the opportunity to say what had become blindingly obvious to me in the last few minutes. 'We're mates, Robbie, we should never have tried to be anything else. Let's not pretend either of us are heartbroken. You've just proved what a good friend you really are, let's keep all that and forget about trying to be anything else to each other. Go to Peterborough, make a big success of the new place, and maybe Sonny's Bar is the answer to my prayers right now. Even after I prove my innocence I can't go back to Grayson's so it looks like I'm definitely going to need a new job!'

It was a strong argument. I was making a lot of sense, even Robbie had to admit it. He swallowed down his food and started to run through all the pros and cons of my idea. There weren't many cons, if I could convince his bosses to give me a chance. And Robbie was happy to help me prepare a pitch, give me all the info I would need. He even offered to be on the end of a phone to give me any support I needed once I got started. If my lightbulb moment worked out, he could go to Peterborough, Sonny's would get an enthusiastic new manager and I wouldn't ever have to face creepy Guy Grayson again. Result.

Chapter Five

The first few weeks working at Sonny's Bar were a slog, but I threw myself at it like it was a life raft in a stormy sea. I tried not to think too much about the ongoing police investigation and steered well clear of Grayson's Jewellers on the advice of cautious Calum Crutchley, my wonder-boy solicitor. Calum advocated a calm and measured approach which jarred with my instinct to go into Grayson's and demand a full explanation from gormless Guy as to why he'd framed me for a jewellery heist I did not commit. If I thought about it too much my blood would start to boil, so I tried very hard not to think about it too much. Even harder was the urge to go and see the man I considered to be the real boss of Grayson's, Guy's father Gordon. What must he and Morag be thinking? Surely, they couldn't believe I was a thief? Although, as Calum rather accurately pointed out, the police had found a stash of expensive jewellery from the shop under my mattress and Guy was Gordon's flesh and blood. I was going to have to tread very carefully if I didn't want to make the situation even worse. I had to accept Calum had a point – it was going to be very hard to explain – but as the days ticked by, I was increasingly desperate to defend myself to Gordon and Morag; until all this they had been a surrogate family for me.

Taking on the challenge of running Sonny's Bar was a welcome distraction from all of that. Simon and Gill Drummond had been brilliant, giving me a real chance as brand-new manager of the place. They'd really loved all my ideas, my experience on club circuits, and I'd used all my performance skills to convince them I could do the job. To be honest, I was convincing myself at the same time. Managing Sonny's Bar and creating a new venue space for Edinburgh's arty crowd was a big task but I was determined to prove myself up to it. There was something inside me that yearned to do a good job, whatever was asked of me. I might only be a tribute act, not a big recording artist or performer in my own name, but every time I stepped on a stage I wanted to be the best Dolly Parton that I could possibly be. When I took the part-time job at Grayson's I'd listened carefully and applied myself to the work diligently, and quickly became a valued member of staff. I believed in always trying my best whatever I did, which is another reason the accusations of dishonesty had hit me so hard. I kept the police investigation to myself. I knew I hadn't done anything wrong so I just had to hope the truth would come out. I would also be eternally grateful for the faith Robbie had shown in me. Not only had he immediately trusted in my innocence but had clearly done a great job in talking up my abilities and helping me land the position.

I was so determined to prove myself worthy of the responsibility, I'd cleaned the place from top to bottom, reorganised the stock room, got my head around the ordering systems and taken over the social media accounts – posting some of my ideas for attracting new customers. I also went old school, designing and printing leaflets to circulate locally to let folk know we were going to be a go-to place for music and comedy. With the help of regular bar staff, Donald and Stella, I hung some funky framed prints all around the bar area. They looked great against the rough brickwork. I'd found them stuffed in a box on a junk stall when I was wandering around a Sunday market in Stockbridge a few years ago and I couldn't resist buying. They were only a few pounds, but I'd never got around to putting them up in my flat. I suppose I'd thought putting all twelve up at home might make my flat look like an art gallery, but here they worked perfectly. Dotted around, one in an alcove, a couple on the stone columns that held up the low ceiling, they drew the eye to different parts of the quirky space. Each picture was done in an abstract, colourful style featuring musicians, performers, microphones, instruments and spotlights. They were all very stylised and stagey. I'd never seen any other work by the artist, but they created exactly the sort of laid back, showbizzy vibe I wanted to get going at Sonny's. I got Stella to take down all the dusty glass wall lights and while Donald swapped the bulbs for ones with a more golden glow I gave the shades a much-needed wash in warm soapy water. When they were all rehung and we switched on the lights we couldn't believe how much difference it made. Sonny's Bar was looking more inviting than ever.

'Hmmff' Donald said. He was a man of few words but the nod of his head led me to think he was beginning to approve of my tweaks.

Feeling emboldened I even freshened up the toilets with a lick of fresh paint and stencilled some inspirational Dolly Parton quotes on the back of each cubicle door. Well, people do like having something to read when they're on the loo, don't they? Stella needed a bit of convincing but once she saw the white lettering on the dark red doors she had to admit it looked cool. When I stood back to admire my own handiwork I was chuffed. I doubted most customers would even realise the words had come from Dolly's lips but that didn't matter, the quotes stood up for themselves. Some of them were a jokey take on life like, *'If you see someone without a smile, give 'em yours'* and *'If you want the rainbow you gotta put up with the rain'*. Others carried more of a warning; *'When someone shows you their true colours, believe them!'* or *'You'll never do a whole lot unless you're brave enough to try!'* My favourite 'Dollyisms' though are always the inspirational ones. As I finished writing the quote for the last cubicle I paused and considered it. *'Find out who you are and do it on purpose'* ... Was that what I was doing? Was running Sonny's Bar going to fulfil my dreams? Make me happy? I supposed being manager of a basement drinking den was what I did now, but it didn't give me any great answers as to the real Becky Mooney. Who was I? A part-time Dolly Parton performer? A novice bar manager? A jewellery thief? I suppose it would depend on who you currently asked. I'd love to find out who I really was, but Dolly hadn't given any clear instructions on how I was supposed to do that.

In the end, I decided not to use my favourite quote in a toilet cubicle, instead I realised it would be perfect on the black wall at the back of the small stage opposite the bar. It captured the mood I seemed to be in and reminded me of the talent I'd discovered I had for spotting fakes when I'd worked in Grayson's. I just hoped I could apply similar nous in my new calling. With a steady hand I wrote *'Be a Diamond in a Rhinestone world!'* and finished with an exclamation mark flourish.

As I backed away from the stage to take in the full effect a voice suddenly spoke from the doorway, shocking me so badly I dropped my brush, splattering white paint all over my blue jeans.

'I think that's a fine attitude to take, I consider myself a bit of a rough diamond,' said the disembodied voice.

'Donald?' But it didn't sound like the voice of the stocky barman from Stirling. It would have been one of the longest sentences I'd ever heard him utter, and anyway, I detected an American accent mixed with the local Edinburgh burr. He'd rolled the 'r' in rough and there was a crackle in his throat like he was used to smoky bars and shots of whisky. I peered towards the staircase where a red velvet curtain was partially pulled back across the doorway but the figure was standing in the gloom of the stairwell, watching me.

'Hello? Can I help you?' I went into cheery, welcoming mode to cover my rattled nerves. Where had Stella and Donald disappeared to?

'Well maybe we might be able to help each other?' The voice suggested a younger man than Donald, the silhouette wasn't too tall, but I could see he was slim hipped and broad shouldered. He sounded amused but I wasn't sure if he was mocking me, taunting me from the darkness, and it put my back up.

'Well, we'll have to see about that.' I didn't mean to snap but I was fighting the urge to curse at the state of my jeans. I grabbed a towel to wipe my hands and dab at the damage as the mystery man stepped into the golden light of the wall lamps. He recognised me before I had chance to look him in the eye.

His gasped reaction caused my head to flick up and take in the denim-clad legs, western-style checked shirt and mop of wild red hair.

'YOU!' I actually staggered backwards as I realised the ginger menace who'd tried to snatch my bag outside the police station was now advancing towards me with his hand out-stretched. I took firm hold of my paint brush and brandished it towards him in what I desperately hoped was a threatening manner. 'Get back you … you … hoodlum!'

He stopped, put his hands in the air and looked me straight in the eye: 'Don't shoot!'

He was definitely mocking me this time and I thrust my brush towards him, not caring about the arc of white paint flicking through the air as I rattled out questions like machine gun fire; 'What d'you want? There's nothing here to steal you know … have you been following me?' My blood had run cold. This guy looked worryingly familiar – more than our brief run-in on the police station steps merited – and now I could see him more clearly minus the oversized shades. Had he been tailing me over the last few weeks? I tried to rack my mind for where I'd seen him – the supermarket? ... the pub? ... a street corner? There was something about him I found so disconcerting, like there was some memory or other nagging at me but I just couldn't place it. But more fool him! I had nothing worth stealing, although perhaps he'd overheard me talking to my solicitor and thought I was a jewel thief with enough loot to make it worthwhile tracking me down.

A splatter of paint hit the sleeve of his shirt and spattered onto his stubbled chin and across his face but he just shook his red head slowly and put his hands on his hips. His answer came in a sort of cowboy drawl; 'Well someone certainly has a mighty high opinion of themselves. Why in the world d'ya think I'd be following you?'

I didn't have an immediate answer to that. My mind was still doing somersaults to figure out how the man who'd tried to take advantage of circumstances as I'd lain prostrate flashing next week's washing had suddenly materialised in Sonny's Bar several weeks later. It just didn't add up but he wasn't backing off and that was causing my panic levels to rise.

'DONALD! STELLA?' I bellowed desperately hoping to summon someone, anyone to help me. This guy could make a grab for the till at any moment and even though I knew there was very little in there I was damned if I was going to let him take it. Perhaps it was the spirits he was after, I wouldn't put it past him to try and whip a few bottles of the hard stuff from under my nose. I saw his eyes flick towards the alcove behind me as Stella stepped into the bar with Donald following close behind.

'I wasn't sure about her writing on the toilet doors but I actually think it looks pretty good,' Stella was saying over her shoulder, not caring a jot if I overheard the back-handed compliment. She's a tell-it-like-it-is sort, is Stella.

'It'd better not lead to more graffiti,' Donald grumbled in response. Typical Donald.

'What's up?' asked Stella as they spotted me in a stand-off with the red-headed stranger.

'This ... this ... villain is trying to rob the place!' I hissed with as much venom as I could muster, the sight of reinforcements having quelled the panic and let my anger rise to the fore.

'I doubt it,' said Stella.

'What?' I jerked my head towards her and caught her twitching her lips as if trying to suppress a smile. I looked back at Ginger and saw, no ... did he just wink at her? Oh Jesus, were they in this together?

'I saw you were advertising for acts to play here and I thought it might be cool to give it a go, but perhaps I'll come back when your decorator has finished.' He nodded his head at Stella and Donald as he said this, ignoring me completely as he took one of my crumpled leaflets about Sonny's Bar from his back pocket and laid it on the round bar table on his right. With that he spun around, picked up the large guitar case I hadn't spotted that had been propped next to the door and disappeared back up the stairs before any of us had chance to move.

'Oh shit!' said Donald.

'What the fuck?' exploded Stella.

'Huh?' I wasn't sure what was happening but Donald and Stella appeared to be furious from the way they were staring at me with what strongly resembled utter contempt.

'Do you know who that was?' Stella spoke slowly and deliberately as if I was simple, stupid or senile.

I shook my head. I certainly didn't have instant recall for every mugshot on Edinburgh's 'Most Wanted' list, even though I had to admit his was an annoyingly handsome face when I'd looked at him square on.

'That was Tom Coltrane!' Donald breathed the words with a hint of awe.

It took a beat or two for my brain to recalibrate with this information.

'Tom … Coltrane?' I repeated the words to help my mind accept the notion.

Stella was losing patience now. 'Yes Becky, Tom Coltrane, the country music star. The guy who swapped Scotland for Nashville and became a huge hit all over the world! Tom Coltrane! The guy who usually plays to hoards of screaming fans in stadiums. And he was here, in our bar, suggesting he might want to play a bloody gig for us and you brandished your daft paintbrush at him, accused him of being some sort of criminal and frightened him off!'

'You muppet!' Donald ended Stella's tirade with a two-word payoff that clearly summed up their joint opinion.

'But he tried to steal my handbag …' I offered the explanation lamely as Stella bolted for the door, her bright red Doc Martens pounding up the stairs to street level chasing after Coltrane.

'Unlikely,' muttered Donald. 'I've heard that his brother is a copper round here you know!'

'Huh?' I sank wearily onto a nearby bar stool desperately wishing some part of my life would start to make sense. It didn't look like that was going to happen any time soon.

Chapter Six

'So I reckon he thinks you're deranged but I told him you've been under a lot of stress lately coz you're so new to the job.' Stella had taken her time to get back to the bar and from her flushed cheeks and starry eyes I could see she was quite the smitten kitten after catching up with Tom Coltrane. It was the little things that gave her away: she kept checking her reflection in the mirror beneath the optics while she filled me and Donald in on their little chat, fiddling with her blonde punky cut and re-tying the patterned bandana around her throat.

'You told him *what!?*' I was grinding my teeth so hard it was a wonder I could speak at all.

'Well I had to tell him something! You were accusing him of all sorts and, according to Tom, you assaulted him once already at the police station when he was trying to be a gentleman and help you with a bag you'd dropped. He really has the most adorable manners you know, picked up some proper Southern charm from the States, along with that incredible accent ... there's a hint of Scottish burr beneath a cowboy drawl' she tailed off, looking lost in thought for a moment. 'It's like Jack Daniel's Tennessee Honey.' Stella gave herself a little shake and then added, 'He said you fell down the stairs and then jumped up and hit him on the head with an iron bar, or something?'

I closed my eyes at the painful memory, painful for both me and Tom in different ways, and then opened them to find Donald staring at me in shock. 'You committed "Actual Bodily Harm" on Tom Coltrane? Outside the police station? Any witnesses?'

'Well, there was my lawyer and this big copper, a sergeant I think he was,' I grimaced at my latest confession. How the hell did I keep getting myself into situations where I could be accused of criminal actions? Me? The girl who had never even got a speeding ticket ... although that may have quite a bit to do with the fact I've never learned to drive.

Stella stopped fixing her hair and tried to calm Donald: 'Yeah, that was Tom's brother Jack, he's a custody sergeant, he told me. He said they'd been larking about at the top of the steps. You're lucky they didn't get you arrested.' She directed the last bit at me as though she thought they really should have thrown the book at me and that I was lucky not to have been sent straight to jail. I didn't think now was the time to tell her I still might be.

'So he wasn't trying to snatch my handbag that day?' The cogs were whirring slowly but my brain was beginning to understand I must have completely misunderstood the situation outside the cop shop.

Stella rolled her kohl-rimmed eyes but didn't dignify my statement with a response. She was now talking about the fact I'd managed to snatch defeat from the jaws of victory by driving away the biggest draw Sonny's Bar could ever dream to have play our tiny stage.

'Tom's come back to Edinburgh for the first time in years, he said. He lives in Nashville, you know, but he saw your leaflet and just thought it would be fun to play a tiny little local gig in his hometown again, like he used to in the old days.'

'Cool …' Donald exhaled the word in a long breath then shook his head at the magnitude of the missed opportunity.

'So he's gone off the idea now he knows I'm the manager here?' I knew the question was redundant as soon as I said it.

'Well he thought you were some lunatic interior designer we'd hired in at first.' My heart leaped with hope that the situation might still be retrievable until Stella added, 'But I had to tell him you weren't the decorator, you were the boss.' I should have known Stella wouldn't lie, she was truthful to a fault. With the emphasis on fault. But she was persistent, a bit like a dog with a bone, she hadn't given up hope that Tom could be convinced to come back and perform, and boasted they had swapped numbers and she would be talking to him about it again. I highly doubted Coltrane had the same motive for swapping contact details with a swooning hot blonde. Call me cynical but I wouldn't be holding my breath for a superstar of Tom Coltrane's status to ever grace our tiny stage.

I decided to try and win back some favour by giving Donald and Stella the rest of the afternoon off. We'd made good progress with the clean-up and stock check and no customers would be in before six o'clock but I doubted the early dart made much difference to their increasingly low opinion of me. I just couldn't stand any more analysis of what an appearance by Tom Coltrane could have done to put Sonny's on the map and gain me more brownie points than a Brown Owl could ever dream of. Stella had theorised that Coltrane was probably after a publicity stunt of some sort to launch a new album, but so what? Of all the basement bars in all the world Tom Coltrane had walked into mine, dangled the most amazing opportunity right in front of my face and I'd blown it.

I tidied up the brushes and fetched some white spirit to clean up the worst of the paint splashes on the floor. Luckily the worn flagstones were so ancient there wasn't much damage there and I'd managed to avoid splattering any tables and chairs. No, I'd just Jackson Pollocked a Grammy award-winning singer-songwriter but I was trying very hard not to think about that. I was grabbing my jacket from behind the bar when I heard the sound of someone coming down the stairs. My stomach instantly turned a somersault, hoping Tom Coltrane had decided his tiny gig gimmick idea was too good to throw away just because he thought I was a graffiti artist with violent tendencies.

My mouth went dry as the steps got closer. What could I say to a misunderstood musician to make amends? Offer to buy him a new shirt? Tell him how much I loved his latest record? No ... I couldn't do that, I couldn't actually remember what his most recent record was ... damn it. I'd loved his earlier stuff ... his lyrics were witty backed with boogie-woogie piano-playing and honky-tonk guitar, his songs had spoken directly to my country music loving heart. Why then had I not recognised him instantly outside the police station? My only explanation was that I really hadn't expected to see a star of Tom Coltrane's magnitude fooling about on the Edinburgh streets. I had also been rather preoccupied by my own police-related predicament.

I steeled myself to give a much better account of myself at what was about to be our third encounter, third time lucky, hopefully. I also realised I was suddenly conscious of what I must look like. Ridiculous really as, on our first meeting, he'd seen my knickers and my temper, and in the last hour he'd seen me in my painting scruffs. Unless I was dressed up as Dolly Parton I never made much effort with my appearance. I'd got into the habit of being a 'take me as you find me' sort of gal. I liked comfy jeans and practical t-shirts and sweaters and it was nice not to bother about plastering on make-up or bothering much with my hair when I wasn't on stage. I reckoned it was good to let my skin breathe but I was kicking myself I didn't have at least a lipstick to hand right now. I quickly pinched my cheeks and licked my lips so I didn't look too washed out. There wasn't much that ever could be done with my mousey locks. My hair wasn't dead straight but it wasn't properly curly either, it could never seem to make up its mind what it wanted to do. I was currently wearing a red headscarf tied Land Army-girl style with a bow on top of my head. I made the snap judgement that was a better option than revealing what was underneath. Perhaps Tom might think it was adorable. I stepped towards the stairwell and told myself to pull it together: this wasn't a first date, this was an opportunity to nail an amazing coup for Sonny's Bar, so I needed to be polite and professional not pretty and pouty.

But, of course, it wasn't a famous music star coming down the stairs. That sort of thing could only ever happen once in a lifetime not twice in an afternoon, I told myself. I quickly tried not to look too disappointed as Calum Crutchley peered around the red velvet curtain and caught me hovering expectantly.

'Ah, Miss Mooney, there you are, I was hoping I'd catch you here. I have some news and I thought it would be good to deliver it in person.'

I offered the solicitor a drink, even though he didn't look old enough to be served alcohol, but he waved it away. He did indeed have news and for once it was good.

'I've spoken to the detective looking into your case and she says they don't think they have enough to take it forward to the CPS.'

I was still recovering from my forlorn hope that singer songwriter Tom Coltrane would reappear so I just looked at Calum blankly.

'That means they're not going ahead with a theft prosecution. They didn't think Guy Grayson's account of what happened added up against your story and also deduced he'd be a terrible prosecution witness. Called him a bit of a slimy snake, between you and me. You're off the hook.'

I understood that. I let the news sink in. I'd been more tightly wound up than I'd realised: it was all I could do to stop the tears pricking behind my eyes.

'Thank you, really, thanks so much Calum, it's really good of you to come and tell me in person.' My voice was thick but Calum just smiled and nodded. He stood up from the table where we were sitting, his mission now accomplished the boy wonder was on to his next adventure.

'No problem, although ...' he hesitated and sat back down looking at me with an earnest expression on his face. 'This has been a bit of a weird case if I'm honest. You might not be being prosecuted for theft, but you have lost your job and we've no real clue as to why Guy accused you the way he did. The CPS might be content to call it a 'misunderstanding' and accept all the missing items have now been accounted for but there's much more to it if you ask me.'

Calum was right of course and it was the one thing that had been troubling me almost as much as the thought of going to court. What had it all been about? It wasn't an insurance job – the police had retrieved all the items Guy had claimed had been stolen. If he'd simply wanted me out of the way, couldn't he have just fired me? Maybe he needed a proper reason to do that? Is that what all this was about? It seemed a lot more vindictive and personal than that. Calum Crutchley seemed to think so too.

'If I were you, Miss Mooney, I'd watch my back.' With that final warning Calum nodded and stood up again.

'You make it sound like he's out to get me.' I tried to laugh but the sound caught in my throat. Calum got to the stairwell and put his head on one side as if carefully considering what he should say next.

'Now the police have decided not to prosecute, that should be the end of it, but ...'

'But ...?' Did Calum really think Guy Grayson had some sort of vendetta against me? Why? What had I ever done to him?

'You should go and see your old boss, Gordon, is it? I know I told you to steer well clear while you were under investigation but now you're in the clear, it might be wise to get back in touch. Perhaps he said something to the police to help your case. Calum was still talking, trying to convince me to go and see Gordon and Morag, but I was having trouble taking anything in beyond the thought that I'd escaped a spell of incarceration condemned to a diet of porridge.

I snapped back to reality and managed to nod back at him enthusiastically, glad to be given the go ahead from Calum to go and visit the Graysons. I couldn't imagine they were my enemies. I'd missed them. We'd got on so well right from the start. I couldn't bear to think that they might think badly of me or that I'd caused them any stress on top of everything they'd been through with Morag's illness.

As I locked up the bar a feeling of exhaustion washed over me. The relief of having the case dropped had released a ball of tension inside me but the result was I now felt tired to my bones. The crazy second encounter with Tom Coltrane in the last hour now felt like a fever dream ... had it really happened? I knew if I went home right now I'd probably collapse into a big bag of marshmallows and then sleep for a week. That wouldn't do. I needed to come back and join Donald and Stella for the evening shift or they really would think I was the worst boss in the whole world. I had to keep going.

I glanced at my watch: it was only four o'clock in the afternoon. Really? It had felt like such a very long day already. As I reached street level and locked up the bar, the little cake shop along the street caught my eye. Its window was always filled with gorgeous Parisienne-style delicacies. It gave me an idea.

I selected half a dozen of the prettiest fancies and had them boxed up and tied with pink and white striped ribbon. It wasn't a peace offering as such, and it certainly wasn't an apology – after all, I hadn't done anything wrong – but it felt wrong to arrive unannounced at Gordon and Morag's without some sort of gift. They had old-fashioned manners themselves and I couldn't imagine them going to visit anyone empty-handed.

I held the box gingerly on my lap as I sat on the bus to Murrayfield. With any luck Gordon and Morag would invite me in for a cup of tea. I was excited to see them, like a little girl going to visit her grandparents for a special treat. I could only hope they'd be just as pleased to see me.

Chapter Seven

The way Gordon's face lit up when he opened his front door and saw me standing on his step instantly quelled my lingering nerves. Next minute I was being yanked by the hand into the hallway and down to the kitchen at the back of the house.

'Morag! ... MORAG! Guess who it is come to see us? It's our Becky ... Look.' He presented me with a flourish as Morag put her teacup down on the pine kitchen table she was sitting beside.

'Becky hen, come in, come in.' Morag didn't rise from her chair but beckoned me towards her as she waved Gordon towards a large blue teapot standing on the stove. 'Get another cup, Gordon, there's plenty left in the pot. You'll have a cup, won't you, Becky?'

The small kitchen was warmed by the heat coming from the ancient old-fashioned range cooker and I was warmed by the beaming smiles the couple were giving as I opened the box of French fancies and found a place on the cluttered table to put them.

They were so chatty and happy I almost forgot everything that had happened and the fact I no longer worked at Grayson's Jewellers. Morag was telling me the doctors were pleased with her progress, she was recovering well from what she claimed had been a 'mini' stroke. 'Just a warning, really,' she insisted while Gordon took a bite of his coffee éclair and nodded in agreement although I spotted a look of concern flash across his face.

'And what about you, hen? How are *you* doing?' Gordon asked the question but they both looked at me expectantly.

What was the best way to broach this? I took time to finish my mouthful of flaky custard tart and dab my mouth with a piece of kitchen roll, reluctant to break the spell by talking about all the recent unpleasantness.

'Oh well, you know, it's all been a bit strange but I'm okay … I think?' I gave an awkward little laugh and clocked they were smiling at me indulgently.

'Starting a new job is always a bit odd, but look how quickly you settled in with us when you first started, isn't that right, Morag?' Gordon bounced his silver head towards his wife. 'I thought you were heaven sent, a real treasure, didn't I say that, love? You were like finding a rare jewel but I always knew we wouldn't be able to keep you and you'd be on to new adventures before too long.'

Morag was concentrating on pouring a second cup of tea for everybody but when she put the heavy teapot down I noticed she looked as though she was struggling to know quite what to say. Was that because of the after effects of the stroke or something else?

Eventually she found her voice but she spoke uncertainly: 'I told Gordon you wouldn't stay long in an old-fashioned little shop like ours. Oh, I don't mean you weren't well suited to the job, you were a natural with the customers and picked up the business side so quickly, but you were clearly cut out for other things. There's something special about you, Becky, we've always thought so.'

I wasn't sure what to say. They were both saying lovely things, which in any other circumstances it would be a joy to hear but the elephant in the room couldn't be ignored. I hadn't left Grayson's by choice or because a new opportunity had tempted me away. The custard tart I'd just wolfed down was now curdling in my tummy as I fought the urge to tell them just what I really thought of their precious ... predatory son. No parent wanted to hear terrible things about their offspring, that was a universal truth, especially a couple like Gordon and Morag who were so trusting. I remembered how they'd always spoken of Guy and his American family with such longing before his sudden arrival back in Edinburgh after Morag's stroke. I'd got the distinct impression he hadn't made much effort to keep in touch. They'd never had a chance to get to know his wife JoJo and most of what they knew about their teenage granddaughter Kourtney was what they had gleaned from watching her TikTok videos. I recalled Morag trying to show me one once and I'd feigned interest in some shakily filmed make-up tutorial delivered by a drawling teenage girl with swishy hair and gleaming gnashers. Kourtney advised her followers – and Morag was so proud to tell me there were *thousands* – to apply a sweep of different colour shimmering shadow to each eye. I thought it made her look unhinged but I'd managed to keep my opinion to myself that time. Gordon and Morag may not be so fortunate today: I was itching to give them my full and frank assessment of the horrible little family who had decided to relocate to Scotland and their attempts to wreck my life while they were at it.

The uncomfortable silence as I agonised over what to say was eventually broken by Gordon.

'When the police came to see us, I told them straight away, if Becky says she had permission to take those items then that will be the truth.'

Morag nodded slowly and added, 'I told the officer, didn't I, Gordon, it will be some sort of silly mix up. Guy must have got the wrong end of the stick.'

So Gordon and Morag *had* spoken up for me, but couldn't bring themselves to think badly of their prodigal son. It was a tale as old as time but I didn't have the heart to confront them about it. What good would that do me anyway? They were such a lovely couple and they also seemed to hold me in very high regard, despite everything. That was a novelty I wouldn't mind enjoying for a little longer.

I decided to direct the conversation towards my plans for Sonny's Bar and away from the circumstances of my exit from Grayson's. Despite the fact I was desperate to get to the bottom of why Guy had behaved in such a dastardly fashion towards me, I chatted about all the ideas I had and what Stella and Donald were like.

'You'll soon have that place on the map I'm sure,' Gordon said, 'and I bet you'll be booked solid in no time.'

I felt healed by the heat pumping from the range, the hot tea in my belly and the sheer positivity Gordon and Morag were lavishing on me. I didn't get to see my own mum and dad too often, with them living the high life in Spain most of the year. I didn't think I missed them all that much but, being here with the Graysons, I was realising what I was missing. I didn't want to do or say anything that would ruin it. Home wasn't a place, after all, it was people.

Morag suddenly started rooting around in one of the kitchen cupboards. 'Where is that ... I'm sure I put it in here ... maybe it's ... ahh here we go!' She swung around to face us with a pink paper gift bag in her hands. 'I couldn't resist it when I spotted it. It's nothing much ... I just saw it and immediately thought of you.' Morag looked a bit sheepish as she proffered the package towards me.

I took it but immediately felt my face flush. 'Oh you really shouldn't have, Morag, you don't need to give me anything.'

'Well don't open it now, I just thought it might be nice to give it to you sooner rather than later. We didn't get a chance to give you a leaving gift. Open it when you get home, when you feel like it. Hopefully it'll make you smile.'

I sat cradling the gift on my lap for the rest of the visit, keeping Morag's kindness close. As we'd carried on chatting I'd caught sight of the kitchen clock on the wall and realised I had better start making a move. I wasn't on the rota to work a shift in the bar that night but after what had happened earlier in the day with Tom Coltrane I thought it was best if I put an appearance in.

I didn't tell Gordon and Morag about my embarrassing encounters with the famous musician. I didn't want to start a story that began with me on the steps of the police station and ended with me totally messing everything up. Again.

I did confide in them about the recent break-up with Robbie, though, and how that had led to me taking on the job at Sonny's. They seemed more interested in how this would affect my singing career than my love life. Perhaps they had sensed Robbie was never 'the one'. I told them running the bar was my focus now and how I was planning on putting my Dolly stage costumes up for sale. 'There might be another Dolly Parton tribute act out there who could make use of them, or some drama group could make pantomime dame costumes out of them maybe?' I tried to laugh at that but the thought of Widow Twankey or Mother Goose wearing my rhinestones and tassels was actually too tragic for words.

'Oh no, Becky, you mustn't give up on your dreams.' Morag leaned forward looking properly distressed at the thought of me jacking in the tribute act.

'Well I'm not sure singing '9 to 5' to drunken hen and stag parties is anyone's actual dream.' I was sending myself up while talking myself down and Gordon wasn't standing for it.

'You love performing and you're good at it,' he said. I looked at him in shock: how did he know, had he ever seen me sing? 'Quite a few of our customers have seen you perform you know, and they were always telling me how good you are. A couple of them told me you should be on *Top of the Pops*, not as Dolly but as yourself.'

He sounded convinced I could be the next big chart sensation but I couldn't bring myself to tell him the television music show he was on about hadn't been broadcast for years. I also didn't want to admit that dressing as Dolly was the only way I was comfortable on a stage. I waved away the compliments and made noises as though I was only kidding about hanging up Dolly's cowgirl hat.

I arrived back at my flat much later that evening after an uneventful shift at Sonny's. After everything that had happened recently, uneventful was good. Uneventful I liked. Donald and I had split the work, serving a steady trickle of customers until around 9 p.m. when he suggested I get off and he would cover the last couple of hours. Donald hadn't said much all night. Nothing too unusual there, but I was grateful to him for the offer to close up. It felt like he was trying to show there were no hard feelings, although I might have been reading too much into it. No matter, I appreciated the gesture and didn't take much persuading to head home.

The early escape was a good way to end what had been a pretty strange day. Not the only strange day I'd had recently but it had eventually turned into one of the nicest, I had to admit. The threat of prosecution was no longer hanging over me and I was glad I'd taken the plunge and decided to visit Gordon and Morag. I'd thought I needed to get some answers from them, find out more about Guy Grayson's motives but I realised now their goodwill had been more valuable to me than answers. Even though I hadn't received any sort of explanation or insight into the workings of their son's crazy mind I really did feel more positive and cheerful for having seen them.

Back at the flat I headed straight to the kitchen to make myself some tea and toast. Eating so much cake late in the afternoon meant I hadn't been hungry before, but now I was ravenous.

While I waited for the kettle to boil I turned to the pink gift bag Morag had given me that was sitting on the kitchen counter. I remembered Morag saying she'd thought of me as soon as she'd seen it. Whatever could it be?

I dug down into the tissue stuffed into the bag until my fingers found something cold and smooth. I fished it out – a mug – but not any old mug. It was white with a picture of a pair of sparkly pink cowboy boots printed on both sides, above the boots was a slogan in fancy Western-style lettering that read 'What Would Dolly Do?' I was grinning from ear to ear. Bless Morag's heart, I loved it.

I christened the new mug by pouring tea into it and stood at the kitchen counter polishing off a second slice of hot buttered toast as a thought started swirling inside my mind. I'd always thought of my Dolly quotes as mantras, as inspiration ... but not as actual instructions. Perhaps that was where I'd been going wrong. What *would* Dolly do? Was it bonkers to wonder? She'd always been my idol, why couldn't she by my guide, too? I definitely seemed to need one. Dolly's chutzpah and resilience were qualities I not only admired but would love to possess, if only I could have her confidence and sunny disposition, neither of which appeared to be fitted as standard in my particular case.

Dolly had gone from a dirt-poor home in the Smokey Mountains to being one of the most successful recording artists of all time. She was a feminist on her own terms, running her career and business the way she wanted to; presenting herself with big hair, big boobs and an even bigger brain that proved she was no dumb blonde. No wonder I felt even occasionally dressing up as Dolly gave me a lift: it was like being able to tap into some sort of superpower.

As I continued to contemplate the question of what the real Dolly Parton would do if she were me, I wandered into the spare bedroom and looked at the pile of discarded costumes heaped on the bed in there. I'd felt wretched and ridiculous when I'd wrenched each colourful diamanté-encrusted piece from its hanger and flung it into the haphazard rainbow mountain that now loomed before me. It was done in a fit of anger and self-pity. With Robbie gone the thought of carrying on performing in pubs, clubs and at private parties on my own seemed too daunting. But would Dolly Parton have ever given in because she'd been let down by a man? No Siree! In fact, I knew she'd done the very opposite, breaking away from the country music legend Porter Waggoner who had taken her under his wing at the start of her career. All the hours I'd spent reading about her life, watching old interviews and listening to the songs meant I knew the facts of Dolly's story well. But, I realised, it was how I felt when I sang them that taught me something more – I could feel some of her fire and her steel. I didn't have to only ask what would Dolly do, I could also draw inspiration from what Dolly really did do. The Waggoner story was incredible. Porter Waggoner was a huge American music star and Dolly was a regular on his show in the seventies but came to the realisation that she needed to forge her own path. Inspired by the turmoil she felt from having to tell her good friend she was leaving his show she'd written the million-selling hit song 'I Will Always Love You' for him. It was a classy way to deal with a difficult situation. Now, I might not be about to sit down and write a solid-gold classic song but I could take a leaf out of Dolly's book and work out if I should – or even if I could – go it alone. As if that wasn't inspirational enough, Dolly the one-woman hit factory also wrote her most famous song, 'Jolene', on the very same day, in the very same writing session. What a woman.

I reached for a white leather waistcoat covered in tassels and rhinestones and held it up, looking at myself in the mirror with just a touch of Dolly between me and my reflection. Was Morag right? Was I wrong to give up on being Dolly … was I throwing away a dream if I got rid of all the wigs and costumes? Or did Gordon have a point? Could I really be good enough to make a go of it as a singer if I just gave myself a chance?

Right now, I was struggling with the idea of performing at all – as Dolly or as Becky Mooney. Although, to tell the truth, I'd struggled with that last one for years, which was why finding I had the ability to morph into Dolly Parton had been the perfect way to carry on with any sort of showbiz career after I stopped performing with Mum and Dad in the Moonshine Trio. Dolly had come riding to my rescue by letting me hide behind her larger than life persona. Without Dolly I knew I would have jacked in performing altogether and given up on any chance of using my voice. I knew I could sing well enough, but that knowledge hadn't been enough to give me the confidence I needed to face an audience as plain old Becky Mooney.

It had been lovely to hear some praise from Gordon for my singing. It had given me an extra smidgen of self-worth and a bit of a boost, but I knew I didn't have either the confidence or the image to be a solo performer in my own right. I just didn't. It would be foolish to over-estimate my own abilities. I'd never done that and I didn't believe I should start now. But was I ready to give up a life on stage altogether? If I were to chuck out all of my Dolly wardrobe and my chance to live vicariously as her every once in a while, was I throwing the baby out with the bath water?

Piece by piece I began to rehang the glittery, gaudy garments back onto their hangers. Little by little bringing the Dolly side of me back to life. It felt good. So what if I'd lost my Kenny? I decided. I would carry on in my own way, with a solo Dolly Parton tribute act. I didn't need Robbie, just like Dolly had realised she didn't need Porter Waggoner. I could go it alone. I just needed a booking or two to prove it to myself. As I was thinking through all the venues I'd played as a double act, wondering if I should ring them to try to drum up a gig, the penny dropped. I didn't have to spend hours finding venues. I had my own.

It was only a few days until the open auditions I'd organised to draw some new performers to Sonny's Bar. There would be singers, comedians, magicians, and an audience to judge the contestants. Or at least I hoped there would. I would put my hat in the ring and let the crowd decide if my show should go on. It would be the perfect place to showcase my new solo act and let the world (or at least this little corner of it) know that Edinburgh's very own Dolly was back in business and wasn't going to let anything or anyone stand in her way. Yes, I decided, *that's* what Dolly would do!

Chapter Eight

When I came up with the idea of holding an old-fashioned 'Open Mic' or 'Free 'n' Easy' night I figured the tickets would be free and the organisation would be pretty easy. We weren't charging for entrance to the bar for the show but we were aiming to make a good profit on the drinks sold during the evening. By posting on all our updated social media accounts, putting up some colourful posters and spreading the news by word of mouth we felt sure we'd have a good selection of performers coming along. Even if some of them were not so good I thought the crowd would still find it pretty entertaining. After all, didn't everyone always love the terrible early auditions on those search-for-a-star TV shows?

Free 'n' Easy was a phrase I'd grown up with on the old working men's clubs circuit to encourage people to get up and have a go at singing a song, or perhaps playing the piano, way before the days of karaoke. When I was a kid touring with my parents I often heard about the times a local would get up and belt out a showstopper and bring the house down. It would be great to have something like that happen on our night, I thought. I wanted to encourage that old feeling of community spirit at Sonny's, create a place where people knew they could come and always know they would have a good time and be entertained, discover a taste of old-school showbiz in a family atmosphere.

That was my motivation for the event, but then I'd gone and added an extra degree of difficulty and a huge amount of risk by deciding to put my own name into the hat. Stella had decided pulling names out of a hat was going to be the fairest way to pick from all the punters who showed up and I'd backed her – it would give everyone, me included, a level playing field.

'Let everyone who wants to perform stick their name on a piece of paper, we'll put them all in this hat,' she said, quickly retrieving a battered, glittery bowler hat that had been knocking around in the storeroom, as a lot more people than we'd expected started to fill up the tables in the bar. 'That way we add a bit of theatricality to proceedings when the name gets pulled out and we're being fair.' I couldn't argue on either point although Donald did question how we'd handle all the people who didn't get their names chosen?

'Simple, we announce we'll be holding more nights like this and they'll have to come back again.' Stella was confident and efficient and she was being a lot more enthusiastic about this night than I had expected her to be. I hadn't told her, or anyone else about my plan to perform as Dolly and now I couldn't bring myself to – my name may not even get pulled out of the hat. I would need a bit of time to get ready though if it did. I'd stashed my stage gear under a desk in the office and I realised some other performers would also appreciate a bit of run-up time before they took their place on our little stage. Stella agreed that names would be called in batches of three: that way anyone who needed a moment to prepare would be able to take it without us losing the momentum of the night. With all the arrangements in place, we kicked off the night's entertainment with a comedian called Gary Garlic – who did stink a bit at first but the audience gave him a chance and he did get much better. That was sometimes the magic of live performance – feeding off the crowd's energy and finding your stride. In quick succession, there was also an elderly jazz trumpeter everyone adored and an exotic dancer named Trudie who stayed just on the right side of rudie.

Things seemed to be going well as the evening went on. Stella was keeping track of all the performers, with a note of particular ones we might want to invite back. There were more hits than misses, luckily, and the crowd were forgiving rather than vicious with the singers and comedians who didn't quite make the grade. It was a fun, joyous atmosphere, just as I'd hoped it would be.

I'd almost forgotten my name had gone into the glittery bowler until I heard Stella on the mic.

'Next up, in no particular order prepare to welcome to Sonny's Bar ... Jack Tinker, Gabby Wolf and ... Wait ... What? ... *Becky Mooney*?' Stella peered across the heads of the audience with a quizzical look on her face but the bright lights shining towards the stage prevented her from seeing my startled expression in return.

I kicked myself for not using a stage name, but then I reckoned they would have realised it was me soon enough, so I quickly got my head in the game. It was now or never and I'd put myself up for this after all. There was no time to explain too much to Stella, but Jack Tinker wanted to go on second so the order was sorted with comic Gabby Wolf agreeing to go on first, leaving me with the final spot. Phew. I headed straight to the office to get 'Dollified' aware that Stella had barely taken her eyes off me despite Gabby having the audience in stitches from the first gag out of her mouth.

I usually had my Dolly prep down to a fine art but this night I found my hands were shaking as I began to apply bright blue eyeshadow onto my lids. It definitely felt like there was so much more at stake than usual. I needed to prove myself to *myself*, as well as the assembled punters. Could I still bring the Dolly magic minus the Kenny content? I didn't have time to waste on nerves or second guessing. Muscle memory kicked in as I fixed my wig, padded my bra and I was just pulling on a silver cowboy boot as I heard a sound that froze my country music lovin' heart. It was the opening bars to 'Jolene'.

I burst from the office, about to sprint to the stage. Why the hell had Stella allowed the backing track to begin when I was not yet in position? The answer was gobsmackingly obvious when I clocked the incredible sight before me. Large as life and twice as buxom, Dolly Parton was already on stage. She raised the microphone to her lips and began to sing the refrain. It took my mind a few beats to process what was happening – there was *another* Dolly tribute act at the open mic session. I'd never even considered the possibility of that happening. I knew I wasn't the only person to ever dress up and perform as the queen of country music but Robbie and I had felt we'd sort of cornered the local market over the last few years and we'd never encountered much competition. I was clearly up against it now however. This Drag Queen Dolly was good. Really good. Her voice was strong and her outfit was an eye-catching red, white and blue Stars and Stripes jacket and matching mini skirt.

By the time Dolly got to the bit about Jolene's red hair and green eyes I was finding something a bit odd about the performance. I couldn't quite put my finger on it at first but there was something unusual about it that was bothering me. It wasn't just professional jealousy and disappointment, although I was certainly feeling that too. That wasn't what was clouding my judgement, honestly it wasn't. Suddenly I realised what I was finding so strange about the sight before me in the spotlight, Dolly was standing side on to the audience so we could only see her left-hand profile.

Right at the moment I worked out what was weird it all got a whole lot more bizarre. The backing music changed. 'Jolene' segued into 'Islands in the Stream'. Wondering how she was going to handle a duet, I looked towards the restrooms to see where this Dolly's Kenny Rogers was about to spring from to join in with the next part of the medley. Would it be another Amazonian diva striding out? But there was no one else heading to the stage to perform.

Dolly suddenly spun on the spot, switching the profile she was showing to the audience to her right-hand side. In a flash, Dolly in all her gaudy Americana was gone and in her place was a silver-haired singer with a full beard and a light blue suit. Dolly and Kenny were one person! It was a neat trick and the crowd whooped and laughed as Dolly/Kenny sang their duet. Jack Tinker's quirky drag act was not going to be something I would be able to follow with my run-of-the-mill solo spot. I felt my heart sink and a tidal wave of disappointment crash over me. I had to get back into the office and get my second-rate Dolly garb off before anyone spotted me lurking at the back of the room. Luckily all eyes were on Jack, or 'Dolly Partly' as he introduced himself to the crowd who were lapping it all up.

'Shit!' I muttered to myself, Dolly Partly had funny banter as well as a totally original gimmick. There really was no hope and I was now desperate to escape.

I took a big step backwards keeping my eyes on the increasingly brilliant performance as 'Kenny' sang a few lines warning Ruby not to take her love to town while 'Dolly' hilariously interjected with sections of 'Here You Come Again'. It really was a great act.

No one was taking any notice of me, thank goodness, as I stepped back further, but the heel of my cowboy boot landed firmly on the toe of someone standing right behind me.

'Arrgghh!'

'I'm so sorry.' I hissed my apology as I whirled around to face a man who had crept up behind me in the darkness.

'You!'

'Yet another warm welcome. I really should take the hint, shouldn't I, darlin'?' Tom Coltrane winced as he limped towards the back wall. Unbelievably I had injured him for a *third* time.

My horror was further compounded as the famous singer who kept on getting under my feet looked me up and down, taking in everything from the bright blonde bouffant wig to the tip of my one silver western boot. He then flicked his eyes towards the stage and raised a quizzical eyebrow.

'What's all this? Double Dolly night? I didn't realise a Dolly drag dress code was compulsory.'

'It isn't!' I was still hissing at him as I shoved him towards the office door just behind us. I couldn't afford to create a scene at this moment. If the rest of the audience spotted me now it would be excruciating. I had no desire to die a thousand Dolly deaths by attempting to follow the storming set Dolly Partly was delivering.

Tom sort of stumbled backwards and we both landed in the back office so I was able to close the door on the crowd now lustily singing along with '9 to 5'.

My audacious manoeuvre had succeeded in removing the risk of me being seen or of anyone noticing me and a famous singer having a heated exchange of whispered words but, as usual, I hadn't thought through the consequences. I was now trapped in a very small space half-dressed as a poor man's tribute act while Tom looked in astonishment from the closed door and back to me. I could tell he was beginning to figure out the sorry situation.

'I take it what's going on out there has ruined your big moment a bit then?'

He spoke slowly, with a Southern drawl more suited to Alabama than Aberdeen but his mind was quick, I'd give him that, though he clearly hadn't got a clue how painful this was as he stood there mocking me.

'Something like that, yeah,' I conceded grumpily as I wrenched the blonde wig from my hair. I pulled off the lone silver cowboy boot and stood there in my stockinged feet trying desperately to appear dignified in my pink tasselled suede two-piece. It just couldn't be done while my boobs were pointing straight at him like a pair of helium-filled barrage balloons. Tom's eyebrows shot sky high as I reached inside my jacket and swiftly removed two foam domes.

'That's quite an act you have there. What d'you do for an encore?'

The temptation to either burst into tears or swear at him profusely was doing battle inside me but then I caught the look in his eye. I laughed. I couldn't help it. The whole thing was obviously so ridiculous and he looked pretty amused too. You know when you try and laugh quietly it just makes everything so much funnier? Well, that's what happened. We suddenly found ourselves clutching at each other, shushing and giggling until I was gasping for breath.

'Oh, oh … stop it, we need to pull ourselves together.' I was wiping my eyes.

'Well you could try but most of you is all over the floor.' Tom nodded his head in the direction of my hair piece and the false boobies lying at our feet and that set us both off all over again.

It was the sound of the crowd cheering the end of Dolly Partly's storming set and Stella taking over on the mic getting all ready to announce me that stopped our laughter in its tracks. Tom saw the look of pure panic on my face and made a swift decision.

'You stay here, I'll handle this, honey,' he announced and I was pathetically grateful and confused all at once. He was offering to help me: that was something I wasn't used to. And he'd also called me honey: I wasn't used to that either. No one had ever called me 'honey' before but somehow with that cowboy-style way of talking it didn't feel patronising. Instead I found it sort of friendly and possibly even a bit flirty?

Tom read the mixed emotions on my face and leaned in close. 'I can pull focus so no one wonders where you are, I have the technology.' With that he swung a guitar from behind his back where he'd been carrying it as a rucksack. 'I'll be the surprise act you booked to close the show,' he said with a wink and just before heading out of the door and up onto the Sonny's Bar stage he leaned in close and kissed me softly on my hot, pink cheek.

Chapter Nine

It was strange to experience my first live Tom Coltrane gig from inside the back office, just peeping out through a chink in the door after wriggling out of my Dolly Parton outfit and back into my jeans and t-shirt.

The crowd was loving Tom running through a few of his well-known hits. He was relaxed and playing acoustic guitar to accompany himself on some laid-back versions of songs everybody remembered from when they were in the charts a few years ago. It was clear we were being treated to something pretty special; to see a star as big as Tom outside a huge arena or enormous stadium is rare. Here he had no backing singers or stage pyrotechnics, it was just a man, a guitar and a whole load of talent. My spine was tingling with the thrill of witnessing someone so incredible on Sonny's tiny little stage, even if I didn't have the best view from my position tucked out of sight. I knew I could have just gone out there and joined in with the audience clapping and singing along but something made me stay put.

Before pulling up a stool and starting his impromptu set Tom had given me a public vote of thanks for inviting him to come along as a surprise guest. He instantly had the crowd in the palm of his hand and I doubted even Stella or Donald remembered I'd had my name pulled out of the hat to perform now that everyone had been wowed by such a famous professional appearing like a musical magic trick right in front of them.

Tom seemed to be having as much fun as the audience and it made me wonder what on earth he was doing performing in our humble little basement club? Wouldn't he rather be playing to vast crowds of screaming fans? Before I knew what I was doing, I reached for my phone and started googling. Tom's last hit record was further back than I thought, a good five years ago. I hadn't realised he hadn't been troubling the charts for that long. Maybe he was finding it hard to keep the hit records coming; it must be difficult to keep coming up with new stuff to keep the fans interested. Or maybe he was bucking against the executives that ran record companies nowadays and was having 'creative differences' about which path his career should take. There wasn't anything about that online but a few other titbits of information came up as I popped his name into the search; the main one being pictures of his uber-glamorous girlfriend, Hollywood actress Juliana Ripon. She was an absolute stunner, that was for sure, her dark hair cropped into a pixie cut made her eyes look enormous next to her chiselled cheek bones and pouty red lips in the shot that filled my phone screen. I wondered why she wasn't with him? Maybe she was away filming or maybe she was waiting for him at some fancy hotel across town. Either way, I was glad she hadn't come along tonight, only because it would have been even more embarrassing to have my Dolly meltdown in the presence of a goddess like Juliana. I bet Juliana Ripon had never worn a pair of false foam boobies in her life and if she did she certainly wouldn't have yanked them out right in front of poor Tom.

I spent some time flicking through endless photos of Tom and Juliana online – in some of the shots he wore a Stetson cowboy hat which ramped up his macho image considerably. He was pictured with Juliana on red carpets, at awards ceremonies, snapped in downtown Nashville and shopping on L.A.'s Rodeo Drive – good grief, the woman was so photogenic it was ridiculous. I was just thinking what a gorgeous couple they made when the noise coming from the other side of the office door suddenly went up a level. I stuck my head out to see what was going on but there was very little risk that anyone would notice me. Most people were on their feet, whooping and cheering. I couldn't even see Tom at first but then I realised he wasn't in the centre of the stage anymore with his guitar slung around his neck, he'd moved over to where our old upright piano stood at the side and he was playing a mean boogie-woogie. I had no idea Tom was such a great piano player: was the piano stuff on his records played by him? He wasn't playing his own music now though, he was playing some crowd-pleasing cover versions and the place was rocking.

Tom eventually wrapped up the set and sent away so many happy punters I sat in the office wondering how on earth I would ever be able to thank him. He even signed some autographs and posed for a few pictures with people as they made their way out of the basement. As they passed the office door I could hear them raving about Tom, the whole night and the club. Quite a few had been filming on their phones earlier on and had uploaded clips onto social media. The whole night was going to be a huge publicity coup for Sonny's Bar. It was beyond my wildest dreams.

As the crowd dispersed I was about to go out and help with the clear-up but Tom's head suddenly appeared around the door. He looked flushed but his tone was determined.

'Just sit tight and I'll be right back,' was his instruction.

My face possibly showed I was a little surprised to be given orders, I was the manager of the place after all. Tom didn't appear aware of that fact as his eyes darted around the room as though he was looking for something, then he looked back at me with a mischievous look on his face.

'What did y'all do with Dolly?' he asked. 'I was lookin' forward to getting better acquainted with her!'

Back in my jeans and sweater minus the wig and stage make-up I knew I looked radically different to how he'd seen me at the start of the night. He wasn't the first guy to be disappointed with the off-stage version of me, but I still had some of Dolly's spirit lurking in me somewhere so I couldn't resist reaching for a previously discarded foam boob and lobbing it directly at Tom's grinning head as he ducked back out through the door. It landed with a soft thud on the closed door after he disappeared, adding to the ridiculousness of the whole situation.

I wasn't sure whether or not to follow Tom's advice to 'stay put'. Why was I obeying a guy I hardly knew? But I also didn't fancy answering tricky questions from Donald or Stella or bumping into Jack Tinker, in or out of his 'Dolly Partly' character.

So I busied myself straightening up the office, even answering a couple of emails and was rewarded twenty minutes later when Tom reappeared telling me the club was empty, the bar secured, tables wiped down and Stella had given him the keys to lock up now she and Donald had headed home.

'Stella said she'd see you Tuesday,' Tom reassured me after seeing my expression when he brandished the keys. He seemed to be a guy comfortable with taking care of things; I was struck by how unusual it was to encounter a man who appeared so capable and helpful but managed to avoid being condescending. Maybe it was the cross of his Scottish down to earth charm all polished up by his Deep South manners. It was quite a combo.

'Right, okay, thanks.' I stood awkwardly in front of Tom wondering what I had been waiting for, what was supposed to happen now? 'Well, thanks for everything, I'd best lock up now then.' I held my hand out for the keys but Tom didn't hand them over straight away, instead he stood there and smiled at me.

'D'ya fancy a drink?'

As he spoke I suddenly realised I could absolutely murder a scotch on the rocks.

'Abso – bloody – lutely!'

Out in the deserted bar the wall lights gave off a soft warm glow, softening the rough edges of the stone walls and battered wooden tables and chairs. It was nice to have the place to ourselves, it felt familiar and friendly. Tom pulled two chairs up to a table while I fixed us a couple of whiskys.

All at once, sitting in a pool of golden light, sipping scotch with a famous musician felt like the most natural thing in the world.

Tom was easy to chat to. I learned that his sweet Southern manners weren't an affectation, although he'd been brought up near Edinburgh and his father was Scottish, his mother Ellie-Mae was from Birmingham. Not the one down the motorway in the Midlands … the one in Alabama. That explained a lot. He was a curious mix of Scottish ruggedness and Deep South gentleman. He was also a very good listener. I forgot all about his musical prowess, chart-topping success and even his glamour-puss girlfriend as I told him the story of how I came to be running Sonny's Bar; my terrible ex-boss at Grayson's jewellery shop; being dumped by my own Kenny Rogers and how it all led to tonight, trying to make it on my own in the clubs as a solo Dolly. The whole thing wound up sounding like a country music tale of woe.

'You'll be telling me next you've got four hungry children and a crop in the field,' joked Tom as we realised my story could rival Kenny's 'Lucille' as a good ole country story singalong. It had everything required; a villain, some drama, lost love, good times and bad. I'd never thought of my own story in quite that way before but I joked with Tom that I'd been brought up on songs full of heartache and hope performed by my own singing parents. We talked about the skill of country songwriters who took a crazy situation and distilled it into memorable lyrics, and then we speculated about what Dolly could do with a tale of a girl falsely accused of stealing jewellery.

'Oh Ru – by,' I sang, 'just put those diamonds down.'

Tom slapped the table and gave a huge laugh. 'You really are Edinburgh's answer to the queen of country music, aren't ya?' he said, still chuckling. 'Talk about life imitating art,' he added and gave a low whistle once I finished my tale of tragedy and comedy. 'So how good a Dolly are ya really?'

'Huh?' I knocked back the last of my drink and went to get another but Tom laid a hand on my arm. I didn't understand his question. 'What d'you wanna know? I've pretty much told you everything.' His touch had rattled me as much as his question, the heat of his hand on my bare flesh was intense.

'Well, yeah, I get how ya wound up here and I've seen y'all Dollied-up, but what I really want to know is … how much d'ya *sound* like her?' As he spoke he reached for his guitar, propped against a nearby chair. 'There's only one way I can think of for me to find that out.'

He wanted me to sing for him? Right there in the bar? With him playing and me singing? I snorted dismissively and went to refill our drinks but when he started finger picking the notes to 'Little Sparrow' I found myself sitting slowly back down in my seat. Whether it was the strangeness of the day or the effects of the alcohol I'll never know but it was like I'd been hypnotised by the music as I began singing the poignant lyrics of the folksy song straight from Dolly's bluegrass roots.

Once I started singing my initial shyness fell away, my voice soared and I sang the song with all my heart and soul. Tom stopped playing along but that felt right. Dolly herself always performs the song a cappella. The dark surroundings of the bar seemed to stretch away in every direction around me, leaving just Tom and I captured in the warmth of a golden spotlight. There was no other audience, no Sonny's Bar, even Edinburgh itself seemed miles away. There was just me and Tom and the song I was singing. The last notes seemed to hover in the air for a while once the song was sung. I looked down into my empty whisky glass as the last of the ice melted away. Eventually I looked up. Tom was staring at me but I couldn't read the expression in his eyes. After what felt like a very long time he spoke.

'You're not Dolly,' he said, and the blood in my veins turned as cold as the ice in my glass. But Tom wasn't finished; 'You're real good, Becky. Too good to be hiding behind a Dolly wig and tassels.'

My nerves were jangling so loud I was afraid he would wonder what the noise was, so I pretended I was used to handsome, talented men playing me huge compliments and shrugged off his words. I headed to the bar to refill our glasses. Despite feeling a little tipsy I desperately needed another drink and I also needed to shake off the funny feeling Tom's staring eyes were giving me.

'Well gee, thank you kindly sir,' I said with a self-conscious giggle in my 'Dolly voice', but Tom wasn't buying it.

'Becky, I'm serious, y'all need to forget about being a daft tribute act, your voice is too good for just that. Don't ya wanna chance at being yourself out there?' He gestured vaguely in the direction of the Edinburgh streets above our heads as I tried to work out if I was flattered or offended by his words.

'Out where?' I said raising a quizzical eyebrow as I handed him his drink and decided to concentrate on being pleased he said I had a good voice rather than miffed he'd labelled me 'daft'. He was talking nonsense really, not about my voice: I knew I could sing and I knew I'd done a great job on 'Little Sparrow' just now, you could feel it in your bones when you'd sung a song well. But I knew, even if Tom Coltrane didn't, that the world was not waiting for a new singer with no stage presence or image of her own to underwhelm them. But when I said as much to Tom he shook his head vehemently.

'How will ya know unless ya try? Your voice is great, you're used to performing and being up on a stage in front of an audience. Just drop the Dolly part and give yourself a chance.'

Drop the 'Dolly part'? He really couldn't have a clue what he was suggesting and I wasn't sure I would be able to explain it properly. Dolly Parton's outfits were like wearing a suit of armour, for me. Performing as a tribute act had been the only way I'd felt comfortable to carry on with any sort of singing career. Mum and Dad had got me performing with them as The Moonshine Trio as soon as I was old enough, touring the pub and club circuit together for years. I'd taken to it easily as a little one, soaking up the attention and applause from the age of three, but my teenage years took their toll on my confidence. My spots might have cleared up and bouts of self-doubt were less frequent but the scars of both remained. The thought of performing on stage simply as Becky Mooney wasn't something I could imagine ever feeling confident enough to do.

I didn't expect Tom Coltrane to empathise with my dilemma but to my surprise he was very understanding.

'It's not unusual for singers to use an alter ego on stage, y'know,' he said. 'You must know even Beyoncé pretends to be someone else when she's performing!'

I found it hard to believe that a global diva of her brilliance ever struggled with anything like stage fright but I knew Beyoncé channelled a character called 'Sasha Fierce' for her awesome stage performances. I'd assumed it was just part of the game though, I'd not thought about it as protection or for confidence – celebs didn't need that, surely?

'And have ya heard of self-esteem?' Tom asked.

'Of course I've heard if it, I've just not got any!' I was a bit snappy; did he think I was some sort of thicko?

Tom's mouth twitched as though he wanted to laugh. 'No, the musician Self Esteem … she performs under that name but she's really called Rebecca Lucy … something.'

My insides shrivelled with embarrassment but I jerked my head as though I'd just remembered exactly who Self Esteem was. Cringe. I took another gulp of my drink and as the warmth of the whisky flowed through me my embarrassment began to fade and the sense of what Tom was saying started to take hold in my mind.

'Do you have a stage persona?' I was genuinely curious. Was this technique the difference between artists who achieved greatness and those who didn't?

Tom shrugged but suddenly he looked sad, vulnerable even.

'No, I never needed anything like that, I've always found being on stage thrilling, energising … although lately …' He looked around as though he was scared of being overheard and although we were completely alone he stopped talking.

'Lately?'

Tom stopped turning his glass around on the table and slowly looked up as I repeated the word. It hung in the air between us and the air felt charged with crackling electricity. He wanted to tell me something, I could tell, and the connection between us felt so real I could almost see it. I held his gaze and waited. I had no idea what was coming. Then he kissed me.

Chapter Ten

I was used to waking late on a Sunday morning feeling pretty knackered. For the last few years Saturday nights had usually meant playing a show and then driving back through the night from whatever pub, club or party venue we had plied our Dolly & Kenny trade so we could crawl into our own beds.

Sometimes Robbie would come back to my flat, although that had been far less frequent recently. Both of us increasingly seemed to prefer our own space, the joy of sleeping diagonally or rolling onto a cool pillow more pleasurable than stretching out and finding a warm body beside us. Or rather, more preferable than find each other's warm body.

But this Sunday morning was different. In fact, *this* Sunday morning was unlike anything I had ever experienced.

As sunlight chinked though unfamiliar curtains and I sensed morning light across my closed eyelids I was dimly aware that something was different. Everything was different. I was different. My mind wasn't groping for my usual to-do list for the day. I wasn't waking thinking about what I had to do, what I should be doing or even what I *could* be doing. I had fallen into the habit of keeping myself busy at all costs starting from the moment I woke until I eventually submitted to unconsciousness at the end of a non-stop and yet, all too often, unremarkable day. I think it's what you do when you aren't completely happy with where you are in life.

But I wasn't thinking about any of that now. I wasn't re-hashing the past or over-thinking the future. My mind was crystal clear, my body felt blissfully relaxed and I had the overwhelming sensation that life was good. That's what really great sex can do for you. I was totally in the moment.

As soon as Tom kissed me I knew there was only one way the evening was going to end. He'd been tentative at first, his lips soft and fleeting on mine. It wasn't enough. I'd leaned in and pressed my lips more urgently against his. The response had been instant, his hands in my hair, his tongue pushing forward. We both rose from our chairs so we could press ourselves closer together, he'd run his fingers down the side of my body and placed his hand at the small of my back pulling me in even closer. I'd kissed my way down to his neck, finding the spot just below his ear that made him gasp when I licked and nuzzled there.

His voice was hoarse when he'd said, 'My hotel isn't far.' I hadn't needed convincing and told him so, replying with gusto, 'Thank God!'

We could have gone for it then and there in the bar ... I can't say I wasn't tempted, and there was unmistakable urgency in his tone. But the stone flagstones and basement chill would have forced us to settle for something too hard, too fast. Neither of us wanted it to be like that. Hard and fast is sometimes exciting but it's very rarely completely satisfactory. We wanted more.

We made the right call.

The taxi ride was hot as hell. Kisses on lips, necks, even fingertips when we weren't using them to touch each other, pushing back unruly hair, stroking each other's faces. His hand lightly on my breast, mine firm on his thigh. We sped through the dark streets locked in a bubble of lust. There was only him and me; everything and everyone else had melted away until Tom had to give the cab driver directions, but he soon focused his attention right back to me. I wasn't the slightest bit concerned about what the driver might think about our backseat antics. He was nothing to me, and in that moment Tom was everything. His eyes ate me up and I had to stifle a moan as he muttered, 'Rebecca … what are ya doin' to me?'

The fact I was having such an effect on him blew my mind. Why men ever think 'playing it cool' is a turn-on is a mystery to me. Seeing Tom so clearly aroused in the back of that cab sent me completely weak at the knees.

I rolled onto my side now and extended a leg with my eyes still closed. My toes found another leg, warm, solid, hairy. It felt like the sexiest leg I had ever known. I let my eyes flutter open and there he was. It wasn't a dream. Tom lay on his back with his face turned towards me, one arm flung behind his head and his blue eyes looking directly into mine. His red hair was messed up, he had the beginnings of stubble on his chin and an expression on his face that gave me hope he was planning to ravish me all over again. I had never seen anything so damn sexy in all my life.

'What a glorious mornin',' he said in a throaty chuckle while in one move rolling on top of me and demonstrating the very definition of morning glory.

Our morning sex was more leisurely, not as frenzied as the night before but still passionate, connected, dirty. I came once while watching his ginger head between my legs and again while straddling him as he gasped my name. At one point I may have reached for the tan cowboy hat that hung on one of the bedposts. It was the ride of my life.

Eventually other appetites emerged.

'Breakfast?' Tom asked as he stood naked at the end of the bed, his tanned body on full display.

I lay admiring the view with the bedsheet rumpled down to my waist. I had no idea what time it was but guessed it must be late morning already. 'Mmm, I could eat.'

We toyed with ordering room service, the temptation to stay in bed was strong, but once food had been mentioned we both needed sustenance immediately. With little further discussion we pulled on clothes and headed out to find coffee and, hopefully, a full Scottish breakfast.

It looked sunny and warm outside but I only had the navy long-sleeve sweater I'd been wearing the night before. As I reached for it Tom opened a drawer and threw me a faded red t-shirt with a 'Nashville – Music City' logo printed in distressed bronze across the chest. 'Suits ya,' he said as I tucked the well-worn, soft fabric into my jeans. I briefly checked myself in the mirror – tousled hair, flushed pink cheeks and eyes bright and clear – and decided I looked and felt more attractive than I had in years.

In the lift we traded our dream breakfast menu items.

'Bacon,' I said.

'Square sausage,' he countered.

'Haggis?' I asked with a raised eyebrow. Had Tom spent so long in America he'd lost the taste for the spicy, crumbly Scottish delicacy? He nodded vigorously showing his taste buds were tingling at just the thought.

'Potato scones!' My final suggestion had Tom licking his lips.

'You're a wicked woman, Rebecca Mooney.'

I rewarded that with a brief kiss before the lift doors opened and we left the hotel with my hand resting snugly in Tom's.

I wasn't used to walking hand in hand with a man. Most blokes I'd ever known hated that sort of a PDA. I also wasn't used to being called 'Rebecca' but I found I was enjoying both unexpected occurrences enormously. I'd never felt 'Becky' suited me all that well. It sounded like a little girl's name, one that went with wearing hair in bunches and buckled round-toe sandals. Some people called me 'Bex' but it never really stuck all that well either; while 'Becky' felt too silly and girly, 'Bex' was too sharp, too harsh. The way Tom said 'Rebecca,' though, made me feel like a new woman. His way didn't sound too formal or like a teacher at school about to issue a reprimand. He rolled the rrr and the name from his lips sounded full bodied and sexy. I'd never heard my name sound like that before. I liked it.

As we moved together through the streets Tom had a baseball cap covering his tell-tale red hair and was now wearing glasses. As we exited the lift he'd taken a spectacles case from his jacket pocket and told me they could be a useful disguise. I suddenly remembered him putting on sunglasses that morning I first saw him at the police station. I'd thought he was posing but of course he was trying to stop people recognising him. It had worked pretty well with me! I thought the tortoiseshell frames he wore now suited him well and gave him a bookish air I found very appealing but he said his record company had told him they'd prefer he used contact lenses if his eyesight ever became a problem for real. Why? Did they think fans wouldn't accept a singer in spectacles? I thought that sounded very narrow-minded but I kept that observation to myself. Since we'd left the bar the night before I hadn't given much headspace to the fact Tom was famous. From the moment he'd kissed me the realness of him had pushed the more ephemeral fact of his fame to the edges of my mind. But back out in the real world I registered it was possible Tom could get recognised at any moment by any passer-by. I may not have clocked he was *the* Tom Coltrane when he was large as life in front of me on the steps of the cop shop, and just clocked him on the head instead, but it soon became apparent not everyone was as unobservant as me.

There were a couple of mums with pushchairs at a bus stop who looked twice and then whispered together and then a bloke making a delivery to a shop who did a massive double take. If he hadn't had his hands full I was pretty sure that guy might have taken his suspicion he'd just seen a famous music star on George Street a bit further.

Tom kept his head down and his hand in mine as we bowled along at a brisk walk. He was obviously practised at dodging unwanted attention. I kept pace and held on tight. It was clear Tom knew what he was doing and where he was going.

We ended up outside a tiny one-room cafe down a side street with 'All Day Breakfast' painted in wonky handwriting on the window. The tables were Formica and the chairs were mismatched but it was clean, the aroma of bacon was enticing and it was quiet.

'I wasn't sure this place would still be here,' Tom glanced around at the brick walls and domed glass counter as he removed his cap and took a seat at the corner table, his back to the room.

We each made our selection from the breakfast items listed on the blackboard menu. 'And toast please,' Tom added.

The stocky guy behind the counter gave a quick nod of acknowledgement as he added that to the ticket but said nothing.

'He knows you, doesn't he?' I said as he turned towards the hatch into the kitchen.

Tom smiled, 'Yeah, I reckon he does, but in here I'm just another customer to him. I'm glad he's still here, that this place is still open. So many things have changed since I was last in Edinburgh.'

That statement opened the floodgates; questions about why Tom was here in Edinburgh were begging to be asked. What was going on with him? Something clearly was. He had mentioned no gigs, had no entourage or PR commitments –

none of the stuff I imagined stars grappled with – but I'd been worried he'd think I was interrogating him. Or even worse, trying to conduct an interview. I hadn't wanted anything to burst the bubble. But buoyed by the best Scottish breakfast I had ever eaten and endless refills of hot, strong coffee I asked and Tom talked. Really talked.

He told me how he felt he was at a crossroads, musically and in life. He explained how the success that had been so hard to come by was even harder to hold onto. 'In the end you're only as good as your next hit song and that next hit is a long time in coming.' It sounded like a lot of pressure, especially when he went on to talk about all the other people who had to be kept happy – executives, producers, managers and publicity people.

He loved Nashville, he'd made a life there for years now and lived in a beautiful home on the outskirts, but said he missed Edinburgh. He showed me a picture on his phone of a gorgeous white clapboard house with a pretty verandah overhanging a large front porch. I almost giggled – it looked like a dream house from a fancy American property show on TV. The charming home was surrounded by trees and abundant flowery bushes in such a picturesque setting it looked like it was straight out of a fairy tale.

'Wow,' I said.

He looked a bit embarrassed then. 'I don't have much to complain about, I know,' he said. 'I don't want you to think I'm the sort to complain my diamond shoes are too tight. It's just …'

I reassured him that everyone has stuff going on nobody else knows about. I knew struggling to get somewhere in life was hard, but I could easily imagine that fighting to stay on top once you'd made it was just as stressful.

'Once that spotlight hits, everyone has an opinion too,' he said.

'So you've come home to reboot? To see if being back where you started will rekindle the flame in some way?'

'Something like that, yeah.' He reached for my hand, 'Though I wasn't looking to start any other sort of fires while I was at it, but … here we are.'

He played with my fingers and I was tempted to climb across the table and crawl right into his lap but I resisted.

Our coffee was topped up once more and the conversation flowed too. He wanted to know more about why I had been at the police station the first time we'd met and so I confessed how I suspected Guy Grayson had created the whole situation to get me into trouble. The only thing I was still trying to figure out was why?

'Did ya knock him back? Was he coming on too strong and his bruised ego couldn't stand the rejection? Men can turn very aggressive if their pride is hurt … Some men that is,' he quickly clarified.

The reality of Guy's creepy manner wasn't something I felt like discussing over breakfast with a man I'd just had incredible sex with. Although I was flattered that Tom instantly assumed another man would find me so irresistible he was driven to trying to get me thrown in jail because I hadn't fallen for his charms. I tried to end that topic of conversation by describing Guy's glamorous American wife JoJo and said it was unlikely Guy would even register me as female next to an Uber-glamazon like JoJo.

Tom's face twitched at that. 'There's thousands of JoJos,' he said. 'Y'all might think they look glossy and perfect but they all look the same to me now. I think L.A. surgeons all use the exact same template for each one, y'know.' He took a swig of coffee from his mug. 'It's not real and it's definitely not sexy.'

'Tell that to Dolly Parton,' I countered.

'Ahhh, she might have fake hair, fake nails, fake boobs and heaven knows what else … but Dolly Parton is the exception that proves the rule,' Tom shot back. 'Dolly's the most real person there is.'

I couldn't argue with that but where did that leave me? Tom appeared to have little regard for the lip-plumped, cheek-sculpted pouting women that came off a plastic surgery production line. I got that. It was quite clear I was not one of those women. No Botox, lip-fillers or fake boobs to be found here. Not when I wasn't in my Dolly Parton costume anyway. Was he trying to tell me he found a woman like me more attractive? More sexy? Was I more his type than the movie stars he was used to? Or was I just a novelty? I pushed the thought away. Surely I didn't really need more proof of his lust after last night and this morning and, anyway, I would also never ask such a loaded, compliment seeking question. I didn't need him to feed my ego in that way but there was an elephant in the room. A very beautiful, slender, drop dead gorgeous elephant by the name of Juliana Ripon.

My stomach did a little flip as I recalled the images I'd found online of Tom and Juliana snapped on red carpets or rushing into exclusive restaurants or theatre first nights. In the heat of passion, I'd pushed all thoughts of Tom's relationship with a Hollywood starlet right out of my mind. But now I'd let the thought back in all the pictures I'd ever seen began to flick across my memory bank one by one. Each image had Tom and Juliana hand in hand, entwined around each other or gazing into one another's eyes adoringly. I didn't like the way the remembered images made me feel.

I weighed up my options. Asking too direct a question about the status of his relationship with Juliana could mark me as some sort of stalker poring over titbits about his love life on online gossip sites. Not ideal. I've always considered jealousy to be a most unattractive trait and had absolutely no desire to give Tom the impression I was eaten up with the most corrosive of emotions. I may have naturally green eyes but I had no intention of becoming a green-eyed monster. No, I was a big girl. Whatever was going on here we were two adults, neither of us married, and I wasn't expecting this to be anything other than what it was – an unexpected few hours, maybe at best a couple of days of sexy fun. Nothing more. No harm done.

So I decided to skip the Juliana question, whatever that question was. Instead I picked up on the comment he'd just made about Dolly. He'd said it with such assurance and warmth it triggered an unexpected thought.

'Wait a minute ... have you met Dolly Parton?' I said. 'Do you know her?'

Tom pushed away his empty plate, leaned back in his chair and grinned.

Chapter Eleven

We left the humble cafe in a lot more style than how we'd arrived. I hadn't spotted him do it but while I was busy paying for breakfast (he fought me on this but I insisted) Tom had somehow summoned his driver.

A sleek and shiny black Audi with tinted windows was loitering on the kerb and a smartly dressed man in his fifties opened a rear door as soon as he spotted us. Was this the same car and driver who had whisked us back to the hotel the night before? The thought struck me that this might be the same guy who had witnessed some rather naughty antics on the backseat as we'd been driven through the late-night streets. It was perfectly possible but I had absolutely no recall of either the man or the car. It could have been Billy Connolly driving a clown car for all the notice I had taken as I'd been rather distracted at the time.

'Hey Iain,' Tom said smiling broadly as we walked towards him, then stepped back and added to me, 'After you, Miss Mooney.'

Iain inclined his head as he opened the car door for me and smiled warmly with no hint of recognition or judgement. Of course, this wasn't the same car and driver. Last night we'd hailed a taxi on the street, I remembered now. Phew.

I couldn't help being impressed however at this smartly dressed driver and gleaming saloon car. It made sense that a star as famous as Tom Coltrane would have a chauffeur on call, despite his enthusiasm for a greasy spoon cafe. I registered the fact Tom must be used to a lot more luxury than I would have ever encountered in my time gigging around the pubs and clubs of Scotland. My experience was limited to The Highlands, not the high life.

The car seats were buttery cream leather, the legroom was insane and there were fresh bottles of water in the seat backs in front of us. I sank into the comfort with ease.

'D'ya wanna know where we're heading?' Tom asked with a barely suppressed laugh.

I'd presumed the car was dropping Tom back at his hotel. I'd stuffed my sweater in my bag and had left nothing else in his suite, in case I wasn't ever going back there. I was more than happy to make my own way home, I wasn't expecting to be chauffeured around.

Tom saw the bemused look on my face and laughed more openly now. 'I swear this isn't a kidnap, Rebecca, but if you've got nothing else planned today there's somewhere I'd love to take ya. If that's okay, darlin'?'

It certainly was. I wasn't presuming Tom and I were going to be seeing a lot of each other from now on but I was more than happy to spend a bit more time with him. He was fun, good company and very, very sexy. I'd take every hour of this fairy tale interlude I could before real life came rushing back in. I settled back in my seat as the car sped north out of the city. Tom said we weren't going too far so I held in my curiosity about the destination and got him to fill me in about his encounter with Dolly Parton instead.

'I'm not claiming we're big buddies or anything like that,' Tom said. 'But Nashville is a surprisingly small place for us musicians. Everyone knows everybody else. I've worked with loads of fellers from her band and I did once bump into her backstage at The Grand Ole Opry.'

I shook my head slowly as I imagined just 'bumping into' Dolly Parton at The Grand Ole Opry. Mind boggling.

'She was tiny, like a little doll, incredibly polite to everyone and as sweet as sweet can be. It's not all a Dolly-act, you know, she really is just the way everyone wants her to be. That's why I say she's the most real of them all. What you see is what you get with Dolly, she doesn't disappoint.' I knew it! But it was still good to hear that Dolly was as charming and authentic as she always appeared.

'Then there was this other time,' Tom went on. 'I was working late in a studio in downtown Nashville and I was really struggling with a song that I just couldn't seem to finish. The chorus wasn't feelin' right so I was playing around with it and getting nowhere fast. The more I tried to nail it the more of a mess it seemed to be. I was getting so frustrated I felt like swingin' my guitar against the wall. I was just about to call it a night as it was getting really late when my producer came through the talkback saying there was someone in the control room who wanted to talk to me. The next thing I know I hear Dolly's voice.'

'Oh my God, Dolly had been watching you work?'

'Yep, she'd wandered in to talk to my producer Vince and I hadn't got a clue how long she'd been standin' there. I was completely mortified as I certainly hadn't been showin' much skill in songwriting up until that point. But then this sweet Southern voice fills the room and Dolly says … *Tom, honey, you're nearly there, don't give up now boy, you're just a whisper away from something great.*'

I gasped. I knew that song. 'That's how you wrote "Whisper Away?"'

'That was the missing piece of the jigsaw,' Tom said nodding. I had the verse melody and some good lyrics but the chorus just wasn't workin' out. As soon as I heard that line I knew it would fit.

'It was a really big hit for you, wasn't it?'

Tom rubbed his hand over his head, ruffling up his hair as he admitted, 'Here in the UK and in the States. Last real hit song I had, yeah.'

I didn't know what to say to that. I wanted to say something like 'until the next one' or 'there'll be lots more I'm sure' but what the hell did I know about hit songs and how to get a record up the charts?

'Did Dolly stick around and help you write it?'

Tom gave a short sharp laugh at that and I was relieved to see the cloudy look on his face blow over. 'I started foolin' around with *"whisper away"* as a lyric as soon as Dolly said it, singing it over and over listening to how the rhythm of the phrase suggested a cool new hook for the song. I'd worked it out in minutes but when I looked up there was no blonde goddess to be seen in the control room.'

'So Dolly didn't realise she'd helped you finish the song?'

'Oh, she knew. Vince said she gave a little laugh as I started using her words in my song. He said she could tell right away it was going to work. Apparently, she told him *"Tell Tom Coltrane he can keep that, no charge"*.'

'That's so cool.'

'That's so Dolly.'

As he said that I spotted we were passing signs for South Queensferry, the port that overlooked the Firth of Forth. It had been a long time since I'd visited the pretty port with pastel-coloured cottages and quirky shops and cafes. I quite fancied having a Sunday afternoon wander around with Tom, pretending we were a regular couple. Maybe this was somewhere he used to come as a child? Or maybe he just fancied playing at being a tourist for the day. Before I could start asking questions about his plans I noticed Tom was looking thoughtful again.

'Perhaps I need a bit more Dolly magic to get me back on track?' He turned to me with his eyebrows raised and a small smile on his lips. 'Whaddaya say, "Dolly"? Could ya see your way to helping a struggling musician out?'

'Me?'

He was in full-on teasing mode now and I feigned mock outrage as he answered, 'You're the closest thing to Dolly Parton I'm gonna find around here, so y'all just have to do!'

I shook my head and laughed and considered telling him to maybe give Jack the one man double-act 'Dolly Partly' a call, but before I could suggest it Iain swung the car off the main road and started driving up a long, overgrown driveway.

'Ahh great, we're here.' Tom looked excited and pointed towards a large red-brick house at the end of the drive. With its huge sash windows, arched front door painted sage green and imposing chimneys towering above, it looked like somewhere a vicar would live in a Miss Marple mystery. A peeling painted sign at the driveway entrance said 'Forthview House'.

Iain turned the car around in front of the house to park just as the double front door opened and a young woman with strawberry blonde hair emerged. She had a child of about four on her hip and a girl aged around seven at her side, both of them red-heads.

I looked at the woman and I looked at Tom.

'That's my little sister, Laura,' he said.

Laura greeted us warmly, a big hug for her brother and a genuine welcome for me. If she was fazed by her brother showing up with a random woman in tow she didn't show it. Maybe it was a frequent occurrence.

The kids, introduced as Reggie and Stevie, threw themselves at Tom who responded with tickles and cuddles. 'Say howdy to my friend Rebecca,' Tom said. They both said 'hello' shyly and then immediately ran off into the garden through the wide open French doors in the massive rustic kitchen Laura had led us into.

'Welcome to the mad house, Rebecca,' Laura said. 'Shall I make us a pot of tea?'

As she put the kettle on and assembled a line-up of four colourful mugs I looked around. The house itself was large and grand but inside it was homely and sort of shabby. The furniture looked like it had been there for decades. All ornate carved wood and faded chintz fabric, absolutely nothing matched. The only modern touches were some pop art pictures and framed music posters on the walls and a few children's toys scattered around. I liked it enormously. As we settled at the table my eye was caught by a painting on the wall, the strong lines of colour depicting a figure with a guitar looked awfully familiar to me: it was very like the collection of pictures I'd hung all around Sonny's Bar. I wondered if it was by the same artist? Such a coincidence, somehow it made me feel even more welcome in the house.

'I'll summon Ferg in the traditional manner,' Laura said as she reached for a broom leaning against the wall by the Aga. She gave three hard thumps on the ceiling with the top of the long handle then stood with her head on one side, waiting. We all waited. I had no clue what we were waiting for.

Within seconds there was a bump on the floor above followed by the sound of footfall creaking across floorboards and then the louder, thumpety-thump of feet pounding down the stairs.

'TOM! ... My Man!' A lanky guy with a wild quiff of brown hair wearing Buddy Holly-style black-rimmed glasses burst into the kitchen. His stubbly face broke into a huge grin as he pulled Tom in for a hug, his oversized paisley-patterned shirt flapping around his skinny body as he gave me a friendly wink.

It was easy to feel at ease with Fergus and Laura and despite them having such obviously easy banter with Tom, I was instantly included and never made to feel surplus to the conversation. It turned out they'd heard of Sonny's and had been once or twice before I took over, and they eagerly promised to pay another visit soon now they knew that I was in charge. They filled me in on how Ferg had been friends with Tom since high school. 'That's how I got to know Laura,' Fergus said.

'He might even make an honest woman of her one of these days,' Tom said as Laura swatted at him with a tea towel. I didn't get the impression Laura was the sort of woman who was living her life waiting for a big white wedding. She wore denim cut-off shorts with a sleeveless white t-shirt, armfuls of bangles and a cool collection of silver pendants around her neck. She looked pretty, but powerful.

'Ow!' Tom pretended to be hurt by the thwack from Laura's towel whip and then as if he was reading my mind said, 'Her middle name is "feisty" you know …'

Laura grinned and said she had considered 'Feisty' as a name for her daughter at one point. 'But in the end, we went for Stevie, after Stevie Nicks.'

'Great name,' I said. Could this couple be any cooler? 'And Reggie?' I hardly thought it likely that Ferg and Laura had named their youngest after one of The Krays. I knew there must be a story behind the choice but I was struggling to think of appropriate inspiration.

'Ahh well, Reggie was inspired by our song.' Fergus looked at Tom and then me before he added, 'Every couple ends up having a song, don't they?' I knew exactly what he meant but I'd never been in the sort of relationship where we nominated a slushy song to be 'our tune'. Although I supposed Robbie and I could have said 'Islands in the

Stream' was ours; it must have qualified after we sang it together as Dolly & Kenny so many times. Ferg glanced at Laura then and started laughing. 'Go on Laura, you know you want to …'

Laura narrowed her eyes for a moment and held his gaze. She looked quite serious before suddenly slapping her hand on the table and bursting into the opening line to 'Wild Thing'. She had a strong, raspy voice not particularly melodic but what she lacked in musicality she made up for in enthusiasm. She might be small but she was mighty.

'Wild thing … I think I love you,' answered Fergus in reply to the impressive impromptu performance given by the mother of his children.

I burst into spontaneous applause. Why on earth had I presumed Ferg and Laura's song would be soppy and romantic? 'Of course! Reg Presley and The Troggs! I love that song.'

Ferg and Laura grinned at each other, then at me.

'Excellent!' Tom said with real satisfaction. 'You passed the initiation test. They'll let us stay now. That's a relief.'

I laughed at that. He meant stay for just a little while, didn't he? My mind started working overtime as that thought struck me. I hadn't been home since Saturday morning when I'd set off for work around lunchtime to get things ready for the open mic night at the bar that evening. That seemed a hell of a long time ago. I'd made full use of all the free toiletries in Tom's hotel room and I was wearing the fresh Nashville t-shirt that he'd loaned me but I didn't want to push my luck. I was proud to be low maintenance but even I had some standards.

I quietly asked Laura if I could use the bathroom and grabbed my bag as she pointed me down the hall. Once inside the downstairs loo I quickly checked to see if I had enough of my 'emergency kit' stashed in my slouchy blue leather handbag. It was amazing how much I could cram inside the well-worn leather of this thing. Robbie used to call me 'Mary Poppins' as I'd often yank assorted stuff from its depths. Years of gigging had taught me you should always try to carry certain things at all times in case you were unable to get home after a show or decided at the last moment to stay over somewhere. I already knew I had a small tube of toothpaste and a travel toothbrush in my make-up bag as I'd used them last night and again this morning, along with a spritz from the small bottle of perfume I always had with me. Tick. Also in there would be bronzer and a face brush to bring a bit of colour and shimmer to my face along with a couple of lipsticks and a small tin of Vaseline which could be used on eyelashes and eyebrows. Tick. Tick. So far so good. I dug around a bit deeper into the bag feeling around for a small drawstring bag. It should be in there but sometimes I needed the contents of my emergency kit and then forgot to replenish the supplies. Aha. Bingo. Safely tucked at the bottom of my trusty bag, two pairs of spare knickers, one pair of socks, two panty liners and three tampax. No high maintenance woman could survive with such limited supplies but they would adequately suffice for low maintenance me.

Despite carrying an emergency travel kit, I wasn't used to being 'whisked' anywhere by a bloke, but hey, I decided I might as well enjoy it while it lasted. Meeting family members of a man I was seeing was also a brand new one on me. No relationship I'd ever had before had led to family get-togethers, Christmas with the in-laws or holidays en famille. Things had never progressed that far, even with Robbie. I'd got used to the idea that meeting someone who I'd want to do that sort of thing with was never going to happen. My mum had told me so often that meeting a soul mate, like she had with my dad, was such a rare thing in life that I'd simply stopped believing it was ever going to happen for me. After a spell of car-crash relationships with mad boys, sad boys and bad boys, I'd given up. My relationships, few as they were, had since then been pretty unremarkable, Robbie included. But at least that way I wasn't getting my heart broken anymore.

Not that I was thinking Tom was going to be my one true love. Oh good grief no. This was a very unexpected but lovely interruption to my regular life. I was sure normal service would be resumed very soon but for now I was prepared to go with the flow with a man who was fun and exciting, had a lovely sister and a cool friend. Here in this ramshackle house it was even harder to think of him as a star, I realised. I could let myself treat this like a holiday romance in my own city. Why not? Now I knew I could keep myself clean and presentable if the opportunity to stay over occurred, I was up for it. Whatever the world threw at me now I was ready. Bring. It. On.

Well, that's what I'd thought as I emerged from the loo to see Tom, Ferg and Laura with their heads bent conspiratorially over a large biscuit tin in the middle of the kitchen table. As I came back into the room three pairs of eyes swivelled in my direction and I had the distinct impression they had been talking about me.

I had thought I was ready for anything but did Tom have more up his checked shirt sleeve than I had bargained for?

Chapter Twelve

Standing in the doorway with Tom, Ferg and Laura all staring at me I suddenly felt awkward for the first time since Tom had kissed me. The way their heads had all snapped in my direction as they instantly stopped talking was most disconcerting. Now they were looking at me, wearing expressions on their faces I was finding impossible to read.

What was I doing here? How was I hanging out with a famous country music star and why had he brought me to meet his family? We'd been getting on so well together and I had been enjoying his company so much I hadn't stopped to wonder why Tom Coltrane ... *the* Tom Coltrane ... had plucked *me* from my regular life and whisked me to South Queensferry with no warning or explanation. Should I be worried? This wasn't something that happened every day, so what was his game here? Should I at least ask questions?

Before I had chance to work out what question it was I wanted to ask, the blue leather bag I had slung over my shoulder started to make a weird buzzing sound and judder.

I saw Tom bite his lip as though he was trying not to laugh.

'Oh good Lord ... it's not ... I think ... oh it's just my phone ... My phone must be set to vibrate!' I tore the bag off my arm and started to search desperately through the contents to locate my mobile and show them all I wasn't carrying anything more offensive than an iPhone. 'There, you see ...' I held the phone aloft and saw they were all desperately trying to hold it together and not dissolve into fits. I could feel my face was glowing red but even I could see the funny side.

'Well, what if I was a part-time rep for Ann Summers anyway?' I said boldly. The best way out of any embarrassing situation is often to own it – I'd learned that much from years on the stage and of course from Dolly. No one ever got the better of La Parton, she'd beat you to the punchline of any joke at her expense and it would be a helluva lot funnier too. I feigned an air of dignity and returned to my seat at the table, selected a shortbread finger from the biscuit tin and just before I nibbled on it added, 'A girl's gotta earn a living after all, there's no shame in it.'

Tom shot me a beaming smile and I was relieved to feel back in the room and among friends now I'd seized the day and cracked a joke.

The questions I'd wanted to ask concerning what they'd all been talking about were forgotten as Laura launched into a hilarious tale of a kid at Stevie's primary school who had once brought his mum's 'Rampant Rabbit' to Show and Tell. The story prompted several follow-up lines of inquiry from us all – the poor mother was apparently still trying to live it down – but then I glanced down to my phone where the screen was face up on the table. What were all these messages that kept popping up on the screen? I started to scroll through in case there was some emergency I needed to know about.

'Everything okay?' Tom had noticed my attention was diverted to the phone and asked with genuine concern.

'Err … yeah … I think so. Actually it's a bit more than okay I think.' I picked up my mobile and listened to a couple of the messages.

The pings that were coming in thick and fast were all about Tom's impromptu performance at Sonny's Bar on Saturday night. With everything that had happened since, I'd almost forgotten that Tom had taken to the stage and given an incredible show in our little underground bar. Unsurprisingly several people had filmed him and the footage had been shared all over. Sonny's Bar had gone viral, we had thousands more followers on all our social media platforms and I'd even had a couple of voicemails from newspaper reporters and TV stations wanting to interview me about what had happened and find out more about what Tom Coltrane was doing back in Edinburgh.

'Wow, that's great … isn't it?' Laura said. She looked at me uncertainly as I hesitated and I looked towards Tom for reassurance. Did she mean great for Tom or for Sonny's?

'I suppose so,' I said while I kept looking carefully at his face. Was this okay with him? Had he known this was going to happen? Would he mind the bar benefitting in this way? What if he thought we were just using his name to build our profile? I remembered then that he'd only come into the bar in the very first place because he'd found one of my leaflets advertising we were looking for fresh talent to come and perform at Sonny's. On that occasion I had splattered him with paint and he'd made a fast exit, but he had returned on Saturday night of his own free will, hadn't he? And he'd brought his guitar with him. He must have always intended to take to the stage, even though in the end he'd stepped in to save my face when I couldn't face going on as the second Dolly Parton act of the evening.

'I just hope the footage is decent quality,' he said. 'Can I see?'

Tom and Fergus pored over the clips I'd been sent and Laura found some more and we all watched them on her iPad.

'That's cool, man,' Fergus said as the footage of Tom playing a mean boogie-woogie on our ancient upright piano played out. 'I haven't seen you hit the keys like that for a long time.'

Tom's focus on his own performance was intense but he grinned at that, 'Yeah man, that's one of the things I wanted to talk to you about.'

'I reckoned this wasn't just a social call,' Fergus replied. I had no idea what he meant but he and Laura were smiling encouragingly at Tom and the conversation was still incredibly good-natured. My disquiet about what ulterior motive Tom might have resurfaced but as my face showed my obvious confusion Tom winked at Fergus and stuck out his hand.

'C'mon, Rebecca Mooney, it's time to show ya why I've brought you here,' he said.

As Ferg bounded towards the stairs like an excitable Labrador, Tom grasped my hand. 'Don't look so worried, darlin,' he said. 'This house is full of surprises ... and they're all good.' With that he gave me a smile that melted all my concerns clean away and, leaving Laura to play with the kids in the garden, I let him lead me to the wooden staircase.

We climbed first one, then a second shorter flight of stairs until we reached a landing with a door painted black with silver stars stuck all over it.

'The kids' idea of interior design,' Fergus said over his shoulder as he opened the door and we followed him in.

I don't know what I'd been expecting but it certainly wasn't what I found behind the starry door. The attic room was enormous, taking up almost the entire footprint of the house and stretching up into a criss-cross of wooden beams that took your eye up to the vaulted ceiling. I spotted a grand piano standing on a faded Persian rug, racks of guitars against one wall, two full-size drum kits, assorted keyboards and all manner of other music paraphernalia here and there in the space. As I swept my gaze around I realised at the far end there was also a large control room behind a pane of glass and a couple of smaller vocal booths. Along the side wall were three huge picture windows all giving beautiful views across the Firth. I could even see the incredible red cantilevered Forth Bridge in the middle distance. It took my breath away a bit.

'This is the recording studio of dreams,' I said.

Fergus looked delighted at that and Tom had a huge smile on his face as he headed for the black grand piano and ran his hand lovingly down the keys.

'Have you got something you're working on you want to show me?' Ferg asked him, but Tom quickly shook his head.

'Maybe later,' he said. 'It's all about Miss Mooney for now.'

'Me?' My voice came out as little more than a squeak.

'She's got a really great voice, but I don't think she knows just how good it is. I was thinking we could record a little somethin' and let her hear what she sounds like. It's not her voice that needs work … but her self-esteem needs a bit of a boost.'

Tom was talking about me to Fergus but his eyes never left my face. He was watching me warily, almost as though he was scared I might bolt.

I'd been taken off guard, that was true, but the idea of recording something in this amazing studio was not unappealing. I'd never been inside a recording studio before and I'd never heard myself properly. Occasionally someone would record something on a shaky phone and upload it onto YouTube but it was never very good quality and I was always performing as Dolly Parton anyway, never as myself. I knew that's what Tom was aiming for. He wanted me to perform as me, Becky Mooney, and listen to how that might sound. I had to admit, I was curious too.

Within minutes Ferg had set up a mic but when Tom asked me what I wanted to sing I suddenly felt ridiculous. Without my Dolly disguise, my usual repertoire felt all wrong. Tom picked up on my hesitation immediately.

'Don't do any Dolly,' he said. 'We know you can impersonate her but we need to hear your own voice, you'll be too tempted to go into your 'act' if you do your usual set.'

That made sense but it didn't solve the problem of what song I should sing. Fergus's voice came through from the control room. 'There's no rush, guys,' he said. 'Just have a play around until you find something that feels right. You tell me when you're ready to record.'

So Tom sat down at the piano and played a few bars, and straight away I recognised the Patsy Cline song 'Walking After Midnight'. I loved that song and couldn't resist singing along. He segued then into a few more country standards and we jammed our way through as many hit songs as we could remember. Sometimes I'd suggest one, other times Tom played a few notes and I joined in as soon as I recognised it. It was fun and an excellent way to warm up.

Eventually I called a halt. 'I really enjoyed the Linda Ronstadt number,' I said, 'maybe we could record that one.'

Tom swung his eyes towards Fergus who was still sitting in the control room behind the glass. I saw him pull a slight face.

'Oh!' The penny dropped and I realised Ferg had been recording the whole time. Before I could rail at the two of them too much, my voice filled the room as Ferg hit the playback button and we all listened as I sang the rocky Ronstadt hit 'You're No Good'. Ironically, it sounded pretty good.

Ferg stopped the track before the end and then jumped through a few of the other tracks he'd captured as we'd performed, and played back snatches of a few of them. I was surprised how soulful I sounded on 'I Hope You Dance' and Tom said he loved the rasp in my voice in the grittier tracks and it was great to hear myself really let go and have fun in Kid Rock's 'All Summer Long'.

It was a cheeky trick but I had to admit that not knowing I was being recorded had helped me relax and play around with the music more than I would have done otherwise.

'Hey Ferg, can you find that bit where she sang "Don't It Make My Brown Eyes Blue"?' Tom asked. Ferg did as he was asked and then Tom sat and listened intently with his eyes closed as my voice soared up into the rafters with the song I knew so well by Crystal Gayle. When it finished he opened his eyes and looked into mine. 'Man, I knew it when I heard you sing "Little Sparrow" the other night,' he said. 'We've just got to get ya out from where you're hiding behind Dolly. The world needs to meet *you*, honey.'

I could feel a warm glow spreading through me as I stood there in a shaft of sunlight from the picture window overlooking the water. Tom's belief in me was uplifting and I wasn't daft enough to deny my own ears and judgement; the voice I could hear in the playback sounded good, raw in places perhaps, but I wasn't just singing the songs exactly as I'd heard them done before. I was phrasing slightly differently here and there, feeling the music and interpreting the lyrics. I'd always loved the way country music invited you to sing a song your own way, to lean in and let your own life experience swirl through the music like cream through coffee. From wistful and yearning to playful and bold I was able to hear my own voice in a way I never had before. It sounded good and felt even better.

Tom and Ferg were clearly experienced enough to know when things were on a roll and to keep a vibe going. Now I knew I was being recorded but I was already feeling pretty comfortable so I went with it. We laid down a few more tracks, Tom accompanying me, switching between piano and guitar depending on the number. We went for a take on 'Little Sparrow' at his suggestion but avoided all other, more obvious, Dolly songs.

I don't know how long we worked – if you could have called it work – I hadn't had so much fun in ages. Well not with all my clothes on anyway.

Tom stuck to being my session musician until he started playing the old Martha and The Vandellas track 'Heatwave'. I knew the song from various versions over the years but it never mattered how often I heard it or who sang it, I always loved it and it never, ever seemed to age.

Tom was playing a fast-paced rhythm on the guitar as I sang the lead but then it was like he couldn't help himself as he began to sing backing and harmony. As we really got into it together, our voices answering each other and blending at just the right moments, the door to the control room opened. Ferg emerged and waved his hand, signalling for us to keep going as he leapt behind a drum kit, and then the three of us really got cooking.

We did the number several times, making slight changes and suggestions to each other, refining the takes until we had a track all laid down. Listening to it back we could hardly stand still. Ferg was drumming his hands on the top of the piano, I was jigging about and swaying almost desperate to dance, and Tom was sat on a stool with his knees bouncing up and down, he clearly couldn't keep his toes from tapping. All of us grinning like the cats who'd got the cream.

'Boy, that sounds good, it's like summer in a bottle. You know how people always say if they could bottle a feeling like that they could make a fortune, well guys ... I think we just did it.' Ferg grinned at us both. Tom was nodding along as though he agreed with every word but, as happy as I was to have been part of the recording session, I wasn't sure where that left me. I'd had a taste of something glorious – but where did I go from here? I didn't want to appear ungrateful by saying anything so I kept my mouth shut and just smiled, but what Fergus said next wiped the smile right off my face.

'Do you write your own stuff?'

Was he seriously asking *me* that question? I figured he couldn't be asking Tom since *he* was a well-known singer songwriter with multiple Grammy award nominations to his name. Why would I have the first idea how to write a song?

'From the look on your face I'm taking it the answer is no.' Tom's eyes were crinkling at the corners in that way I was already learning they did when something amused him. It made him look just the right amount of naughty. While I was distracted by a surge of longing and lust Tom added, 'But I think now is the perfect time to start.'

'Huh? Start what?'

Tom came and stood in front of me and put his hands on my shoulders. Was he going to kiss me? I was sort of hoping he might, we'd not kissed in hours and the feel of his hands on me was bringing back memories of the night before. If Ferg hadn't been leaning on the piano only a few feet away I could have pushed Tom Coltrane down onto the Persian rug right then and there. But he was, so I didn't. I might have been discovering my true voice but that didn't make me an exhibitionist.

'I reckon we should try and write something, me and you, right now. C'mon honey, let's give it a go …'

He was serious. Tom Coltrane was asking me to compose a song with him. What the hell was this guy doing to me? Once again, I was forced to ask myself … just what would Dolly do?

Chapter Thirteen

The next few hours were intense and exhilarating as I discovered I could indeed write a song. Who knew!? Working alongside Tom and Fergus, who had clearly had many sessions like this together before, I quickly learned there wasn't a right or wrong way to create a new piece of music, it really was a case of whatever worked for you.

'It doesn't matter what comes first, a lick or a hook, a lyric or just an idea for something the song needs to be about, it can be any of those things, a combination of all of 'em or something else entirely. All that matters is that you find a spark and then try and fan the flames to get the fire burning.' Fergus spoke from experience and explained how he and Tom had sometimes worked on songs from either side of the Atlantic when Tom was over in Nashville and he was here in Scotland. 'A bit like Elton John and Bernie Taupin but with better technology,' Ferg joked.

'Yeah ... although we've not managed to sell quite as many as Elton, especially lately,' Tom admitted ruefully.

'Hey man, what's with the negativity? There's still time to get back up those charts,' Ferg insisted with a look towards Tom that made me think he wasn't used to hearing him being so down on himself.

I decided to make a concerted effort to not bring any more negativity into the room and listened to all the advice and ideas the guys offered and did my very best to throw myself into the process. When else would I ever have the chance to write a song with a famous musician and a producer of Fergus's obvious calibre? I was determined not to waste the opportunity.

I eased myself in by watching how Tom liked to strum his guitar looking for catchy hooks to build up from. Sometimes he switched over to piano and experimented with snatches of melody while he sang a load of nonsense over the top.

For me, the words of a song can really sell it. I suppose that's why I like country music so much. So many of the great country songs have totally nailed it with a clever line here and there, summing up so perfectly something I have experienced myself. You know they say a good country song can just be 'three chords and the truth'. It can also be powerful and poignant but some of my favourite country songs use humour too. Dolly is the queen of all that, of course. I wasn't expecting to be in Dolly's league but I quickly realised I wanted to try to do what she does, find a way to capture a sensation, an idea or a moment in a lyric and build a song from there.

I let my thoughts wander, let all the events in my life filter through my brain, tried to switch off from the immediate and see what emotions and memories floated to the surface as

Tom played and replayed a melody line on the piano. All at once words began to come into my mind, words that seemed to fit the refrain really well. I sang them in my head at first but the expression on my face must have given me away as all of a sudden Fergus said, 'C'mon Rebecca, don't hold it in, let us all hear it.' He must have been able to tell I had something brewing.

'Mean to me ... Mean to me ... don't ever be mean to me ... those bad boys think it's the way to be, but they don't know what you mean to me ...'

Tom nodded enthusiastically. 'Again ... sing that again.' So I did and we were away – all throwing ideas back and forth and building a song based on a situation as old as time.

'Mean to Me' had a steady tempo and room for some great piano twiddles between the verse and the chorus. Tom and I worked together to create a couple of verses. We threw in references to how boys started showing an interest by pulling your pigtails but could end up pulling your best mate. It was just the right side of bluesy and the story reflected a story I knew so often left women disappointed and hurt. It felt like a great start – for once I wasn't bottling my emotions up but actually using bad experiences from my past and using them to feel good about myself.

'I like the fact you're giving the new guy a warning too, saying you've been messed around before but you won't stand for it again.' Fergus spoke as he came out of the control room after we'd recorded a take but then I felt my cheeks flush red as he looked first at me then at Tom. Oh Lord, is that what he thought I was doing? Writing a song to make a point to Tom?

But Tom was laughing, 'It's a good strong message. Lots a fellas need to hear it and far more women wanna give it, I reckon.'

If I was honest, I supposed the reason I was in my mid-thirties and still single was because I'd made my share of terrible choices with men. I'd fallen for far too many 'bad boys' in my youth and that never ends well. Then I'd gone to the other end of the spectrum with Robbie and just sort of settled for what was readily available and convenient – we both had. Surely there was something in the middle – passion that didn't come with a health warning attached – I didn't want to explain all that in detail to Tom and Fergus right now, but maybe I had in a way, by writing the song.

We played around with a few more ideas after that. I sang a line about whisky chasers and being an 'old-fashioned' girl while Tom was playing some licks on an electric guitar. It turned into a really upbeat, jokey tune about a very modern woman who just loved old-fashioned whisky cocktails.

Laura suddenly appeared with a tray of coffee and biscuits, which we all fell on with delight, but there was no desire from any of us to stop what we were doing. The sun was still bright outside but we must have already been working for several hours. I didn't want the day to end.

A coffee later, we got back to throwing ideas around. There were a few false starts but Ferg was keeping track of lines we'd thrown away or snatches of melody that we liked but then didn't use. 'Nothing ever goes to waste in songwriting,' he said. 'You can always circle back and use it again some other time.'

A bit like life, I thought.

The shadows across the wooden floor were starting to get longer when Tom began singing softly about being lost and alone. Quietly, Ferg and I stopped our own experiments and listened. It was haunting and I kept very quiet and still as he stopped and restarted several times, trying to find his way through the song. He went through the opening a few times, painting a picture of someone struggling to find their way. As he reached what would be the chorus he came out with a bittersweet line about needing the moonlight to guide him home. I thought the song was beautiful, both the melody and the words were gorgeous, but it wasn't until he looked up at me as he sang the moonlight line again that I registered any particular meaning that connected it to me. Was he singing this for me? About me? Before I got any daft notions, I told myself it was because my name was Mooney. After all, I'd had enough years of schoolyard jokes about my name, so it was nice that it was finally being used more poetically. Although I couldn't stop myself longing for more. Was he saying that I was helping him through something, that I was the one he was turning to when he felt lost and alone?

I didn't know what to do but Fergus came to my rescue by way of his disembodied voice from the control room. 'Can you give us some harmonies on this, Rebecca?'

I nodded in response and concentrated on finding the best places to add a harmony or an echo call. The song filled the space with longing and emotion and as the sun began to disappear and the light in the room began to change from gold to blue Tom and I sang with each other about love, loneliness and moonlight.

We all descended the stairs a little later to find the kitchen twinkling in lamplight and a huge pot of chilli bubbling on the stove. Fergus and Tom chattered excitedly about the songwriting session to Laura but I felt I was in some sort of daze. Turns out spilling your creative guts takes it out of you.

Tom got some cold bottled beers from the fridge as Ferg bounded back upstairs to kiss the kids goodnight and then we all sat around the table to tuck in. I was ravenous and the chilli was just what I needed but Laura picked up on how quiet I was. While the boys were eating and chatting away she asked me if everything was okay and I tried to reassure her I was just fine. In truth I was feeling both fabulous and completely disorientated in a succession of confusing waves. There wasn't an easy way to explain all that to myself, let alone to someone I didn't know too well.

Laura had been listening to what the boys had been saying about 'Mean to Me,' the song that had sprung from the line I had sung. She cleverly honed in on what had been my inspiration, asking me more about it.

'Maybe it's just me,' I told her, 'but I've had more than my fair share of guys being mean to me. If they made gaslighting an Olympic sport I'd be able to pick the gold medal winners every time.'

She laughed at that and told me I had a way of looking at the world that lent itself brilliantly to creative songwriting. 'No wonder Ferg and Tom have kept your nose to the grindstone all afternoon,' she said, 'I can't wait to hear what you've all been working on.'

A bolt of panic shot through me on hearing her say that. I hadn't thought further than trying to write a song, as an experiment, a sort of test to see if I could do anything that could ever be compared to composing. I hadn't thought about anyone else hearing it, judging it, even Laura who in the few hours I'd been in her company I'd decided was one of the loveliest people I had ever met. Would I want Laura to hear those songs? Would I ever want to share that raw emotion with anyone?

Before I could respond Tom cut into the conversation with a remark about my old boss, Guy. 'You should write a song about that crazy old boss of yours,' he said, then for Laura's benefit added, 'This was a guy who was so obsessed with Rebecca he got her arrested and tried to get her sent to jail!'

Both Laura and Ferg were gripped by this revelation but I tried to moderate the tone. 'He wasn't obsessed with me, it was just a misunderstanding.'

Tom almost choked on his chilli at that. 'Sorry, Rebecca honey, I don't wanna speak out of turn but it's quite clear that this Guy guy was obsessed. The fact ya didn't immediately fall under his spell and do … whatever it was he wanted y'all to do … is the most likely explanation for why he set the cops on you. He couldn't take rejection and so wanted his revenge.'

I shook my head and tried to protest but Tom simply put down his fork and said, 'I'm not in any way defending him, honey, but I can easily imagine he was so into you he got completely carried away and that's why he lost his cool. I know ya don't even realise it but y'all could easily have that effect on a man.' He carried on tucking into his chilli after that, oblivious to the impact his words were having in the room.

From the corner of my eye I saw Ferg and Laura shoot each other a meaningful look as I swallowed a mouthful of chilli and tried to decide how on earth to respond, but Tom looked up again and carried on, 'I might be joinin' the dots all wrong but I very much doubt what happened at the jewellery store was just a mistake or a misunderstanding. It sounds to me like "Gruesome Guy" as ya called him was either obsessed, or jealous, or had some huge grudge against you.'

I said nothing but then Laura asked me quietly, 'D'you think that's what happened, Rebecca?'

As though I was watching a movie, I allowed some key scenes from Grayson's Jewellers to replay in my mind. It had started with several conversations with Guy where I'd been left feeling weird and uncomfortable. At the time I'd put that down to his arrogant, transatlantic way of talking, deciding something somewhere was getting lost in translation. But then came the times he'd brushed up against me behind the counter, made some rude remarks about the space being too small for the both of us, which made me feel like a baby hippopotamus at the time but all the while he had been pressing himself against me. I'd manoeuvred myself out of reach as quickly as possible and then pretended that nothing had really happened. I'd pretended so well I must have convinced myself. That had only worked for a while though. Eventually he had made it pretty clear that he wanted to add certain other duties to my job description. It didn't feel like polite dinner conversation to point that out too explicitly.

'He was often creepy, but I didn't give him any encouragement,' I said.

'Of course you didn't.' Laura shot back her response instinctively.

'He said and did things in a way that meant, if I'd flown off the handle at what he was suggesting, answered him back or complained to anyone else, I know he would have accused me of over-reacting,' I said.

'Yes, that's the way they do it,' Laura said with feeling.

Tom was looking at me as though he couldn't quite decide what to say next and Ferg was busy examining every spoonful of chilli in forensic detail before putting it into his mouth but Laura's eyes were filled with care and understanding. 'Rebecca, you know as well as I do a bloke like that will have an ego the size of a planet but it can be exploded by the smallest of knockbacks. He would have been pushing his luck, seeing how far you would let him go. It sounds like you managed to close him down tactfully but he would still have registered that as rejection. And he won't have liked that.'

Laura was right, I knew it. How disgraceful that simply by not taking any nonsense a woman could incur the wrath of a man who was so arrogant he thought he could act in any way he wanted and get away with it. Sure, he practically owned the place – but he didn't own me. I thought back to a series of interactions where I had stood my ground with Guy and realised that me making it clear I wasn't interested in his sexual advances must have made him furious. Clearly, he'd taken rejection badly. It explained a lot. Although it didn't in any way excuse it.

'I'm not sure a song called "Gruesome Guy" is gonna be a chart topper,' I tried to break the mood with a joke but I didn't really want to keep thinking about Guy and how my time at Grayson's had come to a bitter end.

Tom picked up on my attempt at a change of tone. 'The real question we need answered right now …' he paused for dramatic effect, 'is do ya have anything urgent ya need to get back to the city for or are y'all able to stay over for the night?' He raised an eyebrow in a way that caused my tummy to flip, and Laura and Ferg immediately started reassuring me that I would be very welcome to stay and we could work again tomorrow in the studio if that was what I wanted.

'Of course, you must stay,' Laura said. 'We've not had the chance to get to know each other much today but maybe I can prise you away from these two for a bit tomorrow?'

That sounded good to me. I sensed Laura was someone who I could really get along with and it was wonderful to feel so welcomed in this colourful, comfortable home. Talking about gruesome Guy had only reinforced how lovely it felt to be away from him and Grayson's, and in this chaotic, musical, happy home. It was crazy how quickly I felt at ease with all of them. Crazy but cool. That sort of thing didn't happen to me too often and I certainly didn't want to cut the experience short. With the knowledge that my emergency overnight essentials were in my bag I seized the moment.

'Well … the club doesn't open on Mondays so I suppose it wouldn't hurt to stick around a bit longer,' I smiled in response to the enthusiastic nods from around the table. Their vibe was relaxed and a bit bohemian. These guys weren't going to worry if I was wearing the same jeans and t-shirt in the morning so I decided to relax into that too.

I had another night with Tom and another day of songwriting ahead of me. The excitement I felt for both were doing more for my mood, confidence and happiness than a change of outfit ever could. I was surrounded by warmth, laughter and music ... what more could I possibly need?

Chapter Fourteen

The next couple of weeks were as incredible as they were unexpected. I went back and forth between Forthview House and Sonny's, alternating between songwriting sessions, getting to know Laura, Ferg and their two adorable kids, while also putting in shifts and overseeing the running of the bar. I suddenly felt like I was living two lives.

I managed to swing by my flat while I was in town and quickly pack a bag with some more clothes and toiletries so that my new friendship gang didn't think I was some sort of down and out, although they simply weren't those sorts of people. Not shallow, or judgemental or worried about designer labels or how much the things you owned cost. It was refreshing to be around; it did occur to me at one point that Guy and JoJo could do with spending time with folk like these but then I ticked myself off for allowing the gruesome twosome to pierce my consciousness in any way.

It felt so wonderful being inside this bubble. It was actually more like a double bubble. There were times I would completely forget that I was hanging out with Tom Coltrane, the famous musician, but then I would remember that not only was he incredibly well known but that I was somehow instantly part of his inner circle along with his sister and best friend. They didn't treat him as though he was any sort of big star so it was easy to let that fact slip your mind, but it didn't make it any less true. When I caught myself suddenly remembering, I would feel like pinching myself. What was going on here? I hadn't shared with anyone I knew what had happened between us, that we'd kissed in the club, gone back to his hotel room, fallen into bed and into this instant relationship where we fitted together like the missing parts of a jigsaw. I hadn't even let on to Stella or Donald. Not that they'd have believed me if I did tell them. I was finding it hard enough to believe myself.

I was also learning that a recording studio was just like a bubble in itself, like its own little world, separate from everywhere else, a sort of safe place where music was the currency and patience was the law. So to be spending so much time at Ferg's Forthview studio, while also staying inside the secret world of me and Tom, definitely felt like a double bubble. I just hoped I wasn't headed for double trouble.

But if I was looking for reassurance from the universe that everything was unfolding just as it should and things were meant to be, I found it one morning in the kitchen of Forthview House. I was making a pot of coffee while Laura took the kids to school and nursery, and found myself taking a closer look at the painting on the wall I'd spotted on my very first visit. The abstract design was distinctive and the more I looked at the guitarist drawn in rough black lines against splashes of red and green the more it reminded me of the twelve pictures I'd bought years ago from a market stall that now hung at Sonny's. I hadn't heard Laura return but her voice caught me by surprise as I tried to read the artist signature in the corner.

'It's not exactly a great likeness but I think I did manage to capture his energy a little.'

I whirled around to find Laura behind me eyeing the picture with her arms folded and a critical look on her face.

'You did this?'

She puffed herself up a little before confirming, 'Yes, it's mine.'

Not only was Laura the artist, the picture was clearly meant to represent her musician brother, Tom. I peered closer so I could decipher the signature. The tiny scrawl said 'Feisty' and I was sure when I returned to the bar it would match the signature on the set of original Laura Coltrane artworks I already owned. I told her about the ones I'd bought and we were both incredulous at the coincidence at first but then Laura smiled at me and simply said, 'It's a sign.' I agreed completely: it did feel as though it cemented our instant connection, and anyway, I'd already learned you didn't argue with Laura 'Feisty' Coltrane.

Back at Sonny's, Stella and Donald were too delighted with the repercussions from the exposure Tom Coltrane had brought to the bar to be overly concerned about what I may or may not be up to when I wasn't with them. I made sure I pulled my weight with a decent number of shifts and liaised with Stella about what to put out on the socials and how to deal with the wider media. The local evening TV news show did a piece about Tom's surprise appearance and used lots of footage of Tom on stage in huge stadiums intercut with pieces to camera by a reporter in our tiny basement venue. They found footage of Tom at Sonny's that some of Saturday night's audience had filmed on their phones and it all made a really great package that promoted the bar wonderfully. It didn't need an appearance from me, and Stella was more than happy to be a talking head while Donald silently wiped the bar down in the background and made sure he was in shot. His fake nonchalant manner made me laugh when I saw the piece go out.

The story of Tom Coltrane's impromptu gig went viral and popped up on national TV spots too. There were radio phone-ins asking people to name famous people they'd seen in the unlikeliest places and a TV panel show debate about the merits of country music, using Tom's surprise gig as a kick off point. Some lunatic attempted to argue that country was the very worst of the music genres, but as the result of all that exposure Sonny's was now consistently packed to the rafters and people were regularly queueing down the block to get in, so I didn't bother getting offended.

I got a fabulous email from my bosses Scott and Gill Drummond congratulating me on getting Sonny's Bar so much publicity. I knew a lot of what had happened was down to luck but I was determined to work hard and capitalise on the opportunities that were coming my way. Several well-known musicians got in touch to ask when they could come and do a gig in our 'famous' basement so I told Stella to start booking them in and advertise it all on our runaway social media platforms. The timing couldn't have been better as the Edinburgh Fringe Festival was now just a couple of weeks away, which meant all kinds of stars were in town.

Every August thousands of visitors descend on our city for a month-long celebration of theatre, music and comedy. Any available space in Edinburgh is turned into a venue of some sort, from cafes and pubs to hotel rooms and even office block receptions or people's front rooms. Makeshift stages are erected, blackout curtains hung and the eternal cry of 'let's do the show right here' can be heard echoing from every corner. We would be too late to get into the official programme of events for the festival but by using social media I knew we would be able to make use of our new-found notoriety and get ourselves a piece of the festival action. I told Stella to start booking a roster of acts for August and also publicise a new, regular Open Mic Night a couple of times a week too.

'There will be loads of creatives and people into performing looking for something to do,' I said, thinking on my feet. 'We might even get some big names coming in and taking to our stage to unwind after their own show. It'll definitely be popular with audience members who've been inspired by shows they've seen. Let's give those people a chance to shine.'

'To shine like a diamond in a rhinestone world?' Stella had answered with a knowing smirk, quoting the Dollyism painted on the wall behind our very own stage.

'Exactly!' I knew Stella was teasing me but I could also tell she thought I was onto something and it felt good to have my ideas given some credit by her.

My head was in an absolute spin with everything that was happening and trying to be in two places at once. I was the old Becky at Sonny's but felt I was becoming someone slightly different as Rebecca at Forthview. At least I had the journey between the two places to recalibrate into what was expected of me in each location and Tom insisted on sending Iain to ferry me back and forth to South Queensferry whenever I needed him which was a huge help. I asked if he could park the big black Audi around the corner from the bar when he picked me up though. I didn't want to complicate matters with unnecessary speculation or questions. I also found it a bit disconcerting to have a chauffeured car at my beck and call. Disconcerting but amazing. I was a bit embarrassed by having a personal driver at first but I quickly decided I could cope with it.

I was in the car heading back towards Forthview early one evening when I started getting a stream of messages from Stella. Then my phone started ringing. I'd been interviewing prospective new bar staff all day. The sudden rush of interest and increase in customers along with our new Fringe plans meant we needed a few more bodies around the place. I'd found a couple of keen newbies who could start soon with Stella and Donald showing them the ropes, put in an afternoon shift myself and then nipped off to where Iain was waiting for me down a side street. It was all a bit cloak and dagger but I didn't feel too bad as things were going so well now at Sonny's.

Stella's alarmed tone on the phone now told me things might not be as rosy as I'd thought.

'Have you seen 'em? There's loads of 'em. I dunno where they've all come from?'

My first thought was we had an infestation. Oh God. What could it be? Mice? Cockroaches? Rats?

'Huh? Loads of what?'

'Terrible reviews, on our own socials, TripAdvisor, Facebook, TikTok, bloody everywhere. Hate-filled utter bollocks. And nasty posts about us too. All anonymous of course. People spewing out disgusting bile about the club, how rank our beer is, the state of the loos. A couple even claim they got food poisoning from our bar snacks. We don't even serve any bar snacks. Unless you count packets of crisps and Nobby's Nuts and I can't see how you can get food poisoning from Nobby's Nuts!'

Stella eventually took a breath and I managed to get a word in to try and reassure her.

'It's just jealousy, Stella, vile people with nothing better to do sounding off because we're suddenly in the news. Ignore it. Don't reply to any of it whatever you do and it will all blow over. It's horrible I know but I'm sure it's just a flash in the pan.'

It took a little while to pacify her but eventually she took my point. I was touched she was so passionately offended about people talking Sonny's down. She was a good egg was Stella. I couldn't blame her for being sceptical about me when I started. Her old manager's ex? I can see why it had taken her a while to trust me. After she hung up I took a little look at some of the posts myself. Despite my words of calm reassurance, I had to admit the criticisms stung me too. This was the last thing we needed just as we were trying to build up our reputation and keep things on the up. I was tempted to answer some of them, despite my advice to Stella to ignore them all. I bit my lip metaphorically and literally as I stuffed my phone back in my bag and tried to rise above the nastiness.

Iain caught my eye in the rear-view mirror. 'Everything all right, miss?'

'Oh, nothing to worry about … I hope,' I answered trying to look like I believed what I was saying.

'Okay, if you're sure,' he said. 'It's not like you to look so worried, you've always got such a lovely smile on your face. A little ray of sunshine you are, no wonder people like having you around.'

I gave him a thankful grin. What a lovely thing to say. But by 'people' did he mean Tom? Who else could he mean? Had he particularly noticed that Tom liked having me around? I wondered what Iain knew about Tom's private life. A driver would surely get to see and hear a lot of stuff while they were driving a famous person. I didn't know how long Iain had worked for Tom: did he work for him in the States or just here in Scotland? Had he seen Tom with a succession of different women? Did he know Juliana Ripon?

With everything else that had been going on I hadn't given too much thought to the Hollywood starlet who was reportedly Tom Coltrane's latest girlfriend. The press had only given Juliana Ripon a passing reference in the articles and reports that had been circulating since Tom's performance at Sonny's had exploded into the media. A couple had mentioned her, some had her aged 25, others at 27. One had wrongly claimed she was in the audience for Tom's impromptu gig but most others reported she was back in the States filming her latest Hollywood blockbuster.

While we'd been hanging out at Forthview, playing daft games with Reggie and Stevie or working on more music with Fergus in the studio, I'd never heard anyone utter Juliana's name. When I was alone with Tom, sitting in the garden late at night with a glass of wine after Laura and Ferg had followed the kids to bed, or when we retreated to our charming bedroom with its sun-kissed yellow wallpaper and soft white pillows, I never wanted to ruin the mood with an interrogation about where Juliana fitted into Tom's life, if she was still part of it at all. Or what if it had all been blown out of proportion by the press as I'd heard loads of Hollywood relationships were? I was too keen to feel his hands on my skin and kiss his lips to dwell on my questions. Sometimes his lips were all I could think about. Tom's voice was known all around the world but when it was just the two of us and he spoke softly, urgently, into my neck, close to my ear, the words from those lips could send me delirious. I adored his speaking voice just as much as his singing voice. I stuck with my plan of not rocking the boat. I wasn't a lovesick teenager who believed every romantic encounter had to be forever. I was having a good time but I wasn't expecting it to last for a long time.

Day by day I was discovering more and more about Tom but I truly didn't feel like I had the right to ask too much more. He was accepting me at face value so I would do the same for him. No other man had made me feel as seen as

Tom did. I was starting to see myself through his eyes and I liked what I saw. I'd never been made to feel like that before. For whatever reason, Tom had brought me into his life and appeared to trust me. To a point. Why would he tell me everything there was to know about his personal life? I completely accepted that would be a foolish thing to do in his circumstances. I could sell a story to the papers in the blink of an eye. Moreover, why would he tell me anything about the private life of another world-famous person, one that I had never even met? I knew he wasn't married to Juliana. I'd seen photos of them together but there was no way of my knowing if their relationship was serious, ongoing or simply a concoction for the press. I sensed Tom was a guy who was in a certain amount of turmoil. Whether that was due to his personal circumstances, his career or a combination of both I couldn't be sure but it felt like the best way to approach things was to let him tell me in his own time.

When I arrived back at Forthview that time didn't seem to be right now.

'REBECCA! Hey Honey!' Tom was leaning out of an upstairs window at the front of the house as I got out of the car and thanked Iain for the ride. 'Quick, get yourself up here, fast as you can.'

I didn't need asking twice and after giving Laura a quick hug hello as she opened the door I ran up the stairs to find Fergus and Tom in the studio looking like two kids on Christmas morning.

'And what have you two been up to?' It was impossible not to smile at the looks of sheer delight on both of their faces. 'Have your numbers come up on the Scottish Lotto?'

'Better than that,' Ferg said glancing at Tom with a look of pride.

'We've been working on "Moonlight Home",' Tom said. 'You've gotta hear it, I've not been this excited about a song since "Whisper Away".'

He jumped up from the piano then, kissed me softly and then pulled me to sit next to him on the stool while Fergus went into the control booth.

Tom's arm was snug around my waist but his leg was twitching against mine as we sat side by side waiting for the music to playback. He was nervous. I could feel it. Was he anxious about the track itself … or my reaction to it? I was going to be the first person to hear a new song from Tom Coltrane and I suddenly felt a wave of anxiety too. I'd loved the beginnings of the haunting track I'd heard Tom begin to compose a few days ago. I hoped I was going to like what they'd done with it now.

I needn't have worried. Tom's lyrics were magical, his voice was first croaky with pure emotion and then soaring and strong with hope and desire. It was beautiful, powerful, but then in the second verse I heard something else. It was my voice. An answering call to Tom's questioning, yearning, looking for answers. It was like my voice was guiding his voice home, out of the darkness to a point of light up ahead. Helping him to find his way home in the moonlight. That was the song. 'Moonlight Home'.

I turned to look at Tom, his eyes were burning into mine. Did he really need me to tell him how good this was? 'D'ya like it?' he whispered. It was a genuine question. He really wanted to know.

'I love it.' I'd never said those words and meant them more. It felt more intimate whispering those three little words into Tom's ear with his body pressed up alongside mine than anything I had ever said to any man before. I could feel my heart hammering and wondered if he could hear it too.

He kissed me again then and with the pounding in my ears from my own heartbeat I almost missed his next words, 'It's gonna be my new single, "Moonlight Home" by Tom Coltrane featuring Rebecca Mooney. What do ya think about that!?'

Chapter Fifteen

Next morning I was awake before anyone, even the kids. I made my way downstairs to the kitchen and opened the French doors to the garden while I made myself a coffee. Then I pulled one of the mismatched dining chairs to the doorway and sat with my bare feet resting on the stone step looking out across the large lawn and slightly unkempt but colourful borders.

The nearest neighbours to Forthview House were a little way away, shielded from view behind tall trees. The closest road was down the long, winding driveway and at that time in the morning I couldn't hear any traffic. The plot the house stood on was elevated but you couldn't see the Firth of Forth from where I sat, the estuary and bridge were only visible from an upstairs window. Here, at ground level, it felt like I was in a hidden oasis. Private and secret, a world away from my real life.

I thought about that some more. What was my real life? Who was I now? It was easier to identify the things I'd left behind; I no longer worked at Grayson's Jewellery shop; I was no longer Robbie's on/off girlfriend (girlfriend? Who was I kidding? We'd been each other's booty call!). Had I also called time on being a Dolly Parton tribute act? That one was harder to know. Up until the Saturday night's open mic night at Sonny's, I had been thinking I could re-establish myself as a solo Dolly artist on the tribute circuit. I'd been planning to get some new publicity material sorted and let some of the agents Robbie and I had often worked with know my new act would be available for bookings. But the unexpected appearance of Jack Tinker as 'Dolly Partly' followed by the equally surprising arrival of music star Tom Coltrane at Sonny's had completely de-railed those plans.

Tom was obviously encouraging me to find a way to perform as myself, Becky Mooney, or Rebecca Mooney perhaps?

Was I starting to find my own voice? But how would that translate into anything that people would be interested in? And was I doing what I'd done too often before and relying on someone else – this time another man – to give me the courage I couldn't find myself. I had so many questions but also the clarity of knowing I didn't have a profile as Becky Mooney, let alone a recording contract; I'd never had the confidence to perform as myself since I was an adult. When I realised I could do a passable Dolly Parton impression, I'd clung to that as a lifeline to help me keep getting up on the stage. My parents had been terribly upset when I rejected my part in the Moonshine Trio and put it down to typical teenage rebellion. I remember pointing out that most teenagers rebelled by getting drunk, staying out late or dabbling in drugs but, with my parents, turning your back on John Denver and Tammy Wynette was much worse than that! Bless them. They'd been so supportive when later on I'd started doing Dolly and launched a new stage act ... for them it was like I'd found my way back from the wilderness, country roads takin' me home.

I'd loved being on stage as a kid and I'd found a way to enjoy it again as an adult. I had developed a coping mechanism but that coping mechanism was Dolly; I wasn't at all sure what would happen if you took that away. My real fear was that I would find it impossible to perform in public without my Dolly disguise. I'd had lots of experience on stage but that experience meant I was realistic about what an audience were looking for. They liked confidence. They liked a strong image and someone who had something to say. That definitely wasn't me. I'd been able to sing in Ferg's studio – but doing the same in public was a different ballgame.

I took a big sip of coffee and tried to still the tremors that were making my hands shake every time I thought about what Tom had said last night. *'It's gonna be my next single. "Moonlight Home" by Tom Coltrane featuring Rebecca Mooney.'* The shock of hearing those words was still reverberating through me. What the ...? Why would ...? How could ...? I simply couldn't find the words to form an adequate question let alone start figuring out any answers.

Instinctively I reached for my phone and sent a quick WhatsApp message to Mum and Dad:

Hey! How you both doing? It's crazy busy here but all good. Love ya x

I wasn't sure if they would have seen the press coverage of Tom Coltrane at Sonny's Bar. Even if it had reached their little enclave on the Costa Brava I'm not sure they would have remembered the name of the place I had told them I was now managing and realise the furore was anything to do with me. They had asked me if the club had a stage when I'd told them about my career change ... for them everything always came back to music and performing. They still entertained locals and holidaymakers in the Spanish bars and clubs, performing once again as the Moonshine Duo, paying tribute to all their favourite country artists with an impressive repertoire of cover versions. Moving to Spain had given them a second wind in their seventies. The climate suited them, they'd found a nice group of mates and the appetite for their sort of entertainment was in good demand there. I was pleased for them and it also gave me a nice place to visit occasionally for a holiday. Still, I missed them.

I was just imagining how amazed they would be if I suddenly rocked up in Cadaques with famous country star Tom Coltrane in tow when I heard a noise behind me and realised I wasn't alone. A tousle-haired Stevie was standing barefoot in the kitchen wearing sparkly unicorn pyjamas that looked two sizes too small, silently watching me.

'Hey Stevie, I love your pyjamas,' I said. 'I wish they made unicorn pyjamas like that in my size.'

Stevie blinked and considered this for a moment before replying, 'D'you like unicorns?'

'Who doesn't like unicorns?!' I exclaimed while beckoning her over to the doorway. 'Why d'you think I'm keeping watch over the garden right now? Early morning is the best time to try and see a wild unicorn, you know. They are very, very shy.'

Stevie's eyes widened at this piece of unicorn information although as a savvy seven-year-old she looked unconvinced at the possibility of a mythical beast sighting. Still, she tip-toed over, peering out at the garden in case a passing unicorn had decided to wander across the lawn. Good girl, I thought, it's always best to hedge your bets.

We debated the unlikely habits of unicorns, fairies, elves and even dragons for a good while. Stevie was a cute smarty pants with a complicated belief system of what could and could not be real which was pretty fascinating. She then announced she was hungry and I helped her get a bowl of cereal and some juice. At some point while she ate her Cheerios and I had a piece of toast with my second cup of coffee we decided that writing a note to a unicorn would be a good way to let them know the garden at Forthview House was a safe space.

'They might think we would catch them and put them in a zoo,' Stevie said, the very thought making her look outraged. I had the feeling she was humouring me more than I was her but we were in the game now.

'It couldn't hurt to make them feel welcome, I suppose,' I told her. 'We could pop it on that tree over there. I'm sure they'd like a picture too.'

We found paper and crayons and began attempting to design a welcome note for unicorns. Stevie contributed some lovely rainbows and was clearly more practised at drawing unicorns than I was. Luckily for me she was too polite to mention mine looked more like hippos.

'What's all this?' Laura came into the kitchen with Reggie on her hip, smiling at the sight of me and Stevie with our heads bent over our pictures. 'It's like an episode of *Art Attack* in here.'

Laura set to fixing breakfast for Reggie just as my WhatsApp alert signalled a reply from Mum and Dad.

'Everything okay?' she asked as she saw me look a bit taken aback by what I'd just read.

'Yeah … yeah, really good … great actually.' I was trying hard to use the right tone to match my words. 'It's … my mum and dad, they live in Spain now but … they're coming over soon.'

The message from my parents was a bit of a surprise. They usually liked to pop over for a few days during the Fringe to take in a few shows and catch up with some of their performer mates, but the message said they were coming much sooner. The end of the week, in fact.

We know about your amazing news. How exciting! Can't wait to see you xx, Mum had written. I presumed that meant they knew about Tom Coltrane appearing at Sonny's Bar. Did that have anything to do with their decision to make a sudden appearance, I wondered?

I tapped a quick reply and made a move to go upstairs for a shower.

'Fancy a top up?' Laura asked, reaching for the coffee pot but I told her I'd already had two cups. 'Ahh … some juice then?' she offered, opening up the fridge and getting a carton of mango juice out. She saw me hesitate and laughed. 'It's just … it's nice to have a new grown-up to talk to at breakfast time, d'you have to rush off so fast?'

I didn't need much persuading to hang out with Laura. As the kids ate breakfast and drew pictures of unicorns and dragons, Laura and I chatted. She was so easy to talk to. She was also pretty perceptive and swiftly figured out I wasn't really up early because I was hunting unicorns.

'Is everything moving at warp speed for you right now?'

I looked at Laura with relief, it was good to have someone to talk to. I hadn't seen my closest friend, Alina, too much lately as she'd moved to Birmingham after getting married last year. We'd been friends since school, her house had been my second home growing up. The busy hubbub of extended family at Alina's with lively meals of delicious Indian food shared around the dining table every night made it somewhere I loved hanging out. Being at Forthview with Laura and Ferg and the kids had reminded me of those times. But Alina never really understood my family's interest in performing. She worked for a big accountancy firm in Birmingham now, which made sense if you knew her. Alina was one of those weird people who actually loved maths. I found that as unfathomable as a quadratic equation. When I threw in the towel with the Moonshine Trio Alina was a great support, but the reality was that she'd actually never got her head around why I was doing it in the first place. Singing and performing had always been my dream career, I'd never had any other ambition growing up. I couldn't imagine Alina would be able to advise me now on how I should reinvent myself for a fresh career in music; even less would she be able to fathom what I thought I was doing hooking up with a famous country music star.

As I suspected, Laura had a bit more insight on both topics.

'Tom's never brought anyone here before, you know,' she said meaningfully as we moved another chair to the open French doors so we could keep an eye on the kids who were now in the garden playing some sort of dragon-hunting game.

She let the statement hang in the air for a moment while I considered how to ask what she thought that might mean. Before I could speak she added, 'He's happier than I've seen him for a long time. More like the old Tom.'

I felt a surge of emotion as I heard that. I didn't like to think of Tom being unhappy, I felt instantly protective of him in a way that surprised me. I knew I liked him, it wasn't just pure lust that was keeping me around, but this lioness feeling was something new. Was I already having deeper feelings for him? That felt dangerous.

'It must be hard trying to keep on top when you're so successful,' I said, adding that I'd gathered he was trying to find his way through a musical dry spell.

Laura considered this with her head on one side. She appeared to want to say something else but was weighing up how to put it.

'Having everyone think they know who you are but hardly anyone bother to really get to know you is not a good way to live,' she said. 'He loves Nashville but not everyone there has his best interests at heart. I know why he's based there but I wonder if he would be happier if he came back home to Scotland?'

It was obvious how close Tom and Laura were. I liked that, it felt good to know how much Tom valued his family. He and Laura and their older brother Pete sounded an interesting mix of their Scottish and American heritage having been brought up largely in Edinburgh but with a mother from the American South. Pete had joined the police force to be a very British bobby, Tom had headed for the homeland of his mother once his music career had taken off and was clearly comfortable as a singing Tennessee cowboy, while Laura herself appeared to be a cool blend of a sassy Scottish gal and soulful Southern belle. I'd never met anyone quite like her.

We chatted about what it was like when Tom first started out and how proud she was of his success. She was careful not to gossip but it was good to get some more background on the real man behind the image. Laura didn't sit on the fence for long though. 'You're good for him, Rebecca,' she said. 'I can tell that already, I think he can too. I hope he's good for you too?'

I wanted to tell her yes, tell her how he made me feel seen and heard more than anyone I'd ever been with before, how he was sexy and funny and being around him made me feel totally alive. But I was mindful that she was his little sister. Given that relationship, it was cool of Laura to ask how I was feeling about things, but I didn't feel comfortable going into too many explicit details so what I actually answered was, 'Uh-huh.'

My reservation wasn't only caused by Laura being Tom's little sister. I was in turmoil over what was now expected of me, not just in our relationship (if it even was a relationship) but with the music we had been creating. It all tumbled out then. I told her all about the song he'd written and how I'd ended up singing backing on the recording and he now wanted to release it.

'If it was just the harmonies on "Moonshine Home" they were talking about I'd be thrilled, delighted, ecstatic … but we've been working on other songs together too and he's got Fergus to record me on some tracks. They say I'm good, that I could put a debut album together. They actually think I've got what it takes to be a recording and performing artist!'

'What a pair of scumbags!' Laura was smirking as she held up her hands in protest. 'Don't shoot me but I'm struggling to see why you sound so outraged about Tom and Ferg having faith in your talent. Trust me, they wouldn't waste their time on you if they didn't believe you were good … great, even. I can't wait to hear your stuff, I've been saying to …'

'Nooooooo!' I could feel hot tears welling and my throat tightening as I cut her off and confessed, 'I don't mean to be ungrateful, truly I don't, but I'm just not up to this. I'm like a snail – I need my shell to protect me.' That didn't really clarify the situation very well and had I really just compared myself to a snail to my boyfriend's sister? I winced, inwardly.

I tried to explain, as best I could, how I understood that having a voice, even a good voice, was only part of what was needed for any sort of musical career. You needed to be able to perform live, promote yourself in the media, be visible as well as audible, and I couldn't do any of that unless I was in disguise. I told her how my teen stage fright had taken over, leaving me unable to face an audience as just myself. Laura listened patiently, asking a couple of questions about how I'd morphed into a Dolly Parton tribute.

'It happened by accident really,' I told her. 'It was a weird sequence of events now I think about it.' I explained how doing Dolly impressions had been my party piece growing up, just for my parents or family. Then one night, years after I'd stopped performing, I went to watch Mum and Dad at a club gig.

'I suppose I missed the scene and enjoyed hanging out in all those bars and social clubs even if I wasn't performing myself anymore. Anyway, Mum went down with a bout of tonsillitis that night and Dad begged me to help him out and go on with him. I refused point blank at first but then he suggested I didn't go on as Becky but as 'Dolly' instead.'

Laura's eyes widened as I described the scene backstage as I'd rifled through assorted wigs in the dressing room to find a blonde one that could pass as Parton-esque, borrowed some make-up and found a tasselled waistcoat and a pair of cowboy boots in the stash of costumes Dad always kept in the boot of his car. I hadn't wanted to let him down so I'd thrown a look together, crossed my fingers and prayed to the queen of country music that I'd get through it.

'It was a bit of a mishmash but Dolly's such a well-known, well-loved character that I only had to add a giggle in my talk and a wiggle in my walk and the crowd lapped it up.'

I looked at Laura and saw an expression on her face that was hard to read: it looked a lot like admiration.

'And how did it feel to be back on stage that night?'

I thought back to how my hands had been slick with sweat as I'd taken hold of the mic and how I'd wished I'd worn a longer skirt that night in case the audience could see my knees knocking. But as soon as I'd put on my 'Dolly' voice and greeted them with a 'Howdy folks!' I'd started to feel better. There had been a gasp of recognition from the crowd, I'd sensed their anticipation that they were about to hear some of their favourite songs and so were happy to see me, and I'd been determined not to disappoint. By the time I'd sung my way through '9 to 5', 'Coat of Many Colours' and 'Jolene,' they were eating out of my hand and a couple of duets with Dad to finish had them cheering.

'It felt amazing,' I said quietly.

'You found a way to do it, good for you,' Laura said. 'And you can find a way to do this, Rebecca, I know you can.'

I looked at Laura sitting there in the morning sunshine as she looked back at me with complete faith in her bright blue eyes. Tom had looked at me in exactly the same way. What was it with these Coltranes that made me want to rise up to the expectations they had of me? I wanted to, I really did, but how?

Laura seemed to be considering the situation for a little while then she took both of my hands in hers. Her face was pale and serious but the sunshine on her gingery blonde hair made it glow and flame as though it was on fire. 'Tom has discovered you, Fergus can capture your voice on record, but I think I can help you with the rest,' she said, quietly and earnestly, 'if you'll let me?'

With my hands still in hers I looked at Laura and marvelled at how this incredible woman was offering her help and friendship to me. A friend like Laura might be as rare and mythical as a unicorn but I needed to believe in her. 'Okay, thank you,' I said.

Laura smiled at me then. 'Excellent,' she said, 'because I have a plan!'

Chapter Sixteen

The first part of Laura's plan was making fresh coffee for Ferg and Tom and letting them know they were in charge of getting Stevie and Reggie to school and nursery. Next, she told me I had half an hour to get myself together before we needed to leave the house.

'Dress in something easy to get on and off,' she instructed. Tom's eyes goggled as she said that and I had to bite back a smutty retort but neither of us said anything. It appeared Tom knew better than to get in the way of his little sister when she was on a mission and I was too intrigued to question her.

We were on a bus heading to an unknown destination before Laura began to reveal any details of her grand plan. We were going shopping. I tried not to look too underwhelmed by this revelation.

'We're not just "shopping",' Laura said reading the look on my face correctly as she waggled her fingers in the air around the word. 'We're not having a girly day out looking for just *clothes*. We are shopping for a new look, an image, we are about to create a completely new persona for you. Clothes aren't just something you wear, they are how you choose to display yourself to the world, they are your armour when you go into battle, your shield from the slings and arrows that might come your way. Wear the right outfit and it lifts your mood, changes your attitude, gives you confidence to be a version of yourself you may never have been before. It worked for Dolly, why wouldn't it work for you?'

She argued the case well I had to admit. For too long the only clothes I'd really given much thought to were the ones I wore when I was imitating Dolly. I'd let my own identity slide so far down my priorities that I'd forgotten how to showcase my own personality. At least I'd remembered I still had one of those. Being around new people who weren't used to me had made me realise I could still be funny, spirited and yes, even sexy when I wanted to be. It helped me realise how important it could be to come out from behind Dolly, before I lost myself altogether.

As the bus jogged along, Laura brought up a series of images on her phone, flicking through pictures of famous singers with their own distinctive looks, asking me questions about what I liked and didn't like about their style. I couldn't help but be drawn in to comparing the merits of Stevie Nicks and Linda Ronstadt, Sophie Ellis Bextor and Taylor Swift. I loved Stevie's swirls of satin and lace, Linda's cotton and denim combos, and the sparkle and sequins rocked by Sophie and Taylor … maybe I could borrow a couple of ideas here and there but I was done with impersonating others: now I had to find a way to be me.

I looked at what Laura was wearing. She was in denim cut-offs and trainers with a long white floaty kaftan worn open thrown over a striped sleeveless vest, her bangles, necklaces and tattoos adding quirks of interest. She looked effortlessly cool compared to me in my boring jeans and t-shirt and I said so.

'Ah thanks,' she said. 'But I wouldn't necessarily dress like this if I was planning to perform on stage. A version of it maybe … with a bit more colour … bolder accessories, a smattering of glitter?' She thought about that for a moment before continuing, 'I know you've never really thought about the image you want to portray on stage as you've always relied on Dolly to do all the work, but it's exciting to now have a chance to show who *you* are.'

She was right. About everything. And now I really thought about it I also knew I hadn't given much thought to how I was dressed when I was off stage either. I'd stopped thinking about my own appearance in any detail. My hair was naturally light brown and I kept it shoulder length as it was easier to stuff under Dolly's wigs. I wore minimal make-up and dressed in simple combinations of jeans and tops. I couldn't even remember the last time I wore a dress.

'There's absolutely nothing wrong with the way you look, Rebecca,' Laura insisted. 'You are naturally gorgeous, you've got great skin, your hair shines and the way you fill those jeans and t-shirts certainly got Tom's attention!'

I grinned at that and wondered if what had really attracted Tom's interest was the moment he caught me in the back room of Sonny's Bar midway between my two personas as I fought my way out of my Dolly costume and returned to being Becky Mooney. I'd even thrown one of Dolly's falsies at his head. Funny way to get his attention ... but it had worked.

Laura was still talking. 'But jeans and t-shirt won't work for you as a stage image. You love performing, Rebecca, admit it ... you might think you developed your Dolly act just to help your dad but be honest, if that was true you would never have carried on after that one night. You want to be on stage, you know you are good enough but you're letting your insecurities spoil it for you. It's time to get past that.'

No one had ever called me out on this stuff before. Laura was hitting so many nerves I was starting to feel like my skin was prickling all over. I was apprehensive but also excited. Was I on the brink of curing my stage fright?

I let myself be swept along in Laura's wake as though I was a rowing boat being towed behind a galleon in full sail. Her white wispy kaftan billowed out behind her as she strode ahead of me through the streets and I followed.

Laura was like a pirate hunting for buried treasure, she could sense when something special was lurking among drabber items, plucking something gorgeous from a rail with a triumphant ... 'Aha!' She had nose for which charity shops to scour, which high street shops might stock quirkier pieces that could pass for high-end designer and then to finish off she led me to a vintage store with three floors of crazy and cool fashion from every era. I'd never experienced a shopping trip like it.

Our first purchases were a couple of waistcoats, one denim and the other black leather. They were on a sale rail in a boutique and I flicked past them without a second glance but Laura seized on them immediately. 'Well, well … what do we have here?' She was holding the denim in one hand and the leather in the other jiggling one then the other as she asked, 'A little bit country, a little bit rock 'n' roll, wouldn't you say?'

I was immediately on board with the idea of pitching my image somewhere in the middle of those two genres and went into the fitting room to whip off my t-shirt and give them a try. They both fitted me perfectly, giving me a neat waist, and when worn with only a bra underneath they looked just the right amount of raunchy. Or so Laura told me, insisting I buy them. When she suggested I could also use them to rock up a flouncy skirt or dress it got me thinking about alternative ways of wearing more feminine clothes but giving them an edge. I loved that idea too.

The next find was a stroke of genius by Laura. We were in a charity shop when she spotted a flash of black and red tartan trouser leg and grabbed it immediately. 'Just try them on,' she wheedled as she clocked the dubious look on my face.

The trousers were vintage Top Shop, a nod to punk with a couple of zips and a touch of leather trim on the pockets. They were a good fit and the slightly stretchy fabric meant they were easy to move in. But I still wasn't convinced. 'Aren't they a bit Bay City Rollers?' I said, pulling a face as I pictured the Scottish boy-band from the seventies.

'I'd say they're more Johnny Rotten than that,' Laura said, before adding with a wink, 'but forget the Sex Pistols, it's about time a true Scottish lass gave tartan a hot new twist.' Before I could protest further she ransacked the rails and found a black chiffon blouse two sizes too big for me and I watched in awe as she knotted it at my waist and pulled it slightly off one shoulder making it instantly asymmetrical and cool. Worn with the trousers it was a definite vibe.

'How did you do that?' I had to admit it was a good look on me, edgy yet feminine, colourful but comfortable to wear.

I added both the trousers and chiffon blouse to my bag and we rewarded our success with a pit stop at a tiny cafe on the edge of an outdoor market where we refreshed ourselves sharing a pot of peppermint tea.

I was enjoying myself immensely. Laura was good company and we'd quickly managed to source some items that were giving me hope that a new stage image was within my grasp.

'Thanks for this, Laura, I don't think I would be brave enough to do this by myself.' She waved away my gratitude but was looking at me with a furrowed brow.

'What is it, have I got a mark on my face?' I reached into my cross-body bag for a compact but Laura told me nothing was wrong.

'I'm just wondering … leave it with me … there was one more place I want to take you … but I'm now thinking we may make an extra stop after Handbags and Gladrags,' she said. She looked at me with a face full of mischief that reminded me of Tom but I couldn't help but be excited rather than alarmed that she was plotting something else. 'Trust me,' she said. And so I did.

Handbags and Gladrags turned out to be Laura's favourite shop in the whole world and it was easy to see why. It was three floors of vintage clothes, shoes and bags but with every corner filled to bursting I was a bit daunted by the task ahead of us. Luckily, as always, Laura had a plan.

'Right,' she said, hands on her tiny hips as she surveyed her domain, 'we don't need more denim, avoid anything too floral, but we could do with some sequins for a bit of sparkle and obviously hone in on any tartan you can find.'

It was an excellent plan. We split up and began working our way methodically through the racks, peering into glass display cabinets and rooting through open travelling trunks along the way. I had a much clearer idea of what I was looking for now and I was hopeful I'd be able to find something myself here rather than rely on Laura and her fashion bloodhound skills.

Over our tea break we had discussed the idea of using tartan here and there throughout my new wardrobe to give it a cohesive look and build up a slight theme. If we could find the right way to do it I thought it could work well. I wasn't a flowery sort of person but tartan and plaid came in so many colour combinations there would always be a way to brighten up any outfit by adding tartan touches.

By the time we encountered each other again over an hour later we both had armfuls of possibilities and it was time for a try-on session behind a gold velvet curtain in the changing room. My finds included an oversized diaphanous blouse similar to the black chiffon we'd bought from the charity shop. This one was red and I'd decided it went equally well with the tartan trousers for a bolder, more colourful look. Laura nodded her approval like a proud mother hen. I'd also found a long, loose duster jacket made entirely of sky-blue sequins. The fabric shimmered and sparkled as I twirled around and it made me feel fabulous even slung over my jeans.

'Snap!' Laura said as I twirled, sorting out a very similar glittery coat from her finds pile, only this one was a silvery fabric. We compared the merits of one against the other but decided they were both too gorgeous to leave behind. They were over the top and showy but I knew they could be combined with less flamboyant fabrics like denim and leather for a grounded yet glamorous look. I just hoped I'd have an occasion to wear them.

Laura was most triumphant about her tartan discovery. I'd almost struck out completely in the tartan department. Everything I'd spotted had been unsuitable or the wrong size. The only thing I had found was a blue and yellow checked man's tie. I wasn't sure why I'd bothered picking it up but I just really liked the colourful design, it was very eye catching. Laura seized on it immediately.

'Oooo what a great idea,' she said lassoing it around my neck and fixing it in a low-slung position. 'You can wear it over a little strappy top instead of a long necklace, or put it with an open-necked shirt if you want a more Annie Hall kinda look. That'll be a great way to put a pop of tartan into lots of different outfits.'

Neither of those ideas had occurred to me but I was liking the touch of tartan theme we were beginning to assemble. Laura, of course, had taken her tartan treasure hunt to a whole different level.

'Behold,' she whispered holding up a deep blue tartan bodice. 'It's Vivienne Westwood!'

I took the corset from her and studied the distinctive folds of fabric across the neckline, the wide shoulder straps and the gold metal zip with its trademark orb dangling from the pull tab at the bust. It was stunning, but did I have the guts to wear it? I didn't dare ask the price, it was surely going to be even more expensive than the sequinned coats ... and they weren't cheap, even though all this stuff was pre-loved. This was going to be a very expensive shopping trip at the rate we were going but I couldn't resist it, I just had to try the vintage Westwood on. Maybe it wouldn't fit and I wouldn't have to worry about the price tag?

Even worn with just my faded blue jeans the Vivienne Westwood design looked absolute knockout, I had to admit it.

Laura said nothing, just nodded her head and smiled. I checked myself out in the mirror. Was that boring Becky Mooney looking back at me? Then I suddenly remembered I'd also found a cool pair of boots tucked in one of the accessories alcoves on the second floor. They were high-heeled ankle boots in black fabric studded with silvery rhinestones. They'd reminded me of the boots Madonna wore in *Desperately Seeking Susan* as soon as I saw them and they looked like they could be my size. I kicked off my trainers and pulled the boots on, tucking my jeans inside the slouchy tops.

Now we were talking. The boots finished off the outfit perfectly. I was a little bit country, a little bit rock 'n' roll, the tartan bodice had oodles of personality and the jeans and rhinestone boots completed a country-and-western-style showbiz look. This could definitely be the start of the new me.

'How d'you feel?' Laura was studying me closely as I stood before the mirror with about a million thoughts whizzing around my mind. I was thrilled with the clothes, the way they made me look was certainly giving me a confidence boost I sorely needed but my brain was already second-thinking the whole thing. How would other people react to me looking like this? Was I too old to be reinventing myself in this way? Was I just setting myself up for heartbreak and disappointment? With Tom? With a new music career? Was any of this a good idea?

Laura could clearly see the doubts creeping in but didn't try to over-analyse me. She waited until I finally gave her question an answer.

'I feel … a bit dazed and amazed,' I admitted.

'Write that down, what a great title for a song! "Dazed and Amazed" by Rebecca Mooney!' Laura said as she came and stood right next to me and addressed my reflection in the full-length mirror in front of us. She put her arm around my waist and gave me a friendly squeeze. 'This is just the beginning of everything, Rebecca. Don't forget, these clothes will be your armour when you present yourself to the world. They are already making you feel good, I can tell, and that will help you so much when you perform. You've made a great start today, but of course, no real make-over is complete without a few finishing touches.'

I wasn't sure what she meant by that but then she stroked my mousey hair and twirled an unruly lock around her finger.

Oh Lord, I thought, as anxiety began swirling inside me again, what on earth could Laura be planning now?

Chapter Seventeen

'C'mon, you know I'm right. We need to put the new image to the test. It's a friendly crowd ... you can do this!'

Laura was doing her very best to convince me but I remained sitting on the end of her and Fergus's bed transfixed at the sight of myself in her dressing table mirror and feeling mildly terrified. She'd insisted on smuggling me into the house, up the stairs and into the bedroom so I could put on one of my new outfits and then give Fergus and Tom the very first glimpse of the result of my make-over. Yet another of Laura's cunning plans ... did they never end?

The reveal idea had occurred to Laura while we grabbed a cheeky glass of wine and a bite to eat at the pub down the road from Forthview House. It had been a long day, we were both starving and we reckoned we'd earned a final stop-off before we returned home to the guys and the kids. It was while we tucked into steaming bowls of pasta that Laura hatched her latest brainwave. I was still reeling from the results of the last part of 'Operation Makeover' and had little to no resistance left.

We'd left Handbags and Gladrags vintage store on a complete high. The pre-loved prices of the two glittery coats and Vivienne Westwood corset had been surprisingly reasonable but then Laura had also managed to wangle a decent discount as we were buying several items. 'You've a new regular customer right here,' Laura told the guy on the till who clearly knew her well. 'Rebecca will be coming back here again for more stage gear, won't you, Rebecca?'

I'd nodded enthusiastically although I was a bit embarrassed by Laura talking me up like that to a stranger. The shop assistant looked pretty impressed at the mention of me wearing stuff on stage though and I made a mental note to seek out Jarvis next time I came into the store. Laura was right, there certainly would be a next time.

As soon as we hit the street Laura pulled out her phone and hailed an Uber. The taxi arrived in minutes and while we were in the back seat heading – goodness knows where – Laura told me she'd already been in touch with her local salon and managed to get an appointment in the next half hour.

'Ruth is a good mate, I've known her since school,' Laura explained. 'She's just finished her last customer for the day but she's cool about sticking around for us.'

'Us?' I didn't think Laura had pulled in a favour from her hairdresser mate because she suddenly had the urge to get a blow-dry.

'Well, yes ... I mean *you*, I suppose,' Laura said while having the decency to look a little bit sheepish.

She was quick to insist she didn't think there was anything *wrong* with my hair, as such, but said I should give myself chance to reconsider my whole 'look' if I was striving for a stronger image. Once again, I couldn't help but agree with her, although while I considered what could be done with my unruly, mousey hair I wasn't coming up with many answers.

'Don't worry about that,' Laura said, reassuringly, 'Ruth will know just what to do. She's great.'

Ruth ran her hands through my hair, looked closely at my bone structure and even rifled through the shopping bags to get an idea of the image we were attempting to create before making a series of suggestions.

The first revelation was that she believed I had naturally curly hair. This was brand new information for me. I'd been fighting my hair for years, struggling and straightening when I apparently needed to use particular products which would do wonders for my waves.

Next, she suggested we lifted my locks with colour. 'You could go blonde,' Ruth said flicking through a chart with a myriad of hair tufts in numerous shades. 'Something with honey tones or a full-on platinum Marilyn?'

It was tempting but I'd never really seen myself as a blonde bombshell like Monroe. Plus, it might just tempt me back to my Dolly comfort zone. The mention of Marilyn made me think of another girl's name however, one who had green eyes just like me …

'Jolene!' I said.

Laura got the reference at once. 'Ahh yes, you already have the ivory skin and eyes of emerald green ... all you need now is the flaming locks of auburn hair!'

Ruth immediately started rifling through the colour chart until we found a beautiful shade of burnished coppery red. I adored it as soon as I saw it, but wondered if it would suit me.

'Suit you? This colour is going to be just perfect on you,' Ruth said and before I knew it the colour was mixed and applied. 'Bye bye mouse, hello foxy,' Ruth said with obvious relish as she finished painting the last of the paste onto my head.

While we waited for the colour to take she shaped my eyebrows and showed me how to create a smoky eye look with a soft brown kajal eyeliner and a touch of mascara. It was incredible how much difference those touches made. My eyes looked greener than ever before.

I was so fidgety in the chair Ruth and Laura decided I should face away from the mirror after my hair had been washed so I couldn't see the results of the colour application until after Ruth had trimmed the ends of my hair and massaged some curl-enhancing product throughout. She then dried it with a diffuser and applied some touches of hair oil to add definition and stood back to admire her work.

'Wow,' she said.

'Really?' I asked.

'Look for yourself.'

She twirled the chair around and I caught sight of myself as a redhead for the very first time.

'Wow! ... I mean ... it's just ... I look so different.'

Laura came and leaned in close to me looking into our reflection in the mirror. 'You were right the first time. You look amazing … Wow is all there is to say!'

So now I sat on the end of Laura's bed looking at a woman with gorgeous red hair tumbling around her pale face and vivid green eyes. She wore the Vivienne Westwood blue tartan bodice top, well cut black satin pants tucked into rhinestone studded ankle boots. Her make-up was classy, smoky eyes, a slick of glossy dark red lipstick and a hint of blush revealing excellent cheekbones. She looked like a performer, like she belonged on a stage or in front of a camera. She looked like she was someone pretty special. The woman was me, but through a new lens. Stage me.

'Let's go.' I'd dithered and delayed but I just needed to get this over with. I needed to gauge the reaction to this new me by walking down the stairs and entering the kitchen where Tom and Ferg were waiting for the big reveal. I wasn't expecting them to be anything but supportive, they were both decent guys after all, but I was pretty sure I'd be able to tell from their expressions if they were disappointed, appalled or were trying suppress a fit of giggles if they thought I looked ridiculous. I wasn't looking forward to having to face whatever I was bound to see in their eyes but it was better to know now than find out the brutal truth from strangers who would have no regard for my feelings.

Perhaps I shouldn't have been too bothered about anyone else's opinion. I thought I looked pretty damn good. Laura had been encouraging, inventive and bold in her suggestions but I hadn't agreed to anything I didn't want to. I'd been thrilled to buy clothes more colourful and outrageous than I'd ever owned before and my hair really was my crowning glory now. Even if I never wore Vivienne Westwood ever again I was keeping the red hair! But I couldn't help caring about what other people would think about a new, improved, revamped Becky Mooney. If I wanted to perform as myself I would have to do that in front of an audience - that was the only way that sort of thing worked to be honest – there was no point being confident in a room all by yourself, you had to be able to carry it off in public. With that in mind I headed down the stairs, took a deep breath and walked into the kitchen.

Ferg's mouth fell open while his eyes were like saucers and I registered Tom do a double take and give a low whistle. I glanced from one man to the other, waited for the sinking feeling to hit the pit of my stomach as I picked up hesitation or rejection to this new version of me. But neither were forthcoming. Instead I could only sense approval, it was written all over their faces and the more they looked the more they seemed to like it.

'You look great!' Fergus said, a big daft grin on his face. His reaction rang true, I truly couldn't detect anything but honesty coming from his direction.

I turned my attention to Tom who was still standing, as though dumbstruck, hands on hips his eyes going up and down my body as though he couldn't get enough of looking at me. As his gaze came up to my face and we locked eyes my heart flipped. He liked it. He most definitely liked it. In three large strides he was suddenly right in front of me. 'Hey you,' he said softly, his voice catching in his throat as he slid his hands up my bare arms making my spine shiver and my legs tremble. 'You look absolutely incredible. I love it. But what's far more important … do *you* love it?'

The question was unexpected but exactly the right thing for him to say and a wonderful thing for me to hear in that moment. I was thrilled he thought I looked good, but even more thrilled that he cared about what I thought, what I felt about taking this step forward. I didn't trust my voice right then so I returned his gaze and smiled and nodded.

'This isn't a new you, Rebecca.' His voice was still soft and low as he spoke. He was smiling back at me but sounded deadly serious. 'This is simply the *real* you, the person who was always there, inside, but now everyone in the world will be able to properly see her.'

He kissed me then and I kissed him back. My head was spinning with possibilities and I felt I was on the brink of something …

Chapter Eighteen

It was another Saturday night at Sonny's Bar and I was in the back office feeling a million times more nervous than I had on the night I'd intended to relaunch myself as a solo Dolly Parton act. Instead of bouffant blonde hair and a tasselled two-piece I now had coppery curls and was wearing my new clingy denim waistcoat with the crazy tartan trousers. I kept looking at the Madonna-style studded boots on my feet and wondered what is was that I was 'desperately seeking'? My mind perhaps? Because I must have totally lost it somewhere along the way ... how had this seemed like a good idea when Tom suggested we debut my revamped look and a couple of new songs right here in the club in front of an unsuspecting audience who had no idea who Becky Mooney was and had very little reason to care?

My stomach was cartwheeling and there was a slick of sweat running down my spine. At least the waistcoat I was wearing left my arms bare so there was no risk of unsightly sweat stains appearing under my armpits. So there was some good news.

Tom had suggested I down a whisky 'for my nerves' before taking to the stage and Stella helpfully said she would fetch me that. Before she went to get it, she tried to talk to me about a spate of nuisance calls to the bar, someone calling and calling but no one ever being on the line but she quickly realised I was not in the mood to take in any new information and gave that up. So I was left pacing the tiny office alone. Well 'pacing' was an exaggeration. The space was so small I could take three small steps before I hit a wall, a desk or a filing cabinet. I was mincing more than pacing. That didn't seem very cool for an emerging country singer songwriter so I stopped.

I had to try and get my stage fright under control. I was hoping the whisky would help, along with the fact the Sonny's Bar crowd would be small and were usually friendly. Laura and Ferg and, of course, Tom had put so much faith in me, had made every effort to bolster my shaky confidence and show me how I could finally step on stage as me and not Dolly. I was desperate not to let them down.

Stella and Donald had given their verdicts on my new look and my plans to sing when I'd shown up earlier, before the punters had started to come in. Donald had said, 'Nice,' with an emphatic nod of his head. Stella had said even less but had immediately given me a great big hug. Both reactions had meant the world.

Tom was planning to sneak in and join me once the show started. Comedian Gabby Wolf was going to be the opening act and then I would be on. I understood the sense of Tom hanging back, it wouldn't do for the audience to think he was planning on doing a repeat surprise performance. My fear of failure was already high, I didn't need the crowd to be disappointed before I even began.

I was barely coping with the suspense and stage fright. Where was Stella with that drink!?

Just then the office door opened and I turned with relief to grab the whisky tumbler from Stella. But it wasn't Stella standing in the doorway, it was Robbie! Seriously!? His timing was as reliably awful as always. He started to stutter an apology and back out of the room and it wasn't until he saw how shocked I looked to see him that he realised he knew me.

'BECKY?!' It was an exclamation and a question all at once.

Bloody hell, this was the last thing I needed and I couldn't help but show my irritation by snapping, 'Hey Robbie, I'm a bit busy right now.'

My erstwhile partner had a tendency to look gormless at the best of times but, on this occasion, he could win an award for most dumbass expression to ever grace the face of a fully grown man. He stood there staring at me with his eyes on stalks and his mouth hanging open. It might have been flattering if I wasn't so preoccupied … and it wasn't Robbie!

What the hell did he want? Why hadn't he called before just turning up? We'd not spoken for weeks, things had been so mad and everything had taken off so well at Sonny's I'd not needed to call him for advice or tips on how to run the place like I'd thought I might have to.

We stood facing each other in a weird stand-off while I debated how to get him to leave. His expression was starting to change as he looked me over, his attitude morphing from shock and surprise to something that looked like … wait … was that scorn I could see written all over his face?

'Good grief, Becky,' he said with a snort, 'what the fuck d'you look like!?'

There it was. The horror of his words and the humiliation of having someone look at me as though I was a bad joke washed over me. I opened my mouth but no words came out. It didn't matter, Robbie was still talking; 'Is this some sort of reaction to our break-up? A mid-life crisis? A nervous breakdown?' With each increasingly insulting question Robbie was looking more and more pleased with himself and I plunged further and further into utter despair.

'Ahh give us a song, Becky!' Robbie was literally laughing in my face as his gaze lingered on my tartan-clad legs for just a little too long. 'Go on …' the sheer delight he was taking was spectacular and he was about to twist the knife even further. 'I'll start you off if you like … Bye, Bye Baby … Baby Gooodbyeeee …'

That did it, I pushed past Robbie and bolted for the exit, sprinting past Stella with my glass of whisky in her hand, as the sound of Robbie singing a Bay City Rollers hit followed me up the stairs of the club and out onto the street. I hit the early evening Edinburgh air gasping and gulping in a desperate attempt to stop myself from sobbing out loud. Now what?

All I could think was that I needed to escape, get away from the club, from Robbie's raucous rendition of the Rollers, which I could still hear even at street level and get out of these ridiculously inappropriate stupid clothes. Where was Iain when I needed him? If only I had a chauffeur-driven car waiting for me right now, although I actually didn't really want to face anybody, not even kindly Iain. I wanted to be on my own, no Iain, no Tom, and definitely no Robbie.

I turned left and began sprinting up the street, I'd get to the corner and there was bound to be a cab I could hail near Cowgate where the traffic was busier. I'd go back to my flat in Stockbridge, lock the door, turn off all the lights and never, ever let anyone in. That was the goal. It seemed achievable. Then I saw them. What the hell!? Mum and Dad were strolling down the street heading straight towards me!

They shouldn't be here. They shouldn't be anywhere near here. They'd said they weren't flying into Edinburgh until tomorrow. I'd managed to dissuade them from coming over before tonight. Once Tom came up with the idea of showcasing me and my songs to Sonny's Saturday night crowd I'd told them to come Sunday instead and they'd agreed. Or at least I thought they had. The sight of them heading my way now proved quite different.

I had seconds before they spotted me. I couldn't risk that. I didn't want the questions – about my clothes, my red hair or why I was running down the street away from my own club. But seeing my parents so unexpectedly was twisting the knife in my guts and messing with my brain. It was tempting to simply hurl myself at them and sob like a baby but I made a split-second decision and ducked into a pub just down from the corner. I burst through the swing doors inside the alcove and tucked myself to the side so I could peep through the small window to watch my parents go past. My heart hammered even harder as I suddenly thought this place might be exactly where they were heading but then I watched as my dad in a jaunty lemon sweater and my mum in pastel-pink slacks sauntered past.

I staggered to the far end of the bar dripping in sweat and brief relief. The smell of alcohol was in my nostrils and I realised I was still craving that large whisky, in fact I needed it more now than I had when I'd been having the jitters in the back office. The place was deserted save for a young barmaid who took my order without making eye contact.

I'd planned to have just the one drink but once I'd tucked myself into a corner behind a carved wooden partition I found it difficult to decide where I would go? If I headed home I'd soon be found by Mum and Dad. They had a key to the flat and must've already been there to drop off their luggage. I couldn't go to Forthview House; my fast exit from Sonny's would be a complete slap in the face for Laura and Fergus my lovely new friends who'd done so much to get me to this point only for me to bottle it.

I sank the first whisky too fast but I ordered another and decided to take my time with this one, sipping it more slowly as I let the warmth of the scotch soothe my rattled nerves. If only I had a comforting bag of marshmallows. They really should stock those as bar snacks in pubs, I'm sure they'd be hugely popular. The panic inside me began to subside, even without the marshmallows, but a more morose mood was blooming as I slipped deeper into my chair and into despair.

Robbie's scornful face kept looming into my mind, the expression on it was one I'd seen before. The trigger for my stage fright and the reason I'd quit performing as part of The

Moonshine Trio when I was just fourteen years old had been a similar reaction from a pair of bitchy girls from school.

I hadn't known Heather and Teresa were in the social club where I was gigging with Mum and Dad. They'd both come along with Teresa's dad who had got into trouble with his ex-wife for previously letting his daughter run feral when it was his turn to have her. So on this particular night he'd insisted on dragging her along to the social club while he met up with his mates and leered over their wives. He'd agreed Teresa could bring a friend to keep her company and out of his thinning hair, he wouldn't have wanted her to cramp his dad-bod, beery-breath style.

The first I'd known that my schoolmates were at the club was after we'd sung a couple of songs. The crowd were receptive and the applause was warm. That's the best you could hope for in a social club where people came along week after week to hang out with their mates no matter what acts are on. They did pay some attention but they were also chatting among themselves and heading up and down to the bar. It was what it was. The entertainment in those sorts of places isn't really the draw, they hadn't bought a ticket to see you specifically, but they did expect value for money for the weekly subs they paid to be a member. As the Moonshine Trio, we prided ourselves on being a popular act that got rebooked often, so we knew what was expected of us and always delivered.

Occasionally we might get someone calling out a request for a song which we'd do our best to accommodate, we were there to please the crowd after all. Hecklers were very, very rare, so it was unusual to hear a couple of voices calling out on that night while Mum introduced our next song. She'd put her hand up to shade her eyes from the spotlight and peered out into the darkened room. 'What's that you're saying, love?' she'd asked pleasantly. Mum was a trooper, it would take more than a woman who'd had a few too many wines to put her off.

'WE WANT BECKY!' the voice had yelled back.

Mum shot a look at me and I looked back at her, mystified and surprised.

A second voice joined in and they began to chant my name while Mum and Dad looked at each other over my head as we stood there in our trio line up. Dad in a Stetson hat to set off his red western shirt with the white fancy piping and shiny black acoustic guitar with the colourful embroidered strap. Mum and I wore matching pastel-pink dresses with handkerchief hems ending just above our white cowboy boots. Our outfits were completed with tan suede tasselled waistcoats and Mum wore a red flower in her bright blonde curls while I accessorised with a red bandana tied at my throat.

'What do they want, Missy?' My dad shrugged and looked confused as he hissed his pet name at Mum while she held up her hand and beamed at the audience.

'Now we're so proud of our daughter Becky, here, she's been part of the Moonshine Trio since she could toddle her way onto the stage, and my husband Carl and I just love to hear her sing too. How about you sing a song for us now, Becky?'

Mum whispered to me then, her mouth away from the mic, 'Sing that new song you like.' I was shocked that

I nipped off to use the loo before getting changed into my civvies for the drive home. At some clubs you had to get changed into your stage gear in the toilets but this club had better facilities so I didn't need to bring my clothes into the ladies with me this time.

I was in the cubicle about to flush the chain when I heard them. Heather and Teresa must have been in a couple of the other cubicles when I came in but now they were at the washbasins and I caught just a couple of words at first as the cisterns of the toilets they'd just flushed re-filled and they ran the taps to wash their hands.

I heard snatches of their conversation, them saying they'd 'never seen anything like it' and something about Mum and I wearing matching white cowboy boots. I was poised to burst out and surprise them, join in with the jollity and let them tell me to my face how much they'd enjoyed it all but then Teresa said; 'It was the funniest thing I've ever seen!'

Heather let out a guffaw and answered; 'Oh my God, I know! What the hell does she think she's doing prancing about like that?'

'Don't forget all those Hell Yeah's and Yee Haw's she was doing too. Couldn't you just curl up and die!?'

There was more. A lot more. They poked fun at what I looked like, how I sang, how utterly uncool I was and then started ripping into Mum and Dad too. I couldn't listen to that.

I opened the door and they caught sight of my reflection in the mirror in front of them as I stood there shaking and pale-faced. You'd think they'd be mortified to be caught mocking me so mercilessly but to my absolute horror they looked … delighted.

'Oooo look now, here she is … how y'all doin, honey-pie? Are you lookin' for your horse?'

Teresa looked like she was going to explode at that, snorting and sniggering while Heather did a mangled American accent.

Teresa pulled herself together a bit and looked at me with a serious face. 'We have to tell you Becky, because we feel it's only right to be completely honest with you … you are really, really shit!'

They stood there staring at me, quivering in delight at their power in that moment, daring me to respond, or break down. I wasn't sure which they wanted but I didn't want to do either in front of their gloating faces. I bolted. Their voices followed me down the corridor back to the relative safety of the dressing room. They were singing the refrain from Green Day's song 'American Idiot' at the top of their voices and screaming with laughter.

School was agony for quite a while after that. Heather and Teresa managed to whip up a new trend for yelling 'Yee-haw' in my direction at any opportunity and hissing 'American Idiot' whenever I passed by. But their re-telling of my country music exploits didn't find an audience for very long. I'm not sure everyone else believed they'd really seen me on stage. I wasn't sure whether to be relieved or insulted by that but it helped to make their bullying campaign falter. The fact that I'd quit the Moonshine Trio and vowed never to go on stage again also took the wind out of their sails. It took the wind out of mine too of course. I'd felt like I was flying that night when I'd stepped forward and taken my place in the spotlight. I'd had the most fun ever, felt like the very best version of myself, but in the harsh strip lights of that ladies' toilet all of that joy had been taken away.

Now I sat nursing my scotch whisky feeling as foolish and embarrassed as I had on that night. Robbie's look of scornful mockery had reminded me so precisely of the looks on those girls' faces. Back then they had made me question everything about myself. Made me reject liking what I liked and doing what I loved. Now here I was twenty years later doing exactly the same thing all over again.

A movement to my right brought me back into the room. I looked up to see Tom Coltrane standing in front of me holding two more glasses of whisky.

'Hey there,' he said, 'mind if I join ya?'

Chapter Nineteen

Tom knew exactly where to find me because I'd been spotted ducking into the pub. Not by Mum and Dad, they'd carried on to Sonny's Bar blissfully unaware of our near miss, but Tom's driver Iain had been on his way to pick Tom up and as he drove past he'd seen me swerve into the doorway.

Tom didn't seem to need much of an explanation as to why I was hiding in the corner of a deserted bar. It turned out he'd got all the backstory he needed from my mum and dad. When he'd got to Sonny's and found I'd scarpered, he'd read the room pretty quickly. It was a skill he first deployed on the open mic night and it had come in super handy again. When questioned, Mum and Dad gave him background info about the night I was humiliated by Heather and Teresa and he worked out for himself how Robbie's reaction to the new me had sent me over the edge.

'Can I just say, for the record, that I think you look amazing. You sure knock me out, Rebecca honey.' Tom gave me a gorgeous wink over the rim of his whisky glass and I managed a small smile in response. 'And while we're telling it like it is,' he added, 'that Robbie fella seems to be a total dumbass!' I snorted a laugh at that. 'I hate to tell you this but he was still laughing to himself when your folks got there. Your mum ripped into him once she found out you'd been about to go on stage as yourself. I reckon you'll see the whip marks from that tongue-lashing for quite a while.'

'What did my dad say?' I could imagine Mum tearing a strip off Robbie. Good for her, he deserved it. But I was worried about how much all this would be upsetting my poor dad. He'd been so happy when I'd found a way to overcome stage fright by being Dolly Parton and he'd always taken pride in the fact he'd helped me to do it. It would have been so lovely to show him I'd found a new way to perform, but as myself once again.

Tom shook his head slowly as he looked at me. 'He said something sorta funny actually. Once he heard you weren't going to dress up as Dolly Parton before taking to the stage he asked what stage name you were going to use.'

I sat back in my chair. 'Use another name? Like what?'

'I don't know. Although now I think about it ...' Tom paused.

'What? Now you think about it, what?'

'Well I've heard ya say you're not actually all that keen on being called Becky. You like when I use Rebecca, don't you ... Rebecca?' He rolled the r and growled the name at me to make me laugh again but I was pondering the notion. A name change? Could I? Should I? It was true I wasn't keen on Becky ... Becky Mooney ... it always sounded like a bratty character in a children's book to me. It didn't suit the sort of woman I aspired to be. But I didn't imagine my dad or mum would be all that impressed if I junked my name, and what the hell would I replace it with? Tom was still looking very thoughtful.

'Tom, what is it? Just spit it out.'

'Well, have y'ever thought that *Reba* is a really cool country-style nickname for Rebecca?'

Reba? I had never thought of that. I liked it. Reba would suit me way better than Becky. Straight away I wanted it. I wanted Reba to be my name. Unlike Beyoncé with Sasha Fierce or Rebecca Lucy Taylor as Self Esteem I didn't want to use Reba as just a stage name, I wanted it to be the new me on and off stage, it just felt right.

'Reba …' I tried it out for size. It rolled off the tongue perfectly. It sounded fresh, brave and full of spirit. That's who I wanted to be. That was me.

'Reba Moon!' It came to me in a flash. There it was. My new name. The new me. A shortened version of Becky Mooney, discarding the bits that were unnecessary and didn't fit me anymore, streamlining and adapting what I already had into something cooler and more exciting.

Tom slapped his hand on the table. 'That's it! You're right. Reba Moon … it's so … you!'

That was decided then. I made another decision straight off the back of it.

'I'm going back to the club. It's time to put Reba Moon on stage.'

Tom said nothing but smiled and nodded as he drained his whisky glass. I was relieved he hadn't put any pressure on me, he hadn't nagged or cajoled or tried to convince me to get myself back on track to perform. But he was there, he'd found me and was there for me, just having his company was balm to my soul. His presence reminded me that I'd moved on from being Becky Mooney with all her hang-ups and now I was ready to tackle life head on. Tom was helping me do that because he really seemed to see me … the real me, whether I was a half-dressed Dolly Parton tribute act, a fledgling songwriter or a sassily dressed 'Reba Moon,' he saw past it all and accepted whatever version of myself I presented to him without scorn or question. It was refreshing, liberating and ultimately empowering. He hadn't saved me – but he'd given me the strength to see I could save myself.

I stood up, leaned across the table and kissed him gently on the lips. 'Back in a sec,' I said. I needed a quick trip to the loo to freshen up. I needed to walk back into the club looking pulled together and in control. I checked my flaming locks in the mirror and reapplied my lipstick. The denim waistcoat and tartan pants combo still looked good. 'Hey there, Reba,' I said to my reflection and registered the simultaneous reply. Mutual greetings done between the real and reflected versions of myself, I felt as ready as I'd ever be to face the music. Literally. It was now or never. Dolly had told me to *'Find out who you are and do it on purpose,'* and it finally seemed like I'd found the way to do that. Reba Moon was who I was and it was time to show the world what she was all about. Some of the most important people in my life were at the club and if I could face them and perform as the new me, I would be able to do anything.

I walked back to the table where Tom was waiting. 'You coming?' I said.

'You bet, Reba,' he replied.

Chapter Twenty

I stood behind Sonny's tiny stage in the darkness as Tom spoke into the offstage microphone to introduce me.

'Good evening folks, welcome to Sonny's Bar, the hippest, most happening joint in Edinburgh. What you're about to see doesn't happen every day, you're about to witness the debut of Scotland's very own country music queen ... please welcome to the stage ... REBA MOON!'

Jesus ... no pressure then, I thought. But actually, his big intro fired me up. There was no point doing this half-heartedly and so, after taking a deep breath, I stepped through the curtain and into the spotlight.

I started with 'Mean to Me', the first song I had ever tried to write; it seemed appropriate in the circumstances. Robbie may not have been in the same league of bitchiness as schoolgirl bullies Heather and Teresa but I was relishing the opportunity to fight back at last. I had no idea if Robbie was still in the room but something told me he was lurking at the back, waiting for me to mess this up. I wouldn't be giving him the satisfaction of seeing me fail.

Tom and Fergus had prepared backing tracks for me to work to. I was used to performing that way and I was able to read the room and choose how I wanted to play my set. Eventually I knew I would love to perform with a live band but this gig was all about getting up on stage and seeing if I could simply face an audience as myself. The way they cheered my opening number spurred me on. I sang the Linda Ronstadt number 'You're No Good' next. My blood was up, injecting passion into my performance, and my voice felt well-oiled by the whisky. I'd never felt so powerful on stage before. It was just me and the music.

'Old-Fashioned Girl', the song I'd written about a whisky loving woman who keeps one step ahead of the chasers went down a storm. The lyrics I'd written made even more sense now I was singing them live than they'd done when I wrote them. It was like my whole set perfectly summed up who I was, what I stood for and where I was in my life. How had that happened? It was magical to experience. They say songwriting can reveal things you didn't even know about yourself: that certainly seemed to be true for me, it was quite the revelation.

The crowd were so receptive and I was feeling so in command I risked a bold move and hoped Tom wouldn't mind when I invited him to join me up on stage. At first, he looked reluctant – as if he didn't want to steal the spotlight. But when I saw his eyes crinkle as he smiled, I knew I'd persuaded him. As he stepped up out of the darkness his eyes were gleaming with pride and happiness and when our fingers brushed as I passed him a mic I felt a tingle of electricity that wasn't connected to the equipment.

As we duetted on 'Heatwave' I realised I was sharing a stage with a famous music star and more than holding my own. To see Tom work at such close quarters was pretty awe inspiring. His voice was rich and melodic and his charisma and stage presence just fabulous, but there was still space for me and instead of hiding, instead of being someone else or wanting to be somewhere else, I filled it well. The way we took turns with our parts, just like we had in the studio with Fergus, worked seamlessly. We were having such fun the audience got swept along with us and we finished the number to thunderous applause and cheers.

Tom leaned over and whispered into my ear as the cheering continued. 'This is your night, Reba, don't let me take that away from you.' I wanted to kiss him so badly but I wasn't going to give the audience that much of myself, that would have to wait until we were somewhere a lot more private. It was cool of him to worry about upstaging me but I wasn't worried about that, not at all. Instead of a kiss I whispered back, "Moonlight Home"?'

Tom stepped back and looked into my face with his eyebrows raised as if to ask if I was sure. I grinned and nodded and we needed no more words to be spoken between us. Tom went and sat at the piano to play and I leaned over the top watching his fingers as they played the beautiful opening to his brand-new song.

The audience quietened into hushed expectation as he began to sing the words to the haunting tune about being lost in the moonlight. He sang looking up into my eyes and

I joined in with the harmony that led the song to its final destination. There was a split second of silence after the last note ended and then the crowd erupted again. Tom jumped up from the stool with a look of both triumph and relief on his face. How he could ever have doubted his own talent and skill was beyond me ... and yet ... I knew all too well how easy it was to put barriers in your own way. I hoped the ecstatic reaction of the Sonny's Bar crowd to 'Moonlight Home' would show Tom the song had a big future ahead of it but Tom was already wanting to put the spotlight back on me.

'I hope you've saved something for an encore,' he said with his lips once again so close to my ear it made my pulse race. As he jumped back down off the stage he went and stood next to my mum and dad who I could tell were glowing with pride and happiness. I swept my eyes around the room taking everything in. I caught sight of Stella and Donald behind the bar looking rather thunderstruck. Robbie was sitting on a stool at the bar and managed to catch my attention by raising his glass to me and giving a slight tilt of his head, not exactly an effusive response but wait ... what? Was that Fergus and Laura at the back of the room? I'd no idea how long they might have been there but they were now waving madly at me with huge smiles on their faces looking a million times more supportive than Robbie.

There was only one song I could think of to close the set, only one number that I really wanted to perform right now. I flicked the playback machine to the track and as the music began I tapped my black-heeled boot, swung my tartan-clad hips, threw back my flaming red hair and gave in to being the totally unapologetic country music artiste Reba Moon with a triumphant performance of 'Red Neck Woman'.

They say there's no such thing as an overnight success but that one night at Sonny's felt like the start of something good ... although I was aware not everyone was finding the sudden appearance of 'Reba Moon' easy to deal with.

The crowd loved my set and I was showered with praise and compliments by people I'd never met. The people who knew me best, however, didn't seem quite sure what to say or do once I'd come off stage and stood in front of them face to face. My mum and dad were full of hugs and backslaps at first but then seemed far keener to know when they would be able to perform on Sonny's stage themselves and kept asking if they would be able to sing alongside 'Reba Moon'? It was quite disconcerting, especially as my mum kept waggling her fingers in the air to indicate quote marks every time she said my new name. It was dawning on me the reason they'd been so mad keen to come to Edinburgh was because of the publicity the bar had been getting. Now Tom was sprinkling some celebrity stardust around they were suddenly keen as mustard to come and spend time with their darling daughter. It felt like they were sort of missing the point.

Stella and Donald said very little. No surprise there, but while I expected it of Donald he actually blurted out, 'That was great,' which sounded pretty heartfelt and genuine. Stella radiated something I suspected was jealousy because of how much she'd fancied Tom herself. I didn't think we'd made it obvious we were sleeping together, but people do have a habit of putting two and two together and making four. Also, to be fair, they wouldn't have been wrong to think we were shagging. We were. I still blushed when I remembered.

I think Robbie was actually planning to sidle out without saying anything to me at all. Sod that. I got between him and the exit. Let him look me straight in the eye and say I hadn't done a good job up there. But people can always surprise you. He couldn't level too much criticism at my performance and I was clearly comfortable with my new look, whatever he thought, so he took a different tack altogether. 'You better watch your back,' he said with a faux-fatherly look of concern and then he leaned closer and spoke slowly as though I was hard of thinking as well as hard of hearing. 'You do know you're being used as a publicity stunt, Becky? Obviously.' He shook his head and raised his hands as if to say, 'Don't shoot the messenger'.

My mouth fell open at the audacity. The absolute cheek of him! I knew exactly what he was driving at, that Tom Coltrane was using me and the bar to attract attention to himself. I knew the truth was a little more nuanced than that. Tom may have thought a big star like him playing a tiny bar like ours had some quirky appeal for a bit of news coverage or social media attention but I now knew Tom's instincts had a more meaningful motivation. He had wanted to rediscover his roots, connect with an audience in an intimate space and remember why he had fallen in love with music and performing in the first place. I hadn't known any of that the first time he'd walked into the bar, but I knew it now. The fact we had also connected with each other the way that we had wasn't part of any publicity stunt, I was sure of that. Tom Coltrane didn't need me for that and what had gone on between us didn't feel fake in any way. I was only just starting to realise that despite his superstar status Tom Coltrane felt like the most real person I had ever known.

I was struggling to think of a strong enough retort to Robbie's accusation and that made my blood boil even more. I looked him straight in the eye and simply said, 'Well you know what they say, Robbie, all publicity is good publicity ... and by the way, the name is Reba.' He just looked at me with the slightly baffled expression he did so well.

Tom had overheard our exchange and came and stood defensively at my shoulder and added, 'Shouldn't you be collecting dirty glasses in ... Peter-burrow, is it? Don't let us hold you up, Bud,' dismissing Robbie with that remark and slipping his arm around my waist at the same time. 'I need you to meet someone real important, Reba,' he said to me, emphasising my name as we turned away from Robbie and his outraged face.

Was Robbie jealous because he realised Tom and I were sleeping together? Because I'd just conquered my stage fright fears ... without him by my side? Because Sonny's Bar was fuller than he ever would have seen it during his time as manager and was fast gaining a reputation as *the* place to be in Edinburgh? Or was it a combination of all the above? I thought I could count on Robbie to be a mate whatever happened, but where was that friendship now? I had to leave those concerns to one side as I got drawn back into the room.

Laura and Fergus managed to fight through the throng and throw their arms around me before apologising for having to rush off straight away to relieve their babysitter. I wished they didn't have to go. I felt like I could really be Reba with them without it feeling weird. I realised it was a lot easier being Reba *on* stage than it was off. I hadn't expected that.

The 'important person' Tom wanted me to meet was from the London office of his record company. A middle-aged man in chinos and a paisley shirt blew my mind when he started talking about a potential recording contract and at that point I thought I might pass out. He also wanted to know how soon he could get paperwork done for me so they could release 'Moonlight Home' as Tom's new single with me as a featured artist. I was in a spin but he kept saying there were '*commitments*' in Nashville that Tom needed to attend to '*A-sap!*' He mentioned the name *'Waz Monsoon'* a few times who I understood was Tom's manager but it was hard to keep up with everything that was being said.

I wasn't sure if it was the adrenaline from the show, the amount of whisky I'd drunk earlier or the weird mix of reactions that had come at me from all directions once I'd stepped off the stage but people's faces began to swim in front of my eyes and I started to feel hot and clammy. The basement bar had become incredibly claustrophobic. Tom noticed my discomfort and pressed his hotel key card into my hand.

'I'll call Iain, he'll pick you up and take you to the hotel … if ya want?' That sounded amazing. I didn't want to go back to the flat where Mum and Dad were going to be staying and have them bombard me with more questions than I wanted to answer right now. I wanted to get out of Sonny's 'A-sap' as the record company guy had put it. Tom even offered to head back to Forthview House so I could have some 'space' as he thought I seemed a bit overwhelmed. It did sound blissful to have a fancy hotel suite all to myself but he was the one person in the world I didn't feel the need to get away from. He agreed he'd have one drink with the record company guy and then meet me at the hotel later.

'Au revoir,' Tom said pointedly. I was aware he was advising me to make what's called a 'French Exit'. Tom was giving good advice and I took it, slipping away without any further fuss.

Within minutes I was enveloped in the luxurious comfort of Tom's chauffeur-driven car speeding through the dark city streets. The clammy, claustrophobic feeling was easing and I thought I was feeling clearer headed, but then I saw her. Tottering along the pavement in sky-high glittery platform sandals was a woman with a blonde beehive and a distinctive wiggle in her hips and jiggle to her tits. It was like looking at a previous incarnation of myself all dressed up as Dolly Parton. The car sped by too quickly for me to get a proper look at her face but the walk, the stature, the hair, were all spot on. It wasn't very likely that the real Dolly Parton was wandering around Edinburgh late at night and all alone. I'd dreamt of Dolly for years and the only explanation I could think of for what I'd just seen was that I must be hallucinating. Great. That was all I needed. Now I was seeing things.

When I woke the next morning Tom was fast asleep by my side. I must have crashed out before he came in. I lay perfectly still so as not to wake him but my mind was whirring so fast I was worried the noise of all the different cogs turning might do it anyway.

The thought most prevalent in my manic mind was that I'd done it. I'd stood on stage without Dolly as my disguise and held a room and won them over. I'd faced my fears and the relief and excitement I felt about that was real. But as Dolly herself would say, *'If you want the rainbow you have to put up with the rain'*, and despite last night being the most fun I had ever had on stage there were a few people who clearly wanted to rain on my parade. The question now was whether I was going to let them.

When Tom rolled over and pulled me into his arms it became a lot easier to forget about everything other than his lips, his fingers and every other part of his insanely sexy body. He growled my name into my hair and I drove him wild when I told him how much I loved what he was doing to me. Everything and everyone else faded from my mind until I was only aware of me and Tom, just the two of us, as we rocked and rolled together on that king-sized bed.

Afterwards we lay together until Tom felt compelled to break the post-coital spell.

'There's something ya need to see,' he said, his voice coming from above my head where it was resting on his bare chest. I giggled until I realised he was being serious. He reached out an arm and grabbed his phone off the bedside table.

Social media was alive again – and not just with the latest secret Tom Coltrane gig. This time the websites were buzzing with rumours about me and Tom. Some snatches of my performance last night at Sonny's had gone viral but the speculation about whether Tom and I were an item was the subject getting most attention across various platforms.

'Tom Coltrane's Sexy Scottish Songstress.' I read the strap line from one post aloud and froze. I'd seen the movies – was this the bit where the big star is told by his bosses to go home on the next plane? The part where he explains he and the girl are from different worlds that can't ever meet? I took a breath and looked up at Tom who simply raised an eyebrow.

'That's showbiz, honey,' he said.

He didn't seem bothered by the gossip. Instead he was actually concerned about me. 'This isn't my first rodeo,' he smiled. 'But I know it's a lot to face. Are you okay?'

'Sexy Scottish Songstress? I've been called worse,' I responded.

Robbie's words about being used as a publicity stunt lurched from the back to the very front of my mind. As did my response to him which still held true. If I wanted to break through as an artist in my own right, these stories wouldn't do me any harm. They weren't significantly untrue, so we would hardly be in a position to sue anyone over the content. Reading further down they were actually accompanied by some great compliments and positive reviews of my songs and performance. One even described me as the best thing to come out of Scotland since Walkers Shortbread. I'd take that.

'All publicity is good publicity?' I framed it as a question but by repeating the line I'd given to Robbie last night I was letting Tom know that I wasn't going to be getting hysterical about a bit of gossip on the internet.

'That's ma girl!' Tom grinned.

But his reply prompted another, probably far more important question in my mind. Was I 'his girl'? Or was that position already filled by a Hollywood actress who went by the globally known name of Juliana Ripon? It was time to bite the bullet. Reba was proving to be a whole lot braver and more direct than Becky and I decided that was a good thing.

'What will Juliana Ripon think about these stories if she sees them?' I sat up and looked directly at Tom's face to gauge his reaction after raising the spectre of Juliana. The bedsheet tumbled around my waist but I sat defiantly naked as Tom rubbed his hand over his eyes before they swept over my breasts and then met my gaze. He pulled a slight grimace at the mention of Juliana's name but I couldn't be sure if he was irritated by the thought of her or by the fact I'd been bold enough ask.

'You've got nothin' to worry about on that score.'

That didn't really answer all the questions that were circulating in the air around us. Here we were lying together in sex-rumpled sheets while somewhere on the other side of the Atlantic a gamine and gorgeous young actress may soon be learning all about me. Tom and I were definitely no longer in our bubble. The protective shield around us had burst and the really big question was ...' would we be able to survive without it?

Chapter Twenty-One

It was an impulse decision to get the bus out to see Gordon and Morag in Murrayfield later that morning. I couldn't really explain to Tom why I wanted to do it but he didn't put up any resistance to my desire to head off on my own to see my former bosses. He offered to get Iain to drive me but part of the appeal of the trip was the time I could spend alone on the bus just turning things over in my mind and trying to figure out how I felt about it all.

Gordon and Morag's place felt like a safe space to return to after a night of unexpected outcomes. I tried not to dwell too much on how I should have felt my own flat, where my own parents currently were staying, should have been the location calling to me most. But it wasn't. For now, I wanted to put off my next encounter with my parents. I loved them dearly, of course I did, and I knew they loved me too, but their lives had always revolved more around their love for being on stage than their love for me. Don't call the NSPCC,

I wasn't a neglected child, but I wasn't always their priority. That's okay – it made me independent in many ways.

Parents are tricky customers for everyone, I knew that. Sometimes the fact they've known you from birth is a hindrance, rather than a help. The whole, *'haven't you grown'*, *'you never used to like olives'*, right through to *'you know Sandra and Kevin's son Jason is a lawyer now? Such a lovely lad ... you'd like him if you gave him a chance ...'* No chance! That kind of twaddle had really ground my gears over the years. The more they spouted nonsense like that the less information I revealed about what was really going on in my life.

I know most parents' motives are good, mine included, and that they usually have your best interests at heart, but all too often they are basing their help/advice/opinion on outdated information. The person you used to be, no, not even the person ... the *child* you used to be. Now my parents lived mainly in Spain it didn't really help them know me all that well. Last night was only the second time they'd ever met Robbie. That was partly my fault: Robbie and I had never had the kind of relationship where meeting the prospective in-laws had been appropriate. How crazy then, that they'd already met Tom ... not that I was imagining that's where our liaison was heading! Marriage!? God no! I pulled the emergency stop on that train of thought and instead began considering that maybe I should make more effort to spend more time with Mum and Dad in the future. Maybe?

I parked that thought too while I looked ahead to seeing Gordon and Morag. The fact they'd met me as an adult had given them a head start in taking me at face value, judging me on my personality and abilities as they were now. It had been refreshing to be with a couple who took to me so quickly and always saw the best in me. Gruesome Guy had done his best to wreck that, of course, but thank goodness he hadn't managed to succeed.

The last-minute plan to head to the Graysons meant I was turning up empty-handed this time. No French pastries boxed and tied with ribbon to present on the doorstep. Hopefully they wouldn't mind me just dropping by and would be as pleased to see me as I was keen to see them. I hadn't been able to make too much effort with my appearance either. I was still wearing my tartan trousers and black studded ankle boots from last night but I'd borrowed a simple black t-shirt from Tom – his stock must be getting low as I'd not given him back the red Nashville one I'd swiped before yet. Together with my new red hair the overall look was slightly punkier than how Gordon and Morag were used to seeing me. I didn't mind that at all, it felt like a good visual blend of the old Becky and the new Reba.

I was learning fast that Reba Moon wasn't just a costume I was wearing for the stage. Now I'd given myself permission to appear publicly as Reba it was like I had finally released the real me into the world. I realised that, as Becky, I had allowed life to happen around me, living my life on the edge of the action and not putting myself at the centre of things often enough. As Reba I was now the one driving the action. I was fed up waiting for things to fall into place by themselves and was making decisions and taking steps to get to where I wanted to be, in my musical career and in my life. Becky always had hopes and dreams but

Reba was the one who was going to try and make those dreams happen. I'd proved as much to myself when I'd finally had the guts to bring Juliana Ripon into the conversation with Tom. I hadn't got a definitive answer about how things stood with Juliana but he had said I had nothing to worry about and that he would 'deal with it' – whatever that meant? Once I announced my intention to go and see the Graysons he looked a bit relieved and said something about having to make some calls to his manager and 'other folk.' I wondered if one of those calls might be to Juliana? Then I thought about the 'commitments' the record guy had been bandying around. There was clearly a whole lot to Tom I didn't know yet.

While we ate our room-service breakfast Tom and I had also spent a bit more time talking about the variety of responses my performance had prompted from the people who had seen my Reba Moon debut. Tom was tactful about my parents' enthusiasm for wanting to perform themselves.

'Ahh, they seemed a fun couple, I suppose you can't blame them for wanting to get in on the action,' he'd said. I thought he was being overly generous but, if I'd started moaning about how the night should all have been about me, me, me, I was aware I could easily sound like I was being a total diva. I reckoned I should save that sort of behaviour, at least for a little while; I wasn't quite in Mariah Carey's league yet.

Tom had found Donald's taciturn approval and Stella's sulky silence completely hilarious. 'They'll come around,' he'd said, grinning like an idiot when he realised Stella's issue with me stemmed from her having the hots for him. 'She's only human,' he'd said with such glee it was hard to reconcile with the fact that he was a country music star with lustful fans all over the world. It just proved that men were men however famous they became, which is what I think I said as I swatted him with a pillow.

He wasn't as amused by Robbie's behaviour and to be completely honest neither was I. After declaring Robbie a 'dumbass' after their initial encounter, Tom had now concluded Robbie was a 'dumbass, a dick, and a disrespectful dork'. He stopped short of asking what the hell I had ever seen in him, which was good – one, because it would have been a tricky one to answer and two, because I didn't feel Robbie's bad behaviour should be any reflection on me and my previous life choices as Becky Mooney.

'Ya do have to be prepared for this sort of thing now, Reba,' Tom had said in a much gentler tone than the one he'd used about Robbie. As I poured a second cup of coffee from the pot he'd talked about how any sort of attention caused ripple effects through your life. He said fame didn't necessarily alter the person who was famous but it really could affect people around them. His voice was filled with sincerity as he spoke and I knew he was talking from personal experience as well as giving me a realistic explanation for some of the things that had occurred the night before. I wasn't 'famous' but appearing on stage alongside someone who was as well known as Tom had already made people start to look at me in a different way. Tom assured me this was just the start; 'Stick with me, kid, we're gonna make you a star!' he'd joked. But I felt as though

I was on the brink of something exciting, risky but potentially wonderful.

I considered all of this as the bus jogged along on its way to Murrayfield, as well as wondering how Gordon and Morag would react to the new improved me? I doubted they would have seen any social media so I was keen to tell them in my own words about my butterfly from a chrysalis moment and hear their honest reactions.

As Tom and I had finished our breakfast our conversation had eventually turned to what still felt to me like the biggest talking point of all. The bombshell statement to end all bombshell statements. The suggestion of a future recording contract for Reba Moon from record company executive Steve Bannister. I knew he might have just been telling me what I wanted to hear so he could get my signature and approval to release Tom's new single – but it was like pure magic to me. It wasn't a childhood dream – it was something I'd never even dared to dream.

I had the card he'd given me tucked into my back pocket. I didn't know people still handed out business cards anymore but Steve seemed to have a bit of an old-school attitude – I quite liked that about him. So bearing that in mind plus the fact he was the only record company executive to ever have shown any interest in signing me – to a real bona fide label too – I had agreed to 'schedule a meeting' with him. *'Schedule a meeting'* – listen to the jargon I was using already! I'd made Tom laugh when I told him he may have created a monster who would soon be demanding baskets of puppies and bowls of blue smarties everywhere she went! He hadn't looked too worried about that and told me he might adopt the same demands for his tour rider going forward. 'So long as you're included alongside them,' he had added.

When I told Gordon and Morag about conquering my stage fright and the possibility of securing a recording contract, I thought they might explode with excitement. It was easy to see where the phrase 'bursting with pride' came from as they practically danced me around their kitchen. It was just the sort of reaction I had hoped for and it finally gave me the chance to feel the same thrill and let joy surge through my veins. I thought about what Dolly had once said: *'You always want your people to be proud of what you have accomplished.'* If Dolly needed that kind of validation then maybe it wasn't that surprising I also needed to see someone I considered 'my people' be genuinely impressed by what I had done to give myself permission to enjoy the moment. Thank heavens for Gordon and Morag.

I shared some of the footage of my performance that had been uploaded onto YouTube with them and told them I'd even started writing my own songs.

'Oh hen, that's so wonderful. Didn't I always say you could do anything you put your mind to?' Morag was smiling broadly and her cheeks were glowing pink. It was so good to see her looking well and happy.

I told her how much her gift of a 'What Would Dolly Do?' mug had spurred me on, prompted me to adopt Dolly's can-do attitude and get back on stage.

The sun was shining and the August weather was finally warm so we sat outside to drink our tea and chat some more.

Gordon apologised they didn't have any champagne to offer but we were all so giggly and our spirits so high that I didn't think anything fizzy would have made us any giddier. But just as they were telling me, yet again, how proud they both were of me, a big dark cloud appeared. It wasn't a change in the weather that threw a shadow over our fun but the sudden appearance of Guy.

Guy walked into the garden from the passageway at the side of the house with such a thunderous look on his face it made me wonder how much he had heard of our conversation before making his presence known. His parents didn't seem to notice the look of murderous intent he threw me and appeared delighted to see him.

'Hello Guy, how lovely to see you! Come and listen to Becky's incredible news. Oops, sorry it's Reba now, isn't it, hen?' Morag smiled indulgently at me and then clucked around offering Guy a cup of tea or a slice of cake. Guy stayed standing and rolled his eyes in response to her attempts to get him to join our mini celebration.

I didn't feel much like celebrating now Guy was glowering at me. I hadn't seen him since the morning he'd had me arrested and accused of theft, and my concerns about his motive had been pushed to the back of my mind with everything that had been happening. Now, there Guy stood, in the flesh, still looking as suntanned as when he'd landed from California ... which probably meant it was out of a bottle or from a sun bed ... a Scottish summer, no matter how pleasant, couldn't possibly turn you that shade of mahogany? But my mind wasn't pondering how Guy maintained his tan, it was turning over the hope that Reba, the new me, might be able to handle Guy better than Becky, the old me, ever had. There was one way to find out.

I decided to break the ice with what I thought was a harmless question. 'How's everything at the shop?' I asked in what I thought was a pleasant tone.

'None of your damn business!' Guy snapped before sneering, 'I would have thought you'd be too busy getting your clutches into your new famous boyfriend to worry about how many watches and necklaces we're currently selling at Grayson's!'

'GUY! Don't be so RUDE!' Morag and Gordon sounded shocked and both instantly barked reprimands at their sullen son who looked as though apologising was the very last thing on his mind. Instead of addressing me, he first shot a scornful look at his parents. 'This all looks very cosy,' he said, his voice dripping in sarcasm. Then he turned to me. 'What are you even doing here?'

Before I could answer for myself Gordon jumped to my defence. 'Becky ... I mean, *Reba* is a good friend, more than a friend actually, she's like family to us. I don't know what's got into you lad, but you need to apologise. In fact, it seems you have quite a lot to apologise to her for so now is a good opportunity to do so.'

Gordon's stern tone cut no ice with Guy and his mother's distressed face didn't appear to be affecting him either. He clearly had no intention of building any bridges with me. Even as Reba, it didn't seem fair to have a showdown with Guy over his vindictive vendetta. I may have craved revenge on him but the last thing I wanted to do was have a slanging match in front of his parents, especially after the joy they'd surrounded me with.

I left as soon as I could after that while simultaneously trying to reassure Gordon and Morag I was absolutely fine and there was nothing to worry about. Guy said nothing during our rushed farewells and their continued apologies for his behaviour. It was upsetting to see them so mortified but I couldn't leave without attempting some kind of parting shot for Guy's benefit. 'I'm glad you came to Edinburgh, Guy,' I said before exiting the garden the way he had come in. He looked a bit taken aback at that. 'No, really I am. Perhaps spending a bit more time with your lovely parents will teach you some proper manners. Any manners at all would certainly be an improvement.'

I turned on my heel then but as I got halfway down the side entry I heard Guy splutter with undisguised rage and yell after me, 'You're NOT family and you NEVER will be so you can get that notion right out of your head! I don't want to see you around here ever again … YOU GOT THAT!?'

I got that. How could I fail to when his words were ringing in my head, but I didn't dignify them with a response.

I got to Sonny's around lunchtime, unlocked the door and made my way down to the deserted bar. I needed to keep busy and wanted to make myself useful. It was the only thing I could think of to do. I had a change of clothes somewhere in the back office, sweatpants and a t-shirt suitable for wiping down tables, restocking the optics and cleaning the toilets. I threw myself into the mindless but strangely satisfying work and walked out of the spotless ladies' room about an hour later.

I sensed an intruder in the main bar area before I actually saw them. In my agitated state I must have forgotten to lock the street-level door behind me when I'd come in and now someone was sitting at a table in the corner of the bar and they were watching me.

The shock of discovering I was not alone made me gasp but, as my eyes focused on the person more keenly, I felt winded like I'd just had a punch to my guts. This wasn't a random stranger.

Sitting primly on a bar stool, one peep-toe sparkly mule swinging from her foot was the one and only Dolly Parton.

Chapter Twenty-Two

There certainly was only one Dolly Parton in the world, and I knew her story inside out. The woman who had fought her way from an impoverished childhood in the Smoky Mountains of Tennessee to become an American icon; a singer, songwriter, actress and philanthropist whose name and image were synonymous with the very best of country music. I also knew that Dolly wasn't scheduled to visit Edinburgh right now so what was she doing sitting in my bar?

From her tumbling blonde hair to her tiny waist and gravity-defying bosom more than a billion people across the world would be able to recognise Dolly Parton in an instant. All except for me, that is. Because of course it wasn't the actual, bona fide, real Dolly Parton sitting in Sonny's Bar that day. It wasn't the one and only; instead it was one of the many, many lookalikes Dolly's talent and fame had spawned across the globe. Didn't I know about those all too well, having been in that club for years myself? Now this one was sat looking at me, her head on one side, with a quizzical look on her face.

'What's a gal gotta do to get a drink around here?' Her accent was pure Southern. I did a double take, wait a cotton-picking minute ... was I wrong? Was this really Dolly after all? I'd thought I'd been hallucinating when I drove past her the other night but was I jumping to the wrong conclusion to immediately presume this must be an imposter, an impersonator, an impressionist of the highest calibre?

'Dolly?'

Dolly slapped her hand down on the table and threw her head back releasing a burst of laughter. 'Not quite, sweetie, but thanks for the vote of confidence, maybe you could write me a five-star review for my show.'

Dora, as she turned out to be, was an actress and she'd brought a play she'd written all about Dolly to the Fringe Festival. It was Dora I had seen making her way to her digs after a late-night show at The Assembly Rooms. Her play was called *Dumb Blonde?*

'The question mark in the title is important,' Dora told me after I'd fixed her a white wine spritzer. 'As Dolly herself would say ... she ain't dumb ... and she ain't no blonde either.' Dora nodded her head in agreement with the sentiment Dolly often expressed after years of being treated with disdain by the country music industry and society as a whole. Those who had taken Dolly for a fool in the past were the ones left looking foolish now, I thought.

Dora apologised for gate-crashing the bar before we were open but I waved away her offer to leave. It felt like fate had brought yet another Dolly to Sonny's, like a moth to a flame, and once I revealed my own past life exploits as a Dolly tribute singer Dora and I instantly bonded and she told me to call her 'Dorrie'.

'That's what everyone calls me ... smashing Dora and Dolly together ... I like it and it's helped me shake off all those daft *Dora the Explorer* jokes.'

'You're just who I needed to see right now, Dorrie,' I told her as we clinked glasses, 'although you did give me quite a fright.'

'You look like a woman with a lot on her mind,' she said. 'You wanna offload?'

'Oh, I wouldn't know where to start,' I told her. Could I really confide in Dorrie about all the crazy things going on in my life right now? My brand-new image, the launch of a fledgling music career, a bitter ex-boyfriend and a crazy Californian with a vendetta against me? It all sounded mad when you listed it and that was before you even got to the bit where I was mixed up with a world-famous country music star.

'Is there a man involved somewhere? Where there's trouble there usually is.'

Dorrie almost choked on her spritzer when I grimaced at that and answered, 'Not one man ... three!'

'Oh honey, you can't keep all that bottled up, why don't you tell me all about it.'

So I did. Not all of it. I kept the stuff about me and Tom Coltrane back but I told her all about gruesome Guy and how Robbie, my ex-Kenny Rogers partner had gone all Coward of the County and now also seemed to have it in for me.

'I don't know what I did to either of them to make them hate me so much?' I wailed, but Dorrie fixed me with a steely stare.

'Really? You really don't know what you did to make them both so mad at you?'

I really didn't. But it turned out Dorrie did. Gently but firmly she explained it all to me from her objective perspective and everything finally started to make some sense.

Guy was clearly a creep who had taken huge offence at my obvious revulsion at his odious advances, that much we both agreed. But it wasn't just rejection that had motivated his plan to have me arrested, according to Dorrie, it was jealousy over my closeness to his parents.

'So he comes back from California to find you, a cuckoo in his nest,' she said, giving me such a lightbulb moment, it threw new light on everything that had been happening. 'Not only are you more than capable of running the family business, his mom and dad have taken you to their hearts and clearly adore you. He obviously felt hugely threatened by that. He still does.'

'But he drove me out of Grayson's, so why is he still coming after me? ... I think the nasty online reviews for Sonny's are down to him too.' More things were clicking into place for me.

'Oh I bet they are.' Dorrie was absolute in her conviction that Guy still saw me as a threat. 'I'm afraid the wound Guy believes you have inflicted on him goes deep. He's probably terrified his parents are going to leave everything they have to you in their will, including their precious jewellery shop.'

'That's ridiculous! They wouldn't do that.'

'Well it doesn't seem likely he'll win any Son of the Year awards right now and from what you've told me they are only getting more annoyed with him. It sort of doesn't matter how likely it is that they would, all that matters is whether Guy thinks they might. Remember Reba, he's a paranoid egotist who judges other people by his own very low standards, that's a very dangerous combination.'

I felt a shiver go down my back as Dorrie said that. Was I in real danger from Guy? What more could he possibly do to me? But Dorrie had moved her attention to Robbie.

'Did you ever ask him how things were going in his new job in, where was it? … Peterborough?'

I had to admit I hadn't. 'He didn't really give me much opportunity for that,' I said, still smarting at the memory of his scornful face as he'd looked me up and down and tried to make me feel awkward and embarrassed about my revamped appearance and colourful new image.

'But after he moved, didn't you keep in touch to find out how he was settling in?'

I thought back to those frantically busy days when I was the newly appointed manager at Sonny's. Robbie had been great answering a blizzard of questions I'd sent him when things were still so new and unfamiliar to me. Then Tom Coltrane had walked into the bar, my life and my bed, Sonny's was catapulted into the news and consequently the bar was always busy. My bosses were delighted takings were at a record high and I hadn't needed Robbie's help or advice anymore, so our communication had tailed off. I was ashamed to admit I had no idea how things had been working out for him in Peterborough while I was riding the crest of the publicity wave and conducting a secret affair with a famous musician.

'It doesn't excuse his shameful behaviour but it might go some way to explaining it.' Dorrie was good at this. She had an ability to look at things calmly, while applying wisdom she had clearly learned from experience. It was extraordinarily helpful.

We talked it all over for a while until eventually she eyed me warily and asked, 'And what about man number three?'

I hesitated while internally debating how much I should say about Tom but Dorrie then reached down into her bag and pulled out a copy of the *Scotland on Sunday* newspaper. As she laid it on the table between us I saw a huge picture of Tom and Juliana Ripon plastered on the front with a smaller, blurry picture of me and Tom taken by someone in the audience when we were performing together last night. How the heck had that made the press already? The headline screamed 'COLTRANE DUMPS JULIANA – Heartbreak for Hollywood star as country music hunk is snared by unknown Scottish singer.'

I gulped and my voice was barely audible as I muttered, 'I don't think snared is quite the right word.'

Dorrie looked at me with ... what was the expression on her face? Judgement? Distaste? Envy? I finally managed to meet her eyes but all I found there was sympathy.

'Oh honey, this guy is gonna be trouble with a capital T.'

I felt winded by her words but was Dorrie simply telling me what everyone else already thought? That I'd been suckered in by a big-name celebrity who had used me for a bit of local fun behind his gorgeous girlfriend's back? Tom had seemed pretty calm about the Juliana situation when I'd questioned him that morning in bed, but was he really only palming me off with excuses while he got ready to plead for forgiveness from his movie star muse? Seeing Juliana's face staring out at me from the front of a newspaper really brought home the fact I'd managed to land myself right in the middle of a love triangle. That would be bad enough in any circumstances but the other two members of this particular ménage à trois were celebrities most people had heard of. Being a mistress, someone's 'bit on the side' wasn't the sort of image I wanted my new persona of Reba Moon to have. I wouldn't have wanted it for plain old Becky Mooney either. I started to stutter my defence, telling Dorrie I hadn't planned for things to happen between me and Tom, that I'd got carried away but, before I could carry on, Dorrie held up her hand to halt my flow.

'I wasn't trying to say that Tom is a bad guy. I don't know him, after all, but I don't think someone like you would have given him the time of day if you didn't think he was pretty decent.' Dorrie spoke quickly, her face still showing more concern than judgement. 'What I meant when I said he was trouble was …' she paused and looked down at the picture of Tom on the table between us. He had an eyebrow raised in that way I found so unbelievably sexy and a smile curling the corner of his lips. The way his hair was mussed up told me he must have just run his hands through it, while he had an arm thrown casually, but protectively, around Juliana's skinny shoulders. Just seeing the picture of them like that made me slightly nauseous. Dorrie sensed my unease and took my hand in hers. 'He looks like the kind of man who could break a girl's heart, whether he meant to or not.'

Faced with Dorrie's honest assessment and willingness to hear me out, I told her things then that I'd barely even admitted to myself. I was falling for Tom in a big way. Once I said it out loud I knew it was true. I'd tried to kid myself this was just a bit of fun, that I was seizing the day by having a fling with a sexy singer, that I wasn't foolish enough to expect anything lasting to come of it. When I was safe inside the bubble Tom and I had created for ourselves, that all seemed to make perfect sense. At first the only other people who had known about us were Fergus and Laura and the fact that Tom's sister and his best friend were part of the secret had made it all feel completely normal. But it wasn't really normal at all, I could see that now. I'd told myself that, if anything was amiss, Ferg and Laura were good people who would warn me, tell me not to get too involved, say something to let me know this could never be anything other than a brief episode in our lives; one to be enjoyed but not something that could lead to anything more meaningful or lasting. But, of course, as Tom's little sister and closest friend, Laura and Fergus's loyalties would be to Tom, not to me. I saw that now. The truth was, I really had no idea what I had got myself in the middle of. I'd vowed not to expect or demand anything from Tom Coltrane but that meant I'd not addressed the situation properly or prioritised my own feelings. And I did have feelings, big ones. Was Dorrie right? Was I on course to have my heart broken into a million pieces? Maybe one day soon I'd be forced to write a song about it all.

'You could have a line about how he plucked your heart strings as easily as he picked his guitar,' Dorrie attempted a lame joke when she saw how upset I was but it was beginning to dawn on me this wasn't a situation I was going to be able to laugh my way out of.

'I need to talk to Tom.'

Dorrie looked at me kindly and nodded encouragingly. 'There's a moment in every love affair when the golden glow that surrounds the two of you turns into a harsh spotlight of reality. For most people that's when friends, family or colleagues all start chipping in with their views and opinions about your new relationship. The bursting of that bubble can be hard to take and whether or not a couple survives can depend on how you deal with it. In your case the spotlight is particularly harsh and bright so how you react now is important.'

My God this tiny woman made so much sense! Her similarity to Dolly was not confined to her appearance. My urge to get to Tom, to see him, to feel his arms around me was suddenly overwhelming. I desperately wanted to get back inside our bubble where we laughed, made love and made music together, and weren't troubled by anything or anybody, but I knew those days had now gone. I'd only seen him a few hours ago so how was it possible that I was missing him so much already?

Dorrie was right about how all the attention was testing us but also the intrusion of the press into our perfect, sexy, romantic bubble was making everything now feel tainted and squalid. Instinct told me if I could get to be with Tom, just the two of us, where I could see him, feel him and hear his voice, it wouldn't feel like that anymore. If we were together I would feel okay, I was sure of it. I wanted to reassure him that I wasn't going to buckle under this pressure but more than that I wanted him to reassure me that we weren't having a meaningless affair. I needed to hear him say Juliana wasn't his one true love, that it was over between them and that we had a chance. I was falling in love with Tom but was there any chance that he was falling in love with me too?

I cleared away our glasses and Dorrie and I made our way up the stairs to the street-level entrance to Sonny's Bar. Just before we stepped outside I pulled her into a big hug. 'Thanks Dorrie, of all the bars in all the world I'm so glad you stumbled into mine.'

She hugged me back and then held me at arms' length while she looked me square in the eye from beneath her beautiful, blonde hair-do. 'Everything happens for a reason, don't you think? I was meant to meet you, Reba, to find you here in your hour of need. Think of me as your very own Dolly-Angel.'

'You really are, I can't tell you how much it's helped to talk to you.'

Dorrie began to push the unlocked, heavy door open as she answered over her shoulder. 'Yeah, talking is great but sometimes action is needed more than words …'

I think she was intending to deliver yet another line of Dorrie wisdom but her voice was drowned out by the sudden noise of shouts and calls from a mob of people standing on the pavement right outside our doorway. They leapt into action once they spotted us both emerging into the daylight.

'REBA! … Becky? …. Is Tom Coltrane with you? Have you spoken to Juliana Ripon? How long have you been having an affair? Reba? BECKY!'

I stood like a rabbit caught in the headlights, transfixed by the sight of a throng of reporters, some with cameras, others with microphones, advancing towards us, but Dorrie was quicker to react. Yanking me by the arm she pulled us both back inside and slammed the door shut and this time firmly locked it. It was good thinking, I'd give her that, apart from the fact we were now completely trapped. There was no other exit from Sonny's Bar, no secret tunnel or back way out.

Dorrie took that on board just like she seemed to process all new information, calmly and rationally. 'Right, so we need to figure out another way to get the hell out of here.' Back down in the bar she stood with her hands on her hips, one tiny foot tapping impatiently on the stone floor while she considered the options. I couldn't imagine thinking it over would take her very long as there were *no* other options.

'Aha!' She smacked her hands together and looked at me triumphantly, 'Of course!'

A few moments later I was standing in the centre of the bar area of Sonny's once again all dressed up as Dolly Parton while opposite me Dorrie, minus her brilliant blonde wig, was wearing my tartan trousers and Tom's borrowed black t-shirt.

'Just when I thought my Dolly days were over,' I mused, as much to myself as to Dorrie who was too busy outlining the grand plan to take much notice of what I was muttering. I fiddled with Dorrie's Dolly wig, it really was a lovely one, I'd never worn anything as gorgeous in all my years performing as a tribute artist.

'Stop fussing, it looks fine.'

'But what about you? We don't have a red wig so you won't look anything like me?' I'd let Dorrie talk me into wearing her clothes while she pulled on mine but I wasn't exactly sure why.

Minus her wig, Dorrie's hair was naturally long, straight and fair. She gave a big sigh and rolled her eyes theatrically. 'You've not been listening to me properly, have you? We aren't switching places, this isn't flippin' Freaky Friday!'

She went over the plan one more time. I was decked out in all her Dolly finery … everything fitted well enough, the hot pink pants with their flouncy kick flares were stretchy and had an elasticated waist, thank goodness. The matching cowgirl shirt with white tassels across the back and down the underside of the sleeves fitted better once I improvised some bosom padding … my feet were slightly too big for Dorrie's fluffy mules but no one would notice that. Suitably disguised, I was apparently going to walk out of the front door of Sonny's Bar, not as Reba, not even as Dorrie, but as 'Dolly' the star of *Dumb Blonde?* the *'hilarious yet heartwarming new play full of truth, tenacity and toe-tapping tunes'* – well that's what it said on the stack of flyers Dorrie had removed from her bag and was now shoving into my hands.

'Might as well get some plugs in for the show while we're at it,' she said with a gleam of mischief in her eye, 'you make your own luck in this life, you know.'

I couldn't help but be rather impressed by how quickly she was turning the situation to her own advantage and I certainly had no better plan to offer.

'Okay, but what about you?'

'Once you've made a clean getaway as the queen of country music I'll lock the door behind you and sit tight. They'll be waiting for Reba, but of course Reba has already gone. When I feel the time is right I'll walk straight out and give them a cheery wave.' She demonstrated the cheery wave for my benefit and I felt quite sorry I wouldn't be around the see her wind up the press mob. 'Even if they realise I'm wearing your clothes from earlier and we've done a switcheroo on them, what are they gonna do about it?'

As cunning plans go it was a pretty good one. I took a few deep breaths, got into my Dolly zone and went upstairs to put on a show.

The shouts for Reba died in the mouths of the hacks as I sashayed towards them proffering flyers and flashing a winning smile.

'Howdy fellas,' I trilled, ignoring the fact there were as many lasses as lads assembled, waiting to pounce, 'what a way to make a livin,' eh?' The '9 to 5' line went over the heads of some of them but I was tickled to hear a couple of them groan as they realised they were being snowed by a grifting Fringe performer trying her best to boost ticket sales to her show. The plan was working. I bantered with a couple of the older guys who appeared grateful for a way to ease their stakeout boredom, name-checked the play, the venue and the showtimes. '*Dumb Blonde?* Catch it at the Assembly Rooms on Chambers Street, every night at 9 p.m.'

With a flutter of my eyelashes I flung the last of the leaflets in their general direction, and told them, 'See y'all around, you take good care of yourselves now, y'hear.'

A chorus of good-natured goodbyes followed me down the street as I tottered gingerly to the corner and, once out of sight, exhaled a huge sigh of relief. Dorrie the great pretender had pulled off a perfect great escape plot. The plan had worked and in several different ways good old Dolly had saved me … again.

Chapter Twenty-Three

I let myself into the flat as quietly as possible and was attempting to make my way unseen to the sanctuary of my bedroom with a blonde Dolly wig in one hand and the borrowed pair of fluffy mules in the other when I got caught in the act by my mother.

'There you are!' My mother's powers of observation couldn't be questioned but I found it a little strange she didn't seem to see anything unusual in me creeping across the hallway in a far-too-tight hot pink ensemble. I suppose that's what years flirting around the edges of showbusiness had done to her. 'I was about to send out a search party, why are you not answering your phone?'

With the trip to see Gordon and Morag, my unexpected encounter with Dorrie and then the press siege at the club I hadn't realised my phone had run out of battery. Again. I started to say that but Mum wasn't interested in explanations and cut me off, snapping, 'Never mind about all that, he's been here for the last hour ... waiting for you!' The last part was hissed at me with lots of eye-rolling and jerky head movements in the direction of the closed living room door.

'What? Who's here?' I was picking up now on her agitated state and could see she looked flustered but also rather delighted. That was weird. Oh no … Tom? It had to be. Mum actually looked quite star-struck. What the hell was Tom Coltrane doing in my home, hanging out with my parents? When I'd left him at the hotel this morning after breakfast we hadn't made any plans for him to come to the flat.

'Tom's here?' I hissed back, trying to stop my mum from opening the door to the living room and announcing my presence. Too late, damn it.

For the second time in the relatively short period we had known each other, country music superstar Tom Coltrane was confronted by the sight of me, half-dressed as Dolly Parton with no reasonable explanation on offer. He looked bemused and bamboozled as I entered the room, but then I clocked my dad sitting with a guitar on his knee and I figured maybe Tom's befuddlement might also have something to do with the fact my parents had been 'entertaining' him with some of their Moonshine Trio favourites while they had him trapped three floors up. Oh good grief, no.

'Hey, you okay?' I asked trying to signal both sympathy and a meaningful apology with my face but Tom's expression was not one I was able to read. His eyes went from my bare toes, up my legs clad in pink satin and rested on my chest where the diamanté buttons of my jacket were straining to contain my bust. Tom's eyes widened in surprise at the sight; he knew my own breasts were not capable of such a feat on their own. I was prompted to reach inside the ill-fitting jacket and remove two scrunched up bar towels I'd shoved inside earlier in my desperate attempt to recreate a suitably 'Dolly' embonpoint.

'Are *you* okay?' He asked slowly in a voice that sounded like he thought I might well be nuttier than a squirrel eating a walnut whip.

'We really must stop meeting like this,' I joked feebly as I dropped the bar towels on the floor while recalling our first encounter in the back office of Sonny's Bar. That funny episode, which had brought us together, seemed a million years ago right now.

Mum and Dad, with a sensitivity that caught me almost as much by surprise as everything else that had happened so far that day, pretended to remember they suddenly had to go out.

'We'll give you two some space,' Mum said in a quivering voice while lingering by the doorway unable to take her eyes off Tom until Dad almost frogmarched her out.

I'd been desperate to see Tom myself but now he was right there in front of me it wasn't the way I had imagined it at all. I'd wanted him to put his arms around me and shut everything else out so I could feel the realness of him, of us, but once we were alone he didn't make a move towards me. An unfamiliar awkwardness between us wasn't helped by how ridiculous I felt standing there in a borrowed Dolly Parton costume and when I tried to explain the reason for it Tom sighed with obvious irritation at the mention of the press pack waiting for me outside Sonny's.

'I managed to fool them though and get away, thanks to Dorrie. I dunno what would have happened if it hadn't been for her.' I was waiting for Tom to see the funny side of this situation but he was obviously having a complete sense of humour failure.

'Alternatively, the press now have pictures of y'all dressed up like a Thanksgiving turkey, which are most likely circulating on the internet even as we speak, with captions poking fun at the both of us!' I'd never heard Tom use such an exasperated tone with me before and he wasn't finished. 'Did ya even consider the whole thing might have been a complete set-up? This Dorrie person was just a honey trap, sent to get y'all talking and land a scoop. I can just imagine the fun they'll have on the subs desk coming up with a caption to go with ...' He let the sentence tail off as he waved his hand in my direction but the word that was left hanging in the air was *'that'*, which was not very flattering.

Tom was being rude and I didn't like it. It also rattled me to think there might be the slightest chance there was some truth in what he was saying. I'd told Dorrie everything, not just confirming the rumours that I was seeing the famous singer Tom Coltrane but revealing my true feelings about him; feelings I'd not even confessed to Tom himself. I was regretting how much I had shared with her now; she knew everything about me, my brush with the law and Guy Grayson's weird vendetta against me plus my fall out with Robbie. If she wanted to, Dorrie could write a book about me, not just an article.

I wanted to defend myself and defend Dorrie too but I wasn't sure how to begin. I thought if I could just go and quickly change my clothes I might be able to think more clearly and explain things better but Tom wasn't interested in giving me a chance to do that. 'Did ya say anything to her about me?' he asked somewhat aggressively and the look on my face must have given me away as Tom then launched into a big lecture about dealing with the press and how I obviously didn't have a clue. 'It's best to keep your mouth shut, especially when ya don't know who to trust.'

Trust. The word resonated with me on many levels. He seemed to be insinuating that he didn't think he could trust me. That was hurtful. Maybe I had made some mistakes but I would never do anything deliberately to cause trouble. Surely he knew that? I wasn't sure I was now able to trust him to do that, to think the best of me. How well did we know each other really? Well enough to trust the other, no matter what? It wasn't looking good.

'Why are you here, Tom?' As upset as I was at Tom's rudeness it dawned on me that there must be a reason he'd come looking for me at my flat.

He suddenly looked more shifty than annoyed and began a long and convoluted story that mentioned his American manager Waz Monsoon, a great deal, and ended with him saying he had to go back to Nashville 'immediately'.

There was something he wasn't telling me. I presumed it had something to do with Juliana but he didn't like it when I brought her name up again, asking, 'Have you spoken to her?'

He didn't answer me one way or the other, just shook his head in an exasperated way.

'So you're going back to Nashville to see her?' I thought it was a pretty reasonable assumption to make but at this Tom exploded.

He started yelling about his career, how he had work to do and commitments to honour and not everything revolved around me or Juliana or any other woman and I needed to realise that. He even asked if things were truly over between me and Robbie? Was he serious? As he ricocheted between defensiveness and accusations I was left reeling.

'For God's sake, Reba, this whole mess could wreck everything, just as I was getting back on track with my music.'

He looked like a wounded animal and I felt for him, truly I did. I was witnessing the downside of fame right in front of my eyes, the pressure to keep succeeding, the intrusion into your private life. Just two hours earlier I had admitted to myself for the very first time that I had fallen in love with this guy. Unfortunately, I'd also admitted that fact to a complete stranger and now the repercussions might be about to make the situation even worse. But what about me? I didn't appreciate being referred to as part of a 'mess'. Charming. The longing I'd had to put my arms around Tom was being replaced with a desire to punch him on the chin. I saw red. I was no longer in the mood to tend to Tom's fears or worry about the emotional state of a Hollywood actress I was never likely to meet. It was clear if I didn't look out for myself no one else was going to.

'So did you just come to say goodbye and give me a lecture on public relations or was there anything else?'

That took the wind out of his sails and he opened his mouth as if to say something but then shut it again.

'No? Well, I have to say, Tom, this has been fun but if you've got a plane to catch don't let me stop you.' I don't remember exactly what happened next but Tom made some lame remark about coming over to ask me to go with him to Nashville. It was laughable really, he was clearly trying to backtrack and make himself look like the good guy despite all recent evidence to the contrary. I think I did laugh when he said it which seemed to annoy him.

'You want me to come to Nashville with you? What? Now? ... Well I suppose I am dressed for it!' I scoffed as I gestured to the tasselled country outfit I was still wearing and tried to cover up my breaking heart with a comedic retort. Tom wasn't laughing though and accused me of lacking ambition and not being serious about my singing career. What the ...?! Eventually he even used Dolly against me.

'What are ya going to do once I've gone, Reba? Go back to being a two-bit copycat Dolly Parton, parroting another woman's songs instead of bothering to find your own voice?'

I couldn't bear to listen to any more. If he was leaving on a jet plane why didn't he just get on with it? Why had he felt the need to come around, hurl accusations, ask stupid questions and make me realise he thought I was an untrustworthy, untalented liability. I presumed it was making him feel better about being a two-timing, self-entitled, washed-up loser. I can't remember quite how I put it, but I yelled something that alluded to all of that and the upshot was that in my very first ... and last ... row with Tom Coltrane I got the last word. His only response was the slam of the door as he stormed out.

Chapter Twenty-Four

I was so sick that for several days I couldn't get out of bed. I wasn't malingering, I was properly poorly. A migraine combined with aching limbs meant my whole body hurt. Constant stomach-churning nausea so I could hardly eat and just the thought of food made me want to hurl. I slept a lot which gave some relief from the discomfort but when I was awake I had so little energy I barely got out of bed. I didn't leave the flat at all.

My mum kept up a steady supply of hot drinks, soup and toast, most of which went untouched, but I was grateful for her attempts to stave off starvation. She didn't send for any medical intervention, however, and once I started to emerge from the fug of illness I did ask her why she hadn't called a doctor?

'There's nothing a doctor can do for what's ailing you,' she professed which I thought was rather presumptuous of her because I was sure I must have picked up some deadly bug or virus or something. If she was trying to make out that

I'd been nothing more than 'love sick' then I didn't think she had really understood the extent of my suffering. I'm not saying I wasn't upset about the break-up with Tom. Knowing our short but sweet affair had come to an end was painful but we'd only known each other for a short time and I'd told myself often enough that the writing was on the wall as far as a long-term love affair was concerned. Once the symptoms of my mystery illness started to subside I didn't feel I could indulge the notion I was suffering from a form of grief or even heartbreak. Surely I hadn't loved for long enough for that to be the case?

Whatever the truth of the matter – and as my mother had not seen fit to call for a medical professional we would never now know what it was that had ailed me – I needed to pull myself together and drag myself back to work.

I discovered my dad had been spending the extra time he'd suddenly found he had to spare on his extended visit to Edinburgh filling in for me at Sonny's Bar. He'd always been a natural host and it was good to know Donald and Stella hadn't been left too short-handed while I'd been out of action. My two regular staff members didn't say all that much when I went back into work. That wasn't too unusual for Donald, of course, he wasn't ever what you could call 'chatty'. Stella looked a bit shamefaced, maybe she was feeling a bit guilty about how jealous she had appeared just before my romance with hunky music star Tom Coltrane had come crashing down around my ears. At least she wasn't gloating or glorying in my misfortune, I had to give her that; if anything her tone was kind and considerate but I wasn't in the mood to be pitied.

'Stella, it's fine, you don't have to walk on eggshells around me.'

At that Stella fixed me with her more familiar steely gaze; 'No one is walking on eggshells, Becky, or are we supposed to call you Reba now?'

I stopped setting up the bar and snapped my head up to look at her, the comment had hit me in the solar plexus and I felt winded. Stella took the pause I gave her to carry on; 'I'm not saying that to be cruel in any way, honestly I'm not, but it looked like you'd made some big life decisions, found a way to move forward with a music career and I think it would be crazy to let all that go to waste. The name Reba suits you more than Becky ever did so I'm happy to stick with Reba. The question is, are you?'

Stella was always straightforward and to the point, it was one of her very best qualities and it was clear to me she was speaking, as always, from the heart and with no hidden agenda. She'd also made a direct hit on the very subject I knew I had to address. I told her yes, I was sticking with Reba. Decision made.

'Robbie will be relieved to hear that too,' Stella said carefully, then as she saw me grimace at the mention of his name, quickly tried to explain how much my former partner truly regretted upsetting me so much the night I made my debut performance as Reba Moon. 'We both know Robbie can be a bit of a doofus but he really does care about you, Reba. You just took him by surprise and he's really struggling in his new job. I think he misses Edinburgh more than he thought he would.'

I heard her out; she and Robbie had worked together at Sonny's for a long time and were good friends. It was good to learn he regretted what he'd said and it chimed very much with what Dorrie had presumed was going on, that it was more to do with what was going wrong in his life than what was happening in mine, but I needed to hear a proper apology from Robbie himself before I'd be ready to properly forgive him.

As Stella and I worked side by side setting up the bar we chatted about what I was going to do now. Stella was a good sounding board, listening as I talked through various feelings and potential scenarios about launching Reba Moon into the wider world and chipping in with her own thoughts now and again. It was hugely helpful and rather cathartic. She made some insightful observations that made me think; the first was that I needed to get hold of record company executive Steve Bannister and see if an offer of a record deal was still on the table despite my split from Tom. That was still my voice on that record with him – even if the thought of having to hear that song ripped my heart out right now.

'Your talent has nothing to do with Tom Coltrane,' Stella said. I was grateful for that verdict on my abilities as a performer. She pointed out that although it might have been cool to do more recording or gigging with Tom it could be better if people didn't think I was riding on his coat tails. It was something that had occurred to me too. People could be very quick to judge if they thought I was only getting a break because of my relationship with a famous musician. There weren't many upsides to our relationship ending but maybe that was one. I said as much to Stella with a heartfelt roll of my eyes. 'Every cloud and all that.'

Stella placed her hands on the bar between us and looked me straight in the eye. 'Don't do that,' she said, not unkindly.

'Don't do what?'

'Don't pretend you're not bothered about whatever has happened between you and Tom.' She held up her hand as I opened my mouth to stop me from saying whatever I was going to say. 'Obviously something has gone on and I'm not just talking about some bits of gossip going around on social media. You and Tom, it really was something else, wasn't it? Something very special. The way you were together the night he introduced you on stage as Reba Moon, the connection between you, it was so …' Stella faltered at that point as she noticed my stricken face. 'I'm sorry, I'm not trying to upset you, it's just, I know only too well that finding someone you feel like that about, having them so into you too … what you and Tom seemed to have together, it doesn't happen every day. I was a bit taken aback when I could see how crazy you seemed to be about each other, it was so obvious how proud he was of you and how comfortable you were together. Are you sure it's all over between you?'

I was finding it hard to swallow and didn't trust my voice to say too much so I just nodded emphatically.

'I'm really sorry to hear that, Reba. No wonder you were knocked sideways, that kind of heartbreak hurts like nothing else can. Are you sure you're okay to come back to work?'

The sentiment was genuine and her tone was kind and considerate but Stella might as well have picked up the razor-sharp knife we used to slice the lemons and plunged it into me. She'd seen me trying to put a positive spin on my split from Tom and had skewered that with breath-taking accuracy. Who was I trying to kid? Myself? I certainly wasn't convincing Stella but I had another go, spluttering my retort. 'I had a bug … a virus … some sort of weird lurgy, I was really ill, not … Tom … I mean … it wasn't …'

My attempt to explain tailed off as Stella grimaced and shaking her head said, 'Okay, Cleopatra, play it your way.'

'Cleopatra!?' I was completely stumped. What the hell was Stella on about now?

'Cleopatra,' she repeated speaking slowly, 'Queen of de Nile?'

Ahh. I got it. Very clever. There was a slight smile playing at the corner of Stella's red-lipped mouth and I couldn't help but give a rueful grin back when the penny dropped.

'Actually, forget Cleopatra,' Stella said then. 'You're more like Miss Adelaide from *Guys and Dolls*!'

'You've lost me now, Stella, what are you on about?' I stood back with my arms folded and waited for Stella to expand on this theory. 'C'mon, this had better be good.' I knew what she was trying to do, she was trying to make me face the fact I had a broken heart and cheer me up at the same time. It was a tough task but Stella was a tough cookie. I waited patiently while she gave it her best shot.

Given the floor, Stella did a rather passable, and quite honestly hilarious rendition of 'Adelaide's Lament' from a show I'd always loved, *Guys and Dolls*. Yes it was funny, but it packed a punch too. Stella's sharp delivery really got across how Miss Adelaide's coughs and sneezes are due to the emotional distress caused by her gambler boyfriend's repeated refusals to marry her. That's the thing about a great song – whether it's country or a showtune. The great ones?

They really say something. I sat transfixed as through the medium of musical theatre Stella was making the salient point that psychosomatic medical symptoms could be connected to your love life. She was too clever for her own good, that girl.

With her twangy, nasal 'Noo Yawk' delivery, Stella's performance was as entertaining as it was unexpected. I couldn't help but laugh out loud. 'You're ... good! Really good.' I clapped long and loud while Stella bowed and blew kisses.

'Twelve years of amateur dramatics and a degree in musical theatre at a top drama school wasn't completely wasted then.'

I stopped applauding. 'What?'

It turned out Stella had always harboured huge ambitions to be an actress but after slogging it around the audition circuit in London for several lean years she had finally thrown in the towel when the bit parts didn't lead to a big enough break. The revelation explained an awful lot.

'They say it's the hope that kills you,' she said. 'I think that means if you keep putting yourself up for something, keep tossing your hat in the ring then you are just inviting disappointment and rejection. So I came back to Edinburgh, stopped setting myself up for failure, got a regular job and tried to put all ambitions to be an actress behind me. But do you know what I think now?' Stella sank into a chair and put her chin on her hand and she looked at me with her big, kohl-rimmed eyes. 'I think it's the hope that makes you feel alive. What's the point in living if you don't take a few risks? Once you take the hope away, what have you got left?'

What indeed? I looked at Stella sitting there and saw a very different woman to the one I thought I knew. I understood exactly what she was trying to tell me.

'I'm gonna give that guy from the record company a call. I've come too far to give up on myself now. Reba Moon is here to stay.'

'Good girl! And what about Tom?'

I shook my head. Negotiating a deal with Tom Coltrane was not going to be so easy but Stella wasn't prepared to give up on our romance just yet.

'You said he asked you to go back to Nashville with him?'

I tried to explain how Tom's invitation had felt like an insincere afterthought in the middle of our row. He had clearly been annoyed with me and off the back of accusing me of still being involved with my ex, selling my story to an undercover reporter and embarrassing him with the press he'd suddenly announced I should go with him to Nashville. In that moment it had sounded ridiculous.

'But he still asked you to go. Why would he do that if he didn't mean it? What if you had said yes?'

Well, that was a good point. What would have happened if I'd said yes? There was no way of knowing the answer to that as I had given a very clear, very firm 'No!'

Stella was confusing me more and more now. I was already hazy on the details of what Tom and I had said to each other while we traded insults and argued. What I did remember clearly was standing there in a second-hand Dolly Parton costume and being made to feel like a second-rate singer and a second-rate date compared to the incredible Juliana Ripon.

Stella suddenly slapped her own forehead; 'Oh that reminds me, I meant to say, your mate Dorrie has been in a few times asking after you.'

'Dorrie? What did she want? What did you tell her?'

Stella looked slightly stunned as I bit her head off. 'She wanted to know if you were okay. I said you were off sick. She seems like a real sweetheart and her show is amazing … have you seen it?'

'Huh? You've been to see her show? *Dumb Blonde?* It's a genuine play? She really is an actress, not an undercover reporter?'

Stella looked at me like I was Daffy, Donald and all the other Looney Tunes characters rolled into one. 'Well unless she's the *most* gifted actress the Edinburgh Fringe Festival has ever seen, spent months writing and crafting a musical play, printed leaflets and posters so she could spend an entire month performing in a sought-after venue with the sole purpose of using all of that as a cover story just so she could pick up a bit of tittle tattle on you and Tom Coltrane, then I think it's probably safe to assume that yes, Dorrie is exactly who she says she is and not a gutter press journo trying to pick up a sordid little scoop!'

When she put it like that it was bloody obvious: of course Dorrie hadn't been sent to lure me into a honeytrap!

Stella was looking at me as though she was trying to figure something out.

'I know, I know … I'm an idiot.'

Stella shook her head. 'You're not an idiot but you do have the tendency to do a good impression of an idiot sometimes.'

'Gee thanks!'

'What I'm trying to say, Reba, is you need to trust your instincts more. It seems to me they are very rarely wrong.'

Now she had my attention: Stella didn't hand out compliments like sweeties but I wasn't sure what she was basing that assessment on? Patiently she began to explain.

'When you worked at the jewellers didn't you tell me the old guy said you had a real knack for spotting fakes?'

That was true, Gordon had told me my skill in spotting a true diamond was a gift I had. Maybe it was the years spent sewing rhinestones onto country costumes but to me the real jewels always stood out a mile.

Stella had more to say about how Tom's experience of fame over the years could well have given him an understandable level of paranoia. 'But don't let his suspicions cloud your judgement. Not everyone is out to get you and I think you know the real diamonds among the fakes when you meet them.'

Was Stella right? It felt like she was on to something: why did I not trust my own instincts? I'd known Guy Grayson was rotten from the moment I met him. I'd liked Dorrie at once and my faith in her had proved to be correct. I'd instantly bonded with Laura and Fergus too and I was sure they were good people. They were all real gems, I was sure. But what about Tom Coltrane? Was he a diamond? Or just a rhinestone I'd been dazzled by?

Our conversation was interrupted by the noise of my vibrating phone juddering on the bar. I pretended to ignore it.

'Aren't you gonna see who it is?'

When I hesitated before picking it up, Stella asked, 'Could it be Tom?'

'Highly unlikely,' I told her. 'I've blocked his number.'

'What? Why?'

I found it a hard thing to defend. I barely remembered doing it but in my feverish sickness when the pain in my head was pounding so badly I think I just wasn't thinking straight. Tom had called several times but I cancelled the call rather than answer him. Maybe it was cowardice. Maybe it was self-preservation but I'd eventually hit the block button and hoped it would stop things hurting so much. If only life was that simple.

Stella was closer to my phone than I was and as I dithered she glanced at the screen, I saw the expression on her face change. 'I don't think Tom's given up on you yet, Reba.'

'What? What d'you mean?'

Stella held up the phone towards me so I could see who was calling.

It was Laura, Tom's little sister.

Chapter Twenty-Five

I knew very well it would be pretty impossible to say no to Laura so I didn't even try. I wanted to see her anyway, I'd missed her and I was curious about what she'd said on the phone. She'd made it sound like she had something particularly important to tell me.

We'd arranged to meet early afternoon at a pub down in Grassmarket. It was full on madness in the streets as I fought my way there, tourists packing every area of sidewalk and queueing outside Fringe venues for shows and performances. You see some crazy sights around the city during the festival, from fire-eaters to fan-dancers, everyone has a gimmick to try and pull the punters into their show. On the one hand it was annoying for us Edinburgh natives to be invaded by such lunacy every August but, then again, we'd all missed it so badly during the pandemic years the return to chaos and craziness was a relief. The visitors and the money they spend are generally made very welcome, even though it could take twice as long to get anywhere with them all constantly blocking every inch of pavement space.

I arrived slightly breathless at The Last Drop, one of Edinburgh's oldest drinking establishments named due to its proximity to the location of the last public hangings which took place in the eighteenth century. I hoped there wasn't a particularly sinister reason Laura had chosen such a macabre spot?

The pub didn't look like it had changed much since those days either, with its stone flagged floors, low ceilings and dark, wonky walls. I pushed my way through a gaggle of American tourists blocking the doorway. They appeared to be confused by a number of items on the menu. 'What in the world is "Cullen skink"?' I heard an extra-large man drawl while his skinny wife was equally puzzled by the mention of 'neeps and tatties'.

I found Laura tucked into a corner table next to a tiny leaded window. She looked like a mystical absinthe fairy in a vivid green strappy sundress with shafts of sunlight dancing off her strawberry blonde hair. There were two pints of frothy-headed Guinness on the table in front of her.

'I took the liberty of ordering for you,' she said with a wink. Guinness wasn't my usual tipple but I was glad I didn't have to jostle my way to the bar and the drinks did look rather delicious. 'You look like you need building up anyway,' Laura added as I took my first sip.

'Okay, mom,' I said as I wiped my mouth, and we were instantly back into our usual, jokey banter. I had been worried things might have felt weird between us but it didn't feel strange at all to be hanging out with Laura again.

I was grateful for that – Laura's help and friendship meant a lot to me.

The first thing Laura wanted to tell me was that Tom hadn't sent her and he didn't even know she was meeting up with me. I wasn't sure how to take that at first; was I actually a bit disappointed to hear he *hadn't* sent his little sister as a special envoy? Laura didn't let me think about that for too long because she was already explaining why she had come.

'You two need your heads banging together,' she said and I almost spluttered stout all over the table as I remembered just why little Laura Coltrane's nickname was 'Feisty'. 'You're such a good match for each other, I could see it straight away but neither of you are being completely honest with each other.'

I reeled back at that and started to question what she thought I was lying about but before I got too far she cut me off.

'Have you told Tom you love him?'

I didn't reply, but I didn't need to, Laura read my shocked expression perfectly. How did she know? 'No, I thought not but I know very well that you do. Look how the weight has fallen off you in the last couple of weeks; if that's not love then I don't know what is!'

I had to admit my clothes were hanging looser on me than ever before. It had given me the extra push to discard half of my existing wardrobe of boring and functional items. All my knee-length skirts and drab tops were now hanging in the charity shop while I enjoyed dressing as Reba Moon all day every day. Today I'd pulled on frayed denim cut-off shorts and a white vest but thrown a silky red floral robe over it as a colourful cover-up. The scarlet red of the robe clashed with my coppery hair but I loved how eye-popping the colours were together. Laura obviously approved too.

'You look great by the way, I'm not saying you don't.' She grinned at me and then carried on, 'Men are simple souls, Reba, and he shouldn't need it spelling out that you really are in love with him, but of course he does.' She took a swig of her own Guinness but before she carried on I had a question of my own.

'What lie has Tom told me?'

Laura gulped down her beer and shook her head. 'I never said he lied.'

'You said he wasn't being completely honest with me, that's the same thing.'

'No. No Reba, it's not but …' She seemed to be struggling to find the words to explain exactly what she meant. 'There are some things I think Tom needs to explain but it has to come from him, it's not my place to speak for him.'

'Then why are you here?' I didn't mean it unkindly and I didn't say it in an aggressive way but I really wanted to know … what was Laura trying to achieve here?

She talked for quite a long time then, about Tom and what he was like when they were growing up. Some of it I already knew. They had been a tight-knit bunch, her and the two older brothers. Pete was the eldest and he took on the role of man of the house after their dad did a bunk. He was sensible and responsible, Laura said, so maybe it wasn't that surprising he'd ended up a pillar of the community as a police sergeant in the local constabulary. Laura was the baby and didn't remember being too perturbed by her father's disappearance.

'I had two big brothers looking out for me, I always felt they had my back so I never really missed having a dad.' She added that between the two of them Pete and Tom had most fatherly roles covered. 'Pete would insist on me being home at a decent time, even if he had to come and pick me up himself. Tom was the one I could pour my heart out to, tell him about any boyfriend trouble. Tom would give me a cuddle and tell me everything would be okay and Pete would threaten to punch the guy's lights out.'

'Sounds like the perfect combination,' I said.

I thought Laura was glossing over how tricky life probably was at times growing up in a single-parent family but I knew it would have become much harder for the siblings in their twenties when their mum died after a short illness. Tom had briefly mentioned losing his mom so tragically young but I wasn't sure why Laura was telling me all of this now?

'Pete was always focused on getting into a solid career, something with prospects and a pension. I was the baby, so protected by the two of them that I never really worried too much about anything. For me life was an adventure and I grew up feeling able to be a free spirit. Even when life finally teaches you things aren't that simple, it's very empowering to have started out that way. I believe it gives you wings you wouldn't otherwise have had.' Laura looked thoughtful as she considered this for a moment. She was clearly a talented artist and although the kids now took up most of her time she'd told me she really wanted to carve out some time to paint more dramatic works of art like the ones I already owned.

'And Tom?' I presumed Laura was leading somewhere with all of this.

'Tom was the sensitive one, creative and romantic, he felt things more keenly than me and Pete. Stuff cuts deep with Tom, it's what makes him such a terrific songwriter but it's not an easy way to live. He didn't have Pete's focus or my devil-may-care attitude. I think my mum worried about him the most when she got ill'.

My heart twisted listening to Laura talk about Tom like that. This was the stuff no one else would know about the famous Tom Coltrane, the stuff that never made it into the gossip columns or dawned on the screaming fans who pushed to the front row of his concerts. He did put his heart and soul into his music though, as a songwriter and a performer, so he did reveal his inner self to the world in that way. I agreed with Laura that it did help him to be a great artist.

'Tom needs to be with someone who understands him, someone who sees the real him and can be a true partner.' Laura looked at me pleadingly.

'He already has someone else in his life, Laura, things are more complicated than you are making out.'

Laura closed her eyes for a moment while she gathered her thoughts. 'All I can say about that … is Juliana Ripon is not the right match for Tom … and they both know it!'

There was something Laura wasn't telling me but she wasn't going to be drawn any further. She did have more to say about why she thought I needed to give Tom another chance.

'It's not just your voices that blend well together, Reba, you're good for each other, any fool can see it. You wouldn't cut a record without rehearsing it first, working things through, keeping the bits that work and cutting out the things that don't, would you?' She held her hands palms up and shrugged as if to demonstrate what she was saying was the most obvious thing in the world. 'So you've hit a couple of bum notes recently but with a bit more rehearsal …' she left the suggestion, that all Tom and I needed was just a bit more practice to make things perfect, hanging in the air.

'I don't know, Laura, I do have feelings for Tom, strong feelings, but I don't want anyone thinking I'm using him for my own career. I don't want *him* thinking that.'

'Has he ever accused you of that? Has he ever said he thinks that you're using him?'

I recalled the row we'd had at my flat. I shuddered at the memory of me calling him a 'has-been'.

'You said that to his face?' Laura went pale as I tried to describe the argument.

'I think "washed-up loser" was the phrase I actually used'.

'What did he say?'

Try as I might I couldn't really remember Tom throwing anything back at me about using him, riding on his coat tails or exploiting our relationship to make my own name.

'He said some nasty things, called me a loose cannon, said I was gullible and needed to be more careful who I trusted. He also said if I didn't take my chances now I'd end up back being a two-bit copycat Dolly Parton.'

Laura didn't hesitate: 'Harsh maybe, but fair,' was her verdict.

'Ouch!'

'I get that he was lashing out at you a bit unfairly for all the stuff in the press but you have to see how awful it is for him to have his private life dragged through the mud all the time. He's never really got used to that and I don't think he ever will, he's much too sensitive. The two-bit Dolly line is rude but that's only because he knows you've got so much potential. He was going about it all wrong but he was trying to give you a kick up the arse and bring you properly into his world. He wanted you to go to Nashville with him so badly.'

'He said that?'

Laura drained the last of her Guinness. 'I haven't been completely honest with you either, Reba. It's true Tom doesn't know I'm here and he hasn't asked me to come to see you but he has told me something and, well, he knows what I'm like so I think he knew I would tell you. I *know* he wants me to tell you.' She leaned forward and lowered her voice. 'Tom was serious about wanting you to go with him to Nashville. I think it came out all wrong and the moment was spoiled.'

'I laughed in his face and sort of threw him out. I thought he'd come to break up with me and was just making a hash of it.' An uncomfortable feeling was creeping up my spine as I replayed those moments in my mind. How differently it all could have worked out if we'd both just handled it better. Had I thrown a once in a lifetime opportunity away for the sake of my pride?

'I get that but there's now an offer on the table that you really can't ignore.'

I leaned towards Laura. 'I'm listening.'

'Tom's record company love "Moonlight Home", the song you duetted on. They want to throw everything behind it and make it the biggest hit Tom's had in a long while. They also love the quality your voice gives it, that ethereal sense your harmony brings and the genuine feeling that your voice is guiding Tom's through the darkness.'

'Are you working for the marketing department?' As usual I was using humour as a shield to hide behind. Laura ignored me and ploughed on.

'There have been a few offers for you and Tom to perform the song live, the record company and Tom's manager think it would make a huge difference to sales to secure an exclusive performance and, of course, it would help increase interest in any solo material from Reba Moon too.'

I could understand that Laura wanted to do everything she could to help her brother, support his career and maybe even get us back on track too, but if he really wanted me to sing with him again maybe I needed to hear it from him directly. Shouldn't he have the guts to ask me himself?

'Didn't you block all his calls?'

Ahh, yes, I had to admit Laura made a very good point, and then she said something that blew my mind completely. 'It's The Grand Ole Opry. The Grand Ole Opry want you and Tom to perform "Moonlight Home".'

It took a minute for the whooshing noise in my ears to subside as my brain exploded. The Grand Ole Opry, the legendary home of American country music for almost one hundred years, was inviting *me* to appear? The place that launched the careers of everyone from Johnny Cash to Garth Brooks and of course the country music queen herself, Dolly Parton. I'd grown up reading about it as if it were the stuff of legends. The Opry had started as a simple radio show in 1925 and was broadcast weekly from the Ryman Auditorium in downtown Nashville. By the seventies its popularity and influence meant it had outgrown the modest theatre and a purpose-built concert arena was built on the outskirts of Nashville to accommodate the thousands of devoted fans who wanted to experience The Opry magic for themselves. I knew the new stage was constructed with a perfect wooden circle taken from the old Ryman Auditorium embedded in the centre so that an authentic piece of the original magic was present in The Opry's enormous new home. I couldn't comprehend that there might now be a real chance for me to stand in the spotlight on that magical circle just like all the country music artists I adored had done before me.

Laura was watching the emotions flooding across my face. I didn't know what was going to happen between me and Tom but faced with this opportunity there was only one thing I could possibly say, so I told her,

'Tell Tom I'll be there.'

Chapter Twenty-Six

Within forty-eight hours of hearing that I had a chance of appearing on the hallowed stage of The Grand Ole Opry I was on a plane from London Heathrow heading straight for Nashville, Tennessee.

I'd got over my reservations about hitching my wagon to Tom Coltrane's fame pretty quickly. If anyone was going to have an issue with me duetting with Tom I decided that was going to be their problem, not mine. Stella guffawed loudly and slapped me on the back when I'd told her that. It was amazing how quickly you could turn an argument around when it was necessary, and it was very necessary that I got myself to Nashville and up onto that famous stage. Stella said she approved wholeheartedly.

'A girl's gotta do what a girl's gotta do!' she'd said. I couldn't have put it better myself. She'd also told me she and Donald would cover my shifts at Sonny's. 'Just don't forget to let me know if you're not coming back,' she'd said, laughing. 'I know someone who'd be thrilled to come and have their old job back if you're crowned the next country music queen and decide to live on a ranch in Kentucky.' I pointed out that Nashville is actually in Tennessee but Stella said I was the one missing the actual point. Again, she wasn't wrong.

It had felt like I was setting off for a whole new life the night before my flight when an impromptu gig turned into a sort of farewell party at Sonny's. I had impulsively suggested to my mum and dad that we would reunite the Moonshine Trio before they headed back to Spain and so we did a version of our old show for a packed crowd of festival-goers who were hanging out in the bar. With Nashville to look forward to and everything now feeling like it was moving so fast, it felt like a good way to close one chapter before writing the next.

The punters loved the mix of singalong country hits we sang and it was good to see Mum and Dad so happy. They really did love being on stage and entertaining folk, it was no wonder I loved it too, it was in my blood. I had no qualms about performing as myself this time around. The spell had been broken and I no longer needed Dolly as my disguise. I relished being Reba and I was building up my confidence as a performer all the time. I just hoped I could keep up the forward momentum.

The bar had been jumping by the time we wrapped up our set with a request from the audience to sing 'Take Me Home Country Roads'. It was an oldie but a goody and a healthy number of the crowd seemed to know the words to the chorus and lustily sang along with us. It was a fun night with a friendly crowd and I felt even happier when I spotted

Dorrie standing at the bar. She had to dash off to make curtain-up for her own show but made sure she gave me a great big hug once I came off the stage.

'Oooh you're sooo good,' she said with a beaming smile on her face, 'and your mom and dad are just adorable, what a pair of sweethearts!'

Dorrie was so effervescent and enthusiastic, how could I ever have thought she was a snake in the grass trying to trick me? I gave her a big hug right back and promised to go and see her show once I was back from Nashville. I also agreed that yes, my mum and dad were indeed a pair of sweethearts, bless them.

Just as Dorrie was leaving, Stella had appeared with a large gift bag. 'This came for you,' she'd said putting the rainbow-striped package into my hands then quickly scooting back behind the bar to serve more punters.

I wasn't sure what to expect: was this a leaving present from Stella? That didn't seem her style. Was it something from Laura to wish me good luck on my travels to Tennessee? Could Tom have arranged to send me something to calm my nerves? Due to the time difference and his work schedule in Nashville we'd only exchanged a couple of awkward fairly formal texts about arrangements for my trip. He'd let me know the flight times and said I'd be picked up at the airport. We both knew we needed to talk about stuff properly but there wasn't any point trying to do that over the phone. I'd be in Nashville soon enough, things would be easier to sort out face to face I was sure.

I'd reached inside the gift bag and pulled out ... a bottle of whisky and a monster bag of marshmallows. I'd known who it was from before I even found the note which simply read:

I'm Sorry x Robbie.

I appreciated the gesture but there wasn't time to deal with Robbie and his issues before I caught my shuttle flight from Edinburgh airport to Heathrow. But as I packed in a mild panic I'd found myself squashing the bag of marshmallows into my carry-on case. I hoped I wouldn't need an emergency supply of my favourite comfort food from home, but better to be safe than sorry.

I glanced upwards to the overhead locker above my head where I knew my secret stash was now squirrelled away and tried to resist the temptation to start tucking in immediately mid-flight. The nerves were real now I was mid-way through the nine-hour direct flight to Nashville. This. Was. Happening. I was going to perform on the biggest country music stage in the world. It was crazy. Just a few weeks ago I'd been pedalling my Dolly Parton tribute act around a few northern pubs and clubs, and through a series of weird and wonderful twists of fate I was now about to partner a true music icon in front of an audience of thousands in the home of country music. It wasn't just the music fans in the auditorium I would be singing to either, The Grand Ole Opry is a live radio show broadcast coast to coast in America and listened to all over the world. Gulp. My fingers itched to rip into my monster bag of confectionary and my taste buds yearned for their soothing, squashy sweetness. Nothing can ever feel too bad when you have a mouthful of melting marshmallows … well that's my belief, anyway.

Luckily Tom had arranged a premium economy flight for my journey. It had meant nothing to me when I'd seen the class printed on the ticket – I was only used to budget airline flights to Spain – but the 'premium' in premium economy was the word I should have concentrated on. I was thrilled to find myself in a large leather chair with oodles of leg room. A screen in the seatback in front of me offered a huge selection of film, TV show, radio and podcast options to keep me entertained, and the food was plentiful, tasty and offered regularly. I could get used to travelling like this, I thought, and it all helped to distract me from reaching for the marshmallows.

My mind did keep returning to the subject of Tom. How would it feel to see him again? Would he be waiting for me at the airport? I thought it was unlikely he'd be standing at the gate with a large bouquet and a soppy expression like he was auditioning for a part in a remake of *Love Actually*. I didn't actually want him to, I realised now. It wasn't his style and it would be far too embarrassing for him as a famous musician but also for me too. I'd rather not have the pressure of a public reunion under the circumstances, much better to wait until we could see each other in private. I just hoped it would turn out better than our last meeting in my flat. I'd been desperate to see Tom then, having only just realised that I was falling in love with him, but that hadn't helped at all, and instead of rushing into each other's arms it had all unravelled into a spectacular mess.

So now I was spending the flight time trying to hold my emotions in check and not get too caught up in how much I longed to see Tom again. I knew how I felt but I needed to give him time to reveal his true feelings to me. After talking to Laura it seemed there was something I didn't know, something he was keeping from me. I needed to give him time to reveal whatever it was before I gave away how hard I was falling. Self-preservation was the key now, because just like Dorrie had so astutely observed, Tom Coltrane was the kind of guy who could break your heart, even if he didn't mean to.

I emerged through security at Nashville Airport to see a smartly dressed woman in a grey two-piece trouser suit holding a card with the name REBA MOON printed on it. Tom had sent a driver in a limo to pick me up and Dawn explained that while Mr Coltrane was tied up with filming commitments she'd been instructed to take me to my hotel. There was that word again – commitments. And they usually seemed to be the kind that kept us apart.

I hadn't known until that moment what the arrangements were going to be for my visit, whether I was going to be staying in a hotel or if Tom would be inviting me to stay with him in his Nashville home. I remembered seeing the photograph of Tom's beautiful white clapboard house and felt a twinge of disappointment I wouldn't be heading straight there. But then I reasoned that given the circumstances Tom may have felt it would be pretty presumptuous to expect me to stay there without asking me first if I was okay with that. I decided to focus on the fact that Tom was being a gentleman and appreciate it. I also realised that due to time differences we had landed in Nashville just after midnight local time and very early morning my time. The flight had departed Heathrow at 9.30 p.m. and I had slept a little on the plane but I was pretty exhausted right now.

'Mr Coltrane said I was to take you straight to the hotel now as he thought you'd be tired and would need to rest. He'll see you tomorrow,' Dawn told me as she manoeuvred the large luxury car out of the airport and headed onto the freeway.

I gazed out into the darkness spotting only enormous road signs and occasional bright lights. This was my very first visit to America but I couldn't get any true sense of where I was in the world. I was itching to explore this incredible place I'd always longed to see but right now going straight to bed sounded like the best idea. I'd heard that keeping to the time schedule of the place you were in was the best way to avoid jet lag. Hopefully if I went to bed now I should be fresh as a daisy in the morning and could reunite with Tom bright-eyed and wearing fresh clothes instead of my travelling comfies: that seemed like a smart move for several reasons.

Just twenty minutes after leaving the airport the limo swept into the impressive entrance drop-off area of The Opryland Resort Hotel. Dawn told me The Grand Ole Opry itself was 'right next door' but I was already learning that Americans used our quaint English expressions very loosely. Opryland was a vast complex covering several acres and no matter how much I craned my neck I had zero chance of spotting The Opry theatre 'next door'.

Once inside the hotel I felt like Dorothy Gale from *The Wizard of Oz* stepping out of her little house after a tornado had dropped it in a strange and magical land somewhere over the rainbow. The 'hotel' I was staying in wasn't a hotel in any sense I had ever experienced before. Beyond reception it opened up into a series of vast glass atriums each with a different landscaped theme! As the concierge led me to my room it was like I was wandering through an illustration in a children's storybook. There were picture-perfect buildings of all different sizes surrounded by lush vegetation and a series of bridges and walkways over streams and waterfalls. A beautiful New Orleans-style building on an island housed a full-sized library, other pastel-painted houses contained shops, cafes and restaurants. In my befuddled state I wasn't sure I would ever find my way through the maze of bridges and tunnels to discover all the various attractions being pointed out to me. I truly knew I wasn't in Edinburgh anymore when a full-size riverboat sailed past along the waterway.

'Am I in Disneyland?'

The young man smiled as I gazed around at the five stories of balconied rooms surrounding the Toy Town-style buildings and tropical jungle. 'I like to think it's more like a Hollywood backlot,' he answered. 'That way I can pretend I'm the hero of the movie when I'm showing folk around.' With that, he handed me a small folded map of the inside of the hotel to help me find my way to breakfast the next morning. He was no Tom Cruise but in that moment he became a hero to me.

My room was gorgeous, with a fabulous view from the balcony over the mini world below, but as soon as I spotted the bed I wasn't really interested in any of the cool features like coffee machines or rainfall showers that Carter the wannabe movie star was trying to point out to me. I tipped him generously and he gave me a *Top Gun*-style salute as he left. Cute, but I was doubtful I would ever cross paths with Carter again in the vastness of The Opryland Resort.

The next morning, I consulted my map and then set out to locate breakfast as though I was embarking on a major expedition. Maybe it was a good map or maybe it was just my intense desire for fresh coffee and hot bacon rolls but my mission was extremely successful. I soon had a waitress showing me to my table situated on a tiny island beneath a mountain of rocks with a series of hot springs spritzing and gushing all around me. Carter was right, the place did feel like a movie set, and today I felt like an extra in *The Flintstones* – yabba-dabba-do – this place could make someone feel slightly insane.

My need to eat had been top priority once I'd opened my eyes: I was starving. I'd slept pretty well but I was showered and dressed and sitting down for breakfast by 7.30 a.m. so I wasn't too surprised I hadn't yet heard from Tom. I was on my second cup of coffee when I felt my phone vibrate in my bag – it was a message from Dawn asking me what time I could be ready for her to pick me up? I didn't want to waste a moment. I'd come all this way and as gorgeous and hilarious as I was finding The Opryland Resort I wanted to get out into the realness of Tennessee now. I'd also started to ache to see Tom, it was like I could almost sense the nearness of him now I was on his patch. Nashville was his American home and I badly wanted to see if he was the same here as I remembered him on his home turf.

I quickly texted back saying I could be ready by 9 a.m. I hoped that wasn't too early but I was raring to go and I was already dressed in Nashville-appropriate attire. I wanted to be comfortable in the Southern summer heat but I also wanted to look the part in the home of country music. My strapless white cotton prairie summer dress would keep me cool and the flared skirt ended just above my tan suede western ankle boots. I wore a blue denim waistcoat worn open over the dress and tied back my hair, which was now a mane of wild red waves, with a green cowboy-style neckerchief. I was ready for Nashville, I just needed to find out … was Nashville ready for me?

Chapter Twenty-Seven

No sooner had I settled into the air-conditioned comfort of my chauffeured limousine than driver Dawn threw me a complete curve ball. She wasn't taking me to see Tom right away after all. Instead he'd arranged for me to visit The Country Music Hall of Fame Museum in downtown Nashville. Huh?

Dawn quickly explained that Tom would be tied up with work until early afternoon but he'd thought I would enjoy spending my first few waking hours in the cradle of country absorbing all the musical history the museum had to offer. Hmmm. It was hard to be disappointed for too long. A morning at my leisure wandering through the magical memories contained in the museum sounded like a perfect way to begin my Nashville experience.

'Once you're done I'm to take you to meet Mr Coltrane out at his home in Brentwood, if that's okay, Miss Moon?'

My stomach lurched with excitement on hearing that and I happily told Dawn that would be perfect, so long as she dropped the Miss Moon and called me Reba. Dawn simply nodded politely but didn't look too keen on being more friendly.

I had a few hours to submerge myself in the incredible immersive experience of the museum but the truth was I could have spent days there and it really wouldn't have been long enough.

I began in the enormous and impressive Hall of Fame rotunda, a stunning circular space where name plaques of all the famous inductees were exhibited all around. Beneath the glass dome high above me golden lettering spelled out 'Will the Circle Be Unbroken' echoing the lyrics of the well-known song and symbolising the unbroken circle of country music from its origins right up until today.

Standing within the impressive ring of all those amazing artists that had gone before me I felt welcomed and cradled by a community of artists, performers and musicians. Everywhere I looked I saw names familiar and dear to me … Johnny Cash, The Carter Family, Willy Nelson, Chet Atkins, Patsy Cline, The Jordanaires, Kris Kristofferson, Tammy Wynette … everywhere I looked a music legend was looking down on me, including Dolly herself of course.

There was so much to take in throughout the museum but I lingered by the Nudie Suits and Boots exhibit, where each item of stage wear designed by Nudie's Rodeo Tailors was more intricate and ornate than the last. I particularly loved the cream suit with black music notes on the lapel worn by Hank Williams and the garish blue suit embellished with embroidered covered wagons and desert scenery made for Dolly Parton's former singing partner Porter Wagoner. I knew Porter had been the older, established music star who had given Dolly a big break on his own TV show in the 1960s by inviting her to perform a guest spot every week. With his blond pompadour hair and love for elaborate western clothing, Porter was a very big deal in country music; in fact, he was known for years as 'Mr Grand Ole Opry' he appeared on the show so many times. I'd read all about how Dolly's own fame had grown and their working relationship became difficult but I'd always thought about them as almost mythical figures. Suddenly, looking at their actual outfits, I realised they were real people, making the kind of tough decisions real life throws at you, whether you're a star or not. Porter's wagon suit stood in front of me now, the rhinestones and beads glittering across the sky-blue jacket and two embroidered rifles decorating the outsides of the suit pant legs, and I imagined how imposing a figure Porter Wagoner must have been in his 1970s heyday. It must have taken a lot of courage to stand up to him but Dolly had found her own unique and tactful way. What a woman she truly was.

As I moved along the Nudie costumes I was enjoying learning some of the names of artists I wasn't so familiar with, each one more perfect than the next for a country music star … Hank Garland … Lefty Frizzell … Johnny Dollar … were any of their names real, I wondered, or did they have the colourful imagination of their managers to thank for gifting them a perfect stage name? I didn't think it mattered whether the names were attributed at birth or adopted much later, a good stage name was a good stage name however it came about. Elvis Presley and Dolly Parton had been lucky enough to be born with uniquely perfect stage-ready monikers thanks to their parents, and I supposed I fell somewhere in between in the stage-name stakes. Mum and Dad had christened me Rebecca Mooney and called me Becky but I'd only had to adapt it slightly to create my stage persona – Reba Moon. I tried to imagine a costume I had worn being exhibited one day just like these with my name on a little sign next to it. Or perhaps a plaque in the rotunda announcing the induction of Reba Moon into the Country Music Hall of Fame? I was getting carried away but I had to admit my name now sounded like it fitted the role pretty perfectly.

I wasn't at all surprised to discover a variety of artefacts and references connected to Dolly Parton throughout the museum including costume items, a selection of awards and even some handwritten song lyrics, but one particular Dolly exhibit stopped me in my tracks. Alongside a few more personal items and mementoes of her childhood in Pigeon Forge were a couple of Dolly's old schoolbooks and as I peered into the glass cabinet I spotted her full name written in girlish handwriting ... Dolly Rebecca Parton. Dolly Parton's middle name was Rebecca? How did I not know this? Why had no one ever mentioned I shared my given name with the true queen? Maybe everyone presumed I knew? Did my mum and dad know? Had I been named in Dolly's honour or was it just a weird coincidence? It sent a tingle down my spine to discover this extra connection between us, especially as I'd found out right here, in Nashville.

Time was getting on and I decided to head to the museum cafe to grab something to eat before it was time for Dawn to pick me up and take me over to see Tom. The anticipation was giving me butterflies so I didn't have a huge appetite but I thought it was best to eat a little before setting off. The trouble with that plan was American menus don't really cater for small appetites; the all-day breakfasts, sandwiches and salads all looked huge and came with a variety of garnishes and sides. I chose the avocado toast which arrived topped with pesto, tomatoes and Swiss cheese. It was quite delicious but I could only eat about half of it.

After my lunch Dawn texted to say she was waiting down on Demonbreun Street to pick me up and I was soon back in the car heading over to Tom's Nashville home. I tried to relax and enjoy the ride, taking in the scenery and letting myself finally get excited to see Tom again. I couldn't help it. As much as I wanted to keep my cool, my emotions in check and my desires under control, I now just longed to see him again. I'd missed him so much. Would it be the same Tom that I'd spent so much time with in Edinburgh? We'd got to know each other first in the privacy of his hotel suite when the intensity between us had been intimate and occasionally delightfully indecent. I almost blushed to remember what we had got up to although I didn't regret a single second. Then when we were hanging out with Laura and Fergus at Forthview House I'd experienced a more casual side of Tom; relaxed, friendly and fun. I hadn't been concerned with how famous Tom was because it wasn't related to the person I got to know. Even when we moved into the recording studio and I'd seen close up how extraordinarily talented he was, the main thing I noticed was his drive and professionalism. He'd been so generous, encouraging me to explore my own musicality as a singer and as a songwriter and he made me feel so safe and secure helping me to finally face my stage fright fears and become a more confident version of myself. Falling in love with him had been so easy, not only because of how he made me feel about him … but because of how he made me feel about myself too.

I tried to hold onto that new, confident and self-assured version of myself now as the limo left the built-up Nashville city limits and headed out into the greener landscape of meadows and woodland surrounding the picturesque suburbs.

After about twenty minutes the car slowed and we headed up a tree-lined drive to a large pair of ornate metal gates. A sign gave the house name as 'Braveheart' which made me smile as I knew it must be inspired by the film. Tom might look and sound like an all-American singing cowboy but he clearly never forgot his Scottish roots.

I craned my neck to see ahead as Dawn punched a code into the entry system but as the electronic gates swung open to let us in all I could see were trees and hedges with splashes of red and pink blooms exploding out of the dense green foliage.

The car crunched its way slowly forward across the gravel and as the driveway curved ahead of us I got my first glimpse of the house Tom called home. It appeared even more beautiful than the picture he'd shown me on his phone when we were at a greasy spoon in Edinburgh.

The white clapboard house with triangular pointed facade was nestled snugly in its own verdant copse of trees, bushes and flowers. It really was the very definition of picturesque.

Four wide stone steps led up to a deep front porch with a galleried balcony above held up by four white stone pillars. It looked inviting and friendly but impressive too … just like Tom himself, I thought! I couldn't wait to jump out of the car, run up the steps and hopefully straight into Tom's welcoming arms.

I had my hand on the lever to open the car door when Dawn turned in the driver seat to say, 'Tom is running just a little late but I can let you in. He says to make yourself right at home and he'll be along soon.'

'Ah, right, okay.' I tried not to appear too crushed by the constant stream of setbacks that were preventing my reunion with Tom. I hoped the delayed gratification would be worth it in the end.

Once she'd unlocked the heavy wooden door and pushed it open Dawn simply gestured for me to go inside then wished me a 'good day, Miss Moon' and went back to the car. I watched in amazement as she slowly drove away leaving me completely alone inside the house.

I quietly closed the door and then turned around on the spot taking everything in. I was dying to look around and at least now I had a good opportunity to be nosy while I was here on my own. I was struck at once by how naturally beautiful the house was with polished wooden floors and a mix of white stucco walls and exposed brickwork. The reception hallway was breathtaking and yet welcoming. I stood beneath a burnished bronze hoop chandelier with twinkling golden lights, on one side of me stood a large shiny black grand piano. On the other side, behind a pair of black ornamental metal gates, was a book-lined space created to look like a snug, with huge comfy armchairs and a cream fluffy rug.

Straight ahead was a wide, cream-carpeted central staircase with a white stucco archway either side. I presumed the arches would lead to the main living space so I decided to take a peak. If the entrance hall had taken my breath away what I discovered next blew my mind. The space behind the staircase opened up into a cavernous room with a pointed ceiling that must have been at least thirty feet high making it feel like a cross between a barn and a church. Despite it being a jaw-dropping space, as I looked around the open-plan kitchen, dining and living room zones it also felt warm and homely. Natural sunlight flooded in from the huge floor to ceiling windows making the bright touches of colour here and there really pop and glow. The kitchen area over to my left was a mixture of distressed turquoise cabinets, polished black marble surfaces and mango wood cabinets. It was completely gorgeous. On the opposite side was a full-size pool table and I was thrilled to see a vintage Wurlitzer juke box standing against the exposed brick wall. Right in front of me was a large rustic dining table with twelve high-backed chairs covered in patterned Navajo Indian tapestry upholstery sitting beneath a low-slung wagon wheel pendant light.

I moved around the dining table to discover a sunken seating area filled with squashy brown leather sofas and piles of soft tartan cushions that looked incredibly inviting.

It was hard to tear my eyes away from examining every corner of the room, everywhere I looked there was something interesting to discover. Colourful artwork, quirky mementoes, a rack of guitars, an almost life-sized painting of a majestic stag on a Scottish mountainside surrounded by swathes of purple heather. I could sense Tom's presence and feel his personality in every choice that had been made about the furniture and decor inside Braveheart. I wasn't sensing anything but Tom in this home, the colours, the vibe, the artistic and musical influences … if anyone else had made decisions about how to decorate here I wasn't feeling that at all. I also loved the fact that for all its luxury this was a such an easy space to be in. The open-plan nature of the room, the flow from the kitchen to the dining area, the playful spaces to the chill-out sofas, it all worked so well and would be such a cool, relaxing, fun place to hang out. I really hoped I would have the chance to spend some time here.

That said, I was getting an acute sense of just how rich and famous Tom Coltrane must be to have such a home. A place like this would not come cheap but could only be afforded by someone who had achieved a huge amount of worldwide success. I'd already known Tom was a big deal, of course, but here was the actual evidence right in front of my eyes.

Just as I was thinking about Tom 'the rockstar' my eye caught a flash of brilliant blue outside the window and I spotted a huge oval swimming pool and decorative outdoor dining cabana with lush green lawns beyond.

'Wow,' I breathed the word to myself.

The more I looked around, the more I wanted to see more. How long had it been since Dawn had dropped me off here? I guessed not more than fifteen minutes or so. I hadn't got a clue how much longer I would have to wait before Tom came back. Did I have time to take a quick look upstairs? Should I? Dare I?

There were a couple of arched wooden doorways off the main living space that might well have led to a downstairs bathroom ... or two ... but I decided to pretend I hadn't noticed those and instead headed back to the entrance hallway to make my way upstairs on the pretext of looking for the loo.

The central stairway was carpeted in plush cream so I hesitated with my foot on the first step and looked down at my trusty suede ankle boots. It was one thing to wander around someone's house when they weren't there, snooping and sneaking about behind their back, it was quite another to do so while wearing your outdoor shoes. I wasn't a philistine, for heaven's sake!

I slipped my boots off, placed them neatly to one side of the stairs and padded my way silently up to the galleried landing above. There was a white stucco archway both to my left and to my right so I had to plump for one wing of the house or the other to explore. I went right and opened a couple of doors to discover a room set up as a study and music room and a storeroom full of flight cases, luggage and suit carriers. I presumed this was the place everything got dumped after a tour.

Next, I found what I was ostensibly looking for: a bathroom. It was huge and fully tiled in an eye-catching Art Deco design of pale green and black. A sparkling white roll top bath on claw feet stood in front of a window draped in diaphanous fabric and a huge scalloped mirror hung over the double sink. I moved across the floor feeling like an extra in a Hollywood movie and checked out my reflection in the mirror. The setting was so spectacular I was praying I didn't look too shabby in these luxurious surroundings. I was reassured to see my white dress and denim waistcoat still looked okay and actually made me look quite at home in a country music mansion. The soft lighting through the window made my red hair glimmer but my face did look a little flushed. I ran the tap and splashed some cold water on my wrists and neck to cool myself but it was as I turned off the tap I thought I heard a noise.

I froze at the sink, my hand still on the tap and strained my ears to listen, maybe I'd imagined it. But then I heard the unmistakable sound of the front door being slammed shut. The first thing I'd heard must have been the sound of the front door opening.

Okay, this was it. The moment I'd been waiting for had finally arrived. Tom was home and we'd soon be face to face. No, I realised, that wasn't enough, what I really wanted right now was for us to be in each other's arms. I checked myself over again, slipped my hair out of its pony tail and shook it loose. I dampened the material slightly and tied the scarf cowgirl-style around my neck to keep me cool. That was better.

I quickly made my way back across the landing and started to descend the staircase. It wasn't a bad way to make an entrance, stepping lightly down the stairs with my white dress swirling around me. I'd never felt more like a romantic muse; maybe Tom would write a song about this moment one day, the moment he saw me again after we'd been forced apart and realised that he loved me, couldn't live without me, that we were meant to be together, forever.

I was getting carried away again, so much for keeping my emotions in check, but when I'd thought I might never see Tom again in person it had been so hard to bear. I knew now that I'd never felt this way about anyone before. I was so into Tom it hurt and being in his house, feeling his presence all around me, had intensified my feelings so much I was throbbing with desire to see him again.

I was halfway down the stairs when a figure stepped into the shaft of sunlight shining through the transom window above the door. But it wasn't Tom illuminated in the spotlight before me. It was Juliana Ripon.

Chapter Twenty-Eight

I stopped as though I'd been electrocuted, my hand gripping the curved bannister, my bare feet rooted to the spot in the deep-pile stair carpet. Face to face with a glamorous Hollywood actress I felt like a Beverley Hillbilly in my cotton sundress and no-shoes state. It wasn't simply my clothing that was making me feel uncomfortable, it was my appearance in general; here I was, halfway down the stairs in Tom Coltrane's Nashville mansion, what must Juliana Ripon be thinking?

She eyed me coldly, her huge dark eyes taking in everything from my naked toes to my dishevelled hair. Despite the fact I was looking down on her from my vantage point several steps up I did not feel like I had the upper hand in this situation. Shocked and horrified as I was in that moment I couldn't help being impressed by how beautiful Juliana was in the flesh. Her black hair was short and glossy and her sulky pout was accentuated with dark red lipstick. She was dressed simply but expensively in skin-tight black leather pants and her casually worn oversized silk shirt the colour of buttermilk was falling off one pale skinny shoulder.

'T…t…Tom's not here,' I eventually managed to stutter, trying to force my feet to move.

'I know that,' Juliana snapped. 'I thought it was time you and I had a little chat. Rebecca.'

She spat out my name as though it was poison in her mouth. So she knew who I was. Uh oh. But how did she know I was here alone? How could she? My mind was cartwheeling but I realised too late I'd been betrayed, perhaps even set up … Dawn the driver! It had to be. Perhaps she and Juliana were close, maybe she felt Tom's ex-girlfriend deserved her moment to confront the woman who had 'stolen her man' and so had tipped her off that I was here alone waiting for Tom to come home. An act of female solidarity between women who considered me to be a traitor to the sisterhood.

I wanted to defend myself. But how? I didn't have a complete grasp of all the facts and now I found myself quite literally on the spot I was furious with myself for not making Tom explain exactly what the situation between him and Juliana was. Tom! The thought of him made another question smack me right between the eyes; was he really on his way? Did he even know I was here waiting for him?

Juliana appeared to have more information than I did about that. 'We haven't got long,' she said, 'so I'll get right to the point …' But then she hesitated and didn't get right to the point at all; instead she stood tapping one tiny stilettoed foot on the hardwood floor in obvious irritation. 'Are you going to come down here and face me? You're giving me a crick in my neck staying up there.'

I padded down the last few steps and loitered by the marble bannister wishing I could pull my boots back on; being barefoot was making me feel even more vulnerable. I wanted to push my feet back into my discarded boots, kick up my heels and run for my life down the driveway, flee from Braveheart like a complete coward. But run where? I had no idea where I was and it would take me a good while to even reach the main road ... and then what? I had no choice. I had to stay exactly where I was and face the music.

Once we were face to face Juliana wasted no more time before making crystal clear exactly what she thought of me. According to her I had thrown myself at Tom and he'd merely submitted in a moment of weakness.

'As if he'd look twice at someone like you if he was in his right mind,' she said witheringly. 'For fucksake, just look at you! How old are you anyway? Forty?'

She was a cheeky little cow although I chose not to say so. I certainly did feel plain and ancient compared to her twenty-something luminous beauty but I don't expect fans of her films have ever seen her features twisted into such nasty expressions. Close up and personal it wasn't too pretty. I also suspected her enviable perky bosom was the result of surgical implants, something I'd never felt the need to resort to despite my lack of natural attributes in that department.

As Juliana Ripon ripped into me I decided to keep my mouth shut and take my medicine as politely as possible. Words like 'desperate', 'mistake' and 'bitch' rattled off the rafters above us while the confrontation continued although it felt like Juliana was being made even more angry by my hesitation to defend myself and give her the satisfaction of a real showdown. To be honest, my mind was otherwise engaged as it recalibrated from the disappointment of not finding Tom waiting for me with open arms. I was also pondering what Juliana had been alluding to when she'd said Tom might not have been in his 'right mind'? What had she meant by that? I could have just dismissed it as another low-blow attack, an attempt to undermine the validity of my relationship with Tom, but it had a ring of truth about it I couldn't ignore. I knew Tom had returned to Edinburgh in an emotional state. He was struggling with issues to do with his fame and career, and had confided some of his thoughts about it all to me. He was worried he'd fallen out of love with music but I'd helped him see it was really the music *industry* he was having such a problem with. We hadn't delved too deeply into all that but I did know that hanging out with me and spending time in the studio with Fergus had clearly rekindled Tom's passion for writing and performing. I think focusing on helping me defeat my stage fright and reinvent myself as Reba Moon had also taken his mind off his own problems and given him a new zest for future projects too.

I couldn't possibly explain any of that to Juliana and even if I had I don't think it would have made much difference. According to her she and Tom were made for each other and I was just a meaningless fling with delusions of grandeur. Was she right?

I'd thought I needed to see Tom badly before but now I was increasingly desperate to hear the crunch of car wheels on gravel and know he was about to walk through his own front door and explain what the hell was really going on! He'd insisted I'd had 'nothing to worry about' as far as his beautiful Hollywood girlfriend was concerned. Well it didn't bloody feel like that right now! He'd intimated it was all over between them and I'd believed him. Had I simply fallen for the oldest trick in the book? Heard what I'd wanted to hear? It was certainly looking that way and as the onslaught from Juliana continued I had to face the possibility that I'd never been anything other than an inconsequential bit on the side, like a foolish fan or a grubby groupie. If Juliana's intention was to shame me it was starting to work.

As my stomach grew increasingly queasy and my skin prickled with fear Juliana delivered the killer blow.

'I don't suppose Tom has mentioned that he's asked me to marry him?' Her blue eyes were like shards of cut glass and her voice was as sharp as an ice pick. My blood instantly ran cold. 'No, I thought not.'

Juliana finally appeared satisfied that her mission was complete but as she turned towards the door and started to leave I finally found my voice. 'Juliana,' I said, the name of the movie star actress sounding strange coming from my own lips but I needed to tell her, 'I'm sorry.'

She gave me a pitying look and exited the scene with a final slam of the door.

The noise reverberated around the entrance hall and the inside of my head. The house I'd felt so welcomed by now seemed hostile and my overwhelming desire was to leave as soon as possible. But where could I head for? I wanted to leave but I had nowhere to go. For a split second I fantasised about standing my ground and waiting for Tom to come home so I could give him a piece of my mind. But my mind was in turmoil and if I didn't get away as quickly as possible

I knew I was going to break down and I didn't want to cry now, not here and not when Tom may come back any moment and find me. I couldn't bear it.

My brain was whirling, bile rising in my throat while I tried to work out what to do but then I heard a pinging noise and I remembered I'd left my bag on the dining table in the living room. Was Tom messaging me? Was he letting me know he was on his way and would be here soon? I darted through the archway and snatched the phone from my bag. But it wasn't messages from Tom that I found. Instead I was confronted by a screenshot of the back office of Grayson's Jewellery Shop. It took me a beat or two to realise what I was looking at. It was a picture captured from the CCTV footage that showed me 'stealing' expensive items from my former workplace. There was a message with it: *'Wait until the whole world knows that you are a jewellery thief!'* What the …? Even in my disorientated state I knew this was a direct threat. There was no name on the message and I didn't recognise the number it came from but clearly someone intended to wreck my chances of success. I knew I hadn't ever stolen anything but a picture can tell a thousand words and this particular picture along with any accusations made could cause me enormous damage.

That did it. I had to get out of there. I pulled on my boots, wrenched open the front door and looked at the phone still in my hand, but I knew I couldn't call Tom's driver Dawn. I ran like an escaped convict down the long driveway and by the time I reached the gates my getaway car was drawing up outside. The Uber app had been my saviour and once I'd picked up my luggage from the hotel I'd get it to take me straight to the airport. My time in Nashville was already over.

Chapter Twenty-Nine

I spent the many hours it took to get back to Edinburgh in a state of utter despair about what I had left behind and total panic about what lay ahead of me.

Crammed into a middle seat between two strangers in economy class I'd stuck on a pair of headphones and pretended to be asleep for most of the transatlantic flight but I couldn't kid myself that sleep would come. Instead my mind kept going over and over so many questions. The main one was how I could possibly have got myself into such a terrible situation? The man I was completely in love with was engaged to be married to someone else and if that wasn't heartbreaking enough I'd had to walk away, not only from him, but from a chance in a lifetime to appear on the biggest stage in country music. If I thought about how it might have felt to stand on the famous circle cut from the historic Ryman Auditorium Theatre stage and perform at The Grand Ole Opry a sharp stabbing pain would pierce my heart and make my blood freeze in my veins. The horror of turning my back on that opportunity was something I suspected I may never be able to recover from.

The other matter keeping me awake and causing my stomach to tie itself into knots was wanting to know who was planning to expose me as a jewellery thief? I knew I had committed no crime but people can be very quick to believe what they see and even quicker to judge. If the CCTV footage of me stashing the expensive watches, rings, necklaces and other property belonging to Grayson's Jewellers was made public my reputation would be tarnished forever. There would be no chance of me landing a recording contract and I could kiss goodbye to any hopes of making it as an even moderately successful singer. The truth isn't always enough for some people, social media commentary will more often take the 'no smoke without fire' route. In some twisted way I thought that perhaps it was better I had received the threatening message *before* I had accompanied Tom to The Opry than afterwards. His career didn't need to be blighted with involvement in my murky mess. Yes, I wish he had been more honest with me about how serious things were between him and Juliana but I had gone to bed with him willingly and with my eyes open, so to speak. I'd known he was a famous musician with links to a Hollywood actress and I hadn't expected any sort of exclusivity at the start. I'd told myself it was just a bit of fun. I'd thought I was being so mature, so worldly wise, getting my kicks and then moving on, but of course affairs of the heart are never so straightforward. I hadn't meant to fall in love and I'd deluded myself that our liaison had developed into something more substantial for him too. Well now at least I knew the truth about that and where I stood in the world of Tom Coltrane. I was devastated and upset but more with myself than I really was with Tom. I didn't think he deserved to have his career wrecked by bad publicity by being linked with me. That was part of the reason I had bolted so fast.

Getting over Tom and my missed opportunity in Nashville would have to go on the back burner for now, however, while I wrestled with the issue of who was planning on doing something so despicable as releasing the jewellery shop footage to the media? The obvious candidate was Guy Grayson. He was the one who had framed me in the first place after all. Was he still not content? Was he on a mission to destroy me altogether? It seemed incredible that he was still not satisfied that he'd done enough to hurt me.

As I'd feigned sleep on the aeroplane a couple of other names had also suggested themselves to me as possible candidates behind the despicable threat. The first was Juliana of course. The woman had just revealed herself as my mortal enemy after accusing me of attempting to steal her man. There was nothing as dangerous as a woman scorned and Juliana's dislike and distrust of me had been obvious. Had she researched my past and uncovered something she could use against me? She might not have been sure she had done enough to run me out of town by revealing that she and Tom were engaged. What if I had been more brazen and not so easily intimidated? Sending the text right after storming out might have been her masterstroke. I already knew she wasn't working alone, Dawn the driver had tipped her off about where she could find me, perhaps they were in cahoots over this too?

My third and final suspect was Robbie. I felt a sense of shame in suspecting my former partner, a man I had always considered to be a good friend, but I'd also seen clear evidence of his jealousy, and jealousy was the emotion most likely to turn someone into a monster.

Robbie and I had split up and then he'd discovered I'd replaced him in my bed with the world-famous country music star Tom Coltrane. Ouch! That must have hurt his pride. No man wants to think they can be so easily replaced and certainly not by someone so talented and desirable that girls all over the world have posters of them on their walls! Not only that but I'd made an instant success of Sonny's Bar while he was struggling with his new job in Peterborough and that must have really rubbed salt into the wound. When he had scoffed at my make-over and joked about how I now looked with my newly dyed hair and more adventurous clothes all I'd heard was echoes of the mockery I had endured in my youth and I'd seen red. But I now realised that Robbie had lashed out because of how hurt he was feeling. I wasn't excusing his behaviour but I was beginning to understand it better.

I figured either Juliana or Robbie could have got to Calum Crutchley. It was possible the young solicitor could have been charmed by Juliana or tricked by Robbie into spilling the beans on my past behaviour and then used the evidence for their own ends.

So that left me with three possible candidates for the person who wanted to destroy me; Guy, Juliana or Robbie. How had I become someone with multiple enemies? But even if I could figure out which one of them it was and narrow the list down to just one name I wasn't any closer to working out what I was going to do about it.

Luckily it turned out that I didn't have to. By the time I arrived back in Edinburgh, weary, worried and overwrought, Stella and Dorrie had put their clever heads together and come up with a cunning plan to save me.

'Let me get this straight,' I said, my mind boggling with what they had just tried to explain as we all sat in the deserted basement bar of Sonny's, 'this plan of yours to defeat my arch enemy involves a contortionist, a hypnotist and a ventriloquist?' I shook my head trying to clear my jet-lagged brain. It was almost comical that I thought Dorrie had just said those words: of course that was impossible, but I was also finding it impossible to figure out what else she might have said that had sounded just like that?

Dorrie nodded. 'Yup, that's exactly what I said.' Ahh. She went on to say that as soon as Stella had called her and told her what was going on she'd known just what to do.

Stella looked from one to the other of us with a solemn look on her face. I'd called her from Nashville airport to tell her the edited highlights, or rather the gloomy lowlights of my aborted trip to Tennessee. I'd started with the shock news about Tom's engagement to Juliana Ripon at which point she'd sworn heavily and cursed them both. When I then explained about the picture message I'd received and the threats to expose me as a jewel thief she'd insisted I forward her the messages. I think she'd called Dorrie before I'd even boarded the plane and now here we were seated around a table like three mafiosos in an episode of *The Sopranos*. Sonny's Bar was now the Bada Bing Club and we were hatching a plan to wreak revenge on a sworn rival. What. Was. Happening?

'I knew she was our girl,' Stella said nodding sagely as she clapped Dorrie on the back. 'As soon as I filled her in she swung into action. Aren't you glad you've got us on your team?'

I wasn't sure how to respond to that. The world appeared to have shifted on its axis and, now Stella and Dorrie were instant best buds, they had embroiled me in a complicated plot to neutralise my nemesis and I was struggling to process where a hypnotist, a contortionist and a ventriloquist came into the equation. I had to presume that this was exactly what a nervous breakdown felt like.

'You're looking a bit confused,' Dorrie said.

'Oh. You think?' I shouldn't have snapped at her but seriously, one of us was clearly crazy and the thought that it was probably me was making me quite tetchy.

'D'you want me to go over it all again?' She spoke to me now like I was a small child trying to remember what the big hand on a clock was for.

I swallowed back the retort I was desperate to give and instead answered meekly, 'Yes please.'

Stella and Dorrie took turns to fill me in, fleshing out the detail of their convoluted plot. Somehow, between the two of them they managed to make it all sound slightly more sensible second time around. Both of them were convinced the traitor out to get me was Guy. Robbie could be dumb but would never be so devious and to think Juliana had tracked down the Scottish footage from the States was a stretch that even Dorrie's contortionist mate Tatiana would struggle to achieve. (I hadn't imagined it; there was indeed a contortionist now involved in the latest bizarre chapter of my life.)

'Tatiana has already made contact with our mark,' Stella informed me, sounding increasingly like an undercover cop in a B movie. 'Guy Grayson is such a sleazebag he actually fell for her spiel, just like Dorrie knew he would.'

'Tatiana's skills aren't limited to bending herself into ridiculously impossible positions or folding herself into a small carry-on piece of hand luggage.' Dorrie paused while I think we all imagined a grown woman concertinaed into a flight case ... she took a breath and then carried on, 'She's from Eastern Europe, speaks with a deliciously husky accent and has charms no red-blooded man would be able to resist. Once she made a play for Guy he was putty in her hands.'

So the talented Tatiana had apparently made it her mission to convince Guy she fancied him and then set up a time and place for them to meet for a date. Guy was so arrogant he appeared to take the pass she made at him completely at face value, presumably thinking this gorgeous, young, mysterious woman found him completely irresistible. But the date was a honeytrap, a way to lure Guy away from the jewellery shop where Tatiana had posed as a regular customer and into a world unfamiliar to him, a place peopled by performers, speciality acts and creative artistes. Dorrie had collected them all together for a showdown performance the like of which had never been seen before during Edinburgh Fringe Festival, or indeed anywhere else.

Once Stella and Dorrie had finally finished describing how Guy Grayson would eventually be exposed and his threat against me neutralised, I didn't know whether to laugh or break into spontaneous applause. I did a little of both while also asking, 'It's a brilliant, if bonkers plan … d'you really think it could work?'

Dorrie looked a little hurt at my lack of confidence but Stella fixed me with a steely look. 'What other choice d'you have?'

She was right. The plan was on. It sounded like the start of a joke delivered by one of the many up-and-coming comedians trying to get a break in Edinburgh: *'so a contortionist, a hypnotist and a ventriloquist walk into a bar …'* But this wasn't a set piece in a stand-up comedy routine, this was my life. Tatiana the contortionist, Jeffrey the hypnotist and Freddie the vent arrived at Sonny's shortly after. Soon it would be Showdown!

Chapter Thirty

I waited nervously backstage as the audience took their seats for the Midnight Mischief Variety Show where a bunch of Dorrie's talented mates were getting ready to perform. I say 'backstage' but it was hardly more than a curtained off area in a re-purposed hotel bar – a fancy dressing room at the prestigious Grand Ole Opry it was not. The irony that I should be sound-checking in Nashville's top spot right at that moment was not lost on me. I'd checked my phone – half-hoping to find missed calls from someone stateside trying to track me down, half-relieved there weren't any.

Thoughts of the incredible opportunity I had been forced to forgo and how Tom would soon be performing 'Moonlight Home' without me had to be firmly pushed to the back of my mind. I needed to concentrate on the task in hand, the need to stop Guy Grayson in his tracks and prevent any further attempts to sabotage my life, my name and my reputation. If we could humiliate the scumbag at the same time then that would be an entertaining bonus.

My broken heart was still managing to beat pretty fast as nervous anticipation began to build. I was anxious to see if Tatiana would succeed with even the first part of the plan, getting Guy to come along to take his seat ready for a show he had no idea he was going to be part of.

There were lots of distractions around to help take my mind off my anxiety. Jeffrey the magician, or 'The Great Marveloso' as he preferred to be known on stage, was calming his own nerves by juggling assorted fruit. The sight of oranges, apples and bananas whirling around was impressive enough but when he saw me watching he gave me a wink and boasted, 'I can do it with pumpkins and pineapples too!' I wasn't sure what to say about that so I just gave him a cheesy thumbs-up. He seemed happy with that response.

I'd been so engrossed with the revolving fruit salad I'd missed the arrival of Tatiana and Guy. The first I knew that they were in the building was when Tatiana popped her head around the curtain to say hi.

'It is Reba, yes?' Tatiana's disembodied head addressed me and I nodded to the beautiful face I was confronted by. Her hair was a wild mass of black curls piled high on top of her head and tumbling down over one shoulder, her eyes accentuated by a feline winged sweep of black eyeliner. She stepped around the curtain and I took in her dancer's physique encased in a skin-tight black satin jumpsuit. A pair of sky-high strappy sandals completed her killer look and I noticed they had sparkly gold wings on the heels. I suspected Tatiana was less of an angel and more of a devil in disguise. No wonder Guy had agreed to accompany her to a late-night variety show, I reckoned she could get most men to follow her to the ends of the earth.

There was a quick chat between performers about the running order. Tatiana would be performing at the start of the show: she thought Guy would be more manageable if he'd had a glimpse of her athletic abilities early on. I peeped around the black drapes and spotted Guy immediately. With his bouffant blond bonce and checked sports coat he looked completely out of place in the diverse, slightly grungy Fringe crowd. Was this going to work? It was too late to voice my reservations. Jeffrey, sorry … 'The Great Marveloso' was already stepping onto the tiny stage and telling the audience to expect to be dazzled and amazed by what they were about to see. They should also have been warned to expect the unexpected but Marveloso kept that up his magic sleeve along with some marked playing cards and a length of silk bunting.

I had to admit, Tatiana was absolutely mesmerising when she took her place in the spotlight. Beneath her satin jumpsuit she'd been concealing a whole arsenal of lethal weapons; a tanned and toned body encased in little more than a sparkly bikini. To the sound of a pulsating backbeat she twisted herself into ever more incredible positions and I watched Guy's jaw slacken and his eyes goggle: he was transfixed. So transfixed that when The Great Marveloso made his way back to the stage through the audience, shaking hands with everyone and commenting on Tatiana's wonderful performance as he did so, Guy had no idea that his mobile phone had been lifted from his pocket with impeccable sleight of hand.

Tatiana handed me Guy's phone as soon as she stepped off stage. I felt like I was in some kind of heist movie. Jeffrey had palmed it to her as he'd held her hand for her bow and the first part of Dorrie's plan was now in play. We'd all agreed we needed more than just suspicion before we proceeded with any sort of revenge or public humiliation of Guy. Our hunch about him being behind all the nastiness aimed my way may well be correct but I wanted proof before we took things any further.

Tatiana whispered Guy's passcode to me as she zipped herself back into her jumpsuit. How she had that information I had no idea but there wasn't time to ask before she slipped back out front to take her place next to Guy for the next part of the show. As she shimmied past him in his aisle seat he was oblivious to everything but her destabilising presence.

As I tapped in the code, all the proof I needed was now in my hands. Literally. The phone contained the CCTV footage of me from the back room at Grayson's Jewellers, the vicious messages I'd received in Nashville threatening to share it plus evidence of fake social media profiles Guy had clearly created so he could post vile content and terrible reviews about Sonny's Bar. He also had several candid photos of me taken while I was walking in the street. What the …? Had he been stalking me? My number in his contacts wasn't listed under my name either, instead he'd renamed me 'Bitchface'. Nice.

'Are we on?' Stella asked as she joined me in the curtained backstage cubicle.

'Oh yes,' I told her while I seethed at Guy's unjust hatred of me. What had I ever done to him? Was I not allowed to reject his clumsy advances without suffering these ridiculous consequences? 'It's time to end this nonsense.'

Stella gave The Great Marveloso the cue he'd been waiting for and he gave ventriloquist Freddie Forsyth a big introduction. Freddie's act was hysterical; he didn't use a puppet like a children's entertainer, there wasn't a goggle-eyed teddy, a hairy monkey or a fluffy big bird to be seen anywhere. Instead, he threw his voice into inanimate objects like a wallet belonging to a guy on the front row and a handbag offered by a woman on an aisle seat. The characters he created had loads to say about their owners, not all of it complimentary, but it was so funny no one got offended. Next, he asked for a volunteer to come up on stage. I found I was holding my breath but Tatiana was ready. She was too fast for Guy, he didn't stand a chance once she threw his hand up into the air while batting her lashes at him with a pleading look he found irresistible.

Once Freddie had warmly welcomed a nervous-looking Guy onstage and tried to put him at his ease he produced a strange-looking contraption from a box I hadn't noticed before. Guy hadn't noticed it either and looked pretty alarmed but he couldn't back out now, not while the audience were looking at him and the tantalising Tatiana was watching expectantly.

None of us were quite expecting what happened next however. The weird-looking item was like a mask that covered the lower part of the face. Freddie fixed it in place with straps at the back of Guy's head and suddenly his tanned and botoxed appearance was transformed into a gormless puppet with the large mouth operated by a string pulled by Freddie.

It was impossible to read Guy's full expression with only his startled eyes now visible but I couldn't imagine he was very happy with the squeaky, effeminate voice Freddie now had him speaking in. It was so clever. Freddie was literally able to put words into Guy's mouth.

It started off with Freddie asking Guy a series of increasingly ridiculous questions about his job, marital status and hobbies. It didn't matter what Guy might have wanted to say, his mouth was covered and only the ventriloquist had access to a microphone so his was the only voice we all could hear. Thanks to Freddie and his voice trickery we learned Guy was a window-dresser in a sex shop, was single but ready to mingle and loved to spend weekends morris dancing and grooming his collection of budgerigars. The audience were splitting their sides by this point and I suspected Guy's ego was torn: on the one hand this was all very embarrassing but on the other he was probably getting off on being the star of the show.

At this point Freddie took things up another gear and declared that Guy, or 'Helluvaguy' as he had decided to nickname him, was about to be reunited with the greatest object of his desire.

'There's a very special woman in your life, isn't there, Helluvaguy?' Freddie said and while Guy shook his head back and forth in confusion he appeared to answer in a falsetto voice:

'Oooo, Mister Freddie, how d'you know about her?'

'Oh I know lots of secrets about you, Helluvaguy,' Freddie told him, adding, 'Would you like to meet the object of all your secret desires? The woman you love more than any other? Say the word and I'll bring her on stage right now.'

Beads of sweat had started to form on Guy's forehead and his eyes darted around the room trying to figure out what Freddie was driving at. I could almost hear the cogs whirring in Guy's brain as to whether Freddie was referring to Tatiana sitting in the audience, his wife JoJo ... or maybe ... somebody else?

'Oooo, yes please, Mr Freddie,' was the eager response the audience heard Guy give, despite him closing his eyes and continuing to shake his head vigorously.

With that, onto the stage stalked Dorrie, all made up as the queen of country music, Miss Dolly Parton herself.

Guy jumped as if scalded and started blinking even more rapidly. Did he think for a moment it was me, I wondered? He knew very well I'd performed as Dolly, so that might be his instant reaction. As 'Dolly' sauntered over and he got a closer look, though, he realised he didn't recognise this particular impersonator and I saw his shoulders relax. It was a mistake to be so naive.

Trapped between the two of them Guy was now a puppet and a plaything for two talented performers. Freddie pulled the strings and provided the voice to make it appear Guy was singing, while Dorrie jiggled and gyrated around him and together they performed a very special, quite ridiculous version of 'We've Got Tonight'.

By now the audience were in helpless fits but something oddly unexpected was happening on stage. As the crowd yelped with laughter and guffawed for more, Guy stopped looking quite so pained and forgot all about shaking his head as if to say 'No'. He actually started joining in. The ego on this man really was quite something. Buoyed by all the cheers he was starting to enjoy it! He swayed to the music, puffed out his chest and was even so bold, and foolish, to attempt to run his fingers up and down 'Dolly's' well upholstered body. Dorrie was quick to give his wandering hands a smart slap for that but when that elicited an even bigger response from the crowd Guy just carried on cavorting and carousing.

The applause at the end was thunderous and Guy merrily took his bow gripping the hands of Freddie and Dorrie as he did so.

When Freddie removed the vent mask from Guy's face I was astounded to see a huge grin slapped all over it. The nerve of him! He was too busy peering into the audience to see if Tatiana was in lustful raptures over his comedic capabilities to notice Dorrie wave her goodbyes to the crowd and be quickly replaced by The Great Marveloso who had reappeared, as if by magic, for the grand finale.

It was like shooting fish in a barrel, like taking candy from a baby, the ease with which Jeffrey, sorry, The Great Marveloso, was able to convince Guy to undergo hypnosis. It was utterly breathtaking. We'd all been so worried about this moment: would Guy allow himself to be put into a hypnotic trance? But in the end he rolled over like a puppy about to have his tummy tickled.

'What if he point blank refuses?' I'd asked when I'd first heard this part of the plan.

'Jeff's a bloody hypnotist! Can't he just put a spell on him or something?' Stella had retorted. But she'd had it explained to her, at great length by Jeffrey, the ethics of putting people under hypnosis on stage and how, in any case, a willing volunteer is always more susceptible to a trance-like state than somebody who is resisting.

We needn't have worried. As soon as The Great Marveloso told Guy what an absolute natural he was on stage, how much the audience were loving him and how he would be perfect for the showstopper end part of the show Guy eagerly agreed to be hypnotised.

He probably expected he was going to be made to look a bit daft, maybe do a silly dance, bark like a dog or speak in a foreign language every time Jeff said a certain trigger word. He was soaking up the laughter and the applause in equal measure and he seemed game for anything that was going to be thrown at him so he could carry on showing off to the audience and to Tatiana too, of course. There was a little bit of that sort of end-of-the-pier nonsense right at the start, The Great Marveloso did have to be sure Guy was fully under after all, but once Guy was clearly completely hypnotised the final act was revealed. The Great Marveloso revealed to the spell-bound audience that Guy was about to face a lie detector. It literally was the moment of truth.

Chapter Thirty-One

We all left the Midnight Variety Show later that night with a newfound admiration for the skill of stagecraft. The athleticism of Tatiana, the tongue-twisting skills of Freddy the Vent and the mind-meltingly fascinating work of Jeff the hypnotist all showed how hard performers work to make their incredible acts look easy. I was wowed. But more importantly, I was utterly triumphant. Guy's lies and deceit had been thoroughly exposed to an audience who were transfixed by such a dramatic turn of events. From laughing uproariously at Guy's crazy antics, they went to stunned silence as he admitted in detail all his dastardly deeds. You could have heard a pin drop as the story unravelled in front of them.

What's more, Dorrie's band of vaudeville villain-catchers had made it slick and showbiz. Jeff, or rather The Great Marveloso, had produced the mobile phone he had swiped earlier from Guy's pocket and returned it to him. He explained he hadn't stolen it but he had 'borrowed' it for a reason. One by one he repeated each of the incriminating things he had discovered on the phone and asked Guy to explain himself.

In his hypnotic state Guy had been told he was unable to lie, everything he said had to be the absolute truth. It worked like a charm. Guy didn't even look like he was trying to fight the urge to spill his guts. He readily admitted everything, from having me arrested for a crime he knew I didn't commit to writing vicious one-star reviews for Sonny's Bar on TripAdvisor.

It was decidedly strange to hear him talk about it all in such a matter of fact way. He showed no emotion but he did appear to have complete clarity about the information he was sharing. The audience held their breath as The Great Marveloso led him through the story of how he had developed such a grudge against a woman he'd worked with he'd become obsessed with doing everything he could to hurt her. The real question I wanted answering was why?

Guy gave more than one reason for hating me so much. The first was my obvious revulsion at his creepy advances which had made him feel insulted. 'I'm a good-looking man,' Guy said with a lack of humility that made several people in the audience gasp. 'I'm in good shape and expensively dressed. She appeared to be this mousy little thing when I first met her. I thought her a bit drab to be honest, I'm used to the women in California who are much more groomed and glamorous. I thought she'd be flattered by the attention but she acted like the thought of me touching her made her feel sick.'

I felt prickles of humiliation myself as he described me as 'drab' and 'dowdy', the bloody cheek of him! But I also felt a shiver of pride at the fact he had at least got the message loud and clear that his sexual advances had repulsed me.

So my lack of interest and unwillingness to accommodate his egotistical sexual appetite had annoyed him, so far so typically #MeToo, but there was more. It seemed Guy's dislike of me had deepened into something more hateful when he began to suspect his own parents preferred *me* to him. Ahh there it was, the veil torn back from the green-eyed monster ... jealousy. Pure and simple jealousy, the most corrosive and poisonous of all emotions had driven Guy to continue with a vendetta against me long after he had driven me from working at his family's jewellery shop. But why had that not been enough? Why not stop once I was no longer an employee? Once I'd lost my job why did he feel the need to keep on goading me?

The Great Marveloso gently peeled back the layers of Guy's motivations like an expert chef dissecting an onion and with Guy now programmed to tell only the truth the final piece of this maddening puzzle finally clicked into place. Guy was broke. He had lost his prestigious, well-paid job in California and he'd only answered the call to come home to Edinburgh and take over the family firm because he'd well and truly burnt all of his bridges in the States. There was much more to find out about the scandal that had ended his Silicone Valley career but I had my suspicions about what might have occurred there. Once a sleazebag always a sleazebag in my book.

Despite losing their only source of income Guy, his trophy wife JoJo, and their designer label-obsessed daughter Kourtney had not eased up on their spending. As Guy described how they had been haemorrhaging dollars trying to keep up appearances of a Hollywood-style lifestyle I almost felt sorry for him. *Almost.* The shame he felt in losing his power, status and spending ability was obvious, it was the only thing to pierce his Teflon persona. No remorse was shown for any of his disgusting actions though, I noticed. Yeah, I pitied him but I wouldn't be crying tears for Guy Grayson any time soon.

I did now understand why he'd almost taken leave of his senses as far as I was concerned. He was relying on running the family business to get him out of a hole and, at some point, expected to inherit everything his parents had worked hard for so many years to establish. It was all he had left, pinning his hopes on the Bank of Mum and Dad. But he saw me as a potential rival to all that. Clearly, I could have run Grayson's better, I knew the systems, the stock and the customers and he even admitted I had more of a natural flair for the trade than he had ever demonstrated. I also knew Gordon and Morag had a lot of faith in me. They'd probably said as much to their son but, knowing them, I feared they may have over-egged the praise and made him feel threatened. I had no reason to think I would ever be included in their wills, handed the keys to the shop or bequeathed so much as a diamante hairpin, but Guy was judging other people by his own, double-crossing, low-life standards. So he'd wanted to run me out of town like he was a gunslinger in a bad spaghetti western and along the way had totally lost the plot.

Once it was all out in the open Jeffrey, The Great Marveloso carefully brought Guy out of his hypnotic, truth-telling state.

The audience sat rapt and engaged and the energy in the room was charged with both judgement and expectation. Guy knew the gig was up. He accepted the situation with an incline of his head as Jeffrey explained both to him and the audience that as a professional hypnotist he maintained the highest professional standards and so revealed a trained counsellor was waiting in the wings to speak with Guy.

The audience gave The Great Marveloso a hearty round of applause once Guy left the stage and they filed out of the make-shift theatre space whispering about the astonishing show they had just experienced.

I thought I was going to feel jubilation. Instead I just felt relief. The vendetta was over and any future disruption to my life or threat to my reputation from Guy had just been neutralised. It took time to sink in but, as it finally did, it was a real rush to the head. I was almost drunk on the feeling but Dorrie, Stella and Tatiana felt we needed a proper drink to celebrate.

We made our way down the Royal Mile in pairs, me and Stella following Dorrie and Tatiana, the pavements far too crowded to walk four abreast. It was almost one o'clock in the morning but the Fringe Festival revellers were out in full force now.

Several clubs and bars we passed had music blaring out and there were impromptu performances erupting on the pavements as we tried to navigate our way along. At this time of the night ... or early morning ... lots of the show people themselves – actors, singers, musicians, comedians, performers of all sorts – were out letting off steam after their own shows were done for the day. A sort of Fringe-madness hits town by mid-August, the pace of the festival is relentless and when every day is spent trying to drum up ticket sales and then perform a show (sometimes more than one show) the temptation is strong for cast members to party just as hard as they work to bring some sort of counterbalance to their crazy lives. We were now in the last few days of the festival and the desperation and desire of people trying to showcase their talent was reaching a peak. The air crackled with drama and heightened emotion as the comedy and tragedy of both performance and real life merged and played out all around us on the streets of Edinburgh

Stella and I linked arms as we moved through the madness; there was a real danger we could lose each other if we didn't keep tight hold.

'Your knack of knowing trash from treasure has been clearly demonstrated once again,' Stella said loudly into my ear as we headed towards the Pleasance Courtyard.

I looked at her quizzically.

'You sussed Guy Grayson was dodgy as soon as you met him.'

She was right about Guy. I'd known he was rotten from the moment I'd met him and tonight all my suspicions had been proved to be true. But my rhinestone radar had failed me with Tom Coltrane! I could have sworn he was a genuine treasure, a diamond guy with a pure heart, but maybe I'd just been dazzled by the brilliance of his fame. Stella saw me grimace and she read my mind: somehow, she knew I was thinking about Tom.

'Don't be so hard on yourself,' she said, squeezing my arm. 'You'd have to have a heart of stone to resist that man, it could have happened to any of us.'

I smiled back at her. I knew she was trying to offer me some comfort, after all she'd been attracted to Tom herself as soon as she'd encountered him, but she hadn't fallen as hard or as deeply as I had; she couldn't have any idea how broken my heart felt. But tonight was not the time for wallowing in self-pity about all that. Together with my awesome new girl gang I had succeeded in stopping one man who was determined to hurt me in his tracks. The pain I still felt over Tom couldn't be so easily cured, that would take time to heal, but tonight I wanted to celebrate a win and all I needed were these amazing women who had been there for me and had my back.

We managed to find a table in a bustling outdoor courtyard festooned with fairy lights. The night was warm and the mood felt quite magical as we sipped cocktails beneath a twinkling canopy of roped illuminations under a starry night sky. A DJ was playing music from decks set up on a nearby platform and we were soon up on our feet dancing to a soundtrack of singalong hits, waving our hands in the air and having an absolute ball. I didn't spot Dorrie when she first approached the guy spinning the tunes while he was taking requests and creating a perfect party atmosphere. The next thing I remember was Dorrie grabbing my hand and leading me towards the mini stage where the DJ was stationed.

'C'mon Reba, how about a bit of Dolly and Kenny, for old times' sake?' She thrust a microphone into my hand and, before I could answer, I heard the intro for 'Islands in the Stream' blasting from speakers all around us. I shook my head but only in amusement. This was hilarious: was Dorrie really wanting us to entertain the crowd with an all-female Dolly Parton tribute show? As she kicked off the song, taking the Kenny Rogers part, I realised not only was she serious but also that resistance was futile. Dorrie's voice rang out across the courtyard and the audience squealed and applauded, delighted at this unexpected live entertainment. Four lines in I came in on the song and we belted the tune out together, our voices blending perfectly while everyone whooped and cheered us along.

It was a wonderful way to end the night and somehow it all felt so right. I was up on stage as myself, the new and improved Reba Moon – so much for Guy Grayson calling me drab and dowdy. Tonight shaking back my red hair and dancing around in a new tartan mini dress and western-style boots, I felt every inch the country music star I was aiming to be. It felt good to be singing Dolly too, she was the icon who had helped and inspired me in so many ways. I wasn't planning to go back to being a tribute artist but I'd never forget how much I owed to Dolly, her music and all her homespun words of wisdom. It felt good to be able to honour that in my own way.

I was so in the moment, soaking up the atmosphere, feeling thankful for true friendship and reflecting on all the positive parts of my life, that I didn't notice someone stepping out from the crowd.

The first time I realised Dorrie was no longer next to me on the stage and her microphone was now being held by another hand was when I heard a completely different voice singing along with me.

TOM! Tom Coltrane was standing right where Dorrie had been just seconds before and had seamlessly picked up the duet from where she had left off. Not only that but he was looking into my eyes with complete sincerity as he sang about being so deeply in love that there was no way out.

Startled, I looked around wildly. I had no idea what was happening, how could Tom be here in Edinburgh? He was meant to be on stage at The Grand Ole Opry in Nashville, he was also meant to be engaged to Juliana Ripon, the real love of his life, not here with me singing about sailing away to another world and *this* being the *real thing*.

I missed my cue to come back in with my part of the song, the music carried on and I saw a plea in Tom's eyes to continue with our duet. The words I knew I should be singing carried new and deeper meaning now and Tom saw my hesitation. He lowered his mic and leaned in close. 'It's you Reba, only you, there's no one else I swear, you have to believe me.'

The sound of his voice, the smell of his skin, I felt my legs go weak and my stomach flip. He brought the mic back up to his lips and carried on singing the words of the song. The audience were cheering but he paid them no attention. His eyes were fixed on mine and I could see and hear only Tom. Tom Coltrane was singing the words of 'Islands in the Stream' for me, right to me, as fireworks exploded in my brain and my heart filled with hope and desire. All my senses told me to trust my instincts. Tom wasn't fake, he may well be flawed but even real diamonds have imperfections, it didn't make them any less beautiful in my eyes. There was nothing else I could do. I took a deep breath and sang along with him, our voices joining in a duet about two people who find sanctuary in each other, coming together in a deep and unwavering love while the world carries on in chaos around them.

Chapter Thirty-Two

Our song ended to whoops and cheers from the partying crowd but Tom and I were locked in a moment all of our own. We stood facing each other, neither of us wanting to break the spell, our eyes taking in every little detail. Tom looked so good I couldn't stop staring at him, he was here, really here, right in front of me and I'd never seen him look so damn handsome.

Under the twinkling fairy lights his rusty hair appeared slightly darker than usual and I thought it looked a little longer now too; unruly tufts giving him a dishevelled just-got-out-of-bed look that was irresistible, especially with a stray lock falling over one eye. Oh! His eyes. They were the brightest blue I had ever seen, it was like this guy was lit from within. Forget 'The Great Marveloso' I felt I was being hypnotised just by looking at Tom. He was also pulling off the dreaded double-denim look with absolute ease. A pair of well-worn, tan cowboy boots looked perfect with his faded jeans. The light blue chambray shirt he wore was rumpled like he'd slept in it, but looked so velvety soft I longed to snuggle up against it, especially when I spotted a few studs had popped open revealing a tantalising glimpse of his tanned chest.

I watched his eyes sweep over me as the lights above our heads made my red hair appear flecked with gold. I felt my face flush as his gaze roamed over the tight-fitting bodice of my green tartan mini dress and down my bare legs to the tips of my toes, encased in fringed suede boots. The outfit was sassy and I felt sexy, even more so when I saw the look of appreciation on Tom's handsome face.

'Hell Reba, I missed you so much.'

'I've missed you too.' The truth was impossible to deny and the statement was out of my mouth before I could stop it. But that was okay, I was being honest and they say the truth will set you free. It was time to tell the truth … the whole truth and nothing but the truth. I'd had a lifetime of listening to love songs, singing them and sometimes even believing them. But what happened when the song ended? The dying strains of the backing track had faded away and I knew I had to find out if our hearts fitted together as well as our voices.

Tom grabbed my hand and we left the Pleasance Courtyard at a sprint. As we reached the road we were blessed by the sudden appearance of a black cab with its yellow light shining. Tom hailed it with a whistle and we jumped into the back. I had no idea where we were heading but with Tom holding onto me so tightly I really didn't care.

By the time the taxi pulled up outside my apartment block in Comely Bank Tom had managed to explain almost everything. Despite the fact we had only travelled a relatively short distance across the city it felt like during that journey Tom and I had come a very long way.

He wasn't engaged to Juliana Ripon, he never had been and never would be. The real truth of his relationship with the Hollywood actress was more of a shock to me than her revelation that they were going to be married.

'She was never my girlfriend,' Tom stated. His tone was matter of fact but his words had me confused. What did he mean? I'd seen photos of the two of them, read articles about their relationship, I'd even met the woman and it was not an encounter I was likely to forget.

'It was all fake, a publicity stunt to boost both of our careers. It was one of the stupidest things I've ever done but you have to believe me Reba, there was no romance, it was all just a staged "showmance".'

'Did someone explain that to Juliana? She seemed pretty convinced it was real when she found me in your house?' I was trying to get my ahead around what Tom was saying and at first it didn't really add up.

'She is a pretty good actress,' Tom admitted before going on to also describe her as 'rather volatile'. He then, choosing his words more carefully, told me why he thought Juliana had been so desperate to try and keep their sham relationship going. He said the idea for them to couple-up had first been cooked up by his manager Waz Monsoon and her Hollywood agent Bebe Blair.

'Individually both Waz and Bebe are formidable,' Tom said with a grimace, 'but together they're pretty terrifying. It's no excuse though, I'm not making excuses, I shouldn't have agreed to it. I kidded myself it wouldn't, couldn't hurt and I thought I was helping Juliana. But I should never have lied, not to my fans, not to people around me and certainly not to you.'

The way Tom told it, Bebe was keen to elevate the status of her ingenue actress client and Waz was looking for a way to get Tom some extra media attention. Record sales had been slipping and tickets for tour dates were becoming increasingly difficult to shift. Tom had needed more persuading than Juliana to agree to the deal but he'd thought she was a sweet girl and so he'd agreed to be pictured with her on his arm at various events and let the press make them a new celebrity couple, one that brought together the glitz of Hollywood and the charm of Nashville. Bebe Blair had apparently even tried to get the name *Tomliana* trending.

Tom nodded but lowered his voice and looked furtively towards the glass screen separating us from the taxi driver as though he feared the balding man could be eavesdropping on our conversation. He then told me the secret he had been keeping on top of the one about his and Juliana's unreal romance and the real reason Bebe Blair had wanted to invent a high-profile love affair for her client – Juliana Ripon was gay.

Tom explained how an actor's sexual preference shouldn't make any difference in this day and age but studio bosses and casting directors didn't need much excuse to look along the line for the next actor angling for any part. When he asked me how many gay movie stars I could name I realised there were shockingly few. I knew rumours about some, but an actor or actress who was gay and openly 'out'? That was a short list. As Tom described what a truly risky, back-stabbing business the movie industry could be I began to see why Juliana's need to have a cover story was so important to her.

'I'm sorry I didn't tell you all this Reba, but this part wasn't my secret to tell.' He looked completely anguished and I finally understood why he had been so cagey about what had been going on. He said he thought Laura might have sussed his high-profile affair was not genuine. A little sister would have a nose for something like that, I told him. I was also thinking that it was rather honourable of him to attempt to keep Juliana's confidence, even from his own family, when I realised Tom was saying something else now.

'Sorry, what did you just say?'

'I said … I never expected to fall in love for real … and that's what caused all the problems.' He grinned then and my heart thumped as he leaned towards me.

'Say that again, Coltrane,' I said, grinning back.

'The bit about all the problems you caused?' he said, then as if he could hear my pulse thundering, he gave in, 'Or the bit about falling in love?'

I could have stopped the cab and just stayed there till dawn listening to him say that over and over again. But I knew there was an even better use of our time.

And so we kissed … and kissed … I didn't want to stop.

The car drew to halt on the pavement beneath my flat and he paid the driver, giving him a hefty tip. As we watched the car pull away it seemed to remind Tom of the method Juliana had used to track my movements in Nashville and then seize the moment I was alone in his house to confront me.

'I've fired Dawn,' he said with a shrug. 'She's gone to work for Juliana full-time so don't feel too bad for her.' I have to say I didn't feel bad for her at all.

I did feel a little sympathy for Juliana Ripon, though. Acting was a tough enough profession without having to pretend to be someone else in your real life as well. The stress of all that must be enormous but it didn't justify her trying to wreck my life. As I unlocked the door to my little apartment with trembling fingers I was struck by how close Juliana had come to destroying everything I'd dreamt of. And not to hurt me – but simply out of fear her own cover would be blown. I knew enough about playing a part and hiding behind a role. But right here, right now, I'd discovered what it was to step into your true self. Her affair with Tom Coltrane was pure fiction but here he was right now, standing in my hallway, and the connection between us was undeniably real.

We stepped towards each other, his hands on my waist while I lightly stroked my fingers across the stubble on his chin and then up to his mouth. He kissed my finger tips and his hands moved up my back, pulling us closer and, as our lips met, his hands were in my hair, caressing, massaging. I pulled his denim shirt apart, desperate to expose more skin. His fingers found the zipper at the back of my dress and the tartan fabric was soon pooled around my feet. Undressed and undone we stumbled to the bedroom.

The mid-morning sun was shining through the open shutters of my bedroom when I woke a few hours later. It reminded me of the first time I had woken up in bed with Tom in his hotel following the Free 'n' Easy night at Sonny's Bar. I'd considered that hook-up to be 'free and easy' too back then. I'd had no expectations that it could be the start of something more but as I sensed Tom's sleepy body stir next to mine I knew now I didn't ever want to let him go.

I made us some coffee and when I came back into the bedroom Tom was sitting up in bed, ruffling a hand through his red hair.

'Ahh that's just what we need,' he said as he reached for the mug, 'once we've had this I'll help you get your things together then we can get going.'

My head was still fuzzy and I didn't understand what he meant. Get going? To where?

Tom read my confusion and grabbed my free hand, pulling me towards him. 'I'll ask you properly this time. Will you come back to Nashville with me, Reba? Give me the chance to show you around and show you off like I'd always planned?'

A return to Nashville? That was music to my ears. It's where I'd longed to go for so long and been so sad to leave prematurely. It's where I would have been right at that moment if things hadn't taken such an unexpected turn. Robbie had been drafted in as stand-in manager at Sonny's Bar and I wasn't expected back at work for another couple of weeks, so I gave Tom his answer with a smacker of a kiss.

'Don't just sit there looking all smouldering and sexy,' I told him, 'there's no time for all that, you need to help me pack.'

Chapter Thirty-Three

The driver waiting for Tom and me as we walked out of Nashville Airport obviously wasn't duplicitous Dawn. In her place was a tall African American guy wearing a black suit, white shirt and bootlace tie. He had on a jet-black cowboy hat with silver trim and matching cowboy boots. I loved the modern country vibe he was rocking. With a big welcoming smile and impeccable manners, he introduced himself as Angelo and carefully took the case from my hand. He may have been a giant but he was also clearly a gentleman.

'Welcome home sir, lovely to meet you ma'am,' Angelo said as he opened the door to the back seat of the limo and I slipped inside.

'Angelo is my regular driver but he had a few days off last week. We missed you Angel man,' Tom told him, clapping the big guy on the shoulder as he smoothly pulled the car out into the traffic leaving the airport. Turning to me Tom added, 'Angelo is his name but we more often call him Angel, 'cause that's what he is. This guy has saved my bacon so many times.'

I could imagine he was a very useful man to have around and Angelo seemed to preen in the driver's seat as he heard Tom talking, then he asked Tom if he wanted him to drive 'the scenic route' on the way home? Tom told him we did.

I wasn't heading to a hotel on this trip. Tom had asked if I was happy to stay with him at his house and I'd jumped at the chance to spend more time at the place I'd partly explored on my last visit. I'd been so impressed with how gorgeous and welcoming Braveheart had felt, until my uncomfortable encounter with Juliana Ripon, but I wasn't going to let her spoil my chance of enjoying a stay there now.

Angelo drove the car right into the centre of Nashville and down Broadway just as the sun started to go down. I hadn't had chance to explore the famous street full of music bars, gift shops and stores selling cowboy hats and boots before. As the sky above started to darken, the multicoloured neon lights up and down the strip were starting to light up, creating a twinkling introduction to the music city.

'It's like Las Vegas!' I said, but Tom and Angelo laughed at my naivety.

'You've never been to Vegas, have you?' Tom said. 'This place can get pretty crazy but it's like a sleepy village compared to Sin City.'

Angel nodded in agreement but as I looked at the hoards of people swarming into all the honky-tonk bars I thought it didn't look like any sleepy village I'd ever known. The sound of country music was pumping out from each and every venue with a different band set up in the open windows playing to the whooping crowds inside and drawing fascinated onlookers outside. I was delighted by the fact almost every person out having fun was wearing a cowboy hat and boots: old and young, men and women, tourist or local they all looked the part. It made for an incredible atmosphere I was desperate to be part of.

Tom saw me craning my neck to look out at the sights he was showing me. 'We can hit the strip sometime if you like, there's a back entrance to Tootsies that can come in handy if I don't want to get too much hassle.' That sounded great to me, although I couldn't quite believe a star as famous as Tom would be able to mingle with these music-loving crowds safely. Maybe that's where Angel would come in particularly handy?

We drove away from downtown, leaving the flashing lights and pounding tunes behind us. A few moments later in a less busy part of town Angelo pulled the car over, jumped out and opened the door.

'I wanna show you something,' Tom said, taking my hand. We walked for a few minutes until we were on a wide, pedestrian walkway between huge white metal archways and I realised we were on a vast footbridge spanning the Cumberland River beneath us. 'Don't look back Reba,' Tom told me and so I kept my eyes forward as we walked further out across the water.

After a little while longer Tom's pace slowed and he stopped and faced me. 'I'm so glad you're here honey,' he said, kissing me softly. The twilight sky above us was now a spectacular mixture of deepest blue, purple and pink. Tom gently put his hands on my shoulders and turned me to face the city. The sight was breathtaking, the cityscape of darkening buildings silhouetted against a vibrant rosy sky.

Tom pointed out one peculiar high-rise tower dominating the view and told me it was known as the 'Batman building'. I could see why. The twin spires crowning its square top looked just like the superhero's head.

'Wow!' I could see why Tom had wanted me to see Nashville from this angle. The city was now starting to twinkle and sparkle as darkness descended, it looked completely magical.

'I thought I was done with Nashville,' Tom said as he stood behind me with his arms wrapped around my waist taking in the view along with me. 'When I went back to Edinburgh I could feel my Scottish roots calling to me. I've always felt torn between Scotland and the Southern States, Edinburgh or Alabama? I'm still not sure which one I should make my sweet home?'

I didn't say a word. Tom sounded like he was still mulling over the question in his own mind, not looking to me to give him an answer right now. I let my eyes roam over the beautiful city laid out before me. It was a place bursting with life, music and possibilities. I was keen to throw myself in and experience it all. I even wondered if my own future might lie here? But just as I was preparing to step into this new adventure in the middle of 'Music City' itself, Tom seemed to be considering moving away. How annoyingly ironic.

As we both stood there drinking in the view Tom suddenly snapped out of his confusion and remembered why he had brought me to this vantage point. He nuzzled into my neck making my pulse race and my knees turn to jelly.

'Take a good look Reba,' he breathed softly into my ear, 'it's all there, Nashville in all its glory … and I believe it's yours for the takin'.'

I kept my eyes on the incredible skyline in front of me and tried to focus on what Tom was trying to tell me. I was facing my future as Reba Moon with the arms of the man I loved wrapped around me. But were we destined to build a life here together or were the things we wanted not truly compatible? I was keen to get started on proving I had enough talent as a singer and enough to say as a songwriter to become a part of this world. Only time would tell if I could make it happen and do so with Tom Coltrane by my side.

Chapter Thirty-Four

Tom didn't give me much time for pondering the possibilities of life over the next few days and weeks. He threw himself into showing me the best of what Nashville and the surrounding state of Tennessee had to offer and, just as he had promised, he did his very best to show me off too. He didn't hesitate to introduce me to a bunch of his mates and took me to meet several producers and musicians who were all full of great advice for the newest singer songwriter to hit town.

At some point in the whirlwind of music bars, coffee houses, recording studios, BBQ joints and hanging out with mates at the house, playing pool and dancing to the juke box, it was decided that I needed to stay in Nashville ... indefinitely.

I didn't need much persuasion. Nashville was an easy place to fall in love with. The city had a small-town feel and I'd discovered Southern American hospitality was a genuine thing, everyone I met made me feel so welcome and I just adored hearing 'yes ma'am' and 'no ma'am' everywhere I went. Politeness might cost nothing but I was realising how the manners of the ordinary folk of Tennessee made them as respectful and dignified as some members of the British Royal Family. Maybe it was the people or the big sunshiny sky, maybe it was the music, but I quickly felt so at home in Nashville I knew I wanted more than a holiday here.

I realised I needed to be in this for the long haul. To be an 'overnight success' you really needed to put the hours in. It's funny how things worked out. I was now almost glad that I hadn't appeared with Tom on stage at the new, enormous Grand Ole Opry venue. Surely it would be better to build up to something like that? If I'd performed at the ultimate arena on such a gigantic stage – in every sense of the term – would music fans have accepted me? I didn't want to risk a backlash before I'd even really begun. When Tom offered to try and get us back on the bill I told him what I was thinking and he thought for a moment before saying:

'You know, I think you're probably right. Waz has been on my back about running out on The Opry, but leave him to me, I'll square it with him.'

I hadn't yet met the infamous Waz Monsoon, Tom seemed keen to shield me from that particular experience, but I knew there were calls and emails flying back and forth between them about setting up a tour and the imminent release of 'Moonlight Home'. From what I could tell, he was pretty furious that Tom had decided to fly around the world to explain things to me instead of staying and performing 'Moonlight Home' at The Opry without me. I knew the release date for the single had been put back a little now but

I kept out of Tom's business dealings as much as possible. Tom was much more relaxed when he wasn't thinking about contracts and sales figures, and I figured he was enjoying having me around … I wanted to keep it that way.

I asked Tom's advice about getting in touch with the man from the record company but he told me to hang fire until I'd had the chance to meet his manager Waz. 'You need someone like Waz on your side before you start trying to deal with record companies and contracts,' he told me. 'Waz just lives for brokering the best deals and you'll be much better off if you have representation.' What Tom was saying made sense but I found even the thought of Waz Monsoon slightly terrifying.

It wasn't the only thing making me anxious. Tom hadn't mentioned moving back to Scotland since our first night back, and I could see how much he loved Nashville, but I didn't dare raise the issue in case it was still something he was wrestling with. I knew he missed his family, particularly Laura, Fergus and the kids. Edinburgh was a great city and I could understand how he might feel it was time for a change. Artistic people often needed to keep moving, find new things to inspire them and shake things up every now and again to get the creative juices flowing. I knew that. If Tom was yearning for the Scottish homeland of his father rather than staying close to the American heritage of his Alabamian mother, I would understand. It wasn't what I wanted to hear, but I would have to understand. But I knew, as deeply as I was falling in love with Tom, I had to let this love affair with Nashville play out. Whatever Tom decided, I knew I had to give Tennessee a chance, and decided I needed to mothball my old life, just like I'd walked away from all my old Becky clothes.

Back at Sonny's Bar, Robbie had jumped at the chance to carry on as manager in my place and also asked if he could rent my flat in Comely Bank while I was away. It was the perfect way to free myself up to pursue my Nashville dreams while not burning too many bridges, so I agreed at once. I was also grateful for the income it was bringing in, I didn't want to have to rely on Tom for everything. I'd been around the music business enough to know that waiting around for a royalty cheque for 'Moonlight Home' might be a long wait indeed.

Meanwhile, I was keen to immerse myself in the country music culture, study more of the history, learn from the best. I went back to The Country Music Hall of Fame several times and visited every other museum in Nashville. I took the backstage tour of the Ryman Auditorium, learning all about Thomas G. Ryman, the hard-drinking riverboat captain who had built the Union Gospel Tabernacle in the late 1800s after turning to Christianity and finding God. The distinctive building with its red-brick facade and arched windows trimmed in white was right in the heart of downtown Nashville, so when it eventually became the home of The Grand Ole Opry the fans who flocked to see their favourite country music stars perform sat on the original wooden church pews, prompting The Opry to become known as 'The Mother Church of Country Music'. Amen to that, I thought.

For a true music fan, visiting the original Opry was a special moment, as was standing inside RCA Studio B where so many legends, from Elvis to Hank Williams, Roy Orbison and The Everly Brothers recorded so many of their songs. Dolly herself recorded 'I Will Always Love You' right on that spot in 1973 and I got tingles when I took the tour and realised how closely I was now following in Dolly's footsteps.

As well as soaking up the history, I also threw myself into the new music scene by seeking out the listening rooms and live lounges all around Nashville where singer songwriters played their latest music, talked about the inspirations behind their songs and shared their stories. I was astounded by how many places you could go to hear musicians open their hearts and share their talent. It lit a fire within me and I was constantly jotting down my own ideas and lyrics in a little notebook I now kept with me always. Tom also let me borrow one of his many acoustic guitars. I was very rusty as I hadn't really played since having lessons at school, but it felt so good to have the power to create my own music.

I'd been in Nashville for a few weeks and Tom and I were breakfasting at The Loveless Cafe early one morning, hoping to beat the tourist hoards, when he dropped a minor bombshell.

'How d'you fancy a trip to The Bluebird later?'

The Bluebird!? I'd been dying to go to the most famous listening room cafe in Nashville, but it was such a tiny place and tickets were so in demand it was almost impossible to get in there. I knew people could queue for hours on the street for the chance to get a seat at one of the few tables to watch musicians perform on the tiny stage or seated 'in the round' right in the centre of the room. I would absolutely *love* to go to The Bluebird. I almost choked on my creamed corn and crispy bacon as I tried to tell Tom how much I wanted to go.

'Now, now, the famous Loveless Cafe biscuits are to die for but don't let the breakfast here kill you,' Tom said, laughing as I spluttered.

I grinned and tried to regain my composure, reaching for another of the fluffiest, melt-in-the-mouth biscuits I'd ever tasted and smothering it with peach jam.

'You look like the cat who got the cream,' Tom said, his eyes crinkling in amusement, but just as he had sweetened me up with talk of biscuits and The Bluebird he landed his punchline: 'it will be good for you to finally meet Waz too.'

'WAZ?' I spat a shower of biscuit crumbs over Tom as his manager's name exploded from my mouth.

Tom dusted himself off and laughed out loud. 'Now don't get all bent outta shape. Waz isn't some sort of brute you need to be scared of.'

Hmmm, I wasn't so sure. From everything I'd heard, Waz Monsoon had a reputation as the scariest, most ruthless manager in the music industry. There was a rumour he'd once dangled a rival record boss out of an office window until the poor guy acquiesced to Waz's terms and conditions. The office had been on the 36th floor.

'Well, he can be fierce and uncompromising, that's true,' Tom admitted with a grin. 'But don't forget, even if he is a bit of a monster ... he's *our* monster.'

I wasn't sure that made me feel much better about the prospect of encountering Waz at The Bluebird later that evening. This was the guy who had masterminded the 'showmance' between Tom and Juliana Ripon, after all. I couldn't imagine he'd been very thrilled by my arrival on the scene, wrecking the deal he'd struck with Bebe Blair to gain the couple maximum publicity.

'Don't sweat over that,' Tom said as the waitress refilled our coffee cups, 'things move fast in this business. Waz knows how to roll with the punches. He'll be onto the next deal by now, sniffing out the next opportunity. Waz looks forward, he doesn't look back.'

I tried to take on board what Tom was telling me. It wouldn't do to be too naive about the business side of showbiz after all. I also took the point that it certainly sounded better to have Waz in your corner than have to face him as an opponent.

I decided on a casual vibe for our trip to The Bluebird. I knew it wasn't a fancy place at all and I didn't want to arrive overdressed. I dug out a white silky shirt to wear with my jeans and suede boots and tied my hair up in a high pony tail. When Tom yelled that Angelo was outside with the car I grabbed a leather jacket and ran down the stairs to find him waiting for me in the hallway.

Sometimes just the sight of Tom could take my breath away. That night as he stood waiting for me by the open front door it struck me just how handsome he looked. He wasn't dressed up either, just a plain blue cotton shirt, faded denim jeans and his tan cowboy boots, but as I reached the bottom step he reached for a sandy-coloured cowboy hat to complete his look.

'Oh!'

He turned to face me as I let out a gasp. I'd also noticed he was holding a guitar case in his hand.

'How else d'you think we got tickets to The Bluebird?' he said with a devilish smile. 'Don't worry Reba, tonight is an "in the round" event so there'll be a few other people playing too. You won't have to put up with listening to me all night.'

I didn't know whether to hit him or kiss him. I'd never seen Tom perform a proper set before. The only time I'd watched him on stage was when he'd jumped into my spot at Sonny's Bar and I'd peeped through a crack in the door from the back office. I knew I'd love to see him play a big gig one day, like a huge theatre or arena, but to see him in such an intimate setting tonight would be incredible. I knew big stars sometimes popped up at The Bluebird alongside musicians who were unknown but I never expected Tom was going to be performing tonight. I was so excited I could burst.

'Do I look okay?' I was suddenly worried I might look too casual. Maybe even a bit scruffy? What if someone spotted I was Tom Coltrane's girlfriend and thought me a very poor replacement for a Hollywood starlet?

Tom silenced the self-doubt before it had chance to take hold.

'You look beautiful Reba,' he said pulling me towards him with his free hand and sealing the statement with a soft, lingering kiss on my lips.

'Now get your ass in that car or we're gonna be late.'

Chapter Thirty-Five

When Angelo dropped us off at The Bluebird there was already a line of people waiting outside hoping to get tickets for that night's show. I stood patiently beneath the blue canopied awning over the front door as Tom signed a few autographs and posed for selfies. At least some of the people waiting in vain would have something to show for the hours standing on a non-descript suburban street.

Sandwiched between a jewellery repair shop, a hair salon and a dry cleaners, the cafe venue didn't look that special at all, but I knew stars like Kris Kristofferson, Carole King, Faith Hill, Garth Brooks and Vince Gill had all played this gig at one time or another. Taylor Swift had even been discovered at The Bluebird when she was just fourteen years old. This place thrummed with the memories of such musical moments and Tom Coltrane was about to add his name to the list of amazing musicians who wowed the music-loving crowd.

Once inside Tom introduced me to the other musicians he would be playing alongside, a soft-spoken brunette called

Jessie, a chatty joker named Caleb, and Garrett, who was tall, handsome and rather intense. They all seemed to be dealing with playing alongside someone as famous as Tom in their own way and I thought it looked like a great line-up for the show. They were already bouncing off each other with that instant ease musicians so often have with one another.

I was shown to a seat at a small round table on the edge of the space cleared for the performers where empty stools and microphone stands stood waiting for them. I ordered a margarita and watched as the seats around me filled up quickly with folk as excited as I was to be there.

'May I join you?'

A deep voice from above my head startled me mid-sip but I swallowed down the large mouthful of limey tequila blinking rapidly to stop my eyes watering.

'Of course!' I sounded a lot more husky than usual as the alcohol burned its way down my throat but Waz Monsoon didn't bat one of his chocolate brown eyes as he settled into the wooden seat right next to me and introduced himself.

'Looks good,' he said, nodding towards my drink. 'Make mine a margarita too and another for the lady.'

The busboy hovering at his elbow answered 'Yes sir' as Waz flashed me a smile that showed off his dazzlingly perfect white teeth.

I was determined not to appear nervous or flustered so I smiled and thanked him and then did my very best to chat normally to this music mogul manager. If Waz was some sort of monster he was able to hide it incredibly well. He was very good-looking in a highly polished sort of way. I found him charming, easy to talk to and with a sense of humour that was more British than American. Along with his mid-Atlantic accent he had acquired an appreciation for irony that was lost on some yanks. That was unexpected. We were getting on so well I decided to be very brave and bring up the taboo subject of Juliana Ripon.

Waz gave me an appraising sort of look as I boldly said that I thought Juliana was a beautiful girl but not really *'the right match'* for Tom. There was a long pause, during which I realised I had no idea how to read the expression on Waz Monsoon's face before he replied, 'But you are?'

I held his gaze and my nerve. 'Maybe,' I said. I don't know why I did it, it felt like dangerous territory to get into, but what had happened with Juliana felt like the elephant in the room and I didn't want Waz to think I was some gullible fool who hadn't got a clue what had been going on. Maybe it was just the tequila talking, I'd heard that it was the drink most likely to send someone crazy. Or maybe it was the bolder side of me being brought out by being Reba. I doubted I would have tackled something so head on when I went by the name of Becky. But Becky wasn't here, I was Reba now.

Waz nodded slowly, pursing his lips as though he was giving this matter full consideration. 'Maybe ... maybe, Reba Moon ... there's definitely potential here, I can see that quite clearly.'

I wasn't sure what he meant by that but then the crowd started to applaud as Tom and the other musicians took their place in the centre of the circle and the show began.

It was an exhilarating show to watch, full of banter between the musicians and wonderful musical performances. The crowd loved hearing Tom tell the story of how Dolly

Parton helped him write 'Whisper Away' and his hit song got a great reception when he played it.

There was a brief interval when Tom came over to say hi to Waz and leaned down to give me a quick kiss on the cheek. 'You doin' okay honey?' he asked. I nodded in response.

'Don't worry about Reba, Tom,' Waz told him, 'she can look after herself just fine.' He gave me a knowing wink.

Tom gave me a quizzical look but there was no time to explain as the second set was about to start and Tom took his place back in the circle.

'I think you're right, Reba,' Waz told me as microphone stands were adjusted and guitars tuned. 'You and Tom could make a very cool couple … falling in love with a girl from his Scottish homeland is a great story, the media would lap that up … it could really help Tom's sales in the UK too.'

I whipped my head to look at Waz but he was already leaning away from me, chatting to a sultry-looking young girl in white cowboy boots who had manoeuvred her chair closer to his and was now busy whispering in his ear, no doubt telling him about her own aspirations to be a singer.

For the second half of the show I was a bit distracted as Waz's words went round and round my head and I wondered if he was seriously planning to send out some sort of press release about my relationship with Tom? Would Tom be okay with that? How would I feel about it? Some articles had been written in the press about Tom and Juliana growing apart and spending less time together but the subject hadn't attracted big headlines or much media debate until they 'split'. Was I about to be used as just another pawn in the publicity game to enhance Tom's career? It didn't feel right to have my private life being managed by someone like Waz Monsoon. Whatever Tom and I revealed to the wider world should be up to us, not this sharp-suited, fast-talking manager.

My mind was reeling but I got pulled right back into the moment as I heard Tom begin to talk about how he came to write 'Moonlight Home'.

'Sometimes, as a songwriter and in life, you can feel like you've lost your way a little,' he said as Jessie, Garrett and Caleb nodded with understanding. 'But then something happens to get you back on the right path.'

'Like winning the lottery?' Caleb joked as the audience laughed.

'Yeah sure, that could work,' Tom told him with a grin. 'But it could be just making different choices.'

'Or maybe reconnecting with people?' Jessie offered.

'Yeah, that too …' Tom said. 'Or reconnecting with places, revisiting somewhere that means a lot to us. In my case I did both, I made some choices that were better for me, went back to my Scottish roots, and it helped me remember who I really was. I also met someone and that person really helped me rediscover myself and my love for the music I make. Suddenly I felt I was back on the right path. That's how I came to write "Moonlight Home".'

I realised I was holding my breath as Tom spoke. Everyone always listens avidly to the songwriters in this kind of session, but right now Tom had completely captured everyone's attention.

'The question is, ladies and gentlemen …' Tom was fiddling with the capo on his guitar as he spoke, 'will the very special person, who is here in this room tonight, come up and help me sing this song for you right now?'

My heart thudded in my chest like a tom-tom beating out a distress signal.

'I think that's your cue,' Waz whispered into my ear but then as I looked at his face so close to mine I saw his expression was sincere. He added, 'Go on Reba, take your moment and enjoy it.'

So that's exactly what I did.

As I stepped forward into the circle, Caleb jumped up to drag a stool in for me and Jessie and Garrett hitched themselves around so there was room next to Tom.

'Folks, will you please give Reba Moon a very warm welcome to The Bluebird,' Tom announced into his mic as his eyes finally met mine and he gave me a sexy smile.

All my senses were on fire, everything sounded louder, looked clearer, I could practically feel the blood coursing through my own veins. The fairy lights strung around the walls of The Bluebird twinkled and glowed brighter than any I'd ever seen before, creating a magical space that felt totally separate from the rest of the world. I felt weirdly at home in these unfamiliar surroundings and I could sense Tom felt this was the perfect place to give this song its Nashville debut.

As soon as Tom began to strum the opening chords I relaxed even more, there was just Tom and me lost inside our duet about finding your way through the darkness and following your heart towards the light, towards home.

Once the song was over I made my way back to my seat next to Waz as the audience applauded loudly. It was the most surreal moment of my life but I now knew for sure that the tiny Bluebird stage had been the perfect place to make my Nashville debut. The Grand Ole Opry would have been far too overwhelming. I needed to work up to something like that, if I ever got that far. Here I felt I'd held my own and been completely accepted by the audience and the other performers. I was part of the Nashville music scene now and it felt wonderful.

'I'm sure you'll be seeing a lot more of Reba Moon, folks, but you can tell people you were there for her very first performance at The Bluebird!' Tom said as he and the other performers joined in with the applause before picking up the rest of their set and carrying on with the show.

At the end of the night quite a few people came over to say hi, tell me how much they loved 'Moonlight Home' and said they had enjoyed my performance. That was lovely to hear but I was super keen to know what Waz Monsoon had thought? Unfortunately, as the lights came up, I discovered the seat beside me was empty. Both Waz and the sultry-looking girl in the white cowboy boots were nowhere to be seen.

In the car on the way home Tom laughed when I mentioned Waz's disappearing act. 'Ah, typical Waz,' he said affectionately. 'He's the master of the French exit, got it down to a fine art. Waz can get a lot of people banging his ear in a place like The Bluebird, there's always someone trying to get his attention, so he just picks his moment to disappear.'

That made sense. I didn't mention to Tom that the dark-haired girl in the tasselled micro mini skirt seemed to have got his attention okay and disappeared with him. None of my business.

'He thought you were great though, Reba, I could tell.'

'Really?' I was sceptical but something in me was very keen to know if the great Waz Monsoon really rated me.

'You'll be able to ask him yourself soon enough,' Tom said slipping his arm along the leather upholstery and pulling me closer on the back seat as Angelo drove the car through the darkness. 'If you don't see him before, he's bound to be at The Country Music Awards next month.'

'The CMAs?'

The grin on Tom's face was now as wide as I'd ever seen it, he was beaming with delight as I realised what he was telling me.

'We are going to the CMAs?' I needed to hear him say it, confirm the fact that I would be his plus-one at the biggest night of the year in Nashville. Anyone who was anyone in country music would be at the televised awards event at The Bridgestone Arena and it was always such a glamorous occasion.

'Well if you're busy I could always take Angelo. You'd come along for a hoot and a holler, wouldn't you, Angel buddy?'

Angelo started to join in with Tom's teasing but I cut them both off. 'Oh don't you worry, I'll be there,' I told them firmly.

I could barely catch my breath with all the surprises coming at me, one incredible experience followed by another, but all at once I was thunderstruck by a sudden concern.

'Oh! But what will I wear?'

Tom shook his head but he was still smiling at me. He could have mocked me, told me it didn't matter or that there was nothing to worry about, I'd find something. As if I'd packed anything remotely suitable for a televised awards ceremony like the Country Music Awards? But I was learning fast that Tom wasn't that kind of guy. He knew I needed to know I looked my best to be comfortable enough to walk into that kind of event so he had the perfect answer ready.

'Well I think in a situation like this we will definitely need to schedule a shopping trip, or two,' Tom said. 'Angelo is at your disposal, Reba, he can take you to the very best shops Nashville has to offer and you've got a couple of weeks to find something just perfect. How does that sound?'

That sounded wonderful to me but I couldn't quite find the words to tell Tom how happy and excited I was. I would have to show him once I got him alone.

Chapter Thirty-Six

If I'd been excited when Tom revealed we would be attending the Country Music Awards, it was nothing to how I actually felt on the night itself. I was beside myself.

Just as Tom had promised, he'd arranged for Angelo to drive me to a selection of shopping destinations around the city to find an outfit suitable for mixing with the Nashville music elite. He also offered to tag along and, although I thought the idea of Tom watching me parade around in a succession of fancy clothes might be amusing, I told him I was sticking with my original stylist.

'You're taking … Laura?' Tom looked dumbstruck when I told him that, but when I patted the phone in my jeans back pocket he realised I was planning to FaceTime her once I found some stuff to try on, and looked a bit relieved I wasn't going to drag him from store to store.

Being able to prop Laura up in the changing rooms worked like an absolute dream and with her help I'd narrowed the choice down to two possible looks by the third shop I went to. Any Old Iron was a gloriously glitzy boutique just off Broadway. There were many stylish options, some of them so jewel-encrusted it was sparklier than Grayson's front window, but a friendly shop assistant appropriately called Star helped me navigate my way through the racks of fabulous pieces. It was also lovely to see Laura's face beaming out of the phone screen on FaceTime as I did so. We had a laugh and a great girly catch-up while I rifled through the clothes and she made suggestions about what I should be aiming for. She also told me it wouldn't be too long before we could see each other properly as Tom had invited her and Fergus and the kids over to spend Christmas with us in Nashville. An American family Christmas with Tom in Nashville sounded like yet another dream come true and when he'd asked me if I liked the idea I'd nodded so enthusiastically I must have looked like Woody Woodpecker. The truth was I simply couldn't find the words to explain how it made me feel. It was like I was glowing.

'It's going to be brilliant. Stevie and Reggie are already bouncing off the walls with excitement,' Laura said. I knew how they felt. I was dying to start decorating the house with all the festive decorations I'd found in one of the spare rooms upstairs. I was picturing garlands down the stairs and fairy lights in all the trees and bushes outside the house. It was such a perfect house for family celebrations. Tom said we could go and find a real tree from a nearby farm and, with the house having such a high vaulted ceiling in the living area, I was hoping we could get a pretty big one.

For now, however, I needed to forget about trimming the house and concentrate on making sure I looked fabulous.

With the dress Laura had helped me find I certainly felt the part.

I took one last look at myself in the full-length mirror in the dressing room area just off the bedroom. I'd come a long way since my Dolly Parton dress-up days. I didn't need a bottle-blonde wig and foam dome boobies to cover up my insecurities any more. Now I stood tall, shoulders back and eyes wide open and I was able to see there really wasn't too much I needed to feel insecure about. Sure, there were women in the world who were smarter, better looking or more talented than me, there's always someone somewhere who can best the best of us, but now I knew I needed to recognise and appreciate that I was more than good enough. But though I'd cast my Dolly looks aside, I still kept her words close. Her advice had got me here – and I couldn't wait to see where it took me next.

Now I dressed to suit my personality I felt I looked better than I had in my twenties. I'd found a local hairdresser to keep my hair colour coppery red and I'd let it grow down past my shoulders for the first time ever. Today I'd called in to the salon and let them give me what they called 'a bouncy blow' – big hair was still a big thing in Tennessee – and I loved how glamorous it felt to have tumbling auburn locks.

The dress Laura and Star had helped me choose for tonight's event was simple but stunning; a long, sleek black evening dress with silver trim around the halter neck and one single shimmering silver stripe from the neckline down to the hem. The soft black fabric pooled into a small train at the back but was slightly raised at the front to give a glimpse of the cute silver ankle boots I was wearing. I carried a black velvet clutch bag decorated with glittery stars and wore a pair of starry drop earrings and silver cuff bracelets to complete the look.

Tom let out a long low whistle as I descended the stairs to where he was waiting for me in the hallway. I hadn't shown him any of my purchases when I'd come back from my shopping trip, I'd wanted him to get the full effect once I'd put it all together with hair and make-up. It seemed my instinct was the right one.

'Damn, Reba, what are you doing to me?' Tom never took his eyes off me as I crossed the marble floor to stand right in front of him. He reached for my hands and clasped them between his own and held them to his chest. 'You look so beautiful, honey,' he said.

I told him he was the most handsome man I had ever seen. It was true and I didn't think it was fair that I should receive all the compliments when he was standing there looking so fine. He wore a black suit with white western piping on the shoulders and a crisp white shirt and matching silk tie. His black boots had silver toe caps to match the ornate silver belt buckle at his waist. Without any consultation over our outfits we matched perfectly.

'Your chariot awaits,' Tom said, picking up his black Stetson hat and opening the front door to reveal Angelo standing by the limousine waiting for us.

I'd never walked a red carpet before that night. Unless you include the slightly soggy one someone once put outside Leith social club when Robbie and I performed for a local bigwig's 50th birthday, and I didn't count that as it was nothing like arriving at the CMAs. It was disorientating to step out of the car to camera flashes and names being yelled by photographers and music fans alike. Tom held my hand as I got out of the car and then didn't let it go as we made our way up the walkway to the entrance of the arena. I hadn't expected a red carpet to be so crowded but it was organised chaos as runners and personal assistants wearing trainers and headsets and carrying sheaves of paper scurried about trying to corral music stars into photo opportunities.

Compared to some of the stars I spotted, Tom and I were underdressed. There were some incredible outfits with feathers and ruffles, others revealed so much flesh they were borderline indecent. It was all great fun, though, the country music folk were a colourful bunch and I loved watching the most outrageous parade like peacocks for the benefit of the paparazzi.

Tom held onto me tightly as we posed for a couple of pictures together and an assistant producer carefully wrote down my name. I think Tom thought I might bolt from his side because of all the attention but I was too dazzled by the spectacle around me to be thinking about doing that.

I spotted Kelsea Ballerini, Luke Combs, Post Malone and Miranda Lambert as we made our way inside. I heard a photographer shout Keith Urban's name and turned around to see his wife Nicole Kidman walking the red carpet behind us; she was a vision in a strapless purple gown. I tried to play it cool, but wasn't sure I succeeded. My cheeks were aching from grinning.

I also saw Waz Monsoon, but only from a distance. He gave an enthusiastic friendly wave but then turned his attention back to the bubbly blonde identical twin sisters he was escorting, one on each arm. Tom told me they were tipped to be the next big country chart sensation with their new single 'Mirror Mirror'. I nodded and tried not to be too concerned about whatever Waz was up to. Since my surprise spot at The Bluebird he'd asked me to send him some of my material. I'd been working really hard to make sure I had good demos of my strongest songs before sending them in but I made a mental note not to take too long to submit them. Waz appeared to have a short attention span, I needed to make sure I took the opportunity he'd offered to help me while he still remembered who I was.

After we took our seats in the auditorium Tom leaned in and told me he found it a lot less stressful to attend an event like this when he wasn't nominated for one of the awards. I turned to look at him to see if he really meant that. Wasn't he upset not to have had any nominations for his music this year?

He grinned in response and shook his head. 'It's good to take a step back now and then and anyway …' he raised an eyebrow at me, 'this time next year it might be our turn when "Moonlight Home" is nominated for song of the year.'

I started to laugh, but I realised he was serious. Crikey!

The show started then with a performance from Jelly Roll duetting with Wynonna Judd and we were off. I lost myself in the succession of award announcements interspersed with amazing musical entertainment.

I'd lost track of time but was having the absolute best night when Tom suddenly took my hand. 'Now don't freak out but I think something special is about to happen.'

I realised the host was giving a great big build up to the next person who was due on stage. I'd missed most of what the presenter was saying about the special recognition award and what it was for, but it quickly became very clear that the recipient could only be one very particular person.

'It is a rare and wonderful thing to have someone who is as loved as she is legendary. Tonight, ladies and gentlemen, we honour a true American icon – a woman whose words and melodies have moved millions, whose kindness and generosity have changed lives, and whose larger-than-life personality has lit up stages around the world for over six decades ...'

Oh My God. It couldn't be. But it had to be. Yes it was. As I heard them announce her name, the unmistakeable figure of the one, the only DOLLY PARTON stepped onto the stage. The audience roared and rose as one to welcome her. Finally, it was happening, I was in the presence of my Queen, my Idol, my North Star and ultimate inspiration. I thought I might faint.

I gripped Tom's hand tightly as Dolly addressed the audience, thanking them kindly for whatever honour it was they had just bestowed on her. I didn't know what exactly it was and I didn't much care. She wore a sparkly golden catsuit, the stage lights glinting and glistening off it as she moved, giving her the appearance of a walking, talking Oscar statuette.

'Well it's so sweet of y'all to be so nice to me,' Dolly said. 'Y'know I've been around such a very long time, or so they tell me. I always say I'm as old as yesterday but as new as tomorrow so I don't let it worry me too much. All I know is it's taken a lot of love to make a career like mine happen and

I wanna thank you all for that love and tell you how much I love y'all too!'

The Southern charm flowed from her, washing over the rapt audience who hung on her every word. She was everything you would imagine her to be ... and more. She was just so ... Dolly!

As she thanked the crowd once again and made a move to leave the stage, Tom began to tug at my hand. I was still transfixed, my eyes locked onto Dolly Parton, afraid of missing a moment of her appearance, but Tom's tugging became more insistent.

'Reba, come on ... we need to move, come on, we don't have long ...'

I had no idea what was happening but I had no choice but to let Tom half drag me out of our row, down the side of the audience and towards a door at the side of the stage. I stumbled behind Tom rather blindly as my eyes were still fixed on Dolly's retreating persona as she tottered towards the side of the stage we were heading for.

Before I had time to figure out what Tom was up to, we reached a dead end and a large man wearing an earpiece stepped from the shadows, nodded to us both and opened the door ahead of us. We were heading backstage.

My eyes didn't adjust to the darkness immediately but Tom appeared to know his way. Up a few steps, along a short corridor, through a door into another dimly lit passageway and then through another door, and suddenly a rush of air hit us. We were outside and a few people were milling around a large people carrier that had its engine running.

'Okay, stand here and get ready,' Tom pulled me to one side and we looked back towards a huge dock door that was wide open to a loading bay behind us. I looked around and realised what it was Tom was trying to prepare me for … Dolly Parton was about to leave the building and for some reason he had placed us directly in her path.

I opened my mouth to question his sanity but before I could speak there was a flurry of activity inside the loading bay. A huddle of people was moving as one towards us. All the people around suddenly seemed to jump to attention, car doors were opened, auditorium staff shuffled into place creating a sort of guard of honour and then there she was, the queen herself, thanking folks as she trotted on her tiny feet in sky-high heels towards her waiting car.

She spotted Tom straight away. 'Well looky here,' she trilled and slowed her pace as she drew closer looking up into Tom's face, 'if it isn't Mr Tom Coltrane himself. Hiya handsome, if you've come to pay me my royalties for that track I helped you with I told you I don't want nothin' from you except to see that gorgeous smile of yours.' She was laughing and Tom was too.

'Hey Dolly,' he said. 'I just wanted to say congratulations on your special award.' He leaned down and kissed her quickly on both cheeks.

'Thank you, honey,' she said, 'and who's this gorgeous vision?' Dolly turned her attention to me and gave me a warm smile.

'Dolly, this is Reba Moon, a very talented singer songwriter and a huge fan of yours.'

It took an enormous amount of self-control to stop myself from dropping a curtsey.

'It's so lovely to meet you,' I told her, surprising myself with the coherent sentence I managed to produce, adding, 'You ... your music ... everything ... I can't tell you how much it's all helped me in my life ... I just want to say ... say ... thank you.' I wasn't making as much sense now but Dolly was smart enough to be able to work out what it was I was trying to say.

'Aw honey, that's a lovely thing to hear, thank *you*.' She looked between the two of us then with an amused expression on her face. 'Look at the two of you, a matching pair of redheads! You look so good together. I'm not usually too fond of folk with flamin' locks ...! I'll make an exception for you two though, you look like you belong together. Now look after yourselves ... and each other.' With that, and a cheeky wink she stepped towards her car and was gone.

The next thing I remember, I was in the back of the car being driven by Angelo, speeding away from the Bridgestone Arena. Tom had pulled out his phone, punched in a message and within seconds the sleek limo had swung into the loading bay area and picked us up.

I lay my head back against the leather headrest and let out a long breath.

'You okay?' Tom sounded concerned.

I opened my eyes and turned my face towards him. 'Am I okay? ... Am I okay? What the hell just happened? What did you just do!?' I could feel a lump forming in my throat as

I considered the situation Tom had just engineered … for me. 'Thank you,' I said in a small, quiet voice. It seemed totally inadequate really but I didn't know what else to say. To have the opportunity to give thanks to Dolly for all she had unknowingly done for me meant so very much to me and Tom seemed to get that, he understood and that also meant the absolute world.

He wrapped his arms around me and held me close. 'Your face was a picture, for a moment I thought you were going to pass out.'

I started giggling as I pictured passing out at the feet of Dolly Parton. 'Can you imagine if I'd fallen across her path like I'd been struck by lightning? What would she have thought?'

'I doubt much phases Dolly, she'd probably have stepped over your comatose body,' Tom said as we both fell into helpless fits of laughter.

We were still describing increasingly ridiculous scenarios of what *could* have happened when the car began to slow down and Angelo spoke over his shoulder, asking Tom, 'Shall I stop here now, sir?'

Tom instantly snapped into a more serious mood, answering, 'Yes, yes that's right Angel, my friend. Here is perfect.'

I looked out of the window and recognised we were in the same place where Angelo had parked on the night I first arrived in Nashville. It had been more than two months since then and such a lot of wonderful things had happened in that time.

'Why have we stopped?' I didn't care too much, I was too happy and too in love to mind where I was right now. So long as I was with Tom it felt like everything was just fine.

When he suggested a walk I didn't bat an eyelid. 'Yeah, sure,' I told him and followed him without question as we walked hand in hand along the pedestrian bridge over the Cumberland River.

It was a lovely way to end a wonderful night. The air was cool under the clear, star-studded November night sky. As we turned to look at the bright lights of the Nashville skyline I gave a little shiver and Tom took off his jacket and wrapped it around my shoulders.

'Reba.' I turned to face him as he murmured my name. 'Reba honey, are you happy?'

I looked into his handsome, mischievous face. Was he kidding? Happy was a pretty inadequate word for the way I felt right at that moment. I recalled the first time I'd ever seen him, messing about on the steps of the police station with his police sergeant brother. Hopefully I'd get to know Pete and his wife Helena very soon as they were coming out to join Laura and Fergus for a big Coltrane family Christmas. But when I'd first encountered the brothers horsing around I'd jumped to the conclusion that Tom was a villain and a thief, mistaking his playfulness for something bad and not realising how sensitive and deep his songwriter soul really was. A man who was able to be naughty and funny, yet also soft and emotional; someone who could pour all his feelings into words set to music ... could there be a more attractive kind of man in the whole world? If there was, I'd never met one, especially one like Tom who was handsome and sexy too. I took his face in my hands and gave him a long lingering kiss, but when I pulled away I thought he looked a little anxious.

'Is everything okay?'

Tom didn't answer me straight away and I was too high and drunk on life for anything to bring my mood down but even so a flicker of a question skittered across my mind. Was *Tom* happy? Was everything that had been happening recently only for my benefit? What about him? What did he want right now? To be here, in Nashville, with me? Or was he yearning for something, somewhere or someone else?

I soon had my answer. Tom paused and then took a little step back and gave a small smile. 'Oh Reba, everything is more than okay ... and that's why ...' He stopped speaking and reached forward. I thought he was about to pull me towards him but instead he slipped his hand inside his own jacket, which was still resting around my shoulders and his fingers dove into the inside pocket. Before I knew what he was trying to retrieve he dropped down onto one knee in front of me.

'Oh!'

Right there on the bridge, with a backdrop of Nashville's city lights sparkling and twinkling like rhinestones behind him, Tom opened a small black box to reveal the most beautiful diamond ring which glittered and glistened in the starry moonlight.

'Reba Moon, I love you to the moon and back again, will you marry me?'

He'd taken my breath away and for a second no words would come.

'D'ya need time to think about it? Maybe consider ... what would Dolly do in these circumstances?' There was mischievous Tom again, teasing me as I stood there, giving me the moment I needed to pull myself together and give him my answer.

'I don't think I need Dolly's help with this one,' I told him, reaching for him and pulling him to his feet as his jacket fell from my shoulders. 'I love you so much, Tom, you absolute diamond! Yes … yes … of course I'll marry you.'

Three Months Later

I'm standing at the side of the stage at the Ryman Auditorium in the heart of Nashville. Peeping around the curtain, I watch as the audience file into the place known as 'the mother church of country music' and take their seats on the wooden pews set out in semi circles.

Tonight is a sell-out show and a heady atmosphere of excitement and expectation is already building. If only these walls could talk ... the sights they've seen and the sounds they've heard ... practically every country music star you've ever heard of has stepped onto this stage and entertained their devoted followers.

As I sweep my eyes across the stage I picture Johnny Cash, dressed head to toe in black, standing wide-legged and tall; Patsy Cline decked out in her traditional western-style blouse performing right here in 1963 just days before she was tragically killed in a plane crash; Hank Williams, Charley Pride and Loretta Lynn have all graced this stage and, of course, the queen herself, Dolly Parton, has appeared right here on countless occasions.

The twists and turns that have brought me here, to this place and to this moment, all began with Dolly and it feels appropriate to pause now and give some thanks to the incredible woman who has been my inspiration.

Tom and I have decided to stay living here in Nashville and our wedding is set for June. We don't want to wait too long before getting hitched as we've talked about starting a family of our own, something both of us had thought might have passed us by. The wedding won't be a big or fancy affair; we turned down Waz Monsoon's offer to get us a lucrative magazine deal. He didn't seem to mind too much. I think he understood we just want close friends and family, some good Southern cooking and lots of great music. We flew over to Spain for New Year and invited my mum and dad of course. Laura, Fergus, their kids Stevie and Reggie and all the Coltrane gang will be there too. My childhood best friend Alina will be flying in from Birmingham with her husband Nathan. Stella and Dorrie are going to be my bridesmaids and are insisting they should wear fancy cowboy boots with their dresses ... I think that's a great idea.

I feel Tom move in close behind me and wrap his arms around my waist.

'Are you ready, Reba?' he asks and I tell him yes, I'm ready to step out on stage to perform a full set of my own songs to an audience for the very first time. When Tom and Waz told me they wanted me to be the support act for Tom's new tour I had to pinch myself, but they said they were sure I was ready. I've come a long way from the tribute circuit in

Scotland's pubs and clubs to being a breakthrough artist in Nashville with a new recording contract and an album of my own music ready to be sold from the merchandise stand in the foyer. Traditional vinyl sells better than streaming links here so I hope someone will read to the end of the liner notes I've included on the album; past the thanks I put in to all the friends who've got me here, and down to the last line I couldn't help but include. A plea to anyone who is feeling lost or missing their sparkle to try asking themselves, what would Dolly do? She's changed my life, and I hope, somewhere, someone else may find the help they need by using Dolly as their guiding light.

As if Tom can read my mind, he gives me a squeeze and whispers into my ear, 'Nashville doesn't need another Dolly Parton, but we all need a brand-new Reba Moon … Go get 'em, Reba!' And that's exactly what I intend to do.

Suzan's debut rom-com *Shake It Up, Beverley*, **is a Beatles themed story which received 5* reviews from fans and a personal 'thumbs up' from Sir Paul McCartney!**

Beverley, a Beatles-obsessed fifty-something mother of three gets into trouble when she goes looking for love on a dating website. Can 'Beatles Bev' ever find a man to love as much as she loves Paul McCartney? It's not looking good when her antics become a talking point on a daytime TV talk-show!

Reader reviews:

'A perfect holiday read, sit back and enjoy the tale.'

'Anyone who wants a laugh-out-loud, witty story that is relatable and highly entertaining, this is the book for you!'

'A poignant and hilarious story. Suzan Holder is a novelist to watch out for.'

Suzan takes us behind the gates of Elvis Presley's Graceland in her tale of a young girl searching for the truth about her beloved Nana Rose's link to the King of Rock 'n' Roll in her second novel Rock 'n' Rose.

Daisy's grandmother makes a shocking confession about Elvis that triggers a journey to Memphis. Will Daisy solve the musical mystery and is a moody motorcycle cop called Blue the answer to her dreams?

Pack your Blue Suede Shoes for a rockin' rom-com.

Reader reviews:
'If you love a good romcom then order it today. I guarantee you won't be able to put it down.'

'A wonderful book about family secrets, following your dreams and finding out who you really are.'

'Made me want to hop on a plane to see Graceland. Left me with a big smile on my face!'

ABOUT THE AUTHOR

Suzan trained as a newspaper journalist and worked on regional and national newspapers before moving into TV production. She worked on a variety of television news and lifestyle programmes and was Series Producer of ITV's network daytime talk show *Loose Women*. Alongside her writing, Suzan is a regular on radio and TV and in print.

Her debut novel, *Shake It Up, Beverley*, was adapted from her own stage play inspired by Beatles fandom, while her second novel, *Rock 'n' Rose*, takes a trip to Memphis and the world of Elvis.

Married to musician, actor and presenter Noddy Holder, Suzan has one son, two step-daughters and two step-grandchildren. She loves music, dancing, dirty martinis and clunky (rather than cowboy) boots.

Find Suzan online on Instagram, X and Facebook.

For more unmissable reads,
sign up to the HarperNorth newsletter at
www.harpernorth.co.uk

or find us on socials at
@HarperNorthUK